Covert
Matters

Covert Matters

A Novel

Steve Dimodica

This is a work of fiction. The names of existing people, places, intelligence organizations and military units have been used in this book, but the reader should remember that this is a novel, and any resemblance to actual events or existing intelligence reports is purely coincidental.

Published by Johnson & Hunter

ISBN 13 Digit 978-1-933598-36-9
ISBN 10 Digit 1-933598-36-0

Cover photo by Kent Knudson/Photodisc/Getty Images

Printed in the United States of America

How Covert Matters may be
best disclosed, and open perils
surest answered.

---- *William Shakespeare*

Acknowledgments

As in any heavily researched endeavor, I owe a debt of gratitude to a number of people: Bob Donoghue, Mike Riley and Bob Ryncarz—longtime teammates and fine operators in SF; Jim R and Paul J for many years PM staffers in the old DDO at Langley; Mark Dimodica, brother, and formerly of the US Secret Service; Kevin T at the FBI, Dennis L of ATF; and Peter M a top linguist and code expert at NSA—thank you all for your advice, insights and your continuous efforts to keep America safe.

I

14 July 1989
Longmeadow, Massachusetts

"HOW DID YOU find me?"

They sat at a wooden picnic table, in the middle of a playground, surrounded by dozens of laughing children.

"It wasn't easy . . ."

The man named Fairchild loosened his silk tie and unbuttoned the collar of his dress shirt. He looked across the table at the lean athletic figure. Except for the grey hair and lines near the eyes, the playground counselor could pass for a man twenty years younger.

". . . you look well," said Fairchild honestly.

The counselor smiled self-consciously. "I work at it." His eyes wandered off into the distance; a faraway look that focused on nothing in particular. It was an excuse, a way to avoid eye contact, and hence the inevitable.

"Why here?" asked Fairchild, genuine curiosity in his voice.

The grey haired counselor shrugged as his left index finger raised upward and touched a thin, white scar that creased his cheek. He had a rugged face, handsome in a way that women found appealing.

"I don't know. Regrets, I guess. It's one of the things I gave up."

"Children?"

"Yeah, kids, a family . . . you can't buy back the years."

He suddenly looked directly at Fairchild, a signal that they could begin.

"Have you been reading the papers?" came the question.

"A bit, mostly local fare, the *Post* is hard to get."

"I bet." Fairchild spread a copy of a two week old *New York Times* on the picnic table. "Page thirty-six."

He waited as the counselor started flipping through the newspaper. A puzzled frown spread across the hard face and caused the white scar to crinkle.

"Lower left corner," continued Fairchild.

"A Soviet Diplomat and a Syrian National were taken into custody last night by FBI agents . . ."

The counselor looked up from the newspaper. "I still don't . . ."

"NSA intercepted a burst transmission emanating from the Soviet consulate in San Francisco. It was directed at a fishing trawler off the coast." Fairchild paused and checked his watch before continuing.

"And?"

"And then, we had a massive double accident on the Santa Monica Freeway at rush hour . . ."

"I'm listening."

"In both the east *and* westbound lanes, simultaneously, at the same mile marker."

The hard eyes squinted. "Disruption operations?"

"Paralysis," nodded Fairchild. "And then Customs scooped a cache of automatic weapons off loaded from a Siberian oil tanker in New Orleans."

The counselor's mind raced as he considered the disjointed facts in silence. "The thread?"

"We didn't have one until the Mossad fed us a brief that tied it all together. As usual, their information proved quite convincing. It seems that one of their deep cover assets in North Africa *foretold* of certain occurrences."

"I'd be leery of anything the Israelis told me; they have their own agenda."

"We were," nodded Fairchild in satisfaction, "in fact we discounted their input almost entirely—despite the coincidence—until . . ."

The counselor's eyebrows raised.

"Until?"

"Until it was separately confirmed by a reliable source."

"Who?"

"The Brits."

The counselor exhaled in silence.

"And?"

"And we're going to be hit, but we're not sure how, or where."

The counselor digested this for a moment.

"But you know *when*?"

"Sixty days, give or take."

A little boy approached the picnic table, tears in his eyes, his pants torn and stained at the knee.

"Mister Tucker," sniffed the child, "Billy Logan won't let me play baseball with them. He threw me down in the dirt."

Swiveling in his seat, the counselor picked up the child and sat him atop the wooden bench. Then he rolled up the boy's pant leg and surveyed the knee. He smiled, "You'll be okay, Johnny." He blotted the child's tears with a handkerchief, then cleaned the knee. "Now you go back over there and tell Billy Logan to let *everyone* play . . . and you tell him that if he picks on someone smaller than himself, then I'm going to pick on him, okay?"

A reassuring smile came to the boy's face. He nodded and went running off.

Fairchild look amused. "Mister *Tucker*?"

A flip wave of the counselor's hand excused the lie. "Old habits."

"Evidently," nodded Fairchild, smiling. "Can you leave it?"

"Do I have a choice?"

"Sort of . . . but this is big, Jay. People are *scared*."

The eyes wandered off again, gazing at everything, yet nothing. Finally after what seemed a very long time, he looked back at his visitor. "I'll need a Second."

"We've prepared a list, there's a lot of people under contract who . . ."

"No, I want my own, someone outside the circle. Someone you can't touch."

A deep sigh permeated the air, hanging there between them like a barrier.

"Thanks for the vote of confidence."

"Do you blame me?"

Fairchild looked down at the picnic table before answering. "No, I suppose not. Who'd you have in mind?"

"Someone who costs . . . and so will I . . ."

"I told them you'd be ambivalent, so I won't haggle."

"Six figures."

"Done," agreed Fairchild quickly.

The counselor's eyebrows raised in surprise. "You *are* scared."

"Desperate." There was a quiet intensity in his voice.

"There's something else . . ."

"Go ahead," nodded Fairchild, clearing his throat.

"The After Action Report from Colón."

Fairchild hesitated, slowly shaking his head. "They'll never allow it. It's compartmentalized; need to know."

"Bullshit," mumbled the playground counselor.

"Jay," answered Fairchild, "you've got to put it behind you, or . . ."

"Tom," interrupted the counselor quietly. There was a smoldering intensity to his voice. "You don't seem to get it. This is not *my* problem. I'm retired. I don't need your money. I live three blocks from here in a rented old Colonial. People mow their lawns, and the kids ride their bikes to school on sidewalks. It's a sleepy little town—and *that's* just the way I like it."

"Sounds exciting," offered Fairchild, a hint of sarcasm in his voice.

The counselor sighed. "It will do. These days, that's about as much excitement as I crave."

"Okay," conceded Fairchild after thirty seconds. "You get the report—*after* you complete the assignment."

Now it was the playground counselor's chance to be surprised. "Are you authorized to make this offer?"

"Yes," shrugged Fairchild calmly, "they suspected you'd have some reservations."

"But they figured I'd come around for the right bait?"

"For the right compensation . . . the Agency's shrinks take their work very seriously."

Their conversation lapsed momentarily. "Uncensored and uncut—no sterilization," said the counselor finally.

"Agreed, complete and unabridged, people, places, times—warts and all. Of course you'd have to read an *EYES ONLY* version, which means traveling back to Headquarters and being locked in a vault for a couple hours at Langley when this is all over."

There was another lull in the conversation as the grey haired counselor mulled the information. Finally, his gaze fixed on Fairchild, a look of calm resolution. "They don't figure I'll make it back—it's *that* bad."

The visitor leaned forward and straightened his silk tie. "They don't know you the way I do." Fairchild stood and extended a business card. "I'll give you two days to tie things up. Call me."

~~~

IT WAS A glitter palace, downtown, the type of discotheque that catered to the singles crowd—and was proud of it. The clientele embraced the full spectrum; from the young Wall Street traders, to the pro-jocks, to the fashion set.

In the corner half-hidden by the spill of the dim lights, strategically placed to survey the ladies, stood a young man. He was handsome in a dark and threatening way, a foreigner; European clothes, strange mannerisms, a heavy accent. He exhibited an air that was at once arrogant and disdainful. Yet, the way he wore his clothes—to include a dress shirt unbuttoned to his navel, and heavy jewelry—suggested a pronounced insecurity. And it seemed, under closer inspection, that they were mere props in his act to appear confident.

After twenty minutes, he sighted an attractive blonde who seemed slightly intoxicated, unattached, and not too discerning. He moved in.

An hour passed.

"So tell me, Saoud," said the flight attendant as she lighted her cigarette, "this job where you travel so much . . . how often do you get to visit New York?"

"As often as I like," shrugged the foreigner nonchalantly. He reached up and tugged at his thick, black moustache. "I prefer Los Angeles during the winter and Monte Carlo in the spring."

"Hmm, Monte Carlo," purred the blonde, lapping up his arrogance, "and I thought I'd travelled . . ."

"It is nothing," trifled Saoud. "I speak many languages, meet many women . . ."

The blonde reached up and ran her long, manicured fingers along the foreigner's chest. His thick hair was matted together, soaked with sweat from their trips to the dance floor. She raised her fingertips upward and purred, licking drops of perspiration from each finger. "Uhmmm, I like your cologne."

Their eyes met and he noted the saucy, intoxicated look that rimmed her Sclera.

"Irene?"

"Yeah," responded the blonde absentmindedly over her shoulder to her girlfriend.

"It's one-thirty, I'm tired, we have an early call . . ."

"You go ahead," nodded the blonde indifferently.

"Irene . . ."

"Go ahead, Sue, I'll be alright . . . won't I, Saoud?"

"Of course," shrugged the foreigner.

"Are you sure?" pressed the second flight attendant.

"Yes, Sue, I'm a big girl. Go ahead. I'll meet you for coffee tomorrow morning."

"Okay"

The blonde's friend stood, mumbled goodbye and started across the room.

They danced two more times, one fast and one slow; and it was during the romantic ballad that their groping became more intense. Saoud pressed his aroused shaft against her thigh, rubbing his organ sideways along her leg as he cupped both of his palms around her buttocks. The blond responded, nestling her face into his hairy chest, seductively licking the sweaty follicles. Finally it ended, and they returned, hand in hand, back to the bar.

Irene reached up and gripped a thick gold medallion that hung from the foreigner's neck. "What is this," she asked turning the unusual piece of jewelry in her fingers, "Is it real gold?"

"Of course," sneered Saoud defensively.

"But it feels so soft."

"That is because it is twenty carat gold, unlike your American gold that is only fourteen carats."

She inspected the medallion more closely, examining the crossed Arabic swords, superimposed on a palm tree. "Where did you get it?"

"Saudi Arabia," mumbled Saoud.

"Oh," exclaimed the blonde in surprise. Her hands raised involuntarily upward to stifle a drunken giggle. "Are you some kind of sheik?"

"No," snapped the foreigner draining his drink. He reached forward and gripped the back of Irene's neck, pulling her forward. "I am a tiger," he whispered. "Now show me your hotel room and I will show you my power."

The blonde purred seductively and he flipped a wad of cash on the bar and led her from the discotheque.

When they arrived at her room, Saoud curiously walked around and inspected all her doors and windows. Finally, satisfied, he removed his suitcoat and threw it on a chair. "Come here," he commanded as Irene kicked off her shoes.

"Just a minute," laughed Irene teasingly. She started undressing on the way to the toilet.

A strange look of anger contorted his face. "*Come here*," he repeated intensely.

"In a minute," giggled the blonde as she shut the bathroom door.

Saoud paused for a moment, his rage seething uncontrollably. Then he crossed the room in three quick strides and flung open the door.

"You *are* a tiger," laughed Irene drunkenly without looking up. She was busy pulling the pantyhose down her sleek, shapely legs. After she tugged the nylons from under her feet, she straightened, and was immediately startled by the glare of uncontrollable fury that constricted his features.

The foreigner reached forward and grabbed a fistful of Irene's long blonde hair. He half dragged, half pulled her from the toilet, and before she could scream, shoved her sideways into a chair. Then he motioned with a small pistol that seemed to appear from nowhere. His brown eyes danced as Saoud surveyed the frightened, cowering woman. "You will start, by licking my toes. Clean them with your tongue, whore. And then, slowly lick every part of my body until it is clean. And while you lick me, *American*, you will repeat: *Allah Akbah*. Do you understand?"

The woman nodded, a confused, frightened expression on her face. Saoud yanked viciously on her hair and placed the barrel of the pistol under her chin. His voice assumed a snarling, venomous texture. "Say it, *Yankee*, whore!"

"Allah Akbah."

And with that she knelt and started licking his soiled, perspiring feet.

THE LIMOUSINE TURNED down the side alley in the elite upper M Street section of Georgetown. This was old money, the real power behind Washington politics; all in a town that fed on power. More than any other city in the world, the nation's Capitol nurtured itself on it's own influence. And the subliminal power brokers that lived, prodded, and directed the nation's affairs beyond the spill of the media, beneath the surface of the political limelight, carried out their tasks on the fringe of Academia—away from the perceived corridors of power that existed in and around Pennsylvania Avenue. This was a way to protect the genuine decision-makers; men and women content to do their jobs, and let others take the credit.

A tall man stepped from the front passenger seat of the limo and took a long, appraising look up and down the alley. He had the hard, obvious look of a protector; a man whose career was spent watching over the health and safety of others.

When all seemed clear, he looked up to a second floor balcony of the brownstone. The French doors were slightly ajar, and even in the late afternoon sun, the silhouette of a second man could be seen through the crack.

With a nod, the man on the street spoke into his lapel. There was a pause, and then he raised his right hand upward and pressed against the hearing device in his ear. He nodded a second time and then moved to the driver's side of the limousine and opened the rear door.

Tom Fairchild stepped from the back seat and walked to a ground floor side door. It opened automatically to reveal a dapper manservant standing in the threshold.

Without a word, they paced down a long Persian carpeted hallway and entered a study. An old woman sat idly, facing him across a Queen Anne coffee table. She nodded a general greeting and lowered a cup of tea. "You're late."

"Yes," nodded Fairchild unperturbed, "Flight was delayed."

The answer hardly appeased the woman, yet she didn't press the issue.

"Are we secure?" inquired Fairchild as he reached into his briefcase and sat down.

"Yes," nodded the woman, positioning a pair of glasses on her nose, "we swept a half hour ago. Report."

"He's accepted . . ." answered Fairchild, ". . . as you suspected he would."

The woman nodded, satisfied.

"But," continued Fairchild, "there is a complication . . ." he looked at the woman expectantly. ". . . besides seeing the After Action Report, Jay wants his *own* Second."

"I'm not surprised," said the woman.

Fairchild conceded her forethought with a nod. "But if he doesn't *trust* us, then why did he consent?"

"He's doing it for *himself*, not for us," explained the woman. She tugged off her eyeglasses. "After what happened, he'll never trust the *people* that work in the system again."

"But he still does believe in the system, doesn't he?" inquired Fairchild.

"If you're asking, do I think he's any threat of going over to the other side, the answer is *no*, I don't think so. But after what happened, he holds a grudge, and he won't trust the *people* again, because last time, they let him down."

"And it hurt," added Fairchild reflectively.

"Precisely."

"So he'll use his own," continued the intelligence officer. "But won't this remove an element of control?"

"Yes, but I see that as a variable we'll have to live with."

For a moment Fairchild sat in silence, thinking.

"Uncomfortable Tom?"

Fairchild looked up, meeting the old woman's eyes. "Yes . . . I wonder if it is prudent."

"Not entirely," agreed the woman, yet you said yourself that he was the best. These are dangerous times. In terms of calculating the tradeoffs, I see little alternative. Who will he take?"

"As a Second?" Fairchild mused for a moment. "I think the Greek."

Now the woman hesitated for a moment before answering. "I thought he had retired."

"So had Jay," countered Fairchild.

"Touché," nodded the woman, a small twinkle in her eye. She stood, a signal for the intelligence officer to leave. "I have some reading to do. I'll need to pull up his file . . . keep me posted. Benjamin will show you out."

"Yes ma'm," nodded Fairchild as he watched the woman glide from the study, her step decidedly more youthful than her years.

II

18 July 1989
Corfu, Greece

KEFEE.

It's a word that has special emphasis to the Greeks. Loosely translated, it means "possessed by the spirit of happiness." And nowhere is the concept of *Kefee* more pronounced than on the Ionian Island of Corfu.

This was the blessed "land of the Phaeacians" in Homer's Odyssey. Here, the shipwrecked Odysseus swam ashore to be gratefully welcomed by Princess Nausicaa. She bathed, dressed, fed, and entertained Odysseus before loading him with gifts and conveying him in sleep along the coastal sea-road back to his own home island of Ithaca.

For this reason, the lush, colorful island of Corfu had become the symbolic refuge for the professional adventurer. It is an international playground and a romantic paradise; from the glamorous discotheques to the secluded beaches, the swank Achilleion Casino to the elegant gardens of the Spianadha. There is something for everyone on Corfu. And, just possibly the most enchanting endeavor is to sit and idly watch the fireflies blink in unison—an unusual phenomenon that buffers the evening stars in a bright kaleidoscope of light.

Jaycott walked slowly along Vassileos Konstantinou, the picturesque boulevard that hugged the shoreline outside Kerkyra Town. Behind him, the flowered Spianadha and the old Venetian fortress stretched above the spectacular still, blue water of Garitsa Bay. The sun seemed to draw the bright colors of the gardens upward and then reflect them down into the sea, thereby creating a picture of such radiant beauty, that even the locals were captivated by the sight.

It was a walk that Jay always savored, and his thoughts briefly retreated to his wife with whom he first experienced it. So few years earlier, yet so very long ago. A moment of sadness gripped the playground counselor, and two minutes passed as he paused beside the low stone wall that served as a tide-breaker, and looked off across the water to the mainland of Greece.

A kilometer from the Hotel Cavalieri, he turned right onto Mistropolitou Athanassiou and after another short walk approached the wrought-iron gate of an old Venetian mansion. It was a three storied home of understated elegance; a renovated guesthouse of sturdy balconies and shuttered windows that possessed a clear, unobstructed view of the Mediterranean.

He knocked at the heavy oak door and was promptly greeted by a stunningly attractive woman. She had raven black hair and slightly narrow eyes that spoke of Oriental descent. Yet, her high cheek bones and aquiline nose suggested European blood.

"Kaliméra."

"Is Theodori home?"

"Né," nodded the woman, stepping aside and motioning him into the foyer. "Who should I say is calling?"

Her effortless switch to English surprised him. "An old friend," he replied.

The woman nodded demurely and started up the long winding staircase that led to the second level. Her lips pouted ever so sensuously as she glided away, leaving him with a stirring in his loins. She was truly beautiful. And knew it.

He glanced around to clear his mind, taking the opportunity to study his surroundings. The entrance parlor was a throwback to British aristocracy; high ceilings, Persian rugs, a glowing crystal chandelier. For a moment, he just stood motionless, his eyes drinking in the quality of the furnishings; the obvious expense.

"Héreté," came a booming voice from above, "a truly joyous occasion!"

Jay looked up to see the dark, swarthy features of the home's owner. The short, muscular build hadn't changed, yet the curly hair had started to thin.

"Ishmael comes home!" A broad grin of genuine delight spread across the powerful Greek's face. The squat legs quickly descended the stairs and with unabashed affection, he bear-hugged his visitor.

"Theodori . . ."

"Look at you," laughed the Greek as he gripped the taller American by the shoulders and stood back, examining him at arms-length. His gaze was long and appraising, and then with a playful slap to Jay's flat stomach, he bellowed again. "Héreté, still whipcord hard. How does he do it?!"

With a wink and a jerk of his head, Theodori led him down the hall and through a pair of sliding Rosewood doors.

The first floor study, like the parlor, was a picture of splendor; floor to ceiling bookcases, matching leather armchairs, and a huge mahogany desk. In the center of the room stood a large atlas of the world.

As Theodori motioned towards the armchairs, he gave the atlas a casual spin. Then, before the globe slowed to a complete stop, he lifted open the top spherical half of the atlas and exposed a bottle of Seven Star Metaxa and two cognac snifters.

The brawny Greek sidled up to the second armchair and sat down opposite his visitor. Then he poured a two finger pull into each of the snifters and nodded. "Ya'sou." They clinked glasses and then flung their heads back; draining the snifters in one swallow. Jay set his snifter down on the small side table that stood between the leather armchairs.

"You've done well." His eyes roamed the study noting the select and expensive artifacts. The room, like the home, suggested a well-traveled man with an eye for quality.

"I am Mediterranean . . . my home is my haven."

Jay examined his old friend with curiosity. "Italian shoes, French cologne, a Swiss watch . . . and your car, German?"

"British," bellowed the Greek in obvious delight. His laughter filled the room with a rumble of amusement. "I traded in my Porsche for a Jaguar.

They joined in laughter as Theodori refilled the snifters.

"But you haven't mentioned my most prized possession?"

A look of confusion twinkled Jay's eyes as he quickly started searching the study. As if on cue, the sliding doors opened and the beautiful woman entered, effortlessly carrying a tray of food. The cling of her peignoir heightened the shapeliness of her figure; firm breasts, a slim waist, and tight rounded buttocks. Jay felt his loins stir again as she bent forward to uncover a variety of hot dishes. She looked up and smiled—although not quite a smile, more a parting of her lips; but still an acknowledgment of his obvious interest.

With a deferential nod to the Greek, she turned, and walked gracefully back out of the study. As the Rosewood doors slid closed, Theodori again burst into a thunderous round of laughter. The brawny man's bellow startled Jay from his mesmerized gaze, until he realized quite self-consciously, that the woman's beauty had captivated him. He followed Theodori's hand and suddenly understood.

"Her?!"

"Of course," acknowledged the wealthy Greek. "She is unquestionably my *most* prized possession. She is gorgeous, yes?"

"One of the most beautiful women I have ever seen," admitted Jay honestly.

"And absolutely incredible in bed," bragged Theodori in a hushed whisper, "*Incredible.*"

Jay shook his head in chagrin. Then he shifted in his chair, uncomfortable, hoping that the action would somehow disguise his embarrassment.

Ignoring Jay's discomfort, Theodori laughed again, and motioned to the delicious aromas that circled from the plates of heaping *sofrito*, *pastitzio*, and *tirópitas*.

"Eat, zesto, eat my friend."

A meaty hand nudged Jay back towards the food.

SOVIET POLKOVNIK (COLONEL) Viktor Papaha stood in the dusty streets of Ashabad and lighted a Marlboro cigarette. He was average height, lean in build; possessing the short hair and gaunt look of a serious soldier—unlike the well-fed card-carrying party bureaucrats in Moscow.

He puffed lazily on the American cigarette, his display an obvious sign of privilege and position, and watched as a convoy of T-72 tanks rolled along. The churning of the heavy metal tracks caused the acrid air to clog with dust and grime.

The Polkovnik wore the uniform and beret of a VDV (Airborne) officer. However, unlike the typical paratrooper, his overcoat was without the distinguished Guards badge that had been awarded all eight Soviet Airborne Divisions at the end of World War II. Thus, Papaha was either assigned to an Air Assault Division . . . or that of some *other* specialized unit.

In truth, the Soviet Colonel commanded a brigade of *Reydoviki* for the Second Chief Directorate of the General Staff, also known as the GRU. His Reydoviki were a hardened Brigade of elite combat troops used in secrecy under the direction of Soviet Military Intelligence. These Special Purpose Troops, or *Spetsnaz*, were the Russian version of the U.S. Special Operations Forces.

For the past two months, Papaha had been directing his men in a regional subversive campaign, attempting to undermine the Muslim partisan support for the independence of several border republics of the USSR.

The campaign had been largely unsuccessful, apparently forcing the disparate guerrilla tribes into a more cohesive resistance; and three days previous, he had been ordered from Taskent to the far western city of Ashabad; a mere two miles from the Iranian border.

Papaha watched bemused as a huge Russian tank ground to a halt in the middle of the street, causing the rest of the convoy to stop short. Six or seven hatches popped open simultaneously as the various tank commanders peered ahead to see what caused the delay.

An old man, his eyes filled with glaucoma, had tripped with his wooden cart into the path of the armored monster. Immediately, an enraged liaison officer ran over and started to beat the old man with a nylon whip, screaming Turkmen dialect phrases at the helpless villager.

Finally, two soldiers dragged the old man from the dusty street, and the impeded tank, its path now clear, cranked up its engine and jolted forward.

Papaha shook his head in frustration and stamped out his cigarette. This was ludicrous. After twenty-three years in the Soviet Army, seventeen as a Spetsnaz officer, Viktor

Papaha had learned the value of human relations. And although he was deeply committed to Socialism, he did not always agree with the heavy hand of Communism, even now, under the auspices of Glasnost and Perestroika. The scene he had just witnessed undermined all their efforts. To see a soldier beat one of his own countrymen, in order to impress his Soviet mentors, was typical of why Papaha's Reydoviki had been summoned to the border republics in the first place. The mushrooming resentment of the local population towards the Soviets had left the regular Army largely ineffective. The Muslims would strike, and then melt into the hillside, disappearing amongst the local population. Papaha had been called in to direct counterinsurgent operations, and had found the locals so hateful of the Russian "invaders" that his efforts had quickly escalated into a mirage. And, now the Soviet military machine was bogged down in a barren region of blurred loyalties and religious fanatics. Moscow's Lebanon. Such actions only served to escalate the nationalist fervor of the border republics.

A click of boots, and Papaha turned to see a Sergeant standing at attention. "Comrade Colonel," started the soldier as he held out an envelope. "There has been an urgent dispatch from Taskent."

Papaha examined the NCO for a moment, and then snatched the message from the man's grip. He tore open the envelope and quickly scanned the telegram. His eyes squinted, momentarily absorbed in the information. Then he stiffened and turned, crumpling the telegram in his fist as he started up the road.

"Comrade Colonel," exclaimed the Sergeant.

Papaha stopped, whirling on his heels, his eyebrow curling at the obvious tension in the NCO's voice.

"My orders were quite specific, Comrade Colonel," added the man quickly, "I must watch you destroy the dispatch before accompanying you to headquarters."

Polkovnik Papaha surveyed the Sergeant for a moment. There was a respectful, but firm look of surety in the NCO's face. His orders *were* quite specific. They left no room for deviance.

Expressionless, Papaha produced a butane lighter and struck a flame. They watched together as the corner of the crumpled telegram caught fire. It burned for five seconds until the Polkovnik dropped the ashes to the ground and crushed the remnant with his boot.

"Is that satisfactory?"

"Yes, Comrade Colonel," apologized the Sergeant, "but my . . ."

Papaha raised a hand in the air indifferently, cutting off the explanation. "Let us go. We do not wish to keep the General waiting."

HE HEARD THE noise because he never slept very well—at least not anymore; not since Ellie. It was a problem that Jay had finally owned up to. For the first two years, he pretended that his insomnia was the result of living too close to the edge; that strange precipe that operatives taunted, constantly wavering between highs of euphoric danger, and lows of desolate boredom.

But more recently, Jay acknowledged that Ellie's body was intoxicating—not only because it was sexually exciting, but also because somehow he found it deliciously secure; a contoured body that he wrapped himself protectively around until drifting off into blissful abandon. Jay missed that, as he missed so very much that she offered. Her death had created an emptiness in his life; a hollow vacuum.

Jay turned his head, ever so slightly—so as not to let the intruder realize his awareness—and scanned the darkness. His eyes combed the deepest recesses of the bedroom, striving with his night vision to decipher shapes. There, standing near the door, was Theodori's woman.

She looked at him for a moment, her lips parting just a bit, and she seemed to thrust forward from the shadow. Then, just as quickly as she had arrived, without saying a word she was gone.

MIKHAIL GORBACHEV STRODE to the podium to address the gathering. Seated before him were the members of the Politburo and one hundred and fifty Regional Party First Secretaries. It was a hostile crowd.

Four months earlier with his political reforms on track following the March elections, he seemed at the peak of his personal power. However things change, sometimes quickly. A few days earlier, several hundred thousand coal miners in western Siberia, the Ukraine, Vorkuta, and Karaganda had gone on strike. It paralyzed Soviet heavy industry. Simultaneously, Nationalist violence flared between Armenia and Azerbaijan, there were riots in Uzbekistan, and the Baltic states were pushing for secession. To top it all off, Prime Minister Nikolai Ryzhkov, purportedly Gorbachev's partner in *perestroika*, was agitating Politburo members.

As Mikhail cleared his throat to speak, the crackling undercurrent of a potential riot bubbled beneath the surface. Six minutes into his speech, the attacks began. First to interrupt was Yegor Ligachev, a ranking Politburo member; then surging forward was the Moscow party chief, Lev Zaikov, bellowing in a deep, angry voice; followed by Vitaly Vorotnikov of the Russian Republic; and then Leonid Bobykin from the region of Sverdlovsk. On and on it continued, one after another, a chorus of disenchantment and frustration—all attacking *perestroika* and its architect. The fervor burned to a fever pitch, and the existence of the Soviet Union as a federation was on the brink of oblivion.

AT THIRTY-SIX, Anna Lyalin was past her time as a competitive swimmer. However, years of training and two bronze medals in Olympic competition convinced her superiors that she should coach. Thus, the Central Army Sports Club, or ZSKA, continued to retain her services long after Anna had hung up her swimming goggles for the last time.

That Anna held the rank of Major in the Red Army surprised few. The Soviet Union had the greatest collection of "amateur" athletes in the world. Nonetheless, the fact that fourteen years earlier Anna Lyalin had been recruited into the

GRU for Spetsnaz training might surprise some. As a cover, her lithe figure, glowing cheeks, and long blonde hair still exuded good health. Yet through the years, her athletic competition turned coaching duties were routinely interspersed with a full syllabus of studies necessary to operating behind enemy lines: marksmanship, linguistics, cryptology, and the covert passing of information.

The GRU found that the ease with which Soviet amateur athletes moved through host countries served their purposes well. And Anna's many trips to western countries and international sporting events conveniently placed her in a position of incalculable worth to the GRU in the event of an outbreak of hostilities. Thus, it was of no particular surprise to Anna when she was approached at poolside by a young male trainer assigned to the Soviet Swim & Dive Team.

"Comrade Lyalin."

Anna ignored the young man as she stood barefoot, curling her toes in the spill of chlorinated water that formed a puddle. She was absorbed; eyes focused, whistle perched between her teeth, hands thrust deeply into the pouch pocket of her sweatshirt. The trainer shifted his gaze from Anna's stern face to the three female athletes that glided through the water.

"Comrade Lyalin," said the trainer again, this time reaching up to touch Anna, tapping her on the CCCP letters stenciled across the back of her sweatshirt.

"Da!?" bellowed Lyalin spitting the whistle from her mouth. Her shoulder and back muscles tensed. The trainer recoiled, watching her from behind as she continued to curl her toes in concentration. Anna's hard, bathing suit covered buttocks seemed to flex with each stroke the swimmers took; back and forth, cutting through the water like human torpedoes.

He took a half step to his rear, expecting one of Anna's strong legs to fly backward and kick him in the groin . . . she was known to hate interruptions during training. When he was satisfied that he was safely out of range, the trainer extended a sealed envelope. "I was instructed, Comrade Lyalin," he began in a loud voice, "to inform you that this is *most* urgent."

Anna turned and looked over her shoulder to see the trainer holding the envelope out at arm's reach. She snapped at the letter and tore open the envelope. Anna read the code word twice, then reached for the whistle that dangled from a cord around her neck and gave a long blow.

The girls stopped swimming. "Showers and massage for all three Petr, then dinner and *bed*. No late night American television—especially for Yolanda, she looks sluggish . . . and spend extra time on Barin's shoulder, she is favoring it."

"Yes Comrade," nodded the trainer.

Anna Lyalin whirled and padded barefoot through the puddles to the locker

III

19 July 1989
Algiers, Algeria

ALGIERS, THE WHITE City of North Africa, owes its nickname and much of its heritage to an old neighborhood of glittering stucco-on-brick houses and sparkling minarets that crowd together along an eight hundred meter hillside. For the better part of five centuries, the high white walls of this section have protected smugglers, pirates, scoundrels, and spies. The teeming streets and vibrant pace of the Old Quarter lend a certain aura to the neighborhood. Rich in romance and steeped in intrigue, its glamorous energy churning subliminally below the surface, the old section bristles with a history whose very name evokes fabled apparitions: The Casbah.

It is home for rebels and a haven for refugees. And although the years have seen the walls erode, the garbage collected, the population mushroom, and the narrow streets shrink, the Casbah still displays the romantic fervor of revolutionaries. It was here that the shackles of French Colonialism were ruptured, and a nation was born. The Casbah is at once both the heart, and the soul of Algeria.

Saoud walked down Rue Ben Ali, a twisted smile contorting his dark features. He stopped outside a 16th century building and started up the first of three flights of stairs. The stench of collecting garbage and urine flared his nostrils, causing him to cough. Things hadn't changed. At the top of the stairs was a wooden door whose frame was artistically carved in a pattern of diamonds and flowers. Saoud knocked in code. A shadow passed by the peephole and he knew that someone was studying his face from beyond the door.

The door suddenly opened and swung inward. An attractive young woman ushered Saoud into the room. It was a large foyer, its wood-beamed ceiling sheltering a tiled floor. Scrubbed white walls were festooned in bright colors of green, yellow, and red, with a picturesque teal-blue mosaic painted in the center.

Saoud ignored the magnificent interior, the exquisiteness of the room a sharp contrast to the decaying stairwell outside. Rather, his eyes riveted to the tight skirt of the woman who led him through yet another door carved with flowers and jewels. They stepped onto a balcony that overlooked a large courtyard in the center of the building—an architectural feature peculiar to all Casbah homes. In the middle of the courtyard, a brimming fountain spouted water skyward in a gentle spray.

On the south side of the balcony, idly looking down at the fountain as he tossed crumbs of bread to the pigeons, stood a flat-faced, impeccably dressed man. He looked up to see Saoud's eyes wander lustfully after the young woman. A hardness came to the flat features, and then as the pretty brunette closed the door behind her, leaving them alone on the balcony, the man spoke.

"Look all you wish, Comrade Issan, but don't ever touch."

A look of defiance crept into Saoud's expression, but he stifled a reply before it left his mouth.

"*Ever*," repeated the flat-faced man emphatically. His features seemed to sharpen into a cruel grimace. This caused Saoud to back down and look away. The Soviet *Rezidentura*, was one of the few men who could intimidate Issan. "What have you to report?"

"Our contacts are in place," answered Saoud, relieved to change the subject, "in Florida. They await your word."

"Patience, Comrade. The time is not right . . . not yet."

"And what does Moscow wait for?"

The Russian dropped his last piece of bread and turned. The neat fit of his British wool suit belied his stocky build. There was a distinct tone of superiority evident in his voice. "Comrade, *you* are not in a position to know such things . . . I am not in a position to know such things. We do our jobs, together, because our goals are the same . . ."

"To bury the American pigs! The insolent Yankee swine who . . ."

"Enough, Comrade," interrupted the Soviet in a quiet voice. His patience was waning. This was the most important assignment of the Russian's career, and its success centered on the cooperation of a hot-headed psychotic with dreams of Islamic vengeance. The Rezidentura raised his fingers and massaged his temples. He needed a drink, a stiff glass of

Vodka. "Go to your hotel and await my contact. We still have more to arrange." The Russian looked up at the taller Arab. "And be discreet in your behavior, Comrade, we are close to a great success, a success that will liberate the Muslims from the yoke of American tyranny—forever."

Saoud's eyes changed color, like two black coals beneath a bed of burning embers. A smile curved Issan's lips and moustache. He nodded, "Fi aman illah."

"Dos Vidania," replied the Soviet. He turned, the movement an act of dismissal.

JAYCOTT PULLED UP short outside his friend's Victorian mansion and slowed to a walk. Sweat dripped from his eyebrows, matting the thick grey hair to his forehead. He strode in a circle, his lungs heaving from the exertion, allowing his body to gradually cool from the run. Finally he paced across the street, hands on hips, his plain grey T-shirt stuck to his chest.

The morning glittered, the bright Corfiote sun bathed the cobblestone streets and sandy beaches; its warmth and security beckoning the flowers to open their petals skyward until the island was covered in a rainbow of color.

Jay stood at the low stone wall and gazed off across Garitsa Bay. He felt a powerful attraction to this island. There was such peace, such tranquility here. A serenity unmatched by any place he had ever been. It was easy to see the appeal that it held for Theodori.

He kept walking, his eyes looking up to the Spianadha, and the gardens of the Esplanade. Finally, after five minutes, he ambled back across the street and lay on the green grass in front of Theodori's home. Jay forced himself through a series of freehand exercises; push-ups, sit-ups, stretching. This worked up another lather of perspiration, and finally, after twenty minutes of non-stop effort, Jaycott stood and brushed off his sweatpants.

He circled around the back of the Victorian mansion and entered the large private garden which adjoined the house. On the veranda, drinking a cup of thick Grecian coffee, his eyes absorbed in a newspaper, sat Theodori. As Jay approached, the heavy Greek looked up and a broad smile crossed his face. "Good day, my friend. How did you sleep?"

"Fine, thanks," nodded Jaycott.

"Look at you, training first thing in the morning. Such discipline." Theodori patted his paunch affectionately. "Now me, I start my diet tomorrow. On the mainland."

"The mainland?"

"Peloponnesus," nodded the Greek, folding his newspaper. He looked at his wristwatch. "And it is time. My plane is leaving." Theodori stood. "The house is yours. My staff will attend to your needs." He picked up a small suitcase from beneath the table. Then Theodori's meaty hand reached out and gripped Jay's shoulder. "I'm glad you have come. Give me a few days to prepare, and then we shall see to this assignment of yours. Yes?"

Jay nodded and patted Theodori's forearm. He knew better than to argue. Every agent had his own pre-operational routine; strange habits or personal quirks that were as much superstition, as they were practical preparations. And the Greek's required him to visit the home of his ancestors on Peloponnesus.

With a wink, the burly Theodori entered his home and was gone.

Jaycott sat alone for a moment, taking the opportunity to pour himself a cup of coffee from the warm pot. A house woman stepped out onto the veranda. She carried a plate of fresh fruit and freshly cut flowers. With a smile, the old woman set the fruit plate in front of Jay and changed the day-old flowers with the new ones. Satisfied, she smiled again and disappeared back into the house.

Jay started to peel an orange, savoring the peace and solitude of the veranda, as the sun warmed his face.

He looked up to see Theodori's woman step out onto the veranda. The bright sun illuminated her face and seemed to cause her raven hair to glisten. She was beautiful. Dressed in a thin, cotton skirt and peasant blouse, she suggested wholesome sexuality. Her clothes clung in all the right places, gracing the swell of her breasts, her firm buttocks, the shapeliness of her thighs. She wore a pair of open toe sandals, their patter softly clicking as she crossed the carved stones.

She sat at his table, and demurely tugged her long black hair into a roll so that it lay across her right shoulder. Then she smiled in a polite but indifferent way. "Good morning."

"Good morning," replied Jay.

She helped herself to a cup of coffee before breaking a lump of sugar in half with her spoon, and slowly stirring it into the black Grecian liquid. "Did you sleep well?"

Jay's mind raced. For a moment he was overcome by a wave of confusion; muddled thoughts, and distorted impressions from the night before. He was filled with self-doubt. Did it happen? Had she realty visited his room to look in on him? Was it a dream? Thoughts, faces . . .

He decided that she had really come, but that it was a protective gesture. Theodori, that great burly Greek, the consummate guardian, had asked his woman to look in on his friend; to make sure that his guest slept peacefully. It was nothing more. And Jay realized, to his chagrin, that his wishful longings were not shared, just the polite service of a host and his staff.

"Yes . . . quite well," nodded Jaycott as he glanced back at his orange.

"You rose early," she added, testing her coffee, "is that normal?" The polite question was accompanied by a dazzling smile. It was at once mocking and yet natural, so that when spoken with her slight accent, it had the touch of innocence.

"Yes," nodded Jay, searching her face for a hint of sarcasm. There was none.

She leaned forward and, in a very American posture, placed both elbows on the table. "Why?"

"Why?" mumbled Jay, his dark eyebrows knitting. He looked at her curiously and shrugged, popping a piece of orange in his mouth. "Habit, I guess."

She nodded, satisfied with the answer, and reached for Theodori's newspaper. "I'm glad. You won't mind then if we get an early start."

Now Jay sat forward, the surprise on his face quite evident.

"An early start for what?"

"Your introduction to the island," she said demurely. "For your safety."

Jaycott sat in silence for a moment, piecing together the handiwork of his friend. "He's very well known."

"And respected," added the woman, realizing that he understood.

"And everyone knows you're his woman."

She nodded. "So we spend the day visiting around the island, showing your face, saying your name, and if anyone should come asking . . ."

"Theodori will know."

"Precisely." The smile again, mocking yet natural. "Is an hour enough time for you to shower and change?"

"Plenty."

"I'll see you then." She finished her coffee and stood, folding the newspaper under her arm. "May I call you Jaycott?" Her accent emphasized the second syllable.

"Sure, or Jay, it doesn't matter."

She nodded, "I am Katerina," and left.

THE MIDDLE-AGED ENGINEER sat at the workbench in his basement, calmly stretching a piece of green wire along a tape measure. He carefully snipped at the electrical wire, cutting it to size. Then, just as he turned his attention to the radio cassette player on the bench, his wife knocked gently on the door.

"Come in."

She too was middle-aged, with several streaks of grey lacing the long hair that stretched back into a bow.

"How's it going?" she asked, taking a moment to survey the detonators, batteries, circuit boards, and electronic equipment that lay spread across the workbench.

"Slowly, but we have time," admitted the engineer without looking up. "Any word on my C-4?"

"Mother says *soon*," offered the wife, referring to the pliable plastic explosive of her husband's question.

To their neighbors in the quiet New Jersey suburb, they were a rather ordinary, somewhat dull American couple. In reality, they were each a Lieutenant Colonel in the Red Army, controlled by the Illegals Training Centre of the GRU.

Unlike Soviet agents, who are actual inhabitants of a host country, recruited for either political or monetary reasons to work for Soviet Intelligence, Illegals are actually Soviet citizens posing as foreigners.

The husband and wife team migrated to the west in a typical yet laborious fashion; three years of immersion training in Moscow where they lived, conversed, and acted as Americans around the clock. This was followed by an indirect journey; Moscow to Czechoslovakia, to Cyprus, to Oman, to Hong Kong, to Hawaii. The entire process took nine months, with each step of the trip acting as a cutout, enabling the couple to change identities, alter cover stories, and build a history.

In California they settled for two years to legalize their existence; adding credit cards, driver's licenses, club memberships, and even managing to "meet and marry". Naturally, this further backstopped their paper trail as "true" Americans.

Finally, the couple moved to New Jersey and after a stint working for a construction company, the civil engineer and his wife purchased a large hardware store in the suburbs. It wasn't long before he hired a capable manager to run his business, and this in turn allowed the couple to take numerous vacations away from home. Their eventual success as small business owners became rather academic, and through the years the Illegals Centre in Moscow covered any cash shortfalls. However, as Intelligence Officers, they blossomed; after all, this was their *raison détre*. Of course, the fact that the GRU held their two sons as "insurance" back in Moscow didn't hurt.

"Have they changed our timetable?"

"Not yet," frowned the wife, "it looks like we're still on schedule."

The engineer lay his wire cutters on the benchtop and surveyed his work. Then he sighed. "I can't do anymore without the C-4."

The wife draped an arm over her husband's shoulder and kissed the back of his balding head. "Enough my Gennadi," she whispered, "time for bed."

The use of his Russian birthname—in direct violation of GRU policy—was reserved for their intimate moments. The engineer's eyes twinkled as she stroked his tired neck muscles and nodded towards the door. He followed her up the stairs.

IT HAD TAKEN them the better part of an hour to slowly work their way up Marasli, past the Monument of Menekrates and the huge public gardens. Then they turned right on Mitropolitou Methodiou and into the "Hora" or the central part of Kerkyra Town. The wide open stores and elegant shops were filled with tourists, most of them European. Colorful weavings from Metsovon, jewelry from Janina, copper and brass from Macedonia, rugs from Arahova—a veritable shopper's paradise; all catering to the international jet set.

Katerina led Jay through the mid-morning throngs of tourists in a graceful, if somewhat deliberate path. She introduced him to shopkeepers, tavern owners, local businessmen, and civic officials. It all had the look of coincidental contact, but as the morning wore on, Jay's appreciation for Katerina's talents grew. She switched effortlessly between languages; at one moment Island Greek, the next Italian, and finally back to English for his benefit. Her demeanor was cordial, even friendly, but always with a hint of reserve; Katerina flashed that dazzling smile in a way that seemed to innocently mock each person they met, so that

Jay could never quite get a handle on her demeanor; or the thoughts that seemed to constantly belie her actions.

Finally, after several hours of needless errands and countless introductions to the locals and regular tourists, she took Jay by the elbow and nodded toward the Spianadha, the large esplanade that separated the town from Garitsa Bay.

"You must be hungry Jaycott," her eyes twinkled with mischief, "and bored."

Jay glanced at his wristwatch and nodded. "The shops will be closing soon. Do you think we've accomplished enough?"

"Ne," she nodded, using the colloquial expression for yes, "for now."

She chose a restaurant on one of the quaint little streets off of Georgiou Theotoki. They dined lazily on grilled fish and a carafe of hyma, the local, unbottled wine. Both were excellent. Their lunch conversation served to refresh Jay's knowledge of the island, the local customs, and any changes that had transpired in the four years since he and Ellie had first walked its cobbled streets. The memories returned, and Jay grew melancholy.

Katerina seemed to sense his mood. Without saying a word, she reached forward and took both of Jay's hands in her own, and gave a slight squeeze. The spontaneous gesture of warmth seemed to ease the formality between them. Jay raised his head, and looked Katerina full in the face. Her eyes seemed to hold his for the longest moment, and there was a depth, a sincerity to the woman that had not been evident on the veranda early that morning, or during any of the role playing amongst the townspeople.

"We have one more stop, if you are not too tired . . ."

"Lead on," agreed Jay, as he reached into his pocket for a handful of Drachmas. She shook him off and signed the check, motioning to the owner. "To logoriasmo!"

The balding man nodded as he wiped his hands on a stained apron. "Evharistó Katerina, Kalispéra."

They crossed the wide boulevard of Kapodistriou to the Liston mansion on the edge of the Spianadha, and ducked under its arcades to avoid the afternoon sun. It was the height of the season and the Kafenions of the huge mansion bustled with tourists, all clamoring for seats and cold drinks amid the shaded café tables.

Katerina was on her mark again, weaving between the scattered chairs of the arcade, introducing Theodori's "good" friend, showing Jaycott's face, repeating his name. She engaged in quiet conversation with many locals, always gesturing toward Jay, touching him in a polite but familiar way, demonstrating a platonic affection that ensured his acceptance amongst the townsfolk. The visitor was obviously a very special friend to the respected Theodori.

Twenty minutes later, they finally settled into two large wicker chairs at the end of the shaded arcade and ordered Koulourákia and Zitsa. Katerina tugged at her blouse to create an airpocket, and then she hiked up her skirt a few inches, kicked off her sandals, and placed her heels on the edge of the seat. Katerina then started to massage her tired feet as the coiled sweet breads and wine arrived. The sheen of her shapely legs flexed with each movement, and it caused

Jay to stir uncomfortably. He felt that familiar flutter in his loins and for a moment he fought the urge to offer Katerina assistance. Instead, he busied himself by filling their wine glasses. After three minutes of alternately rubbing her toes and massaging her feet, Katerina folded one ankle under the opposite knee and smoothed her skirt.

Jay smiled. "We covered a lot of ground today."

Her eyes seemed to twinkle as she tilted her head in an odd way, and then Katerina's face lighted in that glorious smile. She took a sip of wine, and then replaced the glass and picked up one of the long twisted sweet breads. "You have a nice smile Jaycott, you should do it more often."

Jay was taken aback by her observation. He studied her appraisingly, yet she only gazed, expressionless. "I didn't realize I did it so seldom."

Katerina nodded. "That's the first time since I've met you." She nibbled on the Koulourákia.

Jay studied her a few more seconds before changing gears. "What do you know about me?"

"Very little," she admitted, "only what Theodori told me . . ."

"Which was?"

"That you are an American, and that I should trust you completely."

"Is that all?" asked Jay leaning back in his chair. He took a long pull on the glass of wine.

She looked down at the table for a moment before answering. "He said that you saved his life once, that you came back for him, and you should not have."

Jay thought back to the operation many years earlier that Katerina referred to. "He was on my team, I was responsible."

"He said that you made a tactical error."

Jay smiled again, reminiscing over the event. "I suppose he's right."

"And for this reason, Theodori is alive, so I thank you."

Jay nodded, "You love Theodori."

The statement caused Katerina to hesitate, and she chose her words carefully. "I have a great loyalty to Theodori, he is very good to me."

Now it was Jay's turn to hesitate. He looked at Katerina for a few seconds as she started nibbling again on the sweet bread. He wasn't quite sure whether to pursue this line of conversation, so he retreated. "Did he tell you anything else about me?"

"No . . ." she looked up again, fixing his eyes, ". . . yes. He told me that if you seemed distracted, or even sad, that I should not worry—it was nothing that I did."

Jay set his wine glass down and exhaled. He spoke so softly that Katerina could barely hear him. "Theodori is a very wise man."

She nodded, and then sat forward to put her sandals on. "We should go. I hope you do not mind taking a taxi; I am afraid my feet have had a full day."

Jay was surprisingly tired himself. "Of course." He started to reach for some money when she shook him off again. Katerina signed the tab and instructed the waiter to call for a ride.

They drove back to Theodori's Venetian-style home in silence. The old island woman met them at the door. Katerina spoke to her in Greek, outlining various instructions, to which the woman nodded several times. "Lenoris will see to your needs. She will draw your bath and has left a copy of an English newspaper in your room. She will serve dinner at eight o'clock if that is okay?"

"Fine . . . will you be joining me?"

"O'hi, I am afraid not. Tomorrow we will go to Paliokastritza on the other side of the island, with lunch at Lucciola's, it is popular with many of the locals. Tomorrow night we go to the Achilleion Casino, that should round out your introduction to the island. Thank you for a pleasant day Jaycott."

Jay nodded, and watched Katerina glide gracefully up the long staircase. For a moment he stood transfixed, his mind distorted by a jumbled collection of thoughts and feelings. Then he followed the old woman to the guest quarters on the first floor.

Once inside, Jay poured himself an inch of Metaxa from the bottle at the bedside table. He sipped in sparingly as he opened the shuttered windows to allow for a sea breeze. Then when the old woman Lenoris finished drawing his bath and left, he stripped out of his clothes and sat naked on the bed.

Jay's lean, sinewy frame appeared hard even in a relaxed state; and he absentmindedly stroked a deep red scar along his ribcage as he read the front page of the International Herald-Tribune. Finally, he lay back on the bed and exhaled.

"Thank you for a pleasant day," mumbled Jay to himself. He realized, somewhat amusedly, that he was jealous of his good friend Theodori. And then, with a touch of shame, he admitted that for the first time in nearly two years, he longed deeply for a woman other than Ellie.

IV

IT HAD BEEN a strange few days for Viktor Papaha. As
a career soldier he understood and practiced—although not
always agreed—with obedience. But, the circumstances
surrounding his sudden and secretive departure from Ashabad
were strange even by Army standards.

The Commanding General in Taskent was quick to
demonstrate irritation over the Spetsnaz Colonel's orders;
men in power consider themselves privileged, and that
privilege included information—not the lack of it.
Unfortunately, Papaha could offer no explanation as to why
he was suddenly being ordered back to Moscow. This only
served to frustrate the General more, as he assumed that the
Polkovnik had pulled some strings to get himself reassigned
from Turkmenistan. The Commanding General saw it as a
ploy by the elite Spetsnaz officer, to protect himself from the
disgrace of a rapidly deteriorating situation in the border
Republics. When the efficiency reports were filed, the
General would be unable to lay the blame off on Papaha and

his unsuccessful control of the Muslim guerrillas, due to insufficient time in-country.

The orders addressed to Colonel Papaha read simply:

Polkovnik Papaha, V.I.

Return to Moscow immediately.

It was signed by Colonel General Aleksandr Grigorevich Pavlov, First Chief Deputy of the Second Chief Directorate of the General Staff.

Accompanying Papaha's orders was a telegram addressed to the Commanding General himself that just as briefly instructed him to expedite Papaha's return to Moscow by any means possible, even if it meant providing use of his personal car or plane.

"Friends in high places Colonel?" sniped the Commanding General, his frustration oozed.

Papaha shrugged and pulled a pack of Marlboros from his pocket. The slight disrespect incensed the General, but at this point, Viktor no longer cared.

"Aleksandr is an old family friend," lied Papaha, "there was some talk of a European posting."

Mention of a desirable duty assignment caused the General to bristle. As a former Armor officer he had never gained an appreciation for the work of Spetsnaz; and through the years his few brief associations with them had always been at the insistence of a higher command. They were renegade cut throats in his mind; and they always seemed to be scurrying about in the middle of the night, disappearing for days at a time, unaccountable to anyone, and cloaked in a veneer of secrecy. Not the way a war should be fought fumed the General as Papaha lighted his cigarette. He preferred an open battlefield at midday, fifty tons of steel squaring off, tank against tank, strength versus strength.

And so it went. Viktor was shuttled all the way back to Moscow from the far border Republic, and left to wonder why the First Chief Deputy of the GRU—a man he had never even met—had summoned him. His curiosity was compounded by the instructions he received upon arrival back in the capitol. Rather than approach the Khodinka Field Headquarters of the GRU, he was told to appear in Cathedral Square inside the Kremlin walls at noon the following day—in civilian attire.

Polkovnik Viktor Papaha inhaled deeply on his cigarette, idly watching the throngs of newfound tourists scurry about the Square, busily snapping photographs of everything and anything. The Rodina was experiencing an identity crisis. Viktor likened her tribulations and those of President Gorbachev to the former Czar, Peter the Great: doing everything in their power to drag, push, and cajole this xenophobic, sleeping giant of a nation into the next century. But it had been Viktor's experience that people can't always cope with change—certainly not if it occurred too rapidly. And the stresses imposed by the dissolution of the Warsaw Pact, and the jump-starting of a moribund economy were threatening to rupture the country. Mother Russia was at a crossroads, and the Spetsnaz officer was not sure she would survive.

The chimes of the clock on Spassky Tower signaled high noon.

"Good afternoon, Comrade Colonel."

Papaha turned to see a nondescript man break away from the crowd. The man offered a hand.

"And who are you," asked Viktor, ignoring the hand and stubbing out his American cigarette on the stone that lined the Square.

"I am Boris," replied the man as he dropped the proffered hand. His tone took on a more formal cadence. "I am here at the request of the First Deputy Chief. You are to follow me."

With that, the man turned and started across Cathedral Square towards the Great Kremlin Palace.

In minutes they were inside a small office, one of the 700 rooms in the former residence of the Czars. There were no windows, or even furniture, except for two straight backed wooden chairs and an old desk. The man nodded at one of the chairs. "Sit. Wait." Seconds later Papaha was alone.

"Comrade Colonel," came the voice as the door opened. A nattily dressed man entered the small office and took the seat across from Viktor. He lay a thick dossier that he was carrying on the desktop and leaned back in the wooden chair. Then he removed his glasses and started to wipe them carefully with a handkerchief. "I apologize for the lack of amenities Colonel, but under the circumstances we must place security first."

"Then why aren't we at the Aerodrome?" Papaha's reference to the Khodinka Field Headquarters building caused the man to replace his eyeglasses and sit forward.

"I shall explain . . ."

Viktor shifted in his seat and withdrew his pack of cigarettes. Then he lighted a Marlboro, loosened his tie, and unbuttoned his shirt collar.

The dapper man smiled. "Uncomfortable in those clothes Colonel?"

"I'm a soldier . . . are you Comrade Pavlov?"

"Nyet," smiled the man, "I am Lieutenant General Guryenko. I head the Illegals Training Centre. I am here representing Comrade General Pavlov. And you . . ." he opened the dossier ". . . have been chosen to serve the Rodina in a very *special* way . . ."

Guryenko absently flipped pages in the dossier, a dossier that he had long since memorized. ". . . I see that you never attended the Lenin Komsomol Higher Airborne Command School in Ryazan as *most* Spetsnaz officers do, you were graduated from a military engineering school as a lieutenant, and were commanding a penal company when we discovered you . . ."

"Yes, Comrade General," nodded Papaha inhaling on his cigarette.

". . . and you have spent considerable time in three North African countries: Algeria, Tunisia, and Egypt—where you taught yourself *English*, why?"

"My Arabic was useless—each country Comrade General, had its own dialect. Tunisians and Egyptians could barely converse. English, however, was universal."

"I see . . . extensive military operations in Lebanon, Iran, Afghanistan, then you attended the Reconnaissance

Faculty of the Frunze Higher Military Academy, before a posting to Kiev."

Guryenko stopped flipping through the dossier and sat back in his chair. "An altogether rapid ascent Colonel—and nontraditional I might add, even by Spetsnaz standards . . ."

Viktor nodded silently, inhaling again on his cigarette.

". . . marked by an uncanny ability to accept *any* mission—and succeed."

Papaha didn't respond. He recognized that his military record was exceptional, even if his personality was a bit irreverent. He disdained politics, and since he was bereft of any influential contacts or privilege, his lofty rank was purely the result of skill, audacity, and an incredible sense of leadership.

Papaha's men revered him; alternately fearing and respecting the Colonel—but always performing the impossible if not suicidal tasks that he assigned.

"There are elements in the Red Army Comrade that fear the worse for the Motherland over this, this . . . perestroika."

Guryenko shifted in his chair, watching Papaha's expression as he spoke. If Viktor felt anything, he didn't show it.

"Some of us, a not altogether small group, are uncomfortable with the rapidity of change in the Rodina. Many of the citizens in the outlying Republics are demanding liberties and freedoms—even to the point of independence— that threaten our very borders, and hence out existence. The crumbling of the Warsaw Pact, the unification of Germany and its meshing under the umbrella of NATO, the revolt of the Baltic states—even your recent posting to Turkmenistan . . ."

Guryenko leaned back and started cleaning his eyeglasses again with a handkerchief. ". . . each day sees us lose another strategic advantage, another buffer zone as our enemies gain ground. Each day sees our defenses a little more weakened, our flanks a little more exposed—and for what? Perestroika? What is this word? Are the citizens better fed? Are there more consumer goods in the stores? Have the prices of *anything* stopped rising?"

Guryenko replaced the eyeglasses back on the bridge of his nose. "The answer to all these questions is *nyet*."

He leaned forward again, resting his forearms on the desk and spoke in a quiet, conspiratorial voice. "We need to slow the pace of change down, Viktor Ivanovich. We need to fortify our defenses in a prudent manner, to gradually ease the tensions, allow for an orderly transition. We need to buy *time*."

Guryenko leaned back again, fastidiously straightening his tie. "Those following the lead of our President and the Politburo have become enamored by their own egos. They court the western media, driven by their believed popularity, while we fall into the hands of the western alliance—giving away, not negotiating—one strategic defense after another. Defenses in many cases forged with Russian blood. Bloodshed in defense of the Rodina.

Guryenko fell silent, allowing Papaha to sift through the rhetoric, but the Colonel's sharp mind had seen the warning signs many times before. He snubbed out his cigarette. "What do you propose Comrade General?"

"A diversion Colonel. An *act* of sufficient force to uncouple the western media from their present love affair with our leaders, and cause them to rattle their sabres. This should be enough to shake our President into reality *before* we are castrated as a nation."

"And where will this *act* take place Comrade General?"

Guryenko smiled. "Where you will get to practice your English Viktor Ivanovich. We are sending you to America."

JAY ROSE LATE following a restless night of sleep and justified not exercising by declaring this morning a "floater." The floater was Jaycott's self-determined holiday from the rigors of continuous workouts. Years before, Jay had recognized the value in allowing his body a little respite from the strenuous battery of running and calisthenics; an occasional day of rest seemed to work wonders. The fact that his hardened physique had long since become inured to punishment didn't seem to matter, because as Jay got older, he recognized his floaters for what they were: a *mental*, rather than physical day off. And today Jay awoke in a lousy mood, so he rebelled, and declared a floater.

Jaycott threw aside the sheet and slowly stretched his long naked torso while still in bed. All the aches and pains of a life of violence seemed to materialize at once, and Jay thought back to an old acquaintance, a former professional hockey player, hobbled in his old age, who complained of waking each morning to 'every check I ever took.'

Stumbling into the toilet, Jay splashed cold water on his face and brushed his teeth. A shower and shave could wait. Then he tossed on gym shorts and a T-shirt and walked out onto the veranda.

Lenoris, the old house woman, was already busy setting out fresh flowers, coffee and fruit. Jaycott gave her a nod and slumped into a chair. He sat idly, allowing the bright Corfiote sun to warm his face and thought about the previous day.

He had traveled with Katerina to the far side of the island and had a wonderful lunch at Lucciola's. Kat had performed her seemingly innocent ritual, gracefully weaving amongst the Islanders; a kind word, quiet conversation, and an introduction of Theodori's "good friend" to each.

Then it was off to walk the sands of Palaiokastritsa Bay, the fabled beach where Odysseus swam ashore, travel weary and shipwrecked, to meet his loving Nausicaa.

Finally that evening, after a nap and light dinner, they had gone to the Achilleion Casino. Katerina had chosen well, as the fashionable, if not somewhat legendary casino was packed with throngs of the rich and powerful. Jaycott had rotated between the various gaming tables, betting modestly, and using the credit from Theodori's house account. All the croupiers knew Katerina, and the locals were further impressed by her cajoling him to up the wager on Theodori's personal line of credit. Jay lost at rouletté and craps, but won big at blackjack—more than offsetting his deficit. He then refused to take his winnings and instructed the manager to post all money to Theodori's account.

Throughout the afternoon and evening, there had been an air of warmth, even occasional affection, between them. Yet the moment they were out of the public eye, Katerina seemed to grow distant, as though a wall of reserve separated them; cutting off a seemingly genuine, if not platonic tenderness. Once alone, Kat's demeanor assumed a disinterested quality.

These sudden changes frustrated Jay, yet they also served to force some introspection. Katerina was beautiful, intelligent, warm and funny, complex—and very *loyal.* But more importantly, even if she wasn't, Jay was. Theodori was Jay's friend, and therefore by any standard, Katerina was off limits. This in turn helped convince Jay, that his apparently strong desire for Theodori's woman, was nothing more than the "forbidden fruit" syndrome: The reason I want her is because I *know* I can't have her. Ultimately, his attraction, his conscience, her demeanor, and their time together, all added up to a fitful night of tossing and turning; and therefore it was quite easy, after nearly a month of uninterrupted daily exercise, to wake up melancholy and declare a floater.

Thirty minutes later, as Jay busied himself with some grapes, Katerina stepped onto the veranda. Her eyes lighted at seeing Jay, and for a moment—however brief—when she smiled, he got the impression again that she was really quite happy to see him. Very quickly, however, the smile faded and her polite yet reserved demeanor took over.

"Did you sleep well, Jaycott?"

"Yes," lied Jay.

Katerina wore a red, off-shoulder blouse that hugged her body above her breasts, and clung to her arms in a large circle; thereby exposing all the supple flesh of her shoulders, neck, upper chest, and back. The thin cotton material tapered down to her waist and again exposed a section of her bare abdomen and navel before Kat's matching skirt fell to her knee. Her hair was pulled back in a gentle braid and draped over one shoulder. The effect was altogether simple yet stunning, and her taunt, bronzed skin seemed to glisten with each gesture as she sat beside him in the sun.

"I thought we might go to Glyfada beach today, if you had no plans."

"Sure." Jay reached forward and plucked another grape from the bowl on the table.

She studied his appearance for a moment. "Have you exercised yet today?"

"No, day off," he shrugged.

"I see, then do you mind leaving in thirty minutes?"

"Not at all."

"Good. I will have Lenoris pack us a lunch. A bathing suit and some dry clothes are all that is necessary. I shall see you shortly."

"Fine."

Polite, businesslike, distant. Jay watched Katerina rise and glide back into the house.

TOM FAIRCHILD WALKED unhurriedly along the cobbled stones of the Faneuil Hall Marketplace in Boston. He wasn't on a particular schedule, and the crowded mid-morning pedestrian traffic made his leisurely stroll all the more sensible, if not downright necessary.

It had taken Tom the better part of an hour to traverse the short distance from the Boston Harbor Hotel, across Atlantic Avenue, under the expressway, and then alternately through each of the three buildings of boutiques and shops that constituted the Marketplace.

Finally, he tired of the game, and buying a bag of stale bread from a mobile vendor, he loosened his tie, took off his suitjacket, and rolled up his shirtsleeves. Then he lazily sat on the nearest park bench and started feeding pigeons.

A few minutes later, he was joined by a short, mustached man of sixty, who dressed unobtrusively like a retiree; dress shirt buttoned to the collar, no tie, slacks, cotton jacket, walking shoes. The man leaned forward on the park bench, resting both hands in from of himself on a polished cane.

"We agreed on an hour," said the short man without looking at Fairchild. Tom glanced at his wristwatch while flipping a piece of the bread out to the throng of pigeons that had gathered.

"Fifty minutes, close enough . . . besides, I picked up your two boys a half hour ago."

"There are three," clucked the older man delighted, "you're getting lazy, and careless . . ."

"Hardly," interrupted Fairchild "but I knew your well-documented paranoia would leave nothing to chance. Are we secure?"

"Yes, yes, we are quite alone."

"Good Moshi, because I've got a lot to do, and I really *would* like to catch the shuttle back to D.C. this afternoon."

With a sigh, the senior Mossad officer ground the tip of his cane into the cobblestone and spelled out five letters: T, H, O, T, M.

"What?"

The short man repeated the letters a second time.

"What the hell's that," mouthed Fairchild in frustration.

"You tell me," shrugged the Israeli, "you're the ones with all the fancy computers . . . we think it's the target."

"T, H, O, T, M—that's it?!"

"That's all we have."

Fairchild let out a slow exhalation and mumbled. "The vaunted Israeli Intelligence."

"Thomas, would you *please*."

There was clear irritation in the older man's voice.

"Yeah, yeah," nodded Fairchild.

They sat in silence for a moment as the American thought about the five letters. "Any language that you know?"

"No, we do not think it's a word, but rather some type of acronym or symbolic code. We don't think it bears relevance to any particular system. I believe you call it *slang*."

"Why?"

"The way that we uncovered it."

"Which was?"

The Mossad officer shrugged. "You wouldn't approve of our methods . . ."

"Probably not."

"Suffice to say," continued the short man unfazed, "we have confirmed its accuracy by at least one other independent source—and *that* source is considered *very* reliable."

"Your *own* man?" Fairchild was a bit amazed. "How many cells have you penetrated?"

"Ah, no specifics Thomas, there is only *so* much that we can share."

The short Israeli stroked his moustache. "Enjoy your flight back. Give my best to your boss, she's a fine lady."

"I will."

"She's Jewish you know."

Fairchild looked at his counterpart for the first time. "What? That's a new one."

"Quite true though, with all the nationalities in her background, she still celebrates Hanukkah each year. I'd say that makes her Jewish, wouldn't you? Shalom my friend."

Before Fairchild could reply, the Mossad officer stood and walked away, leaving the American with his pigeons.

~~~

Driving to Glyfada Beach was a wonderful journey of scenic beauty. Nestled between lush green mountains, towering peaks and the clear blue Mediterranean, Glyfada hid itself on the west coast, a mere ten kilometers from Kerkyra Town.

Throughout the ride, Jay marveled at the ease with which Katerina handled Theodori's powerful Jaguar. The roads were of poor quality, and an occasional glance at the sheer drop of the mountain precipice, warned Jay that a mistake would be fatal.

Yet Kat seemed unfazed, and though they cruised by a number of roadside shrines, where careless—or unlucky—travelers drove off the cliff, she seemed quite oblivious to any danger.

The ride took them twenty minutes, and surprisingly, the popular beach was uncrowded. A few scattered tourists dotted the sand, but most seemed content to congregate around the hotel pool. With picnic basket and towels in hand, they set off for the far end of the long, sandy beach.

As Katerina spread a beach blanket, Jay kicked off his running shoes and tugged at his shirt. He heard a gasp and looked up to see Kat staring at the deep red scar that curved horizontally along his ribcage. She dropped her hands self-consciously from her mouth, yet could not take her eyes off the nasty wound.

"Sorry," mumbled Jay with a shrug, not quite sure how to respond. He sat on the blanket, and reached into the picnic basket for the book he had borrowed from Theodori's library.

"No Jaycott, *I* am sorry . . . it looks so painful."

"Not so much anymore, I guess it hurt a bit when it happened. It only bothers me now on occasion," he smiled, "like when I get it sunburned."

Katerina immediately reached into her handbag and removed a strong sunscreen. "Here, let me."

She poured a liberal amount of thick, white cream into her palm, and after warming, started to gently rub the lotion along the scar. For a few moments Katerina kept kneading the cream into the long scar as if the act itself would make the wound disappear. Jay looked up to see her shaking, and he calmly cupped her hands in his own.

"You really ought to spread that stuff around, this sun is pretty strong."

"I'm sorry."

His gentle prod seemed to pull Kat out of her slight fixation, and she started to apply the sunscreen over the top of his shoulders.

"I never realized," she admitted, kneeling behind Jay. "Theodori had always said that he made his money the hard way. When I asked him to elaborate, he would only say that he did things for people, for governments, that they would not do for themselves . . . some of the locals have mentioned that Theodori had a dark past—but he has *always* been good to me."

"Does that surprise you?"

"No . . . but he keeps much in. He has no friends. He trusts few. The islanders, they like him, respect him, but that is because they fear him."

"Why do you say that?"

"I see it in their eyes . . . no, the only two men that Theodori spoke of, trusted, were you and a Frenchman. I was always curious to meet these two men, and now I have met *you* . . . I wonder if I will ever meet that Frenchman, what was his name? Pierre . . ."

"Richeleau," mumbled Jay.

"Yes, Richeleau . . . do you know him?"

"I did. Pierre's dead."

Katerina stopped massaging Jay's shoulder. "Oh . . ." Then she changed the subject. ". . . you are in very good shape Jaycott, like an athlete. You have the physique of a much younger man . . . on your stomach." She pushed him down and started spreading sunscreen on Jay's legs.

"How old am I?"

"Older than me," she laughed diplomatically.

"How old are you?" grinned Jay curiously.

"Such a question, typical American . . . let me say that I have yet to reach my thirtieth birthday."

There was an expertise to Kat's applying the sunscreen, a steadiness like a massage. But after a few minutes, her strokes seemed to become less strident, and more sensual, and Jay felt his arousal become apparent.

Katerina applied the cream all the way down his legs until she reached his ankles, and then slowly started up again, smoothly stroking the inside of his thighs, shifting her weight atop his buttocks in a straddle, grinding her pelvis into the small of his back for leverage as she covered each square inch of exposed skin—his back, shoulders, neck, and arms.

"Turn."

"You're going to spoil me."

"You are a guest. Greeks are known for hospitality."

"You're not Greek."

"Actually I am, but only a quarter."

Kneeling at his side, Katerina started to rub the sunscreen into Jay's hard chest muscles. She moved slowly, in long strokes, working her way down his abdomen to the flat, rocky stomach, and then to his sinewed thighs. Katerina continued as thoroughly as before, covering each patch of exposed skin all the way to his toes. If she noticed the bulging erection confined in his swim trunks, she ignored it. Finally, with a pat on his shoulder, she announced him finished.

Jay popped open one eye to see Katerina sitting with her back to him on the other side of the blanket. Then she quickly tugged off her shorts and blouse.

Kat's body was even more beautiful than he had imagined. Clad in a skimpy bikini, her unencumbered limbs and torso showed remarkable firmness. There was a great suppleness to her movements, as she liberally spread the protective cream over her taunt flesh.

"Need some help?"

"My back."

Jay relaxed. Just as well. He hoped the water was cold. For a moment, he doubted the wisdom of their beach excursion. A measured distance seemed to creep into Katerina's demeanor, and in a perverse way Jay welcomed it. Her applying the lotion to his body seemed to introduce a new level of intimacy between them; and though it had started innocently enough, there was no point in courting problems. Certainly if she allowed him the same latitude in massaging her body, his control might crumble.

When Katerina had finished covering every accessible part of her skin, she rubbed an extra amount of lotion in and around her face. Then she curled her hair over one shoulder, lay on her stomach, and unhooked the top of her bikini. Jay gently smoothed the sun screen onto her back and watched as Kat seemed to fall asleep.

He napped himself. Then read for a short time. Finally Jay stood and went for a long swim. The guilt of not exercising that morning energized his strokes, but his real adrenaline pulsed with thoughts of the beautiful, half-naked woman that lay sleeping back on the blanket. Again, he tried to make sense of confusing signals; Katerina's massage had in many ways crossed the boundaries of platonic affection. Yet her sudden coolness shortly thereafter, again distorted Jay's perspective. The real difficulty in sorting through the mess, was that now he began to question his *own* objectivity. Therefore, he sought relief in physical exhaustion. When in doubt, tire yourself out. There was seldom a resolution, but by then one was too worn-out to care.

He returned to the blanket to see Katerina fast asleep. Jay toweled himself dry, read for a bit, and then fell into a deep sleep himself.

At one point in his dreams, Jay was sure that he awoke to Katerina reapplying some cream to his back and thighs. There was her sensuous touch, especially around his buttocks, but in his half-slumber he could not quite be sure, so he dismissed the notion.

When he finally did awake, Jay found Katerina setting out lunch from the picnic basket. The cold pack had kept their wine and food chilled, yet they both picked at their meal sparingly.

While nibbling on a piece of cheese, Kat broke their silence. "Do you ever talk about the woman?"

The question caught Jay by surprise. "What woman?"

"The one who you loved?"

Jay looked at her curiously, searching for some motive, some hint of purpose to the question. She gazed back innocently, as thoughts of Ellie flooded his mind. "She's dead."

"Does it hurt you to talk about her?"

"Yes."

A pause, then after a brief instant, Kat reached forward and touched Jay on the wrist. "I'm sorry Jaycott, I don't want to hurt you."

He met her eyes and nodded. There was a profound sincerity in her face. "I know . . . it's a long story, and it was a long time ago."

"Not so long ago, I think. But forget I asked."

"Fair enough."

"We should go," said Katerina, reaching for her shorts. "Too much sun is not good, even with the protection."

Jay nodded.

"I know the manager of the hotel. He will let us shower and change before we start back. We should also have an Ouzo in the bar, some locals favor this area."

They repacked the picnic basket and their possessions before starting back up the beach.

V

22 July 1989
London, England

THE LONDON STOCK Exchange was an electronic marvel that had long since lost its allure as an active hotbed of finance. Gone were the throngs of busy traders running about an arena-size floor feverishly buying and selling stocks for their clients. The Exchange now served more as a tourist attraction, where the public could look down from the windowed gallery into a near-empty floor and watch the rare stock broker stroll from one vacant computer terminal to another. If three people occupied the huge trading floor simultaneously it was a crowd. The picture was not unlike a huge sports stadium hours *after* a championship game.

However, many in the public still clamored for the opportunity to enter the Visitor's Gallery, in the hopes of seeing the organized chaos that typified most major stock exchanges, and thus it became a good location for a "meet".

Tom Fairchild stood patiently at the far end of the Visitor's Gallery, idly peering down at the midday emptiness and inactivity. Seconds later, a very trim man dressed in a worsted wool suit, and carrying a folded newspaper under his right arm, strolled up beside the American.

"They say that this is the future of the New York Stock Exchange."

"Emptiness?"

"Electronic trading. Amazing how computers match buy and sell orders so efficiently, thus alleviating the need for floor traders."

"I'm sure that those in a position to suffer will fight against the change."

To the trained eye the two intelligence officers had just established bona fides. The far recognition signal was the folded newspaper under the approaching man's right arm. The near recognition signal was the challenge and password dialogue about electronic trading. Satisfied, Tom Fairchild immediately launched into what is known in the trade as the *mad minute*. This is where a quick contingency plan is offered, should the two men be interrupted prior to exchanging all their information.

"If I scratch my chin, we break contact . . . meet again, at the bars of the following hotels, in order; Savoy, Ritz, International—one hour intervals on the hour. Good?"

"Quite," agreed the Englishman without preamble. They were both professionals, and knew to get to the important information quickly. "I don't have much, just a series of numbers."

"Numbers?", protested Fairchild a bit surprised.

"Precisely."

"Go ahead."

"20-8-15-20-13."

"Again."

The Englishman repeated the numbers a second time, in a slow, distinct, if not quiet tone, as the case officer concentrated.

"Got it," nodded Fairchild, "Mean anything to you?"

"No," shrugged his counterpart, "We've been running a computer crunch around the clock; permutations, statistical variance, algorithms . . ."

". . . I'd be curious to know what you come up with. Sometimes the crypto people miss the most obvious because it's so simple."

Fairchild nodded a second time. "How good's your source?"

"A B-2 WOG," answered the Englishman. He referred to the classification system that rated both the agent and the information independently. The letter A was the most reliable agent, D the least. The numbers referred to corroboration of the information; one having multiple independent sources of backup, four having none. Thus a B-2 was a time-tested, reliable agent passing well-corroborated information. The *WOG* term was common, if unflattering, British slang for an Arab. Originally, it referred to Egyptians, specifically those laborers who worked on the Suez Canal during the years of English Colonization. These laborers wore coveralls with the letters W.O.G.S. stenciled on the back—working on government service. As the years passed, it came to refer first to any Egyptians, then any Arabic person in general; one of the less courteous mementos of British colonial rule brought back to the Queen's Island.

Fairchild recognized the lead for what it was: solid. They fell silent as Tom continued thinking of the numbers. 20-8-15-20-13.

"Anything else?"

"Afraid not . . . we had a bit of a bloody row getting that much."

"I imagine. Thanks for your help Reggie."

"Not to say lad," he handed Fairchild his newspaper. "For the flight home . . . all this traveling, a shame you have to keep this affair out of official channels, it would be so much easier to just chat over at Grosvner Square."

The Englishman's reference to the U.S. Embassy was an acknowledgement of Fairchild's difficult assignment. Using contract employees on a covert operation necessitated avoiding all official U.S. facilities, thereby causing the staffer to log a good deal more time shuttling about to receive information.

Tom took the newspaper and patted the Englishman on the back. With a wink he was gone, leaving his counterpart alone to look down on the empty floor of the London Stock Exchange.

HE SAT INDIAN-STYLE, his squat, thick legs crossed at the ankles, and looked across the valley at the Church of Prophitis Ilias. Sweat poured down Theodori's face, and his thinning, curly hair matted to his forehead. The great lungs wheezed, sucking and blowing deep gulps of air as his reddened face and rapidly thumping heart testified to the level of exertion.

Directly to his rear, rose the hill on which sat the palace of Sparta, long since destroyed, and in the distance to either side, rose the steep mountains of Parnon and Taygetus.

It had been this way for three days—the first two of which he didn't even eat; wake at sunrise, exercise, a slow jog around the barren valley, and then back for his reward: two cups of coffee. Afternoon found Theodori climbing the steep, jagged mountains—barefoot, until his torn, blistered feet were numb with pain. He returned to ample amounts of water and a handful of vitamins. After sunset more calisthenics and then a long walk in the dark to heighten his senses.

Theodori's moments of inactivity were divided between long readings on Sparta by the ancient writer Plutarch, and visiting the various shrines that dotted the valley near the river Eurotas. Sleep was his only salvation; each night collapsing his sore, beaten body and letting the exhaustion overtake him until dawn.

Theodori slept on the ground, in a makeshift shelter, unwashed, unshaven, grizzled and weathered; a cruel, self-imposed penance to purge the years of comfort and excess consumption.

It wasn't long before the goat farmers in the nearby village started gossiping about the burly loner who had materialized again in the valley after years of absence. Finally, on the third day—when he broke his fast—a few curious children came around for a look.

Theodori stooped over a fire, eyeing a curdling black broth that emanated a strange aroma. He stirred the liquid, occasionally seasoning the pot with salt and vinegar, all under the watchful gaze of three young boys. Then he spooned a heaping ladle-full into a bowl and with a nod offered it to the closest child. The boy hesitated, but after mumbles and prompting stepped forward and accepted the meal. Theodori fixed himself a bowl of the turbid stew and winked. The child watched the older man consume a few mouthfuls before tentatively testing the lumpy broth. He half-grimaced.

"What is it?" he blurted in peasant Greek.

"Pork cooked in its own blood," answered Theodori.

The child accepted the answer with a shrug, and motioned his friends closer to the fire. Excited, they all came over and sat cross-legged, imitating Theodori, and alternately passed the bowl between them.

"Where are you from?" asked one of the children.

Theodori looked about the valley and smiled. "Here young one, from the land of our ancestors."

"Here?" protested another, "We have never seen you . . ." the child hesitated before continuing, "Christos, the old goat herder says you are from far away, that you used to come to our valley many years ago."

Theodori nodded, a slight smile curving his lip. "Christos remembers well; I do *live* far away, but this is *home*."

The children sat in silence digesting their black stew and the answer.

"Do you know the story of Thermopylae?" asked Theodori, setting down his half-empty bowl. Before they could respond, he held up his index finger in a professorial way. "In 480 B.C., the Agiad King Leonidas—the Lion—son of Anaxandridas, brother of Cleomenes, led three hundred Spartans against the Persian King Xerxes at Thermopylae. Xerxes was ruler of all Asia, and he invaded Greece with an army of 20,000 men . . ." A glint came to Theodori's eye as he saw them fix their attention, ". . . the story of those Spartan soldiers is a tale of one of the bravest battles in military history . . ."

THE SOVIET REZIDENTURA tugged at his briefcase as he strolled through the Algerian Old Quarter. He had never particularly liked this posting to North Africa, yet he had to admit, the position of Rezidentura—of Chief of the GRU Residency in Algeria—offered certain perquisites to a professional Intelligence Officer. And the subtleties of this assignment, when spiced with the obvious opportunities for promotion, certainly suggested greater days ahead. Brussels, Zurich, *Paris*—all were now in his grasp; and therefore the need to forge an airtight mission, one whose very success was all but assured, became paramount.

It had taken him twelve years to get this Rezidentura; a position that held the Soviet military rank of Colonel. And with that rank came all the privilege, monetary compensation, and administrative clout one would expect.

The Rezidentura mused quietly as he turned a corner in the narrow, cluttered streets of the Casbah. It had been many a long day and late night spent drinking, cajoling, recruiting—three separate postings prior to this, two in North Africa. His days as an Operations Officer and Deputy Rezidentura had served him well, showing a particular talent for identifying and controlling terrorist personalities. Thus he had worked alternately for the GRU's Fourth Directorate, which dealt with Agent Intelligence in Africa and the Middle East; and the Third Direction, which concerned itself with Agent Intelligence in National Liberation movements and organizations. The Directorates and Directions were separate branches, yet in each case they reported to the First Deputy Chief of the GRU. He understood the Arabic mind, and he accepted their sometimes frustrating culture. He spoke a fair amount of their language, and even some of the local dialects, yet his real forte had always been excellent French, and the ability to manipulate fringe personalities.

In the distance he heard the daily call to prayer echo through the Old Quarter. The Soviet scratched his flat face and tugged at his suitcoat self-consciously. The North African countries, by virtue of their European colonization, had always been a bit more tolerant to the vices of western civilization than their Asian counterparts. Alcohol, dancing, and less stringent female dress codes were the norm and did not equate to ostracism or prison. Yet the Soviet had noticed over the last few years, a rise in strict fundamentalism. This had been spawned by the Ayatollah Khomeini of Iran, and a sweeping tide of Pan-Arabic nationalism. Of course, the latent insecurity of Arabic males and their incredible chauvinism towards women helped to feed the fire as well. It was all quite relative to the Rezidentura, who viewed any weakness as a point of exploitation; and the naiveté of his young hotheads always induced them to believe that they were working for the KGB—his Soviet arch rival—a political organization, rather than his GRU, a military one. But in actuality that had always been the case; the KGB got the notoriety—both good and bad, depending upon one's perspective—and the GRU got the successes *and* the power. In any case, the Rezidentura's career would take another leap forward, beginning *today*.

He rounded the corner of an old, white alabaster building and knocked on the door. The peephole passed in shadow, and then the thick door opened. Saoud stood motionless, his gold rings, bracelets, and necklace glittering in the late afternoon sun. With a nod, the stocky Soviet crossed the threshold and started down a long hallway to the rear of the apartment.

The GRU officer entered a small kitchen, to see four young men huddled around a wooden table sipping green Arabic tea. They could have been Saoud's cousins; mid-twenties, thin, swarthy; each flaunting their masculinity like so many mannequins. He greeted them in Berber, an Algerian dialect, shaking hands all around, causing Saoud to beam with pride at the urbane touch of his Soviet mentor. With a sense of anticipation, the Rezidentura met each of their eyes, then he carefully set his briefcase down in the center of the wooden table and snapped open the locks. He pulled three folded maps from within.

"This," he began in flawless French, "is a map of the United States, as you all know." He spread the wall size map across the table before allowing his index finger to trace the coastline southward from New York City to the lower right corner. "And this is Florida, the southeastern most state of the United States."

He unfolded his second map, a large depiction of the citrus state, and placed it over the first map. Then he paused for a moment, sensing their energy, "And this," he whispered melodramatically, opening the third map, "is 20-8-15-20-13—the target."

A collective gasp aired, as the eyes of the young fanatics glowed in surprise. They leaned forward, perched on elbows, and immediately started conversing in excited Arabic. The room brimmed with electricity, as Saoud and his four associates seemed to forget the presence of the Soviet, and became engrossed in their final destination.

JAY STOOD AT the tidebreaker across the street from Theodori's home and smiled. Three sea gulls alternately swooped down on the calm surface of Garitsa Bay and stabbed at the still blue water. He marveled at their ability; such precision, like elegant dive bombers, parodying the German Stukas of World War II, screaming down on the unsuspecting fish in a blur of aerodynamic control and predatory violence.

The sun warmed Jaycott's face as his breathing slowly returned to normal. He'd had another restless night, his mind and his libido filled with thoughts of Katerina.

Following their return from Glyfada beach the previous afternoon, Kat excused herself to attend to some

personal matters. Jay had busied himself by going into
Theodori's study and reading. Later that evening, when
Katerina failed to join Jay for dinner, Lenoris, the house
woman offered little explanation. As the night wore on, Jay
began pacing, moving from one diversion to another,
restlessly alternating his concentration as he longed for her
company. Where was she? What was she doing? Why was
she not with him? Moments became minutes, and minutes
became hours, as Jaycott played back in his mind the
sequence of events of their day together.

Now, the morning after, following a hard run, and
harder calisthenics, Jay laughed self-consciously at himself.
He was like a lust-filled adolescent whose first teenage crush
is a combination of newly awakened senses and unchecked
fantasies. Yet subconsciously Jay knew that he possessed a
much deeper emotional attraction to Theodori's woman.
Pretty faces come and go, only character sustains . . .

Slowly, Jay walked back across the street and circled
the house. On the veranda, Lenoris was setting out a bowl of
fruit, and Jay reached for an orange while collapsing lazily
into a chair. Then the old woman set a serving tray on the
table, complete with a coffee pot, milk, sugar, a Graecian
newspaper, and two unused cups and saucers. At first Jay
busied himself by peeling the orange and he payed little
attention to the tray. Yet after a few minutes, as Lenoris
fussed about her morning ritual of arranging freshly cut
flowers, he noticed a sealed envelope with the word *Jaycott*
printed in clear block letters. He leaned forward, his eyes
searching the old woman's face, and motioned at the

envelope. Lenoris shrugged indifferently and walked back into the house.

Curiously, Jay ripped open the envelope, and read the short message printed in the same clear block letters:

> Dear Jaycott,
>
> Urgent business has required me to unexpectedly leave the island. Lenoris shall see to your needs.
>
> Fondly,
> Katerina

Jay's mouth momentarily tightened in frustration. Then he stood and walked into the house to shower.

VI

TOM FAIRCHILD AWOKE with a start, and for a brief moment he forgot where he was. His eyes scanned the strange hotel room searching for a clue, and then he focused on the opened glass shutters of the portico: Athens; the Grande Bretagne Hotel.

With a nod to himself, Fairchild tossed aside the thin cotton sheet and rolled from his bed. In skivvies and night shirt the Intelligence Officer padded barefoot to the shutters and stepped out onto the portico. He gazed down on Syntagma Square, already bustling with tourists, and watched as three Athenians at a café table fed a few hungry pigeons.

Tom stepped back from the sunshine and dialed room service, ordering himself a large breakfast. Fairchild had long since eschewed air conditioning, preferring a natural breeze whenever possible; and one of the advantages of the Grande Bretagne—in addition to its excellent amenities and central location—was the ability to get an evening breeze by which to sleep.

He passed by a small table and looked at the folded newspaper given to him at the London Exchange. He had meant to read the paper on the flight into Athens, yet the constant travel of the past week made sleep more attractive and he napped instead. Now waiting for breakfast, Tom took the newspaper and sat in an Edwardian chair by the glass shutters.

He couldn't concentrate. His thoughts kept reverting back to Central America. Fairchild had been the Case Officer for an operation to penetrate Panamanian money laundering cells. Jaycott had been the point man.

They had traced several of Manuel Noriega's bagmen between Colón and Cartagena, and matched these with wire transfers between the strongman's personal accounts and several offshore banks. Suddenly, six months of work evaporated; couriers disappeared, numbered accounts closed, and the signature to the wire transfers ended. They'd been compromised. Two days after the rollup began, Jay narrowly escaped a Cartel hit team. However, the Colombians played by their own rules, and just as quickly turned their focus on Ellie Ryan Jaycott.

It was a rainy night in Arlington, Virginia, when the young lawyer for a Beltway Lobbyist Firm was run off the road. To suppress any doubts that it was merely a traffic accident, the Colombians also sprayed her torso with nine millimeter bullets and "left their mark" with a very sharp stiletto.

Fairchild folded the newspaper and set it on the table. He understood Jay's frustration, and although time had dimmed the fire, he doubted the pain had waned. Truth be

told, Tom empathized with Jaycott, and shared with him a
sense of gnawing anger. Colón was some of Fairchild's best
work, and he had believed it an airtight operation.
Considering the depth of Jay's cover, it was difficult to accept
that even the Colombians, with all the Cartel's money, could
dig out Jaycott's identity. This is of course what haunted
Jay—the possibility—if not the probability—that there was
an internal leak.

Fairchild's mind wandered . . . T, H, O, T, M . . . 20, 8,
15, 20,13 . . .

THE BURLY GREEK stepped from the taxi in front of
his home, and surveyed the Victorian style mansion. Theodori
was home. It had been a grueling four days, but the self-
styled masochism of the trip had purged the ghost of
conspicuous consumption, and hardened his mind—while
battering his body—to the demands that lay ahead.

Theo swung through the wrought iron gate, one large
rucksack in hand, and approached his front door. It had never
really been a question of money; Theodori had accumulated
much over the years, and invested well, so as to alleviate the
need to ever work again. His accepting of the assignment had
really been a combination of other factors; loyalty to Jay,
boredom with his easy lifestyle, challenge, and maybe just
the one nagging question of ability. Like an aging athlete,
Theodori wondered if he could still perform at peak levels.
He admitted grudgingly that a step of speed was lost, but
what time had stolen on one hand, it had heightened on the

other. No young buck could even accumulate the treasure chest of experience that Theodori had stored. This was a man of guile; pure, unadulterated, deadly; a soldier of fortune who had confronted—and survived—many of life's seamier moments.

He entered the huge foyer, dropping his rucksack to the clean tile floor just as Lenoris, the housewoman entered. A broad smile creased the old woman's face. They exchanged quick pleasantries in Greek before she scuttled off with Theo's mud-caked rucksack.

He stormed his way into the study surprising Jaycott who had just returned from a late lunch in town.

"Theo?!"

"Ishmael," bellowed the burly Greek crossing the room in three squat strides. He gripped Jay by the shoulders holding the taller American at arm's length.

"Ah, the island works its magic on you my friend. The great wanderer finds a home. Look at you; tanned, fit, rested; all your senses coiled like a well-oiled spring."

Jay took a hard look at his grizzled unshaven friend. Theodori looked haggard; his face sallow and drawn, his eyes lined and furrowed. The rapid weight loss was quite apparent. With a blistered hand, Theo punched Jay gently on the shoulder.

"You look like shit," mumbled Jaycott.

"But I *feel* magnificent!" beamed the Greek infectiously.

Jay joined his stocky friend in laughter. "And you need a shower."

"As we speak Lenoris draws my bath; and tonight I will have a low calorie meal of fish and fruit . . . will you join me?"

"Of course," nodded Jay as Theo opened his globe-bar and pulled out a bottle of Metaxa.

"Only one, as a welcome home treat . . . and tomorrow I will run with you—if you take it slowly," winked the Greek.

Jay nodded again. "Early. I've heard from my contact. He'll be here tomorrow morning to brief us. Things are moving fast!"

"And we'll be ready . . . did my staff take care of your needs?"

"Very well," replied Jay, his thoughts quickly shifting to Katerina, who had mysteriously gone away the night before.

"Good." Theodori downed the Metaxa in a quick pull. "I'll see you at dinner my friend." With a meaty paw, Theo nudged Jay and handed him the brandy snifter. Then he bounded from the study.

IT WASN'T A particularly large room, like many of the chambers in the old Executive Office Building, but it had stature. The fact that it wasn't used very often didn't seem to diminish its importance—that importance derived more from the people who assembled there, and the information they discussed; and like many disparate appearances in government, real power was subliminal. Thus, the group took their name from something as innocuous as the room number. Chamber number forty in the old EOB became the official residence of the *Forty Committee.*

Tom Laughlin, Deputy Director (Intelligence), for the Central Intelligence Agency sat at the head of the conference table. He was the defacto leader of the Forty Committee, by virtue of his position in the senior intelligence service of the nation. All the other committee members chaired the intelligence branch or section in their respective agencies, however, most of these other governmental bodies were not dedicated to full-time intelligence collection and interpretation.

Across from Tom, at the far end of the table, sat John Mullins, Deputy Director (Operations) of the CIA. Tom and John were equals of sorts, and the two right-handed men to Judge William Webster, Director of the CIA and a Presidential appointee.

Around the table respectively sat a Deputy Director of the FBI, the Director of the State Department's office to Combat Terrorism, Senior Analysts from the National Security Agency and the Defense Intelligence Agency, Deputy Directors of the U.S. Secret Service, the Bureau of Alcohol, Tobacco, and Firearms, and the Customs Service, the Deputy Chief of the Department of Transportation, a Deputy Director of the Drug Enforcement Administration, and a Rear Admiral from the office of the Joint Chiefs.

These dozen men represented the pooled Intelligence assets of the United States. Each had sufficient clout at their respective organizations to cut through the red tape. They were also senior enough and experienced enough to realize that the committee's success depended upon cooperation. The traditional obstacles and turf battles that existed in Washington were avoided. This then was a group of dedicated professionals who convened their committee only when a national crisis loomed.

"In front of each of you," began Laughlin, "are transcripts of the latest intercepts that Al and his folks at Fort Meade have picked up relative to our problem." He nodded at the NSA Senior Analyst. "Also, we are now quite sure that the attack will be in-Conus and soon." Laughlin turned to his right. "George?"

The Deputy Director for the U.S. Secret Service, cleared his throat before speaking. "Runner's schedule has been curtailed, which is always a difficult task, but he has accepted our requests."

All the committee members recognized the penchant of the President to travel, and they empathized with the Secret Service's frustration in trying to protect a leader with an abundance of nervous energy. "To that end, we have continued to harden all physical sites, as well as increasing our personal vigilance. All available agents have been reassigned to protective detail."

"Good . . ." nodded Tom, turning to his left, ". . . Paul?"

The Customs representative shuffled his papers. "We have put a virtual blanket around all known ports of entry, much to the chagrin of our tourists. Their impatience at the mounting delays and extra security is palpable; that's to be expected somewhat . . . the linchpin is effective identification and interception of hostiles given the freedom of our system of government. We've been coordinating closely with STATE and DOT to close ranks at our borders."

Laughlin nodded before turning to the Deputy FBI Director, "Russell, what's the status of your surveillance?"

"We have sixteen different known terrorist cells under active surveillance. These of course, are already in-country; some are dormant, some are moderately active. Our problem of course, are those acting under legal status with the protection of diplomatic immunity. Freedom of movement to these people is unrestricted, as is their resupply—they have access to the diplomatic pouch; which of course is sealed and inviolate under international law . . . on another level, we have our HRT team on twenty-four hour alert . . . but don't know where to send them."

The FBI's Hostage Response Team was well trained and well equipped. But you cannot fight an enemy you can't find; and you cannot protect a target unless you know what it is.

"When will Delta or Team Six get involved?"

The Admiral from the Joint Chiefs received a hesitant look from the FBI man. The Constitution expressly forbid the U.S. military from operating within the confines of the United States. Terrorism, or more accurately, the sabotage and subversion that it spawned, was a violation of federal law, and hence fell under the normal domain of law enforcement agencies such as the FBI and ATF. However, given the seriousness of the situation, the expertise of the Army's Delta Force and the Navy's Seal Team-Six were welcome additions. "We have issued a request to MacDill

AFB down in Tampa for small detachments to assist us in an *advisory* capacity. I should note that we have also requested the same assistance from John at Langley, and Bob." He motioned to Mullins and Bob Perkins of the State Department—neither of whose agencies similarly had any law enforcement mandate or powers of arrest.

"Rudy?"

The Senior Analyst at the DIA pulled out a sheet of notes and passed copies around the conference table to each member. "This is a list of our most sensitive military installations in-Conus, predicated on an analysis of NSA traffic that the strike will be here at home. These of course are the easiest to protect given our heightened awareness and the control procedures already in place."

He handed out more pages. "These are a list of political installations, most of which are in and around the capitol area. Again the theory being, that although they are not as tactically important as our military installations, they still possess some C-3 significance. They are secondary in nature, and would pose some disruption to our system of government."

He handed out a third group of papers. "These are a list of major industrial installations, outside the circle of federal protection, that present an inviting target to terrorists. One can expect some type of localized security and police surveillance to assist in safeguarding them. A hit at any of these sights could severely disrupt electric power, water supply, or telecommunications to a given geographic region—not unlike a natural disaster . . ."

Finally he handed a fourth set of papers to the committee members.

". . . and these are major sights of no particular military, political, or industrial significance. They are purely symbolic in nature; places or events with no disruptive tactical or strategic value *other* than they typify the strength or stature of the United States as a nation. They are also the easiest targets to surveille and strike."

The Analyst took a moment to catch his breath. He emptied his water glass in one long swallow.

"We are trying to get some information on a cell or cells that could mobilize a major operation with offshore assistance. We've included all the usual groups; the PFLP, the PLO, the ANO, splinter factions of Hezbollah . . . thus far we've been unable to get a solid line on precisely *who*, or more importantly: *where*."

"John," interrupted the Deputy Director of DEA turning towards Mullins; he normally stayed very quiet, but when he spoke there was a pragmatic respect afforded him that came to someone who spent a lifetime waging a war that many thought unwinnable: drugs. "Due to the severity of the problem, has there been any thought to using unconventional collection methods?"

Mullins' folded hands seemed to squeeze tighter, so that his knuckles blanched. He hesitated for a moment, his thoughts pulsing quickly as if debating how much to share with his colleagues. He took a deep breath before answering. "Yes."

All of the committee members seemed to lean forward in anticipation; their interest sparked. John Mullins had been a somewhat legendary Case Officer, who now controlled the actual human spying apparatus of the United States. He had their attention. "Can you be more specific?" asked the Deputy ATF Director.

Mullins looked across the conference table at Tom Laughlin, his fellow CIA employee. The DDI seemed equally surprised and interested in the revelation. This was nothing new, in a world of secrecy, compartmentalization was constant, even when two senior staffers spent the better part of their day in each other's office.

"By design," began Mullins, "my information is limited, but we are in the process of launching a Probe."

"Launching a *Probe*?" pressed the Admiral, his senses heightened by the use of military parlance.

"Yes," nodded Mullins, "a specialist . . . someone with an excellent track record of attaining results, human results, by exposing himself."

"Excuse me John," interrupted Paul from Customs, "but that sounds rather dangerous. Is it fair to place one of our people in that position?"

"It is dangerous," conceded Mullins, "but in any case, he's not one of ours, not really."

The room seemed to pause in unison, yet before anyone could respond, Tom Laughlin, his eyes riveted on his co-worker, spoke quietly. "A contract?"

Mullins looked up and nodded. "Yes."

"You'll forgive me," asked Bob from the State Department, but this *Probe* of yours, this contract, is he U.S.?"

"A citizen yes, an employee . . ." Mullins shrugged, "not if we don't want him to be. If this implodes, his file hits the shredder."

"Why would anyone ever take on that kind of job?"

"I'm not sure," admitted Mullins, "I let the shrinks worry about motivation, I'm only interested in results."

"Speaking of results," added Russell of the FBI, "do you have any?"

"No."

"Well where's he at, what's he been doing?"

"I don't know," answered Mullins honestly, "nor do I want to. There's too much exposure in this method. We have a completely disjointed chain of command—as I said, by design."

"That's a hell of a way to run a ship," grumbled the Admiral.

"Deniability," offered Rudy of DIA.

"Total. In any event, given the situation, I made a judgment call. Only the future knows if I'll be right."

VII

VIKTOR PAPAHA TUCKED the diplomatic passport into his suitcoat pocket and lighted a cigarette. It was the Spetsnaz officer's first trip to North America, and the dual excitement of western travel and an important assignment flushed the Colonel with a sense of anticipation.

He walked to a far newsstand and purchased two packs of American cigarettes and a local newspaper. The stop-off in Montreal was part of a quick immersion; enabling Papaha to acclimate to western ways, conduct a long map study of the target, grow his hair from the short military cut, and practice his English. The Colonel had a few days to waste, and being a legal entry into Canada, he expected—and welcomed—the inevitable RCMP interest that would follow. He allowed for the "tail," and planned on maintaining a very dull tourist schedule, one that was sure to put the Mountie Counter Intelligence Staff to sleep. This of course would enable him to eventually make an easier illegal entry into the U.S.

A delegate from the Soviet Consulate approached, flashed his identification, and gave Papaha a quick salute. The Polkovnik exhaled, and caught the movement in the background of several plain clothes Mounties. He smiled to himself as the delegate relieved him of his bags. Viktor motioned towards the door.

"The car is near?"

"Da Comrade Colonel, it is parked in the special diplomatic zone."

"Good," nodded Papaha, watching from the corner of his eye to make sure that his Canadian hosts had dutifully made their identification. "The food on Aeroflot was terrible. I think I would like to try this famous Canadian breakfast of bacon and . . . flapjacks?"

"Da Colonel, pancakes," smiled the delegate. "The Canadian lumbermen of the North Country are famous for their hearty breakfast." "Yes, and then I think a very long, slow ride about the city so that I get my bearings."

"Certainly Comrade Colonel, but after the long flight would the Polkovnik not wish to rest before meeting with the Military Attaché?"

"No Comrade, I am in no rush, the good General will understand." Papaha glanced over his shoulder. "To the car, and remember—take your time."

THE MEETING WAS held on the third floor of the Cavaliers Hotel, an honorable old mansion overlooking the Spianadha that in the early twenties functioned as the summer residence for King George II. It still retained a regal aura, a quiet grandeur that when mixed with its traditionally high standards of service, made it dignified as well as discreet.

Theodori paced behind Jay and to his left, their eyes automatically scanning in opposite directions. They had fallen into an operational routine; a natural, almost telepathic interplay; two professionals moving as one.

Inside the hotel, Theo spoke quietly to the young lady behind the reception desk. Seconds later, with a nod, they began a slow, methodical climb up the winding staircase. Again their eyes searched, movements were automatic and efficient, actions were reciprocal. The polished wood and oriental carpeting went unnoticed as the two proceeded skyward.

On the third floor landing they turned right, and with a hand motion, Theo indicated Fairchild's room number. They stopped on either side of the door, using the wall as protection, and Jay knocked twice. From inside he heard the number "five" called out. Jaycott answered with a "two."

It was a simple challenge—password system, always revolving around a single digit odd number. Both the challenge and passwords when added together had to equal the base number before entry was permitted. Failure to respond correctly usually ended in a fuselage of bullets. In this case the base number was seven.

The door opened a crack and Fairchild made eye contact with Jaycott. Then the Case Officer swung the heavy oak barrier inward and stepped backwards. Jay crossed the threshold and Theo followed, the burly Greek taking a final protective look down the hall. He closed and latched the door to see Fairchild place a Walther PPK on a small table.

Theodori crossed the room and curiously retrieved the pistol. He popped out the magazine and retracted the slide to eject the chambered round. Then he slowly squeezed the trigger once, dry firing the automatic to check the tension. Finally, while gripping the handgun in his meaty palm, he twirled the Walther several times for balance. With a frown, Theo gently placed the pistol back on the tabletop and looked up to see Fairchild watching him curiously.

"No stopping power," shrugged the Greek.

"Actually I've never used it," offered the Case Officer defensively, "not my style."

"Evidently not," mumbled Theo.

Fairchild looked back towards a smirking Jaycott. "I take it this is Theodori?"

Jay nodded. "Can we get down to business?"

Theo waved an open hand and the three men settled around a small projector that Fairchild had aimed at the white wall.

The staffer talked for thirty minutes, giving the two man team the sum total of his information. He began with the NSA intercepts, the FBI arrests, and the various leads that had been developed. Fairchild was quick to qualify each piece of information, careful to protect methods and sources wherever possible. He showed still photos of four individuals, adding last known addresses, habits, and movements. Finally after giving Jay and Theo the number and letter sequences, and speculations on how they might be connected, he placed a thin file on the coffee table.

"Burn paper. A summation of everything I've said, plus codes and serviceable drops that we'll use to communicate. Any questions?"

Jay looked at Theo. The Greek shook his head. "No," answered Jaycott.

"Good. One last thought . . . *time* is critical."

"We work our own schedule Tom, you know the drill."

Fairchild nodded, about to say something, when Theo stood and touched a thick index finger to the Case Officer's forearm. There was a menacing expression on the Greek's face.

"Those with clean hands," whispered Theo as he reached up and straightened the knot on Fairchild's tie, "should not advise those digging the ditch, on how to proceed."

With a wink towards Jay, he started towards the door. "Come Ishmael, we don't wish to unnecessarily delay your friend's promotion."

Jaycott grabbed for the file and stood, shaking the staffer's hand. "We'll be in touch Tom." Then he followed the burly Greek from the hotel room.

They walked in silence, descending the winding staircase, past the receptionist, and out onto the street. Finally as they turned right onto Vassileos Konstantinou, the shore road, when Jay was sure they were out of earshot, he turned towards Theodori. "Well?"

"I don't like him."

Jaycott smiled. "You don't have to."

"I don't trust him either."

"Neither do I . . . but then, I don't trust any of them anymore."

"Then why, my friend, do we do this?"

"They have something I want."

"What, money? If you need . . ."

"Information Theo. I need to know what happened two years ago. I've played it over in my head a hundred times, and I'm convinced that there wasn't just a lapse—but a leak. Maybe an intentional leak. They never should have got to Ellie . . . I've been promised the After Action Report, and I *need* to read it to fill in the missing pieces—for her sake."

The Greek grabbed Jay's shoulder firmly at mention of the dead wife's name.

"Then we shall do our best my friend; our very best indeed."

THE OLD WOMAN'S name was Listach. She was seventy years if she was a day, and she was a survivor.

Rochelle Listach had been orphaned at a young age, and learned early on that people were innately selfish. It made her hard. It kept her alive. She had worked for the Agency as long as anyone could remember, and the rumors said she traced her roots all the way back to the OSS.

In many ways, Rochelle was perfectly suited to her job. As on Operations Officer she supervised several Case Officers, each of whom in turn developed and "ran" several different Agents. Listach discharged her duties in a talented, if not calculating manner. She was an independent, unsentimental sort who loved her work yet rejected its romanticism. To her, all contract agents were pieces on a chessboard; pawns to be used as the situation dictated. For Rochelle, accomplishing the mission superseded all other considerations. Some of her peers considered this trait pragmatic, others—who saw the results—ruthless. In any case, it particularly suited the very specialized Paramilitary (PM) Division within the Directorate of Operations.

Unlike its much larger counterpart, the Foreign Intelligence (FI) Division, PM Case Officers didn't spend a lot of time attending Embassy cocktail parties. Scattered amongst the three branches (sea, air, and ground) of the PM Division, were a rather motley collection of specialist—all of whom started as Contract Agents; most of whom had extensive military training. Over time some of the Agents were offered full staff positions; others refused, retired, burned-out or died. PM was the cutting edge of hard operations; and its ranks swelled not with the buttoned down, preppie, Ivy-leaguers of FI, but rather with the Ex-Commandos, Gun-runners, and Air-America pilots that eschewed politics and produced results.

The old woman read the decoded report of Tom Fairchild. She had always demanded detailed briefs on dialogue and interactions from her Case Officers. It helped to clarify motives and frame of mind—a tool she used to properly anticipate actions.

Slowly, she removed her glasses and reached for a cup of tea. The beverage had cooled in the time Listach had read

the long report. With a slight grimace, she replaced the cup
back atop the Queen Ann coffee table and shifted in her seat.
Jaycott clearly presented a problem. Yet he was the best man
for the assignment; and since she held the carrot that induced
him out of retirement, she believed him controllable.
Theodori on the other hand, bothered her. He possessed
loyalty only for Jaycott. Rochelle would have to find the
carrot—or the stick—that would influence his behavior. With
a frown, the elderly lady punched a code back into her
computer. Theodori's résumé reappeared on her screen and
she started scanning the information again . . .

Born in Sparta Greece 1941 . . . parents died fighting
in the Grammos Mountains with the DSE Guerrillas in
1949 . . . raised by Aunt and Uncle in Mistras . . . average
student, good wrestler . . . odd jobs and manual labor
following high school . . . forced conscription into Greek
National Army, volunteered for Paratrooper
training . . . imprisoned and dishonorably discharged after
attacking an officer in a bar room . . . travelled the
Mediterranean for several years before surfacing in
Marseilles, France . . . arrested by Gendarmarie in 1966
following the brutal beating of a longshoreman in a
waterfront brothel . . . volunteered for the French Foreign
Legion to avoid prison . . . from Aubagne to Castelnaudary to
Mont Louis Commando School to Camp Raffalli on the
French island of Corsica, home of the Second Foreign
Parachute Regiment . . . discharged from the Legion in the
early 1970's, he then hired-on as a mercenary with the FNLA
during the Angolan civil war . . . moved to Rhodesia five
years later and served with the Selous Scouts . . . in 1980 he

returned to the Mediterranean and worked freelance in Beirut with several ex-Legionnaires . . . employed alternately by the Israeli Mossad, British MI-6, and the CIA . . . Theodori first worked with Jaycott in 1982 in Lebanon on an Agency contract to locate western hostages . . . they worked together six times over the next four years . . .

FIRST CAIRO, AND then Tunis, nodded Jay, "if nothing shakes, then on to Paris."

"These types always fancy themselves cosmopolitan. I'd start in Paris. The PLO may be headquartered in Tunis, but the control officers like the good life. They prefer Safe Houses on the Left Bank."

"Hiding amongst the students?"

"A natural hotbed of discontent, easy to recruit," shrugged Theodori half amused. "Call it the exuberance of youth."

"Such an old cynic," laughed Jay.

"I never went to college," reminded Theodori. "In any case, you'll have more opportunities in Paris, and it will be easier to cover you. We'll have a much freer hand to operate. The culture is less restrictive."

Jaycott nodded, glancing at the desktop. It was covered with assorted piles of leaflets, codes, and dossiers, compliments of their meeting that morning with Fairchild.

"In the long run, however, our probing in Cairo and Tunis will put out the word. There's more chance that we could force a move in Paris or Rome if some glue was already spread. It's not likely that they'll react too strongly in their own backyard; however, on someone else's turf, they'll be less inhibited."

Theo gave a nod, accepting the logic of Jay's argument and reached for the pile marked *Cairo*. He started leafing through the list of contacts, informants, known double agents and terrorist sympathizers. Although the money and logistical support for such acts usually originated in Tripoli, Tehran, and Baghdad, the more moderate Arab countries of Tunisia and Egypt acted as cutouts or buffer zones. The weapons and personnel—the latter, usually orphans drawn from the refugee camps of Lebanon—were assembled and directed to various European Safe Houses. From there, prominent, easily accessible western targets were chosen. To begin their probe in Cairo and Tunis would not only draw the attention that they desired, but it would surely help to "set up" their work in Paris and Rome later on. By beginning their work in the middle of the chain, they would not only increase their odds for survival (as the hard-line states of Libya, Iran, and Iraq were such closed societies that westerners had tremendous restrictions), but it also allowed for bilateral communication. People in Cairo or Tunis could warn people in Libya and Iran, as well as advise contacts in Europe.

Theo paused to pour himself a small snifter of Metaxa. The doors to the study slid open and Katerina entered. She looked radiant, a beautiful smile filling her face as she crossed the room.

Theodori's hand shot up like a giant stop sign. "No closer."

Jay instinctively sat upright and stretched, using his back to further obscure Kat's vision from the desktop.

She stopped in her tracks, the smile on her face changing to a look of surprise.

"Signómi . . ."

"Sigá sigá . . . tí Kánete?"

"Kala."

Katerina frowned, her features changing again, this time a look of confusion. She looked at Theo for a long moment, expecting some further explanation. There was none. Slowly Kat's eyes shifted and focused on Jay. Her gaze was deep, analytical, yet he also said nothing. Sensing her confusion he simply shook his head from side to side and flipped his palm over.

Kat's eyes shifted back to Theodori who was firm in his demeanor. "Kali nikta," she mumbled, and whirled on her heels.

When the doors to the study slid closed they both relaxed.

"She's not happy," offered Theo.

"She doesn't understand."

"It is for her own protection."

"*I* know, but you must tell *her* that."

Theo shrugged. "I have always taken care of her, she needs no explanation." The burly Greek allowed a smile to cross his broad face. "It is good to see her, my woman, she is beautiful, yes?"

"Very," admitted Jay. "One of the *most* beautiful. And loyal. Treat her well my friend."

Their eyes crossed, and Theo nodded. Then they turned their attention back to the pile of information labeled *Cairo*.

VIII

SAOUD STOPPED OUTSIDE the familiar 16th century building on Rue Ben Ali. He took a quick look around the shadowy corners of the Casbah, searching for a tail. There was none. Satisfied, he started climbing the stairs.

At the top of the third flight, the Palestinian repeated the ritualistic knock on the ornate wooden door. It opened, and the Rezidentura's pretty concubine received the young Arab. She nodded, and without speaking, led Saoud through the foyer. The woman was aware of Saoud's leering gaze; she ignored him as he walked behind her onto the balcony.

The Soviet leaned on the wall which overlooked the courtyard in the center of the building. His eyes met Saoud, and self-consciously the younger man's gaze shifted away from the woman's derriere. The Rezidentura stifled his comment, and continued tossing pieces of dried bread towards the pigeons below.

"It is time, Comrade."

Saoud's face changed expression and his eyes lighted in a mixture of anticipation. The Soviet studied the

Palestinian reflecting on just how filled with hate Saoud truly was. The young Arab was quite unbalanced.

"Come."

The Rezidentura motioned as he tossed his final piece of bread towards the fountain, and led his protégé into a small room at the end of the hall. Inside the bedroom, he reached into a desk drawer and pulled out a stack of four passports bound by a rubberband. Then he handed Saoud a stack of four sealed packets, fictitious histories, one to coincide with each passport.

"Have the men study and then destroy them. They will enter the United States from four different countries, days apart, at four separate locations. Each must follow the instructions *exactly*, taking the full time to break up the pattern of entry by passing through the background countries. From the time of departure until you assemble in Florida there must be no attempts at contact, nothing that will draw attention from the authorities. *Each*, Comrade, must be impressed with the need to remain anonymous during their journey—you *must* stress this . . . understood?"

"Aiwa."

"Good. Remember also, that patience is important . . . we are *so* close."

"In-Shaalah."

"This is the last you will see of me until you return here at the completion of your mission."

The Rezidentura draped his arm over the shoulder of the taller Arab and led him from the bedroom. His tone took on a conciliatory, somewhat fatherly tone. "You will be a hero to your people, and a special friend to the Soviet Union. I should tell you my young friend . . ." the Russian's voice quieted to a whisper and his flat face turned hopeful. ". . . there may be an order of Lenin for you. It carries wealth, prestige, and . . ." the Rezidentura's eyes drifted towards his attractive concubine who stood on the balcony watering plants, ". . . certain privileges."

Saoud studied the brunette lustfully. "We treat our special friends *very* well."

The Palestinian flushed with a new sense of urgency. "You would . . ."

"Even *her*, Comrade."

He slapped Saoud on the back, propelling him towards the foyer. "Dos Vidania."

"Fi aman illah."

With a final look at the woman, Saoud turned and walked towards the door.

ANNA LYALIN SPOKE excellent English, and the fact that she spoke it with an accent was easily explained to the untrained ear. After all, most men wanted to believe that the lithe, attractive woman with long blonde hair was what she pretended to be—a Swedish sales consultant for a European cosmetics company. Men could be so gullible.

It had taken Anna the better part of a week to scope out the appropriate locations and set her plan in motion. What she needed now was a permanent base of operations. The quicker she checked out of her hotel and set up an untraceable residence, the faster she could complete the next phase of her assignment. This was her third night of prowling, and she needed the right subject.

Anna entered the cocktail lounge tentatively. She took a moment to survey the room, her long years of training as an Olympic swimmer having taught her to see peripherally without seeming to. It was a quiet bar, but relaxing. One where local businessmen could stop for a drink before going home. At the far end of the horse shoe bar sat a solitary man. He appeared middle-aged, dressed in a suit, tiredly nursing a highball by himself.

At first, the man didn't notice Anna. She took a seat to his left, making sure to leave a stool between them. When Anna ordered a glass of wine the man glanced over. He noticed as she crossed her legs, the short skirt, the form fitting blouse. Anna's figure was quite impressive—as was her tan. After all this was Florida, and everyone was expected to notice.

They sat in silence, as the lone man self-consciously tightened the knot in his tie and squared in his seat. He nervously sipped several times at his cocktail, each time glancing in Anna's direction. Finally, sensing his interest and noting that he didn't wear a wedding band, she looked up and made eye contact. The man smiled.

"Hi, I'm Paul."

Average smile, average looks, average physique. Everything . . . average. Anna smiled in return.

"I'm Britt."

"Buy you a drink?"

Anna shook her head politely motioning to her glass of wine. It was a nonthreatening gesture. "But thank you anyway."

He nodded.

"Not from around here, are you?"

Anna smiled again, her glistening white teeth brightened her face. "No, I'm from Amsterdam."

"Dutch?"

"Actually Swedish, but the company I work for is Dutch." She had turned sideways to face him swiveling on her barstool so that he couldn't miss her tanned thighs.

"Swedish?"

Now the man turned in his seat. He lighted a cigarette, and then as an afterthought motioned. "Do you mind?"

"No," lied Anna.

"What kind of company?"

"Cosmetics; herbal facial creams, natural ointments— all healthy ingredients."

"Well you're a walking billboard."

Anna cocked her head sideways in a puzzled expression. "Billboard?"

"Advertisement . . . that's a compliment."

"Oh," blushed Anna, "Danké."

"You're welcome," nodded the man. He motioned to the bartender for another drink. "Sure you won't join me?"

"No, thank you."

He took a sip from the fresh highball. "So what brings you to Florida?"

"We are thinking of setting up a U.S. subsidiary. Florida and California are the most . . . logical . . ." she, checked herself, feigning doubt as to her choice of words, ". . . yes *logical* places to start."

"Makes sense. Lots of health conscious people around here."

The man seemed to suck in his stomach and sit up straight on his barstool. "So you'll be setting up shop?"

"Yes, if all goes well . . . but tell me of you Paul, what do you do?"

At hearing his name, the man gained confidence. How anyone so attractive, and so obviously cosmopolitan—Swedish no less—could find him interesting was a surprise. But he was hooked.

"I'm a CPA."

"CPA?"

"An accountant."

And so they talked. For the better part of thirty minutes, Paul told Anna everything about himself; about his failure to make Partner at a Big Six Firm, about the pressures of starting his own practice, about the breakup of his marriage. And Anna Lyalin, Britt, listened; because that's what her instructors at ZSKA taught her to do. *Men like to hear themselves talk, mostly about themselves, so you learn to listen, and they will think you're a great conversationalist.*

Finally, Paul looked up and stubbed out his third cigarette. "Listen, I was going to get some dinner, would you like to join me?"

Anna looked at him appraisingly. "You're sure you are not married—please do not lie."

"Honest," said Paul, crossing his heart, "no wife, no girlfriend, no dog. I live alone."

Perfect, thought Anna to herself.

"Well only if you promise not to get me back to my hotel late. I have an early appointment."

"I promise," nodded Paul eagerly. "I'm a complete gentleman . . . just some good conversation and a *healthy* meal."

"Agreed," nodded Anna.

He paid the tab with a credit card, and then led Anna from the lounge. Paul seemed to stand taller as he walked.

THE OLYMPIC AIRWAYS jet touched down at Anwar Sadat International Airport, Cairo. It had been a short but pensive flight for Jay; a flight interrupted by the obligatory changeover in Athens. Enough time to think, to prod, to question, to consider; without intending to, Jay had become involved in a rather emotional departure between Theo and Katerina. 'Bring my Theodori home safely,' she had said, 'and yourself . . .'

It was Katerina's eyes that betrayed her, that look of reserve mixed with sincerity—so that he couldn't decide if she was including him as an afterthought, or whether she hid a deeper meaning. Their few days together during Theo's absence had been full; active, animated, fun—and now that they were over, Jay realized just how much he had enjoyed Katerina's company. He had grown attached to Theo's woman, and although their relationship had never progressed beyond the platonic stage, he sensed that Kat had indeed shared his sense of intimacy.

Jay and Theodori actually flew on the same flight, although to the casual observer—or even a trained eye—one would never suspect that the two agents knew each other. They sat nine rows apart, in tourist class; again, affecting the low profile that coincided with years of ingrained OPSEC (Operational Security). They never spoke, gestured, or appeared to even look in each other's direction – although on this last count, there were any number of brief occasions when they crossed glances; just to assure that the other wasn't trying to pass along a signal.

The Airbus-300 taxied to a stop and the doors opened. The familiar stench of camel dung filled Jay's nostrils. He stretched as he stood, time to go to work.

Cairo.

TOM FAIRCHILD ENTERED the Shepherd Hotel and turned right into the first floor mahogany bar. It was an old but distinguished hotel overlooking the Nile, that many years earlier had served as Napoleon's headquarters during the French occupation of Egypt.

The Case Officer sidled up to a stool and motioned for the bartender.

"Gin, ice, bottled water with gaz."

A few minutes later a portly Egyptian in a business suit entered the bar and sat next to Fairchild. He was sweating profusely.

"Cairo is horrid in the summer."

The fat Egyptian dabbed at his face with a soiled handkerchief and signaled for a large bottle of beer. Then he lighted an American cigarette. "Air conditioning is one of the more civilized developments left behind by the British."

Fairchild took a long look at the Egyptian. Corpulence was a cultural trait amongst the wealthy; as much a sign of success in a poor country as were wool suits and imported cigarettes—only the rich could afford to eat well.

"Kaif Halak," nodded the Egyptian drinking his beer. "You said it was important."

"We have information that Tel Aviv is launching an operation."

The Egyptian looked surprised. "Am I to understand," he whispered slowly, "that you would offer this?"

"Anything to support the Peace," shrugged Fairchild, "besides it's not against you . . ."

The Egyptian paused as he stubbed out his cigarette. "The hook, as you call it, I couldn't imagine an even-handed play—despite Washington's pretense to the contrary."

"Ma á alesh . . . spare me the second citizen routine, I don't make policy . . . and neither do you."

In-shaallah," mumbled the Egyptian bowing his head and placing an open palm on his chest.

"Who then?"

"Us."

"You?!" The Egyptian could barely control his shock. He considered the revelation for a few minutes as he studied his beer. "Well, I suppose it's not without precedent . . ."

"Yes it is," interrupted Fairchild. "This isn't technology theft or influence peddling. This is a strike."

The fat man wheezed and nervously lighted another cigarette as he lowered his voice to a near whisper. "Fain . . . Emta . . . Europe?"

"No. In the States. At home."

"La. Qif, qif . . . I don't believe it."

"Believe it my friend. There are some hard-line types in the Knesset."

"But why? It makes no sense. You are their biggest ally—their *only* ally . . ."

"Ma á arif," shrugged Fairchild with a flip of his hand.

Suddenly the Egyptian pieced it together. "They will blame Cairo?!"

The Case Officer motioned with an open hand and squinted. "Maybe . . . they're going to blame someone; knowing their agenda, I suspect it will be persons of the Islamic persuasion. What better way to turn public opinion in the States against the Palestinian problem?"

The Egyptian wheezed, the unsettling news causing his heavy jowls to shake. "What can we do?"

"Help us. We know that they have several agents right here on the ground, leaving a trail, tying Cairo into the strike. One agent in particular, a westerner, he goes by the code name Ishmael. The Israelis are using him as a throw-off. He's been making contact with known Islamist cells in and around the city."

"Ishmael," repeated the Egyptian quietly. "We can arrest him."

"No, that will serve no purpose; as a throw-off, he'll move away from the real source; classic misdirection; better to give us everything you've got on current operations. Someone, an Arabic group, is being used by Tel Aviv. Remember, the Israelis will leave an Islamic signature to the operation."

The Egyptian sighed, "Current Operations; that is very privileged information, even for friends." He flicked the right thumbnail on his front teeth before holding the fingers in a pear shape with the tips pointing upward. The combined gestures said 'only a little, be careful.' "What do you have?"

"Not much," admitted Fairchild, "a number and letter sequence whose only discernable match is that they correspond to our alphabet; 20-8-15-20-13; T-H-O-T-M; the 20th, 8th, 15th, 20th, and 13th letters of our alphabet . . ."

"Ma á arif," shrugged the Egyptian in a slow interruption.

"We've run thousands of permutations, Geographic coordinates, date-time groups," continued the Case Officer. "We think it's symbolic."

The Egyptian took a long gulp on his beer as he considered the information being shared by Fairchild. "How would I communicate—not the As-sifaara I-ámrikiyya?"

"La," mumbled Fairchild emphatically. "Stay away from the Embassy, our locals are tight with Tel Aviv. Use the Souk cutout."

"Aiwa, no promises my friend. The beer is on you."

"My pleasure. Shukran. Barak allah fik."

"In-shaallah," whispered the Egyptian bowing his head. "Fi aman illah."

"Ma á as-salama."

The fat Egyptian raised his bulk from the bar stool and patted Fairchild on the shoulder as he exited.

IX

VIKTOR PAPAHA ENTERED the Hancock International Airport and strolled towards the rental car desk. He presented an Illinois driver's license and an American Express card.

"A large sedan for two days." He kept his speech intentionally short, knowing that his accent would mark him.

The Spetsnaz Colonel had entered the United States illegally, using a Canadian passport to pass through Customs, and now switching to U.S. identification. It had been typically disjointed; a few days in Montreal, then a flight west to Toronto, followed by a return east and south to Syracuse. The low profile point of entry coincided with a cardinal rule of movement: never travel in a straight line, and stay in the shadows.

From Syracuse he would drive to Hartford, take a train to New York, a plane to Baltimore, and then a bus to St. Louis. This agenda would give Papaha added time to "clear" any trail, as well as orient himself to the new country.

The lady behind the service desk asked a few questions, finished processing the paperwork for the car rental, and handed Viktor a set of keys.

"Through these doors here, turn right on the sidewalk into the parking lot. Row N, number 24."

"Thank you," nodded Papaha lighting a Marlboro.

"Enjoy your stay in Syracuse, Mister Gorman."

Viktor unconsciously touched at his tinted hair and nodded. His disguise was simple, but effective; colored hair, clean-lens eyeglasses in heavy frames, cheek inserts to thicken his jawline. He had arrived.

America.

THE BAR WAS in a dingy basement, beneath the President Hotel, in a poorly lighted section of the city. Booze was plentiful, because Egypt, like some of her North African neighbors, chose to relax various tenants of Islamic law.

As Jay descended the staircase, his eyes gradually scanned the smoke-filled room. Men, mostly all men; drinking, gesturing, laughing amidst clouds of toxic fumes; their bodies leaning forward, touching, jabbering excitedly in that uniquely Arabic way where one man's nose nearly touched the other's. It was a body language that most Americans would find offensive; an invasion of one's personal space. Yet in a culture that frowns on heterosexual displays of public affection, same sex hugging, touching, and hand-holding between friends was considered quite acceptable.

Jay's eyes roamed, scanning the patrons as a loud rock & roll song began on the stereo. Immediately, groups of young men moved to the center of the room where a makeshift space had been cleared between the tables, and started dancing. The few women in the room, also young, stood, walked toward the crowd and started dancing together. Jaycott used the activity to work his way towards the bar.

"Sir?" asked the bartender in a distinctly British accent.

"Whiskey, neat."

With a nod, the bartender turned and poured a two finger pull of Scotch into an empty tumbler. Jay spread five Egyptian ten-pound notes next to the glass. He looked at the bartender, then at the money. Their eyes met and Jay spoke quietly, but in a clear voice.

"Mustafa Ben A'more?"

The bartender hesitated, the name obviously familiar. He scooped up the cash and motioned for Jay to wait. Then he disappeared into the rear of the bar and entered a room. Five minutes later he returned and placed a folded piece of paper next to Jay's drink. A quick wipe of his hands on a towel and the bartender walked away.

Jaycott unfolded the piece of paper, read the scribbled address, and then tucked the paper into his pocket. He ignored his drink, and with a final look around turned to go.

Out on the street, Jay started walking in the general direction of the address, realizing that a taxi at this time of night, and in this section of the city would be rare—but then he didn't expect things to take very long . . .

There were three of them, and they rounded the corner outside the President Hotel rather quickly. There was no pretense in their walk, they made a beeline straight for Jay; fanning out across the sidewalk to block any avenue of escape.

Jaycott slowed, allowing his escort to close the distance as he neared several parked cars.

"Kaif halak."

Suddenly, a hand grabbed for the back of Jay's head—but Jay was already moving. Spinning, he deflected the arm with a wide circular motion, and continuing the momentum, simultaneously hammerlocked the assailant's elbow, swiveled his hips, and flung the man onto the hood of the nearest car.

The speed of Jay's reaction stunned the other two assailants and they hesitated. It proved costly, because before they could react, Theodori burst from the shadows. Like a train run amok, Theo slammed chest high into the second man who fell against the third. Before either could recover, the stocky Greek had pummeled the second assailant senseless with a blackjack.

The third man rolled on the sidewalk, pulled out a knife, and started to stand. Theo's attention shifted, and moving surprisingly quick for a man of his bulk, he kicked at the attacker's ankles. The third man fell again, groaning in pain as Theo started zapping his knife hand with the blackjack.

Jay had pinned the first attacker—face first—against the windshield. Then he grabbed for the man's testicles.

"Mon Ami," whispered Jay into the man's ear as he nodded at Theodori, "il est tres horrible. Comprende?"

The attacker continued to struggle, his eyes darting wildly, his teeth snapping as Jay squeezed.

"Comprende?"

The man yelped in pain and nodded. Behind them, Theo's grunts and the sound of snapping bone served to accent Jay's words.

"Horrible," repeated Jaycott. He gave another gentle squeeze for good measure and the attacker winced.

Theo sidled up to Jay and rolled his eyes in mock exhaustion, motioning for Jay to wait as he caught his breath.

"Tatakallam Inglizi?"

"Aiwa, aiwa . . ."

"Do you know Mustafa Ben Amore?"

"La . . ." denied the assailant.

"No?!" gasped Jay incredulously as Theo sucked air into his lungs. The Greek winked at Jaycott and reached for the man's elbow.

"Let me break his bones Ishmael."

"La, no wait," blurted the attacker as he felt Theo's meaty hands on his arm.

"Where does he live?" pressed Jay.

"The City of the Dead . . ."

"Let me have him," growled Theo again, his tone deeper, more menacing as his pulse slowed. He gently tapped the man's elbow with the slapstick. "He lies."

"No, no . . . Ben Amore lives in the City of the Dead, I swear!"

The attacker's voice had become strident, his eyes flashing left and right in fear as he tried to discern Theo's moves.

"Listen closely," said Jay in a friendly conspiratorial tone, "you tell him that a man named Ishmael wants to speak to him. You tell him to ask around about me; in Paris, Rome, Beirut . . . people know me, people know of me. Comprende?"

"Aiwa, aiwa, yes . . ."

"Good, now go."

With a nod from Jay, Theodori helped yank the attacker from the hood of the car. Stunned, the man looked first at the calm Jaycott and then at the menacing Greek. "I go?"

"Imshi," snapped Jay with a hard edge.

The man started back peddling nervously, his eyes shifting from Jay, to Theo, back to Jay.

"Shukran . . . Barak allah fik . . . shukran . . ."

He bowed, continuing to backpedal.

"Imshi!"

The man turned and ran.

In seconds the assailant was out of sight. Theo motioned to their left, and Jay followed the burly Greek towards an alley across from the President Hotel. He noticed one of the two assailants beaten by Theo, crawling towards the sidewalk, unable to stand.

"At least he's alive. What about the other guy?"

"He's alive too," huffed Theo, "but I had to take away his fight."

They tumbled into the rental sedan, and sped off.
When they were a few blocks from the scene of the struggle,
an escape aided by the curious habit of Egyptians to drive at
night without headlights, Jay glanced sideways at Theo and
smirked.

"You're slowing down."

"Me?!" cried Theodori, stifling a nervous laugh. "You
took forever to react. I thought I was going to have to fight all
three."

"I was timing my move."

"Zeus, you never heard him."

"You're getting old."

"Your hearing has degenerated."

They looked at each other, and then simultaneously
broke into sighs. Finally, after two full minutes, the tension
easing as the adrenaline drained, Theo looked at Jay. "It was a
good start, don't you think?"

"Yeah," nodded Jaycott, "they weren't prepared for
the hard stuff . . . they were sent to accost us, check us out—
but the level of violence will throw them, it's not their way."

"They will pay attention, yes?"

"Yes, Theo, tonight was a good start."

A moment of silence passed. "We'll have to keep our
wits."

The big Greek nodded and settled back to concentrate
on his driving.

"LET'S GET STARTED."

The small side discussions around the conference table ceased and the other eleven members of the Forty Committee turned their attention towards Tom Laughlin, Deputy Director (Intelligence) for the CIA.

"As we have known for some time, attacks by Islamist international terrorists are neither random, nor spontaneous. They are state controlled. for the most part, the financial and logistical support for these operations is directed by Iran and Syria, with major training camps also located in Lebanon, Libya, the Sudan, Afghanistan, and Pakistan. Khartoum acts as the African Headquarters and coordinates much of its activities through control points in Tunis, Algiers, and Cairo . . ."

Laughlin paused for a moment to survey the expressions of his co-committee members. None of this was new information to the men in the room.

"Several interesting leads have surfaced which may pertain to our problem. Rudy."

The Senior Analyst from the Defense Intelligence Agency cleared his throat to speak. "This is a biographic profile we worked up at Arlington Hall." He slid a *Top Secret* embossed dossier across the conference table to each of the other committee members. They in turn ran a finger along the outside of the thick folders and tore through the sticky security seals, thus enabling them to open the dossiers.

"The man whose picture you are looking at is Polkovnik Viktor Papaha, a full Colonel in the Soviet Red Army . . ." He gave them a moment to assess the large black and white photograph of Papaha. ". . . he is also a very experienced, highly respected Spetsnaz officer. Less than two weeks ago, Papaha was commanding a brigade of Reydoviki in Ashabad, a city on the Iranian border. He was involved in a campaign to eradicate several pockets of resistance amongst the Muslim guerrilla tribes of Turkmenistan, a far western border Republic of the Soviet Union. Then suddenly he disappeared . . ."

A look around the room showed each of the committee members equally engrossed in both the dossier and the narrative.

". . . strangely," continued Rudy "he resurfaced in Montreal."

A moment of silence.

"Rather an odd posting," interjected Paul of Customs, "it's confirmed?"

"Confirmed," nodded Rudy.

"He speaks English," offered Bob Perkins of the State Department, noting an entry in the dossier.

"Self-taught," clarified Rudy. "All his previous postings were Arabic, with considerable time spent in North Africa. But wait, it gets better . . ."

He had their attention.

"Two days ago, he disappeared again."

"He's gone *under*," mumbled Russell of the FBI, a slight edge of frustration creeping into his voice.

"Rudy, could you fill in some of the background for us," asked the Admiral from the Joint Chiefs.

"Sure. In the first disappearance, it caught the attention of Aman, the Israeli Military Intelligence. Evidently, they had a 'black' agent of B-2 reliability who reported Papaha's sudden departure. At the time they thought it odd given that the Colonel had only been in Turkmenistan a short period, and the Reydoviki Brigade didn't receive a new replacement Commander. Under normal circumstances it probably would have been filed in some report and forgotten. *But* as luck would have it, the Israelis were just sitting down for their annual Tsiach—that's short for Tsorech Yediot Hasuvot—a yearly get together of all their intelligence organizations where they plan upcoming events and compile wish lists of necessary information; enemy order of battle, T O & E structure, personnel changes, etcetera *and* it was mentioned."

"Fortuitous," nodded the Admiral.

"Very," agreed Rudy. "In the second disappearance, our verification is the RCMP."

"The Mounties don't *lose* people." added the FBI man tensely. "He's *under*."

The Deputy Director for the Secret Service turned towards Laughlin with a pensive expression. "How do you figure the Soviet angle here, Tom?"

"I'm not sure I do," admitted the Deputy Director (Intelligence). "But I've been at this game too long to accept the idea of a coincidence."

There were several mumbled agreements by the other committee members. Laughlin looked across the conference table to the far end where his CIA co-worker sat in silence. "John, anything you want to offer?"

All eyes turned towards the Deputy Director (Operations). Beneath the surface lingered a palpable curiosity regarding the spymaster and the progress of his 'probe' agent. Mullins glanced around the table and calmly answered.

"No."

THE MINIVAN WAS loaded with clothing, golf clubs, a picnic basket, and various other vacation supplies—in short, all of the paraphernalia that a middle-aged suburban couple might take along on a holiday excursion. However, unseen beneath the folded middle seat, was a false storage compartment. This compartment, padded, airtight, and waterproof, was lined with a special noncorrosive, fire resistant lead filament that rendered the contents impervious to x-rays, electronic shock, and gaseous combustion. It stretched the entire width of the minivan, was eleven inches deep and two feet across.

Packed flush end to end inside the compartment were thirty 1¼ pound blocks of composition C-4; a moldable, high brisance explosive. Due to its detonating velocity of over 26,000 feet per second and a relative effectiveness factor of 1.34 (as compared to TNT), the C-4 was ideally suited for cutting and breaching irregular shaped targets. It also was quite stable, and thus relatively insensitive to shock or friction.

"Kak deela," mumbled the middle-aged woman in Russian as she entered the garage. Her demeanor had taken on a rebellious edge in recent days. Ever since the start of this assignment, Gennadi's wife had intentionally ignored her training and lapsed into their native tongue whenever they were alone. It made for bad habits, which led to mistakes, which ended in compromise. And the more Gennadi complained, the more often his wife spoke in Russian. He bit his lip and answered in English.

"It's going well."

"*Gdye boodyet oodar?*"

He winced, his frustration building.

"We will be told."

"*Oo vas fotoapparat?*"

"Yes."

"*Probkee?*"

"Yes."

"Vodka?"

"Da, Da, Da," snapped Gennadi in Russian. "Why must you taunt me?"

"*Vee moy droog.*"

"You're also my wife."

"That's right," she said finally in perfect English, "and don't you ever forget it. No one loves you as I do my Gennadi. No one."

He paused for a moment and leaned back against the open door of the minivan. His eyes searched his wife's for a brief instant. "Is everything alright?"

"Ya nye yzayoo," she shrugged, reverting back into Russian. She turned and walked out of the garage.

X

2 August 1989
Moscow, USSR

YURI VLASOV WAS a powerful man. He was also a
national hero. Now in his fifties, the former Olympic weight-
lifting champion still commanded respect—not only because
of his imposing size, but because in many ways he typified
the success of the Party. Yet no one in the Congress of
People's Deputies was prepared for this.

It had become the hottest television show of the era.
Day after day, for six or seven hours of live broadcast, all
work ceased as millions of Soviet citizens sat transfixed
watching a relatively small group of liberal reformers push,
prod, insult, and cajole the hard-line conservatives forward.

For a nation conditioned towards obedience and
submission to a ruling elite, this newfound political activism
was a catharsis—yet it also broke dangerous ground. Never
had they seen so many of the young radicals engage in such
virulent political debate. It bordered on scurrility; an abusive,
slanderous, uncontrollable political attack; unlike anything
the citizens of the Soviet Union had ever seen—or dared
contemplate. The roughly four hundred, or twenty percent, of

the People's Deputies engaged in the histrionics gathered strength and courage as the days wore on. They seemed to sense that their crossing over the line left them little alternative but to push forward, penetrating deeper and further into the murky waters of the Russian conscience. This was a battle for the Rodina's very soul, and no privileged Party *apparatchiki,* Army General, or Senior Minister was to be left unassailed.

The upstarts were many; first there was Andrei Sakharov, then Boris Yeltsin the Moscow Party boss, followed by Sergei Stankevich, Yuri Afanasyev, and the economist Gavril Popov. Their frustration knew no bounds, their anger vented unabated. But the most stinging speech— agreed by all—came from the lips of the strapping Vlasov. The beloved Olympian held no political aspirations. His was a tirade from the heart. Here was a recognized national hero, who enjoyed all the perquisites and adulation of the privileged class, condemning *nomenklatura.* He jabbed a thick, calloused finger directly at Vladimir Kryuchkov, head of the KGB, sitting four rows from the front.

"They are a threat to democracy . . . not a service, but a real underground empire which has not yet surrendered its secrets . . ."

Vlasov bellowed in the deep, grunting staccato of a trained weight-lifter. Other members of the Politburo joined Kryuchkov in his shock. The stinging unprecedented attack rendered them motionless; their faces blank, eyes glazed.

Vlasov condemned the KGB's history of torture, murder, and evil misuse of drugs and psychiatric chemicals on political dissidents. He reprimanded the elite for the disappearance of his father, a former diplomat, nearly forty years earlier.

". . . we must honor the memories of our fellow citizens who were victims of excesses and executions . . ."

Finally, he called for the removal of KGB headquarters from Dzerzhinsky Square in downtown Moscow, pushing a thick fist skyward as he condemned ". . . the unforgettable bloody history of the building."

Hundreds of People's Deputies sprang to their feet, clapping wildly, offering a standing ovation to Vlasov as an almost palpable silence blanketed Kryuchkov and his associates. They sat stunned.

To the rear of the large auditorium, quietly assessing the mood of the Congress, sat Lieutenant General Vyacheslav Guryenko, Chief of the Illegals Training Centre of the GRU. He glanced off to his right and made eye-contact with another man six rows removed. Then slowly, almost imperceptibly, he nodded. The second man stood and walked from the auditorium.

THE CITY OF the Dead sits outside the old section of Cairo, a short walk from the Citadel and the Mosque of Mohammad Ali. At first look, it appears to be a typical—if not unusually large—Arabic cemetery; acres and acres of low rise brick and mortar burial vaults protected by a stone wall with an occasional minaret or dome jutting skyward to mark the grave of a wealthy merchant. Dirt roads and dusty paths intersect at odd angles bereft of any pattern, curving circuitously around the decaying monuments and grimy headstones, lending a corrosive feel to what appears a forgotten, seldom visited final resting spot for Cairo's deceased.

Except for the people.

Packed into the endless array of tombs, vaults, and mausoleums are nearly a half million Egyptians; a thriving metropolis of living, breathing, eating, cursing, fornicating, Allah-praising Egyptians. This is their home; and amid the sacred burial ground of someone else's relatives, these families rent an 'apartment' for everyday living. In a city racked by over-population, void of adequate housing, and inured to poor sanitation, sleeping with the dead each night makes sense. In fact, many consider it a rather novel approach to Cairo's chronic construction shortage; why build more apartments when thousands of unused burial vaults, complete with thick walls and solid roofs sit 'idle'.

Thus, in the City of the Dead, children play outside among the grave markers, while inside fathers drink tea perched atop alters and mothers prepare the evening meal on a sarcophagus dining table. It is a uniquely Egyptian solution to a common world problem; and everyone involved from the cemetery caretakers and religious *ulama* who share in the rental profits, to the families of the interred who must give adequate notice when visiting their ancestral tombs (time for the inhabitants of any particular 'apartment' to gather their worldly possessions and disappear for a few hours) regard it as normal.

Jaycott paced along the inside of the protective stone wall aware of the fact that he was a perfect target. He couldn't have offered a trained marksman a better silhouette by which to sight-in. This of course was the reality of his chosen profession. The money was quite good, but if you 'stirred the pot' for a living, you had to accept some repercussions. It came with the turf. The consequences of his agitating could be painful, sometimes fatal—but almost always they were dangerous. Yet despite the risks, there was a distinct clarity to the work. Jay suffered few delusions that other staff employees might possess—promotions, pensions, and headquarter politics were non-existent in his world. Go in, keep pushing buttons until something breaks, deliver the goods, then get out. One only had to trust to skill, luck, and a strong backup—and in Theodori, Jay had a Second whose experience and loyalty was unmatched.

He rounded a corner to see two barefoot children eye him curiously. He ignored them and kept his distance. In many cultures, certainly Arabic, the best point of contact in a random approach was an old man. The theory suggested that on balance, young men were ambitious and hence untrustworthy; children were unreliable; women were taboo . . . but an old man? Odds were good that since he had already lived a life, socialized more freely, and usually functioned as the patriarch—there usually was a greater chance of success.

It took Jay ten more minutes of systematic wandering to locate a suitable subject. Four old Egyptians sat huddled in front of a headstone, the flowing folds of their Galabiya gowns wrapped about their knees. They all seemed to be talking simultaneously, gesturing in the excited, somewhat confusing style peculiar to Arabs. Between them they passed a long water pipe called a shee-sha. "Sabaah il-khair," offered Jay.

"Sabaah il-khair," mumbled the four Egyptians in unison, pausing in their conversation to examine the obvious foreigner. There had been no point in attempting to disguise himself, quite the opposite; Jay stood tall, dressed in expensive dress slacks, sports jacket and aviator sunglasses. Theodori on the other hand, shuffled slowly in the distance garbed in a traditional Galabiya robe and Kefiyeh headdress; his swarthy complexion further covered by a fake beard attached with vegetable glue; his dress, mannerisms and gait offering a natural blend to the surroundings.

"Fain Mustafa Ben Amore?" asked Jay. They exchanged glances without answering.

"Tatakallum Inglizi?"

Still no answer.

"Aish fi?"

One of the Egyptians started to speak when the oldest of the group sitting on a short stool directly to his right made a clicking sound with his tongue and teeth.

Not surprised by their reticence, Jaycott reached into his trouser pocket. His hand came out holding the largest roll of Egyptian twenty pound notes any of the old men had ever seen. He made a rather dramatic gesture of unfolding the roll and counting the crisp new money as he spoke.

"Flous, I owe Mustafa Ben Amore a great deal of flous, and I know *he* would be most appreciative if someone would help me find him . . ."

Jay paused, taking a moment to inspect a note that looked tattered and world-weary—not crisp like most of the currency in his roll. He held the money up to the sun for further analysis, and then with a grimace he crumbled the note into a ball and tossed it nonchalantly back over his shoulder. "Poor quality," he shrugged.

Two of the Egyptians were so startled that they nearly bumped heads lunging for the twenty pound note, yet the oldest man grunted and they both quickly settled back on their haunches in an effort to preserve decorum.

"How much money does the stranger owe Mustafa Ben Amore?" asked the senior man in excellent English.

"Ma a'alesh," shrugged Jay unfazed and unsurprised. Money was truly the international language. "But let's say there would be a healthy commission to the man who could guide me to his beyt."

"Boukra."

"La, 'al-youm. Now."

"Kam?" asked the Egyptian rubbing thumb and forefinger together.

Jay started peeling off twenty pound notes, watching the man's eyes. When he got to ten he stopped and tucked the remaining roll back into his pocket. He then spread the ten notes sideways, fanlike, and extended the currency towards the Egyptian—fully aware that two hundred Egyptian pounds was a great deal of money to a resident of the City of the Dead. As his newfound guide reached for the money—a sign that he had accepted the offer—Jay jerked the currency back, tidied it in one flat bundle like collapsing a deck of cards and tore the pounds in half.

For the second time in three minutes the Egyptians jerked involuntarily. Jay smiled handing half of the torn notes to the old man, and placing the corresponding half into the pocket of his sports coat. "In case we get lost."

"Ta'al," mumbled the guide shaking his head in dismay. Standing, he mumbled a few unintelligible words to his friends. "Ta'al," he repeated extending his right hand, palm down. He scratched his fingers downward in a clawing motion, the Arabic signal 'to come.'

The old Egyptian ambled off in a lackadaisical stroll followed by Jaycott.

They walked for several minutes; a winding path of left and right turns along the dusty roads of the cemetery. Occasionally Jay glanced back to see that Theodori hadn't lost them, conscious to see that his friend was not in turn being followed.

Finally they stopped outside the wooden door to a mausoleum that looked as nondescript as any of the other crypts that crowded the graveyard. The only difference was the Bawwab, or doorkeeper. In this case the Bawwab was a young man in his mid-twenties who arrogantly smoked a cigarette while leaning against a tombstone. He seemed to straighten a bit when Jaycott and the old man approached. The guide motioned for Jay to stop and shuffled forward for a private conversation.

The two Egyptians spoke quietly, occasionally looking back at the well-dressed foreigner. Questions, answers, and then the young man disappeared inside. Several minutes elapsed before he returned and nodded.

The old man shuffled back towards Jay. "Mustafa Ben Amore will see you."

Cloaking his movements with his flowing Galabiya, he nonchalantly offered an open hand, palm up. The inevitable ba'sheesh. Jay winked, and just as discreetly handed the old man the other half of the torn Egyptian notes. "Shukran."

"Fi aman illah."

"Ma'a as-salama."

Jay moved towards the mausoleum door and allowed the young Bawwab to give him a quick frisk. He tugged a large pistol from the waistband at the small of Jay's back and fingered the thick roll of currency folded in Jay's pocket. He looked at the weapon and then pointed at the money. "Ya sa'lehm?!"

"Flous."

The man's eyes widened in amazement. "Flous?"

"Aiwa," nodded Jay, "nuqood."

The man fingered the roll again through the lining of Jay's pocket, then turned his attention to the pistol.

"Be careful, it's loaded."

Not catching the sarcasm in Jay's voice, the Bawwab examined the handgun closely, then straightened himself and motioned. They entered the mausoleum.

The chamber was lighted by dozens of candles, more as a source of illumination than any sense of reverence. On the floor, a thick, double Persian carpet surrounded the sarcophagus at right angles. The stone coffin seemed oddly out of place as it protruded annoyingly in the center of the room. In a strange if not symbolic role-reversal, those present in the mausoleum appeared to forget that the purpose of the crypt was to honor the dead, not provide living quarters to Cairo's overflow population.

Jay removed his shoes, and crossed the carpet to a far corner where Mustafa Ben Amore sat cross-legged propped up by pillows. He eyed Jaycott curiously as the young man who escaped unharmed from the alley several nights previous filled two small tea cups. Ben Amore motioned and Jay sat on the carpet, careful to fold the soles of his feet down and away. The Bawwab placed Jay's pistol on the carpet next to Ben Amore and went back outside.

"Did you come to kill me?" asked the Egyptian glancing at the nine millimeter automatic.

"If I came to kill you, you'd be dead," answered Jay calmly.

Ben Amore's jaw tightened and his pupils narrowed into two dark slits. There was a moment of silence as the two men assessed each other.

"You are either very brave, or very foolish."

"Probably a little of both," smirked Jay. The twinkle in his eye eased the tension.

Mustafa Ben Amore tossed his head back and roared with laughter, an exaggerated display of confidence that seemed to relax the young bodyguards that loitered around the inside of the mausoleum.

He sipped at his tea.

"Ishmael is a name from your Bible, Aiwa?"

"So they tell me."

"Are you religious?"

"Not particularly, but I know the influence of an amir, a mufti, and an ulama."

Ben Amore smiled to expose a gold-capped incisor. "Ahhh . . . and you are wise also."

Jay nodded at the compliment.

"And what service can Mustafa Ben Amore provide to the foreigner called Ishmael?"

"I seek information."

The Egyptian waved his arm, a signal to continue.

"I represent a group of very wealthy businessmen. They hear of a plan to strike a target in the United States. They wish to offer their . . . assistance."

Ben Amore's eyes widened. "And even if I knew of such a plan, am I to understand that your American friends wish to provide *aid* to whomever might initiate such a *thing*?"

"I'm not American," lied Jay. I'm South African. I was born in Cape Town."

The reply puzzled Ben Amore. He digested the information for a few moments. "Explain to me Ishmael, why this interest?"

"Let's just say that we are very concerned with *who*, receives the credit."

Ben Amore took a moment to sip again at his tea. This time Jay joined him.

"That seems a strange request. Why would it matter? Washington would only blame a Muslim group anyway."

"Initially," agreed Jay, "yet it could be arranged so that other *evidence* becomes available. This evidence, with the proper focus, could point at an entirely different party."

"And whom do you think should receive the *credit*."

Jay paused before answering. Then with a smile he said: "Israel."

A glow seemed to cover Ben Amore's face and he leaned back in silence. He looked at Jay with very pensive eyes considering the information.

"I am confused, mut'assif . . . I did not realize that South Africa was on bad terms with Tel Aviv."

Jay shrugged. "They are not, but then, I don't work for the government of South Africa. The businessmen that I represent are from several different countries, and quite frankly, none of them has any interest in politics."

"Well then, why does it matter what country is implicated? What would you and your associates stand to gain?"

Pretending to be incredulous, as if the answer were blatantly obvious, Jay gushed.

"Why money, of course."

"Money?"

"Billions," clarified Jay, noting the continued confusion on the Egyptian's face. "It's like this; every year the United States Congress votes a financial and military aid package to Tel Aviv. The Israelis take the money and use it to manufacture and re-export weapons all over the world. As you know, weapons systems, technology, and security services are some of the few positive contributors to the Gross National Product of Israel. If suddenly Tel Aviv was thought to be involved in a terrorist strike *against* the United States—for whatever reason—then public sentiment would be so strongly anti-Israel, that none of the politicians in Washington would dare support a financial assistance package—at least not until Tel Aviv's non-involvement was convincingly proven. No financial aid package means no new weapons systems, no seed money for Research & Development, no operating funds for the military industrial complex of Israel; thus no exporting of weapons and technology to customers *we* would like to do business with. It's really basic economics—supply and demand. And the rewards to us? Incredible *profits*."

Jay leaned back and slowly sipped at his tea. He could see that Ben Amore's head was spinning as he attempted to separate the plausible from the possible. To a mufti, the concept of monetary gain was at odds with the religious considerations that surrounded a Jihad. But the Egyptian understood enough of global politics to recognize the attraction of vast sums of money. The international arms bazaar was known to generate incredible wealth.

They sat in silence for what seemed an eternity. Then finally, Ben Amore spoke. "I shall consider the offer of your associates, *not* . . ." he quickly added, ". . . that I know of any such planned 'strike' as you call it."

"Of course not," agreed Jay.

Ben Amore reached for the pistol and offered it grip first.

"Fi aman illah."

Jaycott reached forward and took the nine millimeter, pausing for just an extra second with the handgun pointing at the Egyptian. Ben Amore's face contorted and his bodyguards tensed. Then melodramatically Jay snapped his wrist back so that the barrel pointed towards the ceiling. He smirked and stood. "Ma'a as-salama."

Outside of the mausoleum Jay reached into his pocket and extracted his roll of currency. He quickly peeled off half a dozen twenty pound notes and stuffed them into the hands of the young Bawwab. "A shehnil'-aw-lehd."

Surprised, the doorkeeper tucked the money into his shirt and watched him stroll away.

"WILL THERE BE anything else ma'm?"

Rochelle Listach looked up at her manservant and shook her head. The dapper black man crossed the room and retrieved the tray of barely touched food.

"Was the preparation to your satisfaction?"

"Yes Benjamin," answered the old woman somewhat distracted, "it was quite good, I'm afraid I am preoccupied."

She shifted in the seat at her desk and turned from the computer console. "Please take it away."

"Very good ma'm, some tea perhaps?"

Again, the wandering attention.

"Ma'm," he repeated quietly.

The old woman looked up, testy. "What?"

"Anything else ma'm, before I retire?"

"No, that will do, thank you."

"Goodnight ma'm."

She didn't answer, her eyes back on the computer screen, deep in thought. Benjamin walked quietly from the study.

Rochelle Listach's success over the years was attributable to two strengths; the first was an uncanny ability to anticipate actions. She did this by studying people. Rochelle believed that every agent developed tendencies, and those tendencies were an outgrowth of the sum total of their experiences and motivations. Thus, to *know* the players, was to predict their moves under various scenarios. Her second strength was the ability to make calculated decisions. In this regard Rochelle was an anomaly; old but unfazed, ladylike but ruthless.

Following her formal retirement from the Agency, Rochelle was occasionally brought back as a consultant to run particularly difficult assignments. The threat of the first ever terrorist strike on U.S. soil spawned such an occasion.

She pushed her reading glasses back up on the bridge of her nose and continued scanning Jaycott's personnel file . . . weapons specialist with the 5th Special Forces Group . . . missions to North Africa . . . OCS, Ranger School . . . Detachment Commander with the 7th Special Forces Group . . . missions to Central America . . . recruitment by the Agency . . . marriage . . . Colón . . .

Rochelle typed into the computer and expanded the file on the Colón assignment. This affair had been a major turning point in Jaycott's life, and Listach knew that deep in the ambiguities of this file lay the experiences and motivations that governed her Probe. To know the file was to know Jay, and to know Jay was to anticipate his actions . . .

THE TELEPHONE INSIDE Jaycott's room at the Cairo Marriott rang just as he entered. "Yes?"

"You had company." It was Theo's voice.

"How many?"

"Two."

"Level?"

"Amateurs."

"Where'd they pick me up?"

"Just outside the city."

"Where are they now?"

"On the veranda, by the front door. One of them made a phone call."

Jay thought for a moment and checked his wristwatch. "Okay, here's the drill: I'm going to nap for a couple hours, then get up, exercise, and shower. I will leave for dinner at exactly eighteen hundred hours. I'll go straight to Felfellas. I won't return before twenty-two hundred. Does that give them enough time?"

"Yes."

"I'll meet you at the cutout at midnight. Get some rest."

"I will," mumbled Theo and Jaycott heard the line click dead.

XI

THE DELTA AIR LINES jet touched down at Kennedy
International Airport. Gazing out the window in a moment of
quiet reflection, sat Saoud Issan. The Palestinian had taken
nearly two weeks to arrive in the United States following his
departure from Algiers. From North Africa he had travelled to
the Mediterranean island of Malta. Four days later he
departed to London, from England to Bermuda, Bermuda to
New York. At each stop he spent several days to break up the
pattern and backstop his cover. The fact that both Malta and
Bermuda shared a history as well as a political relationship
with Great Britain eased the transition. Since most customs
officers scrutinized arrivals from the Middle East, landing
with a plane load of returning tourists proved innocuous.

He began by landing in Vallettas, a businessman
arriving "home" on a Maltese passport from another
Mediterranean port. Four days later he departed for England,
a former military protector of the island nation. A week of
business in London, was followed by a departure to the
Crown Colony of Bermuda. Finally, a few days of relaxation

led to the final leg to New York. All the while he traveled light and controlled his unnatural desires.

Now, nearly three weeks to the day, Saoud was back in New York. He was filled with a great sense of anticipation as the zero hour approached. Saoud prayed to Allah, that the illegal entry of his other co-conspirators—each arriving in different cities, on different days, under different false passports—would be uneventful. They were so *close*. America would pay, and one day his people would have a home.

"It's been nice talking to you," smiled the woman to his left. "I hope your business goes well in New York."

"Yes," nodded Saoud, momentarily interrupted from his thoughts. She shifted in her seat. The movement caused the woman's skirt to inadvertently hike-up and expose her leg. Saoud leered at her thigh and his loins stirred. He would like to invite the Yankee whore up to a hotel room and humiliate her, but his tight schedule necessitated getting to Florida immediately. "Thank you."

She smiled again and combed her hair as the plane taxied to a halt. Saoud smiled back. T, H, O, T, M. Allah Akbah.

PAUL HERSCH LATHERED the shampoo in his thinning hair. He was the luckiest man in the world. Paul couldn't believe his good fortune; Britt, an incredibly beautiful Swede, was *his* Britt. She wanted *him*. Paul kept waiting to wake from the dream; after years of loneliness following his

divorce he had met and become lovers with a woman that
was way out of his league.

They had dated every night for a week before
consummating their relationship. It had evolved slowly—
seemingly taking forever—heightened by a gradual warming;
little affectionate touches and hugs that increased in both
frequency and duration each night until they finally embraced
in a passionate kiss. Paul's lust was incredible. And Britt
returned his kiss with a fervor that Paul had never known.

Never having had a great deal of confidence with
women, the accountant was reluctant to be too forward.
Instead, he took his time, treating Britt to a whirlwind tour of
fancy restaurants and nightclubs. She encouraged him in
small ways, careful to appear gradually won-over; listening
intently to his stories, appearing to enjoy his company. Britt
made Paul feel special, and more importantly, she made it
clear that he did the same for her. Two nights after their first
real kiss they had gone back to Paul's modest home and made
love all night. *All* night. Britt was insatiable. This was a first
for Paul Hersch. He was as giddy as a schoolboy, head over
heels infatuated with the beautiful Swede, and she seemed to
have eyes only for him.

Thus, it seemed only natural, that a night earlier,
while grilling fish on the back deck, he would catch her cue.
Britt's cosmetics company would be setting up a full-time
subsidiary in the United States. Britt would be in Florida for
at least a year—much too long to stay in a hotel. He would
ask his beautiful Swede to move in with him. Britt was

unquestionably the best thing that had ever happened to Paul, and he would do anything to have her around full-time.

The accountant stepped from the shower and smiled at himself in the mirror. Life was grand. After a quick toweling, he pulled on a terry cloth bathrobe and stepped from the bathroom.

Sipping coffee in the kitchen, Anna Lyalin glanced up from her newspaper and smiled.

"Good morning."

Paul smiled. "Any coffee?"

"Of course," she purred, standing to greet him, "but first give me a kiss."

Anna reached up and wrapped her arms around Paul's shoulders. Her kiss was warm, wet, passionate; her tongue probing his mouth in a series of soft, but lingering penetrations.

"Hmm," she purred again, "you taste so good."

Paul's hands reached under Anna's firm buttocks, lifting up her short negligee. Anna started to kiss his neck, opening Paul's bathrobe, nibbling at his chest.

"Oh Britt . . ."

She licked his nipples; using her tongue, her lips, her fingertips expertly as she descended down Paul's chest, over his abdomen to the soft curl of his pubic hair.

". . . you are so beautiful," he moaned, his eyes watching Anna descend as his shaft hardened.

Anna took Paul's testicles into her mouth, one at a time, running her hands over his thighs. His breath shortened. Slowly, teasingly, she took his shaft in her mouth and started a long, slow rhythm.

THE TELEPHONE RANG and Jaycott paused knowing that his pre-arranged signal with Theo was one ring and then a disconnect. It rang a second time and slowly he uncradled the receiver. "Yes?"

"The meeting you desire is tonight," began the voice in perfect, if accented, English. "The north side of Mikeranos, eleven o'clock, come alone, unarmed." The line clicked dead.

"Bingo," mumbled Jay to himself, slowly recradling the receiver. It had been expected, ever since his meeting with Mustafa Ben Amore in the City of the Dead. They had hit a nerve, and when Jay returned back from his dinner several nights previous, he carefully and systematically searched his hotel room to confirm the 'visitors' that Theo reported arriving. Two listening devices were identified, as well as several disturbed personal items and papers.

From that point on, Jay and Theo communicated by Dead Drops and neutral telephones at pre-arranged times. They also did everything possible to backstop Jay's cover; picking up and shaking various tails, placing long distance telephone calls to Geneva, and contacting other known Islamic cells in and around Cairo. All of this of course would be noted, compared, and disseminated to the interested parties; and when added to the extra 'spin' of disinformation provided by his Case Officer, Fairchild, everyone's ears would be buzzing with the name Ishmael. Which of course, is precisely what they wanted. Time was short, and they needed to reach critical mass as quickly as possible.

The process was actually quite simple: get everyone whispering the same name—even if for different reasons—and sooner or later the real John Doe would stand up. Curiosity always got the cat.

Jaycott dialed Theo's hotel room across town and hung up after one ring. Then he sat at the writing desk and started encrypting a short message. He'd have just enough time to load their Emergency Drop, advising the burly Greek of the scheduled meet that night.

THE ALARM BUZZED and instantly Viktor Papaha was awake. The digital clock read 2:00 a.m. The Spetsnaz Colonel had long ago learned to catnap when time permitted, and thus was quite conditioned to operating at night. He walked into the bathroom and splashed cold water on his face. Already dressed, he slipped into casual loafers, and packed his toiletries into a small nylon shoulder bag. Then he slid a couple of dollars under a clean ashtray for the maid, took a last look around the hotel room, and exited.

Down at the lobby, Papaha casually dropped his speedy check-out envelope in the slot at the front desk, careful to avoid eye contact with the clerk, and turned back towards a side door that led to the parking lot.

Every minor detail of Viktor's 2:00 a.m. departure had been planned, more from habit than necessity. The middle of the night departure of a tired businessman from a St. Louis hotel was not—in and of itself—of any particular interest to anyone. Yet Viktor preferred caution. He quietly climbed into the rental car and drove away.

Six blocks from the hotel, Papaha pulled the sedan into the crowded parking lot of an all-night diner and sidled up to a car in the last row. Quickly, he got out of his sedan with a flat edged screw driver and removed the license plates from the front and rear of the target car. Then he screwed on two license plates that he had stolen several days earlier from a different car in Baltimore. The whole process took six minutes.

Finally, back in his rental car, he exited the diner's parking lot and drove to the Interstate. He would continue nonstop until he reached Knoxville, and then he would abandon the rental car—stripped of any identification—in the middle of a University of Tennessee parking lot. Viktor would then steal an innocuous looking car from the same campus, and switch to the Missouri plates. These were simple risks, but necessary. Papaha needed an untraceable car by which to perform the next phase of his mission.

JAY DROVE THE rental car through the darkness, up the Plateau of Giza, to the tourist lot and parked. He climbed from the car, an expensive camera draped about his neck, and starting hiking up the winding stone footpath towards the Great Pyramid of Cheops. In a few moments, a uniformed Egyptian, obviously caught napping, bounded from the small Guardhouse to the left.

"Qif, lah-za," called the policeman, hurrying to catch Jaycott.

Jay ignored him, striding his way up the stone path.

"Is-tanna," continued the Egyptian puffing as he jogged to catch up, "law sa maht . . ." he grabbed Jay's arm.

"Me?!" Jaycott turned with a look of surprise on his face.

"Mish mum-kin," mumbled the Egyptian as he waved his index finger from side to side gesturing no. He struggled in English. "Closed . . . not possible . . . tomorrow . . . you come tomorrow."

Jay motioned at his camera and then at the Pyramids. "Photo, I must take photographs of the Pyramids. Soo-ra."

"Soo-ra?"

The policeman looked at Jay in the darkness as if he were crazy. "No sun, need sun for soo-ra."

"No," Jay shook his head and pointed to his camera. "Special—mahk-soos—special camera for night. Photo okay special." He motioned for the Egyptian to wait, and extracted a National Geographic Press Pass from his jacket pocket. He allowed the policeman to read the words written in both English and Arabic script.

"Night time good," nodded Jay, pointing again to the long camera lens and then the Pyramids. "Special, makh-sous, photo okay"

The policeman, intent on doing his job and keeping tourists away from the attractions after dark, started to object again when Jay stuffed several Egyptian pound notes into his hand.

"Min fadlak."

"Ma-andeesh meh-ni," shrugged the Egyptian tapping his wristwatch. "Til-tiseh."

"Twenty minutes," nodded Jay in agreement. "Shukran."

"Afwan."

The policeman turned and started walking back to his Guardhouse a little richer. Jay smiled and continued up the stone path. *Basheesh*, the international language.

At the northeast corner of Cheops, Jay turned right and started circling towards Kefren, the middle Pyramid, stopping to snap a few worthless photographs lest the policeman—or anyone else—was watching. Finally, after ten minutes, Jay stopped on the north side of Mikeranos, the smallest and westernmost Pyramid on the Plateau. He walked out from the base of Mikeranos so that he would be easily silhouetted against the ancient stone structure. He studied the flat, sandy desert before him, and smiled, satisfied that the darkness assisted in his precautions.

A short time elapsed before Jay saw the headlights of two cars circle up from the tourist parking lot, their radial tires crunching hard against the gravely stone path that he had walked. They came to a halt thirty feet to his right, their highbeams blinding Jay who had instinctively closed one eye to help preserve his night vision. He heard the car doors open, and saw the shadows of several men fan out to either side.

Jay held his arms limp and away from his body, palms open. Two men approached from the first car.

"Are you Ishmael?"

"Yes."

The first removed the camera draped around Jay's neck and opened his jacket. The second immediately started to frisk him, pausing to tug the large pistol stuck in the small of Jay's back. When they were satisfied, the first man spoke again.

"Wait here."

They walked back into the shadows behind the headlights. There was some quiet conversations and then the two men returned accompanied by a short, heavyset Arab. He wore a tailored suit, was balding, with a thin moustache above jowly cheeks, and spoke with a clipped, almost British accent.

"You were told to come *un*armed."

Jay shrugged, "Sorry about that. It's sort of like an American Express Card."

He could see the jowly Arab's face crinkle. Then his eyes lightened in amusement as he caught the pun. "Don't leave home without it?!"

"Precisely," smirked Jaycott.

The Arab guffawed in laughter slapping his hips, obviously enjoying the joke. The bodyguards seemed to shuffle in the background.

"Can we do something about the lights?" asked Jay.

With a quick gesture the highbeams on both cars were reduced down to parking lights and Jay opened his one closed eye. He noted that both cars were large Mercedes stretch models, and that two other bodyguards sat in the drivers seats of each.

The jowly Arab held up Jay's pistol, expertly slid out the magazine, and with his thumb started flicking the bullets on the ground.

"I commend your choice of weapons . . ." flick, flick ". . . a Sig Sauer model P226 . . ." flick, flick ". . . Swiss design, German manufacture . . ."flick, flick ". . . short recoil, locking lug . . ." flick, flick ". . . single or double action . . ." flick ". . . fifteen rounds of nine millimeter Parabellum . . ." flick, flick, flick ". . . weighing thirty ounces with a barrel length of less than four and a half inches . . ." flick ". . . accurate, reliable, and I daresay . . ." he flicked the final bullet from the magazine ". . . *deadly*." He stopped to look down at the pile of bullets in the sand. "Especially considering your choice of ammunition. What are they, Glaser Safety Slugs?"

"Yes."

"Very impressive," nodded the Arab, "and I suspect you know how to use it?"

"I can get by—in a pinch."

The jowly Arab laughed again and slid back the receiver ejecting the one chambered round. Then he handed Jay the unloaded pistol and empty magazine. Finally, he snapped his fingers and one of the bodyguards returned Jay's camera. The Arab motioned and the two bodyguards backpedaled towards the cars, just beyond earshot.

"Ishmael," he began, "everywhere I go these days I hear the name Ishmael . . . you've become somewhat of a minor celebrity here in Cairo."

"Is that good?" asked Jay cocking his head sideways with a curious look on his face.

"That depends . . . you obviously have some contacts, passable information, plenty of money to throw around. Your actions are bold, maybe even a little crazy . . ." The Arab fixed him with an appraising look as Jaycott raised an eyebrow, ". . . or maybe you're just very committed. The question is, where did you *really* come from, and *what* do you really want?"

Jay shrugged. "I thought it was rather obvious."

The Arab laughed. "Nothing is ever obvious—oh that story about profiting in the international arms markets is plausible enough, but my dear Ishmael, I know something about weapons and money . . ."

The Arab raised his hands outward, palms up, in a self-evident gesture.

"Touché," agreed Jay.

"Why all this need to involve Israel? Certainly you and your associates have another agenda?"

"If we do, we don't discuss it. What does it matter?"

"To me?! Nothing!" laughed the Arab. "I am but a businessman. But where Israel is concerned, you can be sure, there are *always*, many questions."

"Such as?"

"Such as who *are* you? Are you motivated by more than money? Are you actually *working* for Israel, looking to entrap certain parties in another of the Mossad's memorable schemes?"

"This all sounds very diabolical," said Jay his eyes narrowing for effect, but I assure you that neither I, nor any

of my associates, have any connection to *Israel*." He
whispered the last word with a touch of vehemence.

The Arab looked at Jay for a full minute. "Well then,
who are you?"

"Businessmen. Powerful, private, businessmen. Men
who for different reasons *share* many of your concerns,
hopes, fears . . ."

"But who?!" demanded the Arab. "Exactly *who* are
you?"

The bodyguards seemed to stir nervously in the
background. Jay looked towards the cars and the Arab
acknowledged his alertness.

"They could force that information from you."

Now Jay laughed. His confidence in the face of the
threat disturbed the Arab. Casually, he pointed out towards
the vast desert. "What do you see?"

"See? I see nothing; the sands of Giza covered in
blackness."

Precisely. But let's say for argument, out there," Jay
nodded to the north, "in all that blackness, is a man with a
Mauser SP-66, fitted with a special night vision device . . ."

The Arab's jowls contorted as he peered into the
desert. His eyes shifted left to right, then left again, searching
vainly for a human form.

". . . let's say," continued Jay, "that I once saw that
man drop a target at eight hundred meters in high winds.
Let's say that this man, this incredible marksman, is also just
a little bit crazy . . ."

Jay turned towards the Arab. "Before they," he motioned at the bodyguards, "take one step, *you* would be dead. You've got your answer; figure it out."

The Arab's demeanor changed. He peered hard into the night, then back at Jaycott. "I still don't . . ."

"Maybe we are not crazy at all. Who are we? Think about it. We are precise, efficient, financially strong and *very* committed. *Who* are we? We use finely engineered weapons." Jay held up his empty pistol.

"A Sig Sauer nine millimeter automatic . . ." mumbled the Arab, ". . . Swiss design, German manufacture." His eyes seemed to twinkle as he spoke his thoughts. "The Mauser is a *German* sniper weapon."

Jaycott shrugged knowingly and pointed out towards the desert. A look of puzzlement crossed the Arab's face as he stared hard at Jay. "Germans? Are you German?"

"We are *very* committed and we *hate* Jews," whispered Jay in his most menacing voice.

The Arab's eyes seemed to pop out of his head. He blurted the one word answer, his voice betraying a mixture of fear and incredulity. "Nazis?!"

Jay fixed the Arab with a cold stare. The lack of an answer became an answer.

"Nazis," repeated the Arab, almost to himself. His mind was working on overtime. Jaycott had learned long ago, when backstopping a cover to allow for some flexibility. The implausibility of the story made it perversely plausible. The Arab would believe what he wanted to believe. Since most Muslims hated Israelis, it was an emotional bridge to believe that other people shared the same hatred—and the most notorious Jew-haters in history were the Nazis.

"We have our own reasons for wanting to help," said Jay. "We can be of great assistance."

The Arab seemed dumbfounded; almost overwhelmed by his deduction. He stared at Jay, speechless.

"Call me," said Jay. Then he turned and walked away.

XII

9 August 1989
Langley, Virginia

JOHN MULLINS LOOSENED his tie and unbuttoned his shirt collar. It was hot. He lighted a cigarette and frowned. It never ceased to amaze the Deputy Director (Operations) that despite all the money spent on the sprawling suburban headquarters of the Central Intelligence Agency, they could still never seem to get the air conditioning to work right. John took a long drag on his cigarette. Damn oppressive, sticky, Washington summer humidity. He flipped through the Top Secret file on his desk.

"You won't find anything useful in there," said Tom Laughlin entering Mullins' office. John looked up at his counterpart the Deputy Director (Intelligence).

"Remember Dmitri?"

Laughlin rolled his eyes. "How could I forget. A veritable Santa Claus."

"He made my career," nodded Mullins through a haze of smoke, pausing to remember General Dmitri Polyakov, a Ukrainian-born Soviet masterspy, who for twenty-five years supplied the west with invaluable secrets.

"He made a lot of careers," agreed Laughlin, "old 'Top Hat' changed the course of history."

Mullins put down the file, stretched back in his seat, placed his feet atop the desk, and laced his fingers together behind his head. He continued to talk with the cigarette dangling from his lips. "How longs' it been?"

Laughlin shrugged, leaning against the map on Mullins' wall. "A year, maybe a year and a half. No doubt, a bullet in the back of the head—after they bled him dry of course. Probably a welcome end at that point. A nondescript, unmarked grave in some forgotten field—what's that term?"

"Bratskaya Mogila," offered Mullins. The ash on his cigarette was getting dangerously long. They sat in silence for a moment. "I've got a bad feeling on this one Tom . . ."

Laughlin nodded. "Yes, it's got a very definable Russian signature—unusual; typically they confine themselves to providing training and resources. This time, however, they seem to have actual operational involvement . . . if Dmitri were around, he'd have been a great asset."

He watched the long, grey ash fall onto Mullins' shirt. "Those things will kill you."

Mullins ignored him, but sat forward, plucked the cigarette from his lips and stubbed it into a full ashtray. "Do you have anything?"

"No," mumbled Laughlin straightening, "but the Judge is on my ass. He's got to brief the President tomorrow, and we don't have anything new . . . did you hear anything from your *Probe*?"

The last word was said with a touch of sarcasm. Mullins just shook his head. Laughlin turned and exited as quickly as he had entered. The Deputy Director (Operations) rubbed his tired eyes, staring blankly at the file. 20-8-15-20-13 . . . T, H, O, T, M . . .

IT HAD BEEN two weeks. Exactly fourteen days since Jay had left Corfu with Theo and last seen Katerina. So much had happened, and yet in some ways it seemed so recent; her look, her face, her eyes—those eyes—so expressive and yet so cool; a distant window to her emotions. Kat's final words lingered: 'bring my Theodori home safely, and yourself . . .'

Jay missed her, and now, in a quiet, contemplative moment his thoughts returned to Corfu and their time together on the island. This of course was accompanied by a double dose of guilt; for desiring a woman that was not his wife, and even worse, a woman that was the lover of his best friend. In a philosophical way, Jaycott dismissed his hunger as a byproduct of his profession. He understood better than most, that danger heightened passion. Katerina's combination of beauty, warmth, and inaccessibility fueled his desire. Yet it also exposed the emptiness of his life in the two years since Ellie's death. In a sense, he was jealous of the burly Greek. Theo had found a contentment and a comfort that Jay longed for—and despite it all, here was Theodori—a friend to the last—risking everything so that Jaycott could chase the ghosts one last time.

The phone rang.

Jaycott's attention shifted towards his desk, instantly alert. It rang a second time. In one smooth motion Jay was on his feet and crossing the room. He paused until the phone rang a third time and then plucked the receiver from the cradle.

"Yes?"

"We will meet, this morning, eleven o'clock. The Khan El-Khalili Souk."

"The Souk's a big place, where exactly?"

The line clicked dead. Jay stared at the buzzing receiver and then gently recradled the telephone.

THE SOVIET REZIDENTURA sat idly in the small room off the inner courtyard that he had converted into an office. The door was open, allowing the sunlight and sounds of the Casbah outside to circulate upward to his third floor dwelling. He always made it a point to dress in an expensive, tailored wool suit—despite the heat—when meeting any of his subordinates—be they Soviet Operations Officers or locally recruited agents. He believed this touch increased his authority. However today, with no one to meet and no appointments to keep, the GRU officer sat comfortably in a short sleeve shirt and slacks, idly chain smoking French cigarettes. He seemed transfixed by a series of photographs that lay spread across his desk.

Moscow Centre had—in typical fashion—requested a good deal more information than they shared. In this case, they had sent the Rezidentura (and he assumed the same was true for all his Fourth Directorate peers) a package in the Diplomatic pouch. The package contained photographs, some information, and a laundry list of questions—all pertaining to the man in the photos. Although the Centre never mentioned where the pictures were taken, the GRU officer recognized various landmarks and structures in the background and correctly deduced Cairo.

Such requests from the Khodinka Field Headquarters were relatively routine; except that this time the Centre coded the request as *Yavotchnaya Kvartira* or "Secret House." This tipped their hand as to the seriousness of the request. That intrigued the Rezidentura, because Moscow Centre would know, that the Field Offices would know, that Moscow considered the information quite important. To a professional Intelligence Officer conditioned to an unequal flow of information between a Field Office and Headquarters, the subtlety of the "Secret House" code spoke volumes. This man in the photographs had peaked someone's interest in Moscow, and the Centre was casting a broad net to quickly gather information.

The Rezidentura studied the lean, hard face in one picture, a blowup of a head and shoulder shot. The features were rugged, sort of handsome mused the Rezidentura objectively; but the thin scar on the cheek and the wary eyes told a different story. This man in the photographs was very capable.

He flipped through several more pictures depicting the subject in various situations; alone with others, close-up and from afar. The subject was middle-aged, yet tall and athletic in build. Yes, very capable confirmed the Soviet to himself.

"Well Ishmael, whomever you are" mumbled the Rezidentura to the photographs of Jaycott, "you seem to be a very important player of late."

TOM FAIRCHILD SAT at a wooden table in the rear of Casa Botin, a small restaurant just off the Plaza Mayor in the heart of Old Madrid. It was four in the afternoon, late into the lunch hour, and the restaurant was nearly deserted. Slowly, patiently, Fairchild nursed a glass of *chato* and a salad, preferring to eat light as his body was constantly torn between several countries and time zones.

He had been waiting for nearly an hour and Tom had to fight the urge to continuously check his wristwatch. Finally, the front door opened and a dark, swarthy man entered, pausing to survey the room. He made eye contact with Fairchild before moving to a chair two tables away. A second man entered, and he positioned himself in a seat near the front door. A full minute passed, and then a short, mustached man in his sixties entered the restaurant. With the help of his cane, the short man worked his way towards the rear of the dining room and took a seat opposite Fairchild.

"Shalom Thomas," mumbled the Mossad officer.

"Moshi," nodded the American. "A bit of a dramatic entrance, even for you."

The Israeli chuckled in good humor, motioning for the waiter to fetch another glass of wine. He rested both hands on his polished cane and surveyed the beautifully furnished old room.

"This was one of Ernest Hemingway's favorite restaurants."

"I know," said Fairchild raising an eyebrow. "A bit high profile, don't you think?"

The Israeli smiled. "A perfect cover. Hide in plain sight."

Fairchild frowned.

"Really Thomas, where would the two of us blend in better; amidst a bunch of foreign tourists, or in the middle of some little *tascas* surrounded by suspicious Madrilenõs?"

"Point taken," nodded Fairchild.

"Besides," continued Moshi "the food here is quite good."

A moment of silence passed as the waiter brought the Israeli a glass of *chato*.

"So?" asked Fairchild, raising his eyebrow again.

"Four Palestinians left Algiers bound for America at least ten days ago—maybe two weeks. They are each under false identities and passports. Even allowing for cutouts and backstopping, the first of them may already have passed through your Customs.

"The 'Go' Team?"

"One would think. Why expose local assets in the U.S. that could compromise a whole cell; which means they are using imports, which are expendable . . ."

"And poorly trained," interjected Fairchild, "which means the target is probably not a hardened sight."

He thought to himself as Moshi continued the process aloud. "If not a military or significant industrial target, then a symbolic one. Which makes their choice much broader. There are hundreds of possible soft targets."

"And it makes our job that much more difficult."

"My sympathies," nodded the Mossad officer.

"Anything on T, H, O, T, M?" asked Fairchild as an afterthought. "We need a break."

"Afraid not," shrugged the Israeli. "I'm surprised your *Ishmael* hasn't delivered anything; he's been causing quite a stir down in Cairo."

The American gazed at Moshi sheepishly, not at all surprised that Jaycott and Theodori's activities had spread through the Intelligence grapevine—after all, that was the point of a Probe.

"How reliable is this information Moshi?"

The older Israeli gave Fairchild a wounded look and then patted his hand in a paternalistic fashion. "Trust me Thomas, after all, we are allies."

The American nodded. "Any advice?"

The Mossad officer grew pensive for a moment while stroking his moustache. "Try the roast suckling pig, it's really quite good."

The incongruous statement momentarily confused Fairchild. Then he realized this was Moshi's way of ending their meet. He retorted quickly. "That doesn't sound very Kosher."

Moshi lowered his voice to a conspiratorial whisper. "The Rabbi tells me I'm allowed—but only if it's in the line of duty." He drained his wine glass and winked. "Shalom Thomas."

The Israeli stood, cane in hand, and with a slight spring in his step, walked from the restaurant.

THE KAHN EL-KHALILI Souk is a huge open-air bazaar in the heart of the Old City. Unlike a typically well-planned American mall, the central marketplace in Cairo is a labyrinthian maze of narrow streets and tiny alleyways that sell all forms of silks, spices, jewelry, leathergoods, and appliances—literally everything from a silk carpet or inlaid brass pot to a toaster oven.

A 'meet' at the Souk presented a difficult problem. Clearly, the unobstructed lines of sight that enabled Theodori to cover Jay from a distance at night were now non-existent. Use of a sniper weapon was eliminated. This contact was deliberately set in broad daylight, at close quarters, during the peak late morning shopping hour; and to compound their advantage—and Jay's risk—no fixed point of contact within the sprawling bazaar had been established. *They* would find *him*.

Jay's stomach turned. The thought of wandering aimlessly, lost, amid blind corners and dead-end alleys nauseated him. Too much risk. Hell, to task a whole team to tail and cover one man in the crowded Souk was difficult enough, but to expect the lone Theodori to provide security was absurd. Even in disguise he could only follow Jay a short time before eventually being spotted. No, the 'meet' was well conceived.

These musing turned Jaycott's thoughts to another matter. Did they believe his little story of representing Nazi extremists or did they want more accurate information? Did they arrange the 'meet' at the Souk because they feared him, or because it made Jay an easy target? If the latter held true, then a "snatch" made sense, and the torture that would follow his kidnapping would eventually tell them everything they needed to know. Jay had no delusions: everyone breaks eventually.

Jaycott considered the setup at length; analyzing and discarding various scenarios that tended to maximize his exposure. If he was required to walk into the lion's den, he would at least do it on his own terms. His only plausible action was to enter the Souk quickly, locate a neutral position from which Theodori could unobtrusively observe him, and camp out. The risk of course, was that if they couldn't "channel" him into a trap, they might abort the 'meet.' Yet Jay had learned long ago that *no* meet was better than a *bad* meet.

Jaycott spotted Theo as he climbed from the taxi. If he hadn't expected to find the Greek waiting patiently outside the entrance to the Souk, even he would have overlooked him as a local. Theodori's swarthy, stubbled face was wrapped in the traditional headdress known as a Kefiyeh, his thick torso clad in the long cotton galabiyya robe complete with its flowing sleeves, all covered—even in the heat—with a burnous. Right down to his grimy ankles and sockless, dust covered shoes, Theo looked like a true native—an Egyptian to the last.

Jay took a few minutes of laborious counting to pay the cab driver thus allowing the burly Greek to turn and lead him into the main alleyway that marked the beginning of the huge, open-air bazaar.

Jay moved with a purpose, oblivious to the shopkeepers hawking their wares, and quickly overtook the shuffling Theodori who ambled like a broken old man. When Jay was seven steps to Theo's front he slowed, making a point of turning his head in all directions as if to say: 'Alright, I'm here, let's get on with it.' No one approached.

His eyes searched furtively for a static position as they neared the first bend in the alley. The nausea started and Jay once again applauded their decision. Having received the phone call requesting the 'meet' only three hours earlier, he was deprived of an opportunity to perform a reconnaissance of the Souk. He was blind. This was their turf, they had him, and they knew it.

Jay slowed perceptively so that the shuffling Theodori could close the gap. Then, his eyes shifting to either side, he turned left into a second narrow passageway. Souvenirs, trinkets, copper trays and camel-leather bags hung everywhere, but up ahead, thirty steps to his front, the passage widened and Jay saw a few tables and scattered chairs. Lounging around, talking, and sipping sweet green tea were a half dozen locals—Cairo's version of a café. Jay made a beeline for the tables and took the last empty seat.

A bead of sweat trickled down his temple as he ordered tea. Then Jay placed a twenty pound note on the table and motioned for the waiter to refill the cups of every local in the café. To a man, they looked at him in mild surprise. Jaycott grinned. *Stay, drink, enjoy, I love company.* He could see the locals size him up. A well dressed foreigner. Each smiled and nodded; some motioning their thanks with hand raised upward palm turned in, others touched their own chests. Then to Jay's astonishment, Theo shuffled past him, and with the audacity of an elder Egyptian, insistently motioned a younger man from his seat. The *balls*, smirked Jaycott to himself. *Incredible* balls. In New York, an adolescent would have told Theo to 'take a hike,' but then this was Cairo, and the burly Greek always possessed a great sense of rhythm. He knew the Arabic culture, and he always knew how far to push things. It wasn't long before the café owner and several of the older patrons were jabbering at the disrespectful youth to give up his chair. The young man relented and Theodori sat. Seconds later, from beneath his flowing galabiyya, he produced a shee-sha, the long stemmed Arabic waterpipe. He expertly prepared and lighted the pipe, took a drag on the long hose, and passed it amongst his new found friends. Instant kinship.

As Jay exchanged small pleasantries with his tablemates, he noted that Theo had taken the opportunity to reposition himself—ostensibly to pass the pipe. They were barely twenty feet apart, however, Theo clearly was covering everything to Jaycott's rear and left. Therefore, Jay shifted his chair sideways to view his right and front.

For thirty minutes nothing happened. Jay bought another round of tea. Egyptians by nature are not imbued with a great sense of urgency. The term *ma'alich*, or 'never mind' creeps into their conversation with great regularity. When one adds to this cultural trait of procrastination the social obligation of politeness, one understood why Jay's café friends found it difficult to leave. They didn't *want* to go back to work, and they certainly couldn't be so rude as to ignore the foreigner's hospitality. Jaycott would buy tea for whomever and how many until their kidneys burst. He had staked out his corner. The 'meet' would be here—a static contact point where Theo could cover him—or not at all. He had walked into the lion's den. It was their game, but he refused to play by their rules.

"Sa bah it kheyr."

Jay and the two men at his table looked up to see a large mustached Egyptian. He was one of the bodyguards from the first 'meet' at the Pyramids.

"Sa-bah in-noor," they mumbled back in unison.

"Iz zay yak?" he continued looking straight at Jay.

"Bi kheyr, il Ham du lil-leh," nodded Jay noncommittally.

"Our friends are waiting for us," said the bodyguard in English.

Jay shrugged and motioned at the table. "They should meet us here, the tea is really quite good. Besides, I wouldn't want to appear uncivil to my new friends."

The bodyguard's expression changed and his eyes narrowed. Jay returned the squint evenly. Five seconds passed. Then the bodyguard leaned over and whispered to the closest tablemate, pushing some wadded money into the Egyptian's hand. The man motioned to his friend and stood.

They both shook Jay's hand, thanking him profusely for his generosity and walked away. The bodyguard then sat in one of the two empty seats.

"Who told you to stop here?"

"No one," shrugged Jay, "but no one told me *not* to either."

"You should have kept moving. This is too open."

"The Souk's a big place, I was afraid I'd get lost."

"We would have found you."

"You *did* find me," smirked Jay.

The bodyguard's lips tightened and Jay noticed how a large vein in his temple seemed to throb.

"You will come with me."

"No."

Jaycott's answer was spoken so calmly, so quietly, that the bodyguard's frustration increased. "You *will* come with me," he whispered emphatically through clenched teeth, "or we will drag you."

Jay leaned back in his chair beyond the man's reach. "We?"

The question caused the bodyguard to unconsciously glance to the right. Jay looked over his left shoulder and noticed two large Egyptians standing in front of a leather goods shop across the alley.

"I see," said Jay, "friends of yours?"

"Ay-wa," nodded the bodyguard suddenly pleased with himself and exuding confidence.

Jay looked back a second time to make sure that Theo noticed. Then he slowly scanned the crowded stalls that surrounded the café, trying to identify other likely accomplices.

"*Now*, you will come with me Ishmael, yes?"

Jay smiled again and shook his head. "Have some tea." He reached forward and picked up the teapot with his left hand.

The bodyguard slammed Jay's forearm to the table, pinning his wrist and the teapot flat with both hands. The loud crash caused the other café patrons to suddenly take notice.

"Then we will drag you!"

In a blur, Jay's right arm shot upward to the Egyptian's face, his open hand contorted in a claw-like grip. He ripped at the bodyguard's eyes, tearing at the sockets. Blood splattered and the man screamed, reeling backwards out of his chair to roll in agonizing fits on the concrete floor.

It only took a moment for the two accomplices standing across the alley to react. The first man produced a small truncheon, rushing forward to strike Jay from the rear. Suddenly a deafening roar filled the alley—as if a cannon had discharged—and the man's chest exploded in a cratered mass of flesh and bone. All eyes turned sideways to see the grisly Theodori crouched in a balanced Weaver stance aiming a massive Desert Eagle automatic pistol.

The second assailant hesitated, both eyes widening in disbelief as the burly Greek squeezed the trigger again. The force of the .44 Magnum bullet tore into the man's ribcage shredding organs and spewing blood, sweeping the man upward off his feet and crashing him headlong into a crowded café table.

Screams. Shoppers started diving for cover as the stench of gunpowder mixed with the deafening echo of Theo's huge handgun. Jay motioned to his left as he drew his nine millimeter, angling his body at right angles to his partner, moving quickly back in the direction from which they arrived. There was no time for thought, speed was their best weapon; and as Theo jostled to keep up with the faster Jaycott, he glanced back towards the café. Sitting stunned, in a tight semi-circle, their mouths open and eyes aglow, were the patrons who shared the Greek's waterpipe. They watched in disbelief as the disheveled Theo transformed himself from a hobbling old local into a deadly shooter. More alarmingly, he noticed two serious looking men—Trailers—approach from the far side, converging quickly towards the confusion at the café. Theo pushed forward, burrowing quickly into the narrow passage that joined this alley with the main street of the Souk.

They were in the crowd, hiding the weapons with their bodies, their eyes shifting furtively from side to side. The screams and confusion were a plus, but Jay realized that he, more than Theo, was an easy mark. They broke into the main alleyway and instinctively slowed to a fast walk. As many Egyptians were moving towards the café area as away, their curiosity piqued by the noise and gunshots; the anguished cries of emotional people increasing the chaos. It was a shield, cover, and Jay embraced it.

Theodori had fallen several steps behind, his massive pistol hidden in the flowing robes of the galabiyya. Secure in his disguise, he covered the European-dressed Jaycott, knowing that safety lay just a few steps more beyond the entrance to the Souk.

Sirens, a screech of tires, and police were running into the entrance. Jay motioned them into the Souk, pointing towards the far end of the alley, the direction from which he had just come. "Doghir, 'ala tul, imshi . . ."

A large man in a cotton jacket walked towards Jay from the entrance to the Souk. He clearly was not with the police.

"Aish fi?"

Jay motioned with his free hand while hiding his pistol behind his leg. More shouts. The two Trailers emerged from the passageway. They hailed the man accosting Jay, pointing and yelling. He grabbed at Jay's shoulder which proved to be a mistake. Instantly Jay rammed his pistol up under the man's jaw and squeezed off two rounds. The man's head exploded.

Another man from the crowd to Jay's front pulled out a weapon, but before he could take aim the front of Theo's galabiyya recoiled, and the magnum bullet blew a gaping hole in the man's abdomen.

Suddenly they were alone in the middle of the street as the mob scattered in all directions. Theo moved the last few feet towards the entrance and made eye contact with Jay.

"Romulas?"

Jaycott nodded, accepting their secret codeword that initiated Evasion and Escape procedures. They were blown.

Each turned, and moved away from the Souk in opposite directions.

XIII

13 August 1989
Washington, D.C.

"THEY GOT OUT alive."

It was a factual statement. Tom Fairchild returned Rochelle Listach's serene gaze, finding it difficult to read the old woman's expression. Deep behind those thoughtful eyes, he could almost hear the gears of her wizard sharp mind turning—reviewing, discarding, considering. His boss' reputation for identifying probable outcomes was legendary. She seemed to think four moves ahead of the average person, and Tom found himself wondering if Ms. Listach played chess.

Slowly, Rochelle sipped at her cup of tea. "Well, it confirms our choice of Jaycott. He certainly is resourceful. They've gone to ground?"

"Yes," nodded Fairchild, "I imagine they will resurface soon. My guess is either Tunisia or Morocco. The moderate countries are easier to move in. Algeria is a possibility. Libya I tend to doubt."

The operations officer considered this analysis thoughtfully before setting down her tea cup. "I must tell you that the ruckus they've stirred is impressive. There isn't an agent on the payroll or case officer working the region who hasn't reported some version of the events in Cairo. Unfortunately, we still don't have a target site."

"T, H, O, T, M?"

"Precisely . . ." she grew pensive again before speaking. ". . . clearly, they know that Jaycott has a Second."

Fairchild's expression tightened. "The cable traffic would indicate that our Ishmael has presented a bit of a threat," she continued. "I think we must push the situation. We must see who reacts."

"What do you propose?"

"Theodori has a woman."

Fairchild squeezed his eyes shut.

"Will it work," asked Listach in a matter of fact tone.

"I suppose," relented Tom, opening his eyes. "If handled correctly."

"Do you see any alternative?"

The case officer grimaced, his mind a disjointed jumble of thoughts and conjectures. "There must be another way."

"If we had time," agreed Rochelle. "But we don't. *Time* is the one element we don't have. Desperate situations require desperate means."

They sat in silence for a moment.

"Are you okay with this Tom?" Her tone was cold, mechanical. Fairchild looked hard at the diminutive old woman. He nodded.

"Good. As soon as they surface, we'll set things in motion. Benjamin will show you out."

She reached for the hardcover book sitting on the coffee table. The act was a sign of dismissal.

ABD-AL RAHMAN SPED east along Interstate Route #10 in Alabama. The traffic was sparse, and his rental car was surprisingly fast.

For the better part of four days after arriving in the United States, Abd-al had remained quiet in New Orleans. He watched hours of American television in his hotel room, or took long walks in the city—eating the strange food; listening to the stranger music. America was not what he expected, but then, having never set foot in the country before, he was not quite sure what to expect. The boredom grew, yet Abd-al was determined to follow his instructions carefully; for both the Soviet Rezidentura and Saoud his mentor were very explicit about the need to keep a low profile.

Finally, things were moving again, and Abd-al used the solitude of driving to Florida from New Orleans as a release. The rental car had air-conditioning, a wonderful stereo system, and tremendous power. It was a big, fast, fancy American car. Thus, it didn't take the Palestinian long to pop an Arabic tape into the cassette. The electric windows were up, the air conditioning was on, and the chanting music of Umm Kulthum filled his ears. He found the scant traffic along the highway seductive. The speedometer inched forward.

As Abd-al sang along with Umm Kulthum, his head bobbed and his free hand tapped in unison against the dashboard. He kept a wary eye out for police, but the bright sun of a panhandle August obscured his long vision. The speedometer touched eighty miles per hour.

He never saw the pickup truck. Just over a rise in the highway, a rusty, brown vehicle eased into Abd-al's lane from the soft shoulder of the road. The driver of the pickup truck was nearly as surprised as Abd-al Rahman; and the fact that he was moving nearly fifty miles per hour slower than the rental car made a timely reaction impossible. He swerved back to the right as Abd-al slammed on the brakes, yanking hard on the wheel to the left. The combination of speed, a blinding sun, and compressed reaction time proved too much. Abd-al's right front fender caught the pickup truck's left rear bumper and the jack-knifing rental car's momentum carried it sideways into a spin. The inertia started a tumble, and the car flipped, rolling end over end across the highway before ending on its roof, tire spinning, in the passing lane of the interstate.

IN A LARGE corner office at the Khodinka Field Headquarters of the GRU, Colonel General Aleksandr Grigorevich Pavlov sat sipping vodka with his subordinate Lieutenant General Guryenko.

". . . therefore Gorbachev is seeking to appease the Nationalists. This secret meeting was taped at his Dacha."

"And you say Comrade General, that several Provincial Party Leaders were in attendance?"

"Da," nodded Pavlov.

The dapper head of the Illegals Training Centre patiently removed his eyeglasses and began cleaning the lenses with a handkerchief. "You are curious Vyacheslav Tikhonovich?"

"Very, Comrade General," nodded Guryenko with a slight smile.

Pavlov sipped his vodka. "Boris Gidaspov from Leningrad, Bobykin of Sverdlovsk, and Lev Zaikor to name a few."

Guryenko leaned back in his chair and let out a deep sigh. This information obviously surprised him.

"The discussion revolved around the Central Committee Meeting scheduled for next month," continued Pavlov.

"They've postponed it three times."

"Da," agreed Pavlov, "but pressure is building. Gorbachev must control the hardliners or he risks a coup."

"And how, Comrade General, will he appease them?"

"There was talk of setting up a new Russian Bureau in the Party to control the Nationalists."

"With himself as the boss?"

"Naturally Vyacheslav Tikhonovich, you see it all so quickly." Pavlov was smiling. "Gorbachev must court the Nationalists while he continues his reforms."

"So that he can continue to purge the Politburo."

"Da. There is talk of a *list* and the name Chebrikov is always mentioned."

Guryenko caught his breath, the name momentarily startling him. Pavlov noted his subordinate's hesitation.

"Your thoughts Vyacheslav?"

"A dangerous decision," admitted Guryenko. "To attack the chief of the KGB is a frightful proposition—even for Gorbachev."

"Da, but he has teeth of steel."

They sat in silence for a brief moment.

"Of course," continued Pavlov, "if the KGB falls from its current position of influence, then the Red Army reigns supreme."

"Agreed Comrade General, but one must never wound a King."

"Which is why we must continue in our unsolicited support of Comrade Gorbachev. Do you now see how it begins to fall into place?"

"Da, Comrade General," nodded Guryenka.

"So tell me, how are our Illegals progressing?"

"Quite well, all of the Illegals have arrived at the target site. We have not yet made contact with the Executive Agents recruited from Algeria. They are slowly working their way to the target site from four different routes."

"Eta harasho," nodded Pavlov satisfied. He poured two more shots of vodka into a pair of tumbler glasses. "To the Rodina, Vyacheslav Tikhonovich."

Guryenko raised his glass. "Nostrovia, Comrade General."

TUNISIA. THE LAND of Hannibal. The country on the Mediterranean Sea where the Arabic and European cultures collide.

Slowly, Jaycott strolled up the narrow streets of Side Bou Said, the old French Quarter of Tunis, re-familiarizing himself with the unique sights and sounds of the Capitol City. Men in Italian designed sportcoats and slacks swept café entrances while women wrapped in traditional Arabic Kaftans and Abayas carried plastic grocery bags.

It was a dichotomy.

Everything official, from its language, to its religion, to its ethnic background, to its currency was consistent with the other Islamic countries of the world. However, Tunisia was a mere 63,000 square miles of land, populated by 8 million people, sandwiched between the behemoths of Libya and Algeria on the northernmost point of the continent of Africa.

It learned to accommodate.

Tunisia exported some oil and textiles, but possessed nothing on the order of the incredibly rich petrol-dollars of its Arabic brothers. What it did have was a 1,000 mile coastline and several natural seaports, which when coupled with its proximity to Europe, proved a most valuable resource in Tunisia's primary foreign export: tourism.

Jaycott stopped at a small café table on the cobbled steps of the Terrace Tea House. He ordered green tea and looked off from the cliffs of Side Bou Said to the ancient ruins of Carthage below. He scanned the café crowd, noting the various tourists and locals gathered in conversation;

nibbling on food, discussing politics, sipping at drinks as they too enjoyed the panoramic view. But nowhere was Theodori.

It had been an abrupt and risky departure from Cairo four days earlier, but Jay had sneaked under the police dragnet by employing a known blackmarket smuggler. The names and addresses of several such 'businessmen' had been built into Jay's Evasion & Escape plan should the need arise. Tom Fairchild's CIA network proved valuable.

Jaycott sipped his tea thoughtfully. Tunisia was a good choice. As a country she played a moderate hand, taking a hardline against Islamic Fundamentalists, but at the same time permitting the PLO to headquarter in Tunis following the organization's official departure from Lebanon. This non aligned stance permitted Tunisia friends on all sides; a somewhat westernized slant to Islam, and a coastline of affordable tourist hotels for the European traveler. It also, like Cairo, permitted Jay and Theo a more flexible environment for movement.

Jay looked up as a young couple passed his table. When he and Theodori broke into their E&E mode following the shootout at the Souk, they moved separately. Each knew the resourcefulness of the other, and each had memorized persons, places, and points of contacts that could facilitate a fast and illegal exit from Egypt. They had agreed in their planning that they would resurface in Tunisia. For ten uninterrupted days, between two and three in the afternoon, both Jay and Theo would come to this very café searching for each other. If at the end of that period they had not re-established contact, then the remaining partner would abort the mission. In either case, Fairchild would be notified. This was easily accomplished through the use of pre-designated codewords, spoken on scrambled telephone lines, to pre-established dead drops. Everything had been committed to memory. Fairchild would know within an hour of their resurfacing, the exact status, health, and location of his Probe Team.

Except that Jaycott had come to the Terrace Tea House three days in a row without seeing Theodori, and now he started to worry that the burly Greek had not survived. He checked his wristwatch, and after waiting the obligatory hour, prepared to leave. Suddenly, he looked up and noticed a well tanned stocky, curly haired European dressed sportily in slacks, a suitjacket, and Ray Ban sunglasses. Theo reached up and tugged the sunglasses down the bridge of his nose, making a point to look directly at Jay before moving to an empty table. The eye contact was made, and the Ray Ban's pushed back into place. Jaycott smiled to himself. So much for a grizzled old Egyptian shuffling about the Khan El-Khalili Souk in scuffed shoes and a dirty burnous.

Theodori snapped his fingers imperiously at the waiter, flashing a wad of Tunisian dinar paper currency, displaying an expensive gold watch on one wrist, and an expensive gold bracelet on the other. He ordered a large lunch.

Four tables away, Jay relaxed a bit and motioned to a different waiter, pointing at his own empty cup of green tea. "Encore, s'il vous plaît."

The waiter nodded.

XIV

TOM FAIRCHILD STOOD on the small bridge that connected the Ile de la Cité with the Quai St. Michel. His hands fumbled nervously with a long French cigarette as he looked up at the cathedral of Notre Dame and the face of a grimy gargoyle. He flicked an ash from the slender Gitane. From the quay side on the Left Bank, he watched Reginald Parks of the British Secret Intelligence Service approach. As always, the MI-6 officer was trim and nattily dressed in a worsted wool suit, even in the August heat of a Parisian summer.

Reggie stopped next to Tom in the middle of the bridge and gazed out at the Seine.

"The river barges run slow."

"Paris is for lovers and dreamers. Commerce is the curse of the Aristocracy."

"Spoken like a true capitalist," smiled the British Intelligence Officer.

"If I scratch my chin," started Fairchild wearily, dragging on the cigarette, "we break contact and meet each hour, on the hour, at the bars in the Ritz, the Crillon, and the George Five—in that order. Got it?"

"Quite."

Reginald Parks took a long appraising look at his American counterpart. "You look tired laddie."

"I am," admitted Fairchild, flicking his ash into the river. "My body lost track of time zones."

Parks nodded at the cigarette. "I thought you quit."

"I did." The case officer threw the cigarette into the Seine. "I appreciate you grabbing the shuttle on such short notice, Reg; I hope I didn't screw-up your day."

Parks shrugged. "I'm here, it sounded urgent."

"It is," nodded Tom, turning to face Parks. "In the briefcase at my feet is a file on a woman named Katerina Terrass. She lives on the Greek island of Corfu. Her identify and whereabouts must be fed to the other side—but it must appear to be a leak, an inadvertent breakdown in security. The details are included."

Parks regarded Fairchild pensively. "Is this tied to that business down in Cairo?"

Tom shrugged.

"Are those your people?" continued Parks.

Fairchild didn't answer directly. "Reg, I need your help."

"I understand lad. Is she a hostile?"

Again, no answer. The Englishman raised an eyebrow. "You're setting up an innocent?"

The two men stood in silence looking at each other in the Paris sunlight.

"Why us?" asked Parks.

"Why?!" growled Fairchild in a low voice. "Why *not*? Because you're our closest allies, our 'cousins'. Why? Because nobody would believe the French, nobody likes the Italians, nobody *trusts* the fucking Israelis . . . where else do we turn Reg? Who else could pull it off? Who else would Moscow believe?"

Parks chewed his lip for a moment before answering. "This is a bloody awful business."

"It sucks," agreed Fairchild.

Silence ensued. Tom turned towards the river. "Will you do it Reg?"

Parks turned and also faced the river, leaning his elbows on the guardrail and hanging his folded hands over the Seine. "Queen, country, and all that rot," sighed the Ml-6 officer. "Leave the briefcase and be on your way."

Tom nodded and turned. "Thanks Reg, I won't forget this."

"Quite right," nodded Parks, "and get some sleep."

Fairchild wearily started for the Quai St. Michel and the Left Bank.

AMMUNITION. THE GRU Rezidentura sat at his desk in the old Quarter of Algiers and turned a page on the forensic report. Ammunition was the key. He lighted a cigarette and took a moment to inhale deeply. The fact that he was sitting in a hot office, two countries removed, sifting through a Russian translation of an Egyptian incident was totally lost on the Soviet. Years spent in the Intelligence trade had accustomed him to such seeming incongruity. Everything was available for a price; and all manner of private or public employees could be bought, bribed, or both. He highlighted a passage in the report, and made a note in the margin.

It was terribly clear to the Rezidentura that the firefight in the Souk involved at least two professionally trained individuals. Everything about the sequence of events from their actions, to their coordinated movements, to their thoroughness, and finally their successful escape—all indicated a high level of training. But most of all it was the ammo. The ammunition clinched it.

The Soviet set down his pen and rubbed tired eyes. Piled atop his desk was a stack of reports and diagrams including pathology notes on the four victims, the forensic analysis on gunpowder residue, fingerprints, blood stains, shell casings, bullet fragments, and the conflicting eyewitness accounts of a dozen Egyptians. He sucked on the cigarette.

Two types of ammunition had been used. In the first instance, the Egyptian Police had recovered three spent shell casings from a .44 Magnum cartridge. This was odd. Few shooters used a .44 Magnum handgun for the obvious reason that very few shooters could handle a .44 Magnum handgun. It was a beast. The reports told of a grizzled old local suddenly brandishing a massive pistol, and with surprising speed and apparent calm, squeezing off rounds with deadly accuracy—from a practiced marksman's stance. It all sounded very professional, but then Arabs could be excitable and given to exaggeration, and even they watched television . . . except for the ammunition. One didn't so readily excuse their story when one verified that a .44 Magnum handgun had fired three times and claimed three victims.

The Rezidentura then consulted a reference book on small arms from his Operations Center at the Embassy and determined that the two most widely manufactured handguns using the powerful .44 Magnum cartridge was the Smith & Wesson Model 29, or 'Dirty Harry' gun, and the IMI Desert Eagle. One was a U.S. manufactured revolver, and the other an Israeli manufactured pistol. Each was an oversized, intimidating piece of iron whose weight, report, and recoil demanded exhaustive training if a shooter was going to use it with any degree of effectiveness. This shooter had.

In the second instance, the Egyptian Police had recovered two spent shell casings for nine millimeter parabellum cartridges next to the body of the fourth victim. Unlike the .44 Magnum rounds, the nine millimeter were considered quite common. The difference here was not in the *size* of the bullets, but in their destructiveness. The second shooter used a special round—a souped-up bullet—that was chambered for a nine millimeter automatic, but possessed the lethality of a much larger weapon. The key to this ammunition lay in the pathology report.

The muzzle of the weapon had been held under the soft palate of the victim's jaw, at point blank range. There were two entrance wounds. This corresponded to both the powder burns and residue, as well as the two recovered shell casings. However, instead of the two bullets proceeding upward to become lodged in the mass ganglia of the victim's brain, they released some type of high velocity prefragmented projectiles that expanded upon penetration into a cone-shaped pattern. The result was a 100% energy transfer to the victim's skull. Instead of the bullets penetrating the Egyptian's brain, they disintegrated it. Again, it was the ammunition that told the story.

The Rezidentura took a final drag on his cigarette, and then with a pronounced finality, stubbed out the ashes. Across the large desk in the far corner sat Moscow Centre's questionnaire of an American Agent codename: Ishmael. The Soviet had not doubt that it was this very man involved in the shootout in Cairo. In the week since headquarters had mailed the various field offices the *Yavotchnaya Kvartira* request, the Rezidentura had learned something of Ishmael's activities in Cairo. And what he learned he didn't like. Evidently this agent provocateur was engaged in activity directly related to uncovering the Soviet's operation in America; T, H, O, T, M. This perturbed the Rezidentura. They were so *close*, and now Ishmael and his network were demonstrating a rather dangerous proclivity towards attracting attention. That was enough to jeopardize everything that the Rezidentura had worked towards. And it was a risk he could not accept.

TENSION. IT HUNG in the air like a thick, billowing blanket; a wool cover that shrouded the room in anxiety. There was a collective feeling of impotence that seemed to grow with each passing day. These were powerful men; men conditioned to making decisions; decisions predicated on

useful information. They had none; and that fact—more than
any other—caused these men to chafe in frustration. Together
they could marshal an incredible wealth of governmental
resources to combat any foe. They possessed the keys to the
entire U.S. warchest, and yet their inability to discern a target
site left it all for naught. The clock was ticking . . .

Slowly, Tom Laughlin surveyed the other committee
members, pausing to note each man's expression as his eyes
circled the conference table. He gave a slight nod, and cleared
his throat. "Let's get started."

All eyes shifted towards Tom at the head of the table.
"We may have a break." He turned towards the Deputy
Director of the FBI. "Russell."

The Federal Agent stood and passed out eleven
dossiers sliding a thin manila file across the rectangular
conference table to each of the other committee members.

"Two days ago, at three o'clock in the afternoon, a
traffic accident took place on Interstate Route #10, seventeen
miles east of Mobile, Alabama . . ."

Several of the committee members were leafing
through photographs and Highway Patrol accident reports.

". . . one driver, the owner of a pickup truck, lives in
Summerdale, Alabama. He is alive, but hospitalized in critical
condition. The second driver, a Caucasian male, mid-
twenties, Mediterranean descent was DOA. He was originally
identified as a foreign national, traveling under a Spanish
passport, driving a rental car which he contracted when he
entered the United States through the port of New Orleans on
the ninth of August . . ."

The agent paused to ensure that he had their full attention. ". . . in attempting to notify the next-of-kin, the Alabama State Police contacted the local Bureau office, who in turn called the State Department. The Spanish Consulate verified that the passport had, in fact, been reported stolen two years ago in Tangiers, Morocco. We therefore ran a fingerprint request through Interpol . . ."

Russell paused a second time and allowed himself a small victory. He scanned the room.

"And?" questioned the Admiral, voicing their collective impatience.

". . . and, the dead driver of the rental car is Abd-al Rahman Ajaj, a known soldier of the Palestinian Islamic Jihad."

"Bingo," signed Rudy of the DIA. John Mullins lighted a cigarette.

"There's more," added Russell, waiting until the members quieted again. "We sent a forensic team down to the crash site, and went over the vehicle with a fine toothed comb. A false compartment in his suitcase yielded a cryptopad, a series of numbers in a notebook, and a sterile map of Florida."

Jack Belmont of the Department of Transportation was on his feet, moving quickly towards a huge wall map of the United States. He started tracing his index finger from left to right along interstate Route #10 east of New Orleans.

"We've got the cryptopad and the notebook," offered Al of the National Security Agency, "nothing as of yet."

"Ten, maybe fifteen miles from the Florida border. Pensacola . . . Eglin?!" announced Belmont talking aloud with his back to the other committee members as he studied the wall map.

"Possibly," nodded Russell, at mention of the Air Force Base. "It's a viable target."

"Sure is," agreed the Admiral. "Naval training school, flight school, high profile postings . . ."

"We've contacted the Base Commander," continued Russell. "They are on a code yellow alert. We've also sent an HRT team to Florida as a precautionary measure. All high ranking arrivals and departures using Eglin as a point of entry or exit have been re-routed. Rudy is comparing the T, H, O, T, M letter and 20-8-15-20-13 number sequence versus every known code, coordinate and facility designation at Eglin."

Russell caught his breath. "We have judged it necessary to provide the Base Commander with limited information. I might add, that some widening of the circle is inevitable. Some of our leads must be shared as they develop. Clearly in this case, if Eglin Air Force Base *is* the target, we must take every possible step to secure the facility."

The FBI Agent sat down, and for a moment all eyes either studied the dossiers or watched Jack Belmont as he continued surveying the wall map. Finally, Al, the NSA representative spoke. "If we're talking about sharing information, could someone shed some light on that incident in Cairo?" He looked directly at John Mullins of the CIA. The DDO remained impassive, dragging lazily on his cigarette.

"It was our Probe," nodded Mullins, exhaling. "We are not sure how it got to the point of a gunbattle, but it's drawn attention. The best we can hope for now, is that the sponsors of this strike are sufficiently rattled, and will make a mistake."

"I thought the strike had a Soviet signature?" protested the Admiral.

"It does," acknowledged Tom Laughlin, "however, even though sources and methods are Soviet, several inconsistencies lead us to believe that this is an unsanctioned operation."

"A renegade strike?" asked Paul of Customs.

"We believe so," admitted Laughlin, "we don't think it has the blessing of the Politburo."

"Could you amplify?" asked the DEA Agent.

"I'll try . . ." he collected his thoughts for a moment before beginning. ". . . as you know, Moscow has a plate full of problems. Our best estimates have determined that there are at least four power bases developing—and *each* is jockeying for control. If one of these groups is sponsoring the strike—using an Islamist cutout—they can blame another group. The guilty group appears moderate, while the innocent group appears to be extremists. It's a setup."

"And the primary risk to the guilty group, is that we expose them *before* they can blame the innocent group. Then it would backfire," added Mullins.

"We use a Probe to draw attention to the problem before the perpetrators can plant their tainted evidence. What we're hoping is that their fear of exposure will spook them."

"Bait and switch?" asked Bob Perkins of the State Department.

"Precisely. The guilty group fears the attention that our Probe is drawing to their plot; they panic, and they go after him. The hunted becomes the hunter.

"But a strike against the U.S. for the sake of advancing internal politics—that's a bit drastic Tom, even for some of the players in Moscow. They're risking a war."

Laughlin looked across the conference table at the Deputy Director of ATF, and shrugged.

"Actually Larry, they're not. The truth is, that barring a direct military invasion, we'd never go to war over this. Besides, they've attached a False Flag with the Islamist connection."

"Tom," interrupted Rudy, "what precisely is the state of affairs in Moscow right now? Can we get a handle on it?"

The DDI signed. "Think of it this way; in the best of times, when Moscow's leadership is considered stable, Red Square's politics are a can of worms. Their political machinations and shifting alliances in an average year make the crap that happens in this town look like kid stuff. Take that environment and start introducing instability and radical change . . ." Laughlin waved his hand in a matter of fact way, ". . . it's a free for all."

Jack Belmont stuck a blue pin in the large wall map at the crash site on Interstate #10 in Alabama.

"Mister Abd-al Rahman Ajaj was going somewhere in a hurry. I'll start a matrix. If Eglin *is* the target, something else may develop."

Laughlin nodded before speaking. "From this point forward we meet every *third* day, here, at zero, eight, three zero hours. All conversations on STU-3 telephones, all E-mail KG-84 encrypted, no travel greater than two hours driving time from this room. Questions?"

Tom's eyes roamed the conference table. "Good, we're adjourned."

SAOUD HAD BEEN in Miami for three days, and the sight of so many young, scantily clad women incensed him. It was indecent. He worked hard to control his unnatural urges, yet the permissiveness of this society always stirred his hunger. Saoud was scheduled to leave for the target site soon, and although he had been warned repeatedly by the Soviet Rezidentura to avoid any activity that could compromise their mission, the Palestinian knew that Allah would understand. Retribution was necessary. It cleansed the soul.

Saoud paced his hotel room, impatiently sipping a whiskey. The woman was late, and this only seemed to increase his anger. Finally, there was a knock. He raced across the room and flung open the door.

"Hi, I'm Pam."

A pretty blond in a tight halter top, shorts, and spiked beach shoes stood in the hallway, smiling. She looked twenty years old. "Are you John?"

Saoud grunted and motioned her into the room. He quickly closed and locked the door.

"Business first," started the blond in a matter of fact tone, "I do straight, French, and Greek. No S&M, no three-way, and you must wear protection. I have a selection if you forgot them."

She produced a handful of latex condoms from her handbag and placed them on the side table, then kicked off her shoes. Saoud just watched her.

"You have two hours—no more, because I've got a three o'clock class. It's three hundred dollars, in advance."

She smiled again and raised an open hand towards the Palestinian. For a moment, Saoud did nothing. His eyes seemed to glaze over. Then suddenly his left arm swung in a wide arc and he struck the call girl with a vicious backhand. She stumbled, and before the girl could scream, Saoud was atop her. He held a sharp knife at her throat. The venom in his whisper was palpable.

"I decide what we do here, whore!"

The Palestinian grabbed a handful of her hair, and with the knife held tightly against her neck, dragged the college student to the bed. He flung her down face first, straddling her back with the weight of his torso, and started to secure her wrists to the headboard with pieces of pre-positioned nylon cord. Then he stuffed a hand towel in her mouth, and as the young girl pleaded, wound masking tape over the towel.

She struggled helplessly as Saoud sliced open the halter top to expose her back, and ripped off her shorts and panties. For a moment, he rubbed his free hand over her naked back and derriere. He traced her tan lines with his fingertips, alternately probing her anus, her vagina, and then up under her stomach towards her breasts. He squeezed the student's nipples, causing her to wince. Saoud ignored her muffled pleading, and she began to cry.

The Palestinian stood and took off his pants, exposing a bulging erection. Then he walked over to the sidetable and drained his whiskey in one long swallow. Finally, after turning up the volume on the television, he took a long, thick leather belt from his garment bag in the closet. Saoud made a point to position himself where the young girl could see him. Then he lashed the leather belt against the side table several times. The crack of the strap terrified the call girl. Tears poured from her eyes as she lost control. Saoud bent over and whispered in her ear. "You are a Yankee whore." He touched the back of her derriere with his free hand and felt her muscles tense. Her body trembled in anticipation. Then with a huge swing, Saoud brought the leather strap down on her naked buttocks with a resounding snap. Her body seemed to jolt from the bed as a huge red welt appeared across her exposed flesh.

Again and again Saoud struck the call girl, bringing the leather belt down on her helpless body, each time repeating aloud the phrase "Allah Akbah."

XV

KATERINA WALKED DOWN Georgiou Theotoki Avenue doing errands. She stopped first at the Post Office, next the bank, and finally over at the Town Hall. Barely nine in the morning, it was already warm in Kerkyra, and the streets were packed with tourists at the height of the season. Walking through the Hora, or central shopping district, Katerina entered an elegant boutique.

"Kalimerá Philippe."

Surprised, the shopkeeper motioned his sales clerk towards an Italian couple, and nodded to his left.

"Kalimerá Katerina, ti Kánete?"

He led her to the far corner of his shop, pausing to touch an expensive hand embroidered rug from Arahova.

"I am well," she nodded, treating the merchant to her dazzling smile. "Theodori has been gone three weeks now, his business treats him well, né?"

"Málista," nodded Katerina, handing the boutique owner a thick, sealed manila envelope. She continued in a soft voice. "Please see that this is processed today Philippe, it is very important."

"En táxi," nodded the merchant, quickly palming the envelope and dropping it below countertop level, "I shall."

"Evharistó," she touched the back of his hand and turned.

On the street, Katerina was unaware of the tourist who stood window shopping one storefront away. As she turned right on the sidewalk, the man looked across the street and nodded—almost imperceptibly—to a second tourist. The team turned and started down the street following Katerina.

"AL WHO?"

Detective Sergeant Dan McBride of Miami Metro-Dade Police Department looked up from his notes and shifted the toothpick between his teeth.

"Allah Akbah," he repeated to his partner, Slim Moody.

"Don't know the name," shrugged the tall, black detective as he stretched his long legs and placed a well-polished shoe atop the metal desk. "Did you run a rap sheet?"

"I don't think it's a name," added McBride. "I think it's a language."

"Well it ain't Spanish," laughed Moody.

"No," agreed McBride, "sounds like Arabic,"

"Arabic?!" Moody rolled a quarter between his fingers and sat forward. "Danny boy, I hate to tell you, but you've been living and working in *Miami* the last twenty years."

"Seventeen, Slim."

McBride motioned his partner closer. "Listen to this." He switched on a small pocket tape recorder. For the next three minutes they sat in silence, absorbing the distraught, halting testimony of the college prostitute. She was clearly a very scared, confused young woman. As she relived the ordeal, the victim kept repeating the strange phrase that Saoud had chanted as he whipped her unmercifully. Finally, the interview ended and McBride turned off the tape recorder.

"Allah Akbah," mumbled Moody as he deftly rolled the coin. "I guess Arabic's as good a guess as any . . . tell me about it."

McBride leaned back in his chair. "The John arranges for a hooker through an escort service specializing in 'coeds.' Truth be told, the kid really was a college student; a Sophomore at U of M, majoring in Fashion Design."

"A little side action helps pay the bills," acknowledged Moody, "it's been a trend of late. When I was in school, I waited on tables."

McBride nodded, "It's tough to feel sorry for her Slim, until you see her. I've known my share of shit, but this John beat the piss out of her. She's no angel, but this . . . I mean he fucking flogged her Slim. Like a piece of meat."

Moody rewound the tape and replayed it. They listened intently as the hooker retold her story in a shaky voice.

"Ok," said the black detective finally, "continue."

"When he's done," starts McBride again, pulling the frayed wooden toothpick from his teeth, "he pumps her up the butt and blows his load. The girl must have passed out, because she doesn't remember the rape." McBride pauses for a moment looking at his partner. "Is it a rape if she's a pro and is there to turn a trick?"

Moody frowned, considering the question. "Debatable. Clearly you've got Aggravated Assault with a Dangerous Weapon, maybe Conspiracy with Intent. Was she into S&M?"

"No. She even recited her menu. No S&M, no three ways . . . like I said, a college student—honor roll."

"She's a hooker Dan, keep your perspective. If she wasn't tricking, this wouldn't have happened."

"I know, I know . . ." McBride waived off his partner and leaned back sipping at a styrofoam cup of cold coffee.

". . . we've got anal penetration, semen specimens, blood type matching the victim, and a couple of partial thumb and palm prints. The victim was in deep shock when the housekeeping staff found her bound spread-eagle on the bed. The Doc said a couple of more lashes, and it would have been the Homicide boys working the case instead of us . . . how do you figure the phrase: Allah Akbah? Some kind of religious thing?"

Moody shrugged, twirling his quarter. "Beats me Danny. Who knows anymore. The world is full of fruitcakes. You got any leads on the perp?"

"I dumped our stuff into the NCIC network. I'm waiting to see what the Feds come up with. He 'beat feet' in the middle of the night. We've got a pretty good description, and the girl thinks she could pick him out of a lineup . . . one interesting thing, he made a phone call to the four-oh-seven area code. We're running the number."

"Oh," Moody looked up, "sloppy perp?"

McBride put down his styrofoam cup. "I think I'll go over to the hospital, see how she's doing."

Moody stretched his long legs. "I hear that twang in your old heart Dan."

McBride frowned.

"She's a kid Slim . . . maybe it's because I look at her and figure that could be Sara in a couple of years."

McBride's reference to his teenage daughter caught his partner's attention.

"What the fuck," shrugged Moody, "I'll take a ride. It beats paperwork."

The two Miami Metro-Dade detectives stood and exited the squad room.

ANNA LYALIN ENTERED Paul Hersch's home feeling tired, but satisfied. It had been a week since she had moved in with the accountant, and now that her base of operations was secure, the Spetsnaz officer began the next phase of her mission. For the past four days, Anna undertook a hard reconnaissance of the target site. It was important to analyze every aspect of her assignment.

She began by collecting maps; painting a mental picture, committing reference points to memory. Next came hours of driving the perimeter; every highway, every exit ramp, every mile marker. She parked on the side of the road for long periods, sitting and studying traffic flows, clocking regular police movements. Finally Anna walked; inside, outside, back and forth; snapping photographs, drawing strip maps, listening, watching, smelling, touching; constantly monitoring every aspect of the target site the way they had trained her in the GRU.

"Britt?"

Anna Lyalin looked up to see Paul Hersch enter from the kitchen. She forced a smile. The role playing was getting harder by the day, but the end was nearing. "Paul . . ."

"I thought I heard you come in."

She moved towards Hersch and kissed him passionately on the lips.

"How was your day?"

"Very good," blurted the accountant. "I picked up a big referral today from one of my bank contacts." He hugged her warmly. "I swear, ever since I met you, things have been going great." He nibbled on her ear.

"I'm glad," whispered Anna, wincing a bit.

Hersch held the swimming coach at arms length. "Is everything okay?"

"Yes, yes my love, I've just had a long day." She forced another smile. "Scouting locations for our cosmetics stores is tiring work." She kicked off her shoes.

"Well why don't you take a nice relaxing bath. I've got dinner half done. After, I'll give you a massage and . . ."

Paul raised and lowered his eyebrows suggestively. Anna looked up at the accountant longingly, then reached down and groped at Paul's crotch through his trousers."

"You are so good to me." She gave him a quick kiss. "That sounds wonderful."

As Anna pranced off towards the bedroom, Paul gave her an affectionate pat on the buttocks and marveled at his good fortune.

THEY SAT IN a hotel room, perched over a round table, the civil engineer from New Jersey calmly explaining the explosive packages to Saoud Issan.

"There are two charges. Each charge is identical in size, shape, destructive capability and camouflage. The base is fifteen blocks of one and a quarter pound C-4 plastic explosive laid flush on a piece of stiff cardboard. There is block to block contact; three high, five deep—all taped securely under an electronic circuit board. Each charge has a dual detonating system; two electric blasting caps crimped to equal lengths of detonating cord, primed at the center rear of the charge. You'll join the two free ends together at a point fifteen centimeters from the end—here . . ." the GRU officer pointed to a specific spot on his explosive ". . . and tightly tape the blasting cap of the firing system to these parallel pieces of detonating cord."

The engineer looked up to see if Saoud was absorbing the explanation. He scratched his balding head, noting his wife fidgeting uncomfortably in the background.

"Do not, repeat, do *not* attach the electric blasting cap to the detonating cord until just before zero hour. You must be *on site*, and as close to zero hour as possible. Understand?"

"Yes, yes," nodded the Palestinian egotistically at the engineer, "I have done these things before."

The engineer's wife caught her husband's eye and stifled a comment. She was clearly becoming agitated with Issan's posturing of expertise. The GRU officer sighed and patiently pulled out two small hand-held radio transmitters.

"These are remote control firing devices, capable of emanating an electric current of significant power through multiple obstructions up to a distance of two hundred feet."

The GRU officer placed the remote control firing devices into one small leather pouch, the electric blasting caps into a second, and the detonating cord into a third.

"These electronic circuit boards flushed to the blocks of C-4 act as both a beacon and an amplifier to the electric current once the remote control device is activated."

He slid, the two oblong shaped explosives—each the size of a very large gift box—into a blue nylon shoulder bag.

"You see," demonstrated the engineer proudly, "a simple, travel bag that a tourist would carry on a sight-seeing excursion. Small enough to place *under* a chair, or on a table in a crowded room; light weight enough for one man to carry and transport; casual enough so as to not attract attention."

"And deadly enough?" interjected Saoud in a challenging tone.

The GRU officer paused, mentally calculating the kill zone. "It's almost nineteen pounds of plastic per charge . . .

depending on the density of the furniture, each of the two charges should cut a radius of about thirty feet—with collateral damage stretching twice that distance. They'll never know what hit them."

The Palestinian smiled as he fingered the gold medallion that dangled from his neck.

"Are there any questions?" asked the engineer.

"No," answered Saoud. He carefully packed the two nylon shoulder bags into an empty suitcase, and secured the explosive charges with safety straps. Then he snapped the suitcase shut. Next he placed each of the three small leather pouches that separated the remote control firing devices, the electric blasting caps, and the detonating cord into a square briefcase. Finally, Saoud straightened and eyed the engineer.

"You won't see us again," admitted the GRU officer extending a hand, "Good Luck."

Saoud sneered. "Luck is for infidels; I trust in Allah."

The engineer's wife opened the door and checked the hallway. She nodded, and the Palestinian picked up both the suitcase and briefcase in separate hands, and walked from the room.

As the greying wife closed the door she looked long and hard at her husband. "Gennadi . . ."

"It will be alright. We do our job—nothing more. Please pack our bags. We leave for home tonight."

"The Rodina?!" blurted the wife surprised.

"No," the engineer sighed "New Jersey."

XVI

". . . SO THAT WHEN we make the approach, he'll have a point of reference."

"Exactly," nodded Jaycott, leaning back in his chair. They spoke in solemn tones, not quite a whisper, but hushed enough so that their voices would not carry beyond the spill of the table. The coffee shop was bustling with both locals and tourists alike, and amidst the din of the crowd, they were as innocuous as any two Europeans chatting up a business deal.

Theodori finished his cup of sweet green tea in one swallow and frowned. He studied his friend for a long moment. Jay returned the husky Greek's gaze before finally speaking. "Well?"

"I was just wondering Ishmael, if this all goes bad and we have to hit the loop again, will your *friend* Fairchild be there to pick up the pieces?"

Jay smirked.

"Are you suggesting Theo, that he's not to be trusted?"

Theodori nodded.

"And since we're on the subject, I don't like him either."

"I know, but you've never liked any of them."

"I like *you*," protested Theo defensively.

"But I'm not one of them."

"Precisely. They're parasites, paying others to do their dirty work."

"So what does that make us?"

"Whores—at least I am. I've always accepted the realities because it paid well. You, unfortunately, have always been burdened by other motivations."

"Such as?"

"Principles Ishmael. You always need to believe you are making a positive contribution. You want to think that whatever we do is ultimately for a greater good."

"But isn't it?"

"No, my friend," said Theo, "it isn't. We do dangerous things for big money because we have the ability—nothing more."

"You're such a cynic."

"I'm a realist . . . who does the hard thing?"

Jaycott shrugged, reciting the obvious answer. "He who can."

"Evharistó," nodded the Greek. He waved his hand to the waiter, indicating the desire for a bill.

"But now we are involved emotionally, which is bad. We are in this for personal reasons, because they have promised you information about the death of Ellie."

Jaycott bristled, a hard look shadowing his face. "Yes Theo, this is personal, and I make no apologies for that. If you want out, just . . ."

Theodori waved his hand melodramatically. "I don't *need* the money, so I'm obviously here for the same reasons you are . . . and furthermore, I understand. I now know the depth of your passion."

The burly Greek leaned back, pleased with himself. This was obviously new ground for Theo.

Jay's expression turned muddled. "What are you saying?"

"That I realize now my friend, how much I love Katerina."

Theo laughed, more to himself than to Jay, before continuing. "Who would have thought, after all these years, that an old war horse like me would turn soft—but it's true— I miss her."

"Then consider yourself lucky," smiled Jaycott standing. He dropped a few Tunisian Dinar on the table. "You have someone to go back to."

Theo grabbed at Jay's forearm, surprising the American with the intensity of his grip. "Promise me Ishmael, that if anything happens to me, you will take care of my affairs."

Jaycott was momentarily stunned by the emotion in Theodori's voice. It was out of character, unlike the Greek to act melancholy. He patted Theo's hand. "Don't worry, you'll outlive us all."

"Promise," repeated Theo in a serious whisper. His eyes searched Jaycott's.

"I promise," nodded Jay.

"And Katerina . . ."

The mention of Theodori's woman in this context made Jay pause.

"Promise you will see to her safety Ishmael. I have made provisions for her."

They studied each other in silence. The unspoken words passing between them.

"Yes," nodded Jay finally, "and Katerina."

This reassurance seemed to settle Theodori. He stood, his barrel chest jutting forward, a new look of serenity crossing his face. "Kalá, my friend, now let's go pick a fight."

". . . LETHAL TERRORIST ACTIONS against Americans in the years nineteen seventy-three through nineteen eighty-eight." Bob Perkins of the State Department reached forward and lay a copy of the thick study on the conference table. The other members of the Forty Committee looked at the Threat Analysis Division's report. "We define lethal as deadly or potentially deadly. There were one hundred eighty-four attacks, resulting in five hundred and seven Americans killed during that period. All of these are broken into six separate regions of the world: Europe, Latin America, near East Asia, the Aegean, Asia Oceania, and Africa. None of them occurred in the continental United States."

Perkins sat, as the Admiral from the Pentagon stood and held up a thick white and blue manual. "This is Training Circular nineteen dash sixteen, updated through April nineteen eighty-eight. It is titled 'Countering Terrorism on U.S. Military Installations,' and we have assured that the Commander of every installation in the Southeast corridor has received an updated copy. We have also required that every military base, fort, and port worldwide has a current plan and testing procedure in place. As you know, these threats have gone through varying cycles, and we don't want our folks to get rusty or complacent."

The Admiral placed the TC on the conference table and took his seat. Russell Porter of the FBI stood and held up a blue Department of Justice report. "'FBI Analysis of Terrorist Incidents in the United States, nineteen eighty-eight.' This report was prepared by our Terrorist Research and Analytical Center, Terrorist Section, Criminal Investigative Division. It tracks all terrorist incidents from nineteen eighty through last year. The groups primarily responsible are the Puerto Rican OVRP, FARP, the EPB-Macheteros, the Jewish Defense League of Rabbi Meir Kahane, and various white supremacy groups such as the Aryan Nation. We have never had an attributable Islamist terrorist incident in the continental U.S."

The Deputy Director placed the blue FBI report in the center of the conference table beside the other two manuals. Tom Laughlin turned to his left and addressed the Senior Analyst from the Defense Intelligence Agency.

"Rudy?"

The analyst stood.

"To know the enemy's mind, is to know the enemy. To know the enemy and his motivations is to predict his movements. To predict his movements is to prevent their occurrence . . ." Rudy took a deep breath before continuing. ". . . our folks from the Middle East Desk sat down with members of the Rand Corporation and wrote a treatise titled: 'Why Muslim Radicals Hate American Society' . . ." The analyst pulled a thick report from his briefcase and opened it to the first page with a dog-eared corner. ". . . most of the world's one billion Muslims subscribe to the fundamental belief that the teachings of the Prophet Mohammed are the literal truth and only path to God. A small radical faction advocates the use of terrorism as a means of asserting Islam's rightful influence on what they view as a decadent society. Much of this assertive surge—compliments of the Ayatollah Khomeini—is clearly violent and bloody . . ." He flipped to a second page with a dog-eared corner, taking a moment to locate the important paragraph. ". . . what we call freedom, they call licentiousness. It is their different view of freedom that stokes their hate. They hate our alcohol consumption, our loose sexual relations, our foreign policy supporting Israel and moderate Arabic governments. They don't like us culturally, religiously, or politically . . . and the radical is willing to suspend mainstream teachings of Islam, to take violent measures against those people and places where Islam can have an effect both on private behavior *and* public life . . ."

Rudy took a moment to flip to a third page with the corner folded down.

". . . of the many power blocks in the Islamic world currently competing for influence—Sunnis versus Shiites, Iran versus Saudi Arabia, religionists versus secularists—the one constant is hatred of the West; and the United States is the standard for the West. Thus, Americans are the quintessential target for any terrorist strike. To kill Americans in their home, within the sovereign borders of the United States, would prove the ultimate statement."

The DIA analyst placed the treatise on the conference table and took his seat.

Tom Laughlin looked across the room at Jack Belmont of the Department of Transportation and nodded. Belmont stood, moving towards the large wall map of the United States where he had begun a matrix.

"We may have another lead . . . we owe this one to a couple of metro detectives . . . three days ago, a woman was discovered bound to a bed and near death in a Miami hotel room. She was discovered by the housekeeping staff in deep shock. The perpetrator had checked out. The locals confirm that she was a prostitute and the perpetrator was her client. However, the victim states that A—the beating was beyond the scope of her contracted services, and B—it was ritualistic."

"Ritualistic?!" interrupted Paul of Customs.

"Yes," confirmed Belmont. "Evidently the man flogged her with a leather belt while chanting the phrase: Allah Ahkbah."

"God is great," confirmed John Mullins of the CIA, speaking for the first time. "It's Arabic."

A silence fell over the members of the Forty
Committee as the significance of the information sunk in.

"And the day before the incident, the perpetrator
made a phone call to another hotel room. The two metro
detectives fed the info into the NCIC data bank and traced the
call," Belmont stuck a pin in the wallmap, "to here . . . a hotel
room outside of Daytona, just south of the intersection of
Interstate Route number four and Interstate ninety-five."

Two members stood and walked to the wallmap. The
Deputy Director of the Secret Service traced the I-95
highway south from Georgia along the coast into northern
Florida until it intersected with I-4 just west of Daytona
Beach. Then he continued to trace his index finger several
more inches down the map along I-95.

"Oh my God, Canaveral."

"Canaveral?" blurted Rudy of the DIA.

"Cape Canaveral," clarified Belmont. "The Kennedy
Space Center Complex."

There was a disturbing quiet that enveloped the room.

"The hotel room in Miami was registered to a Raul
Fazio. A Spanish name, but he is described as swarthy and
Mediterranean in appearance. He could be Spanish—or easily
be Arabic. The hotel room outside of Daytona that received
the call was registered to a Mr. and Mrs. Ronald Hoch of
Hackensack, New Jersey. They have since checked out. We
have an All-Points-Bulletin placed throughout Florida and
along I-95 north to New Jersey."

"Basic police work now," confirmed Tom Laughlin.
He nodded towards the members representing the FBI,
Bureau of Alcohol, Tobacco & Firearms, and Customs.

"We've got what looks like another viable lead . . . let's run it down. We're adjourned."

MIKHAIL GORBACHEV SAT on the patio of his dacha in Usova, a little village west of Moscow, and sipped vodka. Unlike many Russians, the Soviet President was quite temperate in his drinking habits. But this afternoon he permitted himself a short spirit out of civility. Mikhail was having a rare weekend lunch with his Prime Minister, Nikolai Ryzhkov.

The conversation had turned chilly, and although Ryzhkov had originally been handpicked for his position by the Soviet President, of late, he found himself more at odds with his mentor, than in agreement.

The great success of the March elections had begun to unravel. The coal miners' strike, economic despair, the empty promises of *perestroika*—all had contributed to a shift in Gorbachev's power base, and nipping at his heels were the *nomenklatura*; the self-serving, self-perpetuating hierarchy of the Communist party who made up the Politburo and Central Committee. These were the ultra right-wing bureaucrats of the Soviet Union, who essentially ruled everything, and thus had the most to lose by Gorbachev's drive to tear down and rebuild the Soviet System. They were the most powerful members of the ministries, the Provincial leadership, the Press, the military, and the KGB. And he was attacking them.

"Mikhail, when I was Chief of Uralmash, building heavy machines in Sverdlovsk, we had a saying: 'Don't arrange jobs purely on the basis of efficiency, you must balance efficiency and social security'."

Gorbachev stared at his Prime Minister with a penetrating gaze. His eyes were two black shimmering coals that locked onto Ryzhkov with the power of a laser; never blinking, never shifting; a magnetic energy that looked through the Prime Minister rather than at him.

"Nikolai," said Gorbachev in a very measured tone, the voice deep in his chest emanating upward from his round, fleshy face, "they are dead souls. I will dispense of them as I did Solovyov in Leningrad. Perestroika will *not* be rolled back."

"But Mikhail, we need to find new approaches, new methods to govern the triangle of power, and . . ."

There was an uncomfortable pause by the Prime Minister as he withered under Gorbachev's gaze.

"And?" prodded the Soviet President.

". . . and there is trouble afoot. You read the *Moscow News* article. There is talk of *Vzglyad* doing a piece on television, as well as *Ogonek* and *Moskovskaya Pravda*—it is all around us Mikhail."

Ryzhkov drained his glass of vodka and sat forward, challenging his mentor. "There is talk of a coup."

"You forget your place, Nikolai, you have thrown your hat in with Chebrikov and you waive the KGB ghost before me."

"Nyet, Mikhail Sergeyevich," protested Ryzhkov. "It is the Red Army that bears watching. Who speaks for Yazov?"

The Prime Minister's reference to Dmitri Yazov, the Defense Minister, caused Gorbachev's features to relax. The Soviet President's strength was never grand strategies; quite the contrary, Mikhail Gorbachev's skills lay in footwork. He was quick witted, instinctive, charismatic—a born improviser that could insightfully size up a changing tide of sentiment and react long before his political rivals saw the picture. There had never really been a clear vision by which Gorbachev initiated the painful process of *perestroika*. His strategy had been to point the bow into the wind and sail; changing course by tacking whenever conditions dictated. Like a surfer, he rode the waves, never quite sure when to time the break, always leery of an undertow. He smiled, displaying those 'teeth of steel'.

"Fear not Comrade Ryzhkov, the Defense Minister only *thinks* he controls the Red Army. Knowledge is power . . . and *who* has the knowledge?"

Ryzhkov's facial expression changed. Gorbachev leaned forward and spoke in a harsh whisper, as a teacher would scold a pupil. "Too much attention is on your friends at the KGB. They are easy targets, hated by the masses, thugs in cheap suits . . . but everyone loves a patriot, a soldier, a protector of the Rodina. *Who* Nikolai, amongst the Red Army has the knowledge?"

Like the glow from a fluorescent lamp, the Prime Minister's face illuminated. "The GRU?!"

The Soviet President leaned back without answering and finished the one drink he permitted himself. "Raisa will be here soon." He stood. "Enjoy your ride back to Moscow."

The Prime Minister also stood, his mind racing, his dismissal obvious. "Da Comrade President, Dos veedanya."

"Dos veedanya Comrade Ryzhkov . . . and Nikolai . . ." Gorbachev turned and raised his index finger for emphasis. ". . . you would do well to approach certain alliances with caution. It was I who chose you to be Prime Minister. Ve pon yalee?"

Ryzhkov nodded and watched the Soviet President walk out into the garden.

THEY CAME AT the dead hours of the night, when people reach their deepest sleep and hence, most unsuspecting state. There were four of them, and they moved as professionals; quickly, quietly, and with a purpose.

The first man crouched on the side of Theodori's home, half hidden by the shrubbery. He was dressed in black, a penlight clenched between his teeth, a screw driver and wire cutters in either hand. Carefully, he traced the main battery powered circuit to the primary relay and snipped the wire. Nothing happened. He smiled, and quickly cut two more wires—one blue, and one white. Then he spoke into the tiny voice activated microphone at his throat, "Da, Pashlee."

Two other men, dressed in similar black attire, quickly appeared from the shadows and mounted the steps to the front door. Each wore a pair of Nova General Purpose night vision goggles. One man carried a huge sledge hammer, the other a silenced P-6 automatic pistol. As soon as the alarm specialist joined them on the front porch, the man with the sledge hammer swung the tool in a wide arc, and landed the thick metal head squarely below the doorknob. With a crash, the heavy oak door swung inward, and the three men charged into Theodori's foyer.

At precisely the same time as the sledge hammer struck, the fourth man sitting in a darkened van a block away, turned the ignition key and without the assistance of headlights started creeping the vehicle forward along Mistropolitou Athanassiou.

The first two men were halfway up the staircase when the alarm specialist turned and positioned himself at the far end of the foyer, just inside the long Persian carpeted hallway that led to the downstairs guest quarters. Producing his own P-6 silenced pistol, he backed against the wall and waited.

At the top of the stairs, the two men turned right, never running, but moving very quickly with the confidence that the night vision goggles permitted. They started towards the Master Wing.

Cristos, the local handyman that moved into Theodori's home to provide a male presence for Katerina and Lenoris during periods of Theo's absence, stumbled half asleep down the first floor hallway. He was groggy, still obviously tired when turning the corner into the main foyer. The alarm specialist raised his P-6 and squeezed the trigger three times. The nine millimeter bullets pierced the handyman's forehead, and he stumbled backwards into a curio before collapsing sideways onto the floor.

Upstairs, ten feet down the Master Wing, Lenoris opened a bedroom door to see the first black clad man rush

by carrying his sledge hammer. He ignored her, and before
Theo's old house servant could scream, the second man
raised his silenced automatic and fired. The P-6 coughed
three times, catching Lenoris' center mass in the chest,
knocking her backwards into the wall. Without breaking
stride he joined his partner.

The first man raised the sledge hammer just as the
Master Bedroom door swung inward. Katerina's look of utter
surprise quickly turned to fear; but before she could move
they reacted. The man with the P-6 rushed forward, clamping
a firm hand over Katerina's mouth as the other man dropped
his sledge hammer and pinned both of Katerina's arms to her
sides. They half carried, half dragged Theo's woman
backwards to her bed, using their superior size and body
weight to control her movements. She struggled, twisting
wildly, kicking at the two men, and the motion caused her
negligee to tear. Immediately, the second man seized the
opportunity to grab both legs. He quickly wound duct tape
around Katerina's ankles. Then, repeating the process, he
wound duct tape around her knees. Katerina continued to
struggle, her senses now fully awake, but the two men were
well-rehearsed in their movements.

They twisted Katerina on her side, pinning her wrists
to either hip, and wrapped the duct tape several times around
her waist and elbows. Then they placed a small hood over
Katerina's head, twisting the cowl sideways until her nose
found the air holes, and pulled a chord to tighten the hood at
her neckline.

In one smooth motion, they yanked her up and threw
Katerina over the shoulder of the first man—the larger of the

two. His partner now took the lead, retrieved the sledge hammer, and pistol at the ready, started from Katerina's bedroom.

Down the hall into the second floor foyer, they passed the antique furniture, onto the staircase. The second intruder hefted Katerina effortlessly. He steadied her torso with one gloved hand, while using the other as a guide, sliding it sideways down the banister as they descended the stairs. At the bottom of the staircase, they were joined by the alarm specialist who had secured the first floor foyer. A nod between the three men, and in single file they passed out the door, along the porch to the front walk.

The van glided to the curb and the rear double doors swung open just as the alarm specialist—the last man— tugged Theodori's broken oak door shut behind him. Katerina's torso was placed in the middle of the empty van floor. They covered her, head to foot, with heavy blankets. Then the two men leaped into the back of the van beside her and pulled the double doors closed from inside. The alarm specialist jumped into the passenger seat next to the driver and nodded.

"Gdye lodka?"

"Bleezka. Apasna?"

"Nyet, Pashlee."

The driver grunted and put the van in gear, pulling from the curbside.

The entire operation took four minutes, twenty-three seconds.

XVII

TOM FAIRCHILD SAT on the broken steps under the
Column of Foca looking up at the Rostrums in the Roman
Forum. The Case Officer was tired. It had been constant
motion since the beginning of the assignment, and the
perpetual jet lag was taking its toll. He pulled out a crumpled
pack of cigarettes and rummaged around absent mindedly
until he located a filtered smoke. With a sigh, Fairchild struck
a match and lighted the cigarette, inhaling deeply. Several
minutes passed before he heard the tapping of a cane along
the ancient cobblestones of the Via Sacra.

"Shalom Thomas," nodded Moshi, the diminutive
Mossad officer. From a distance, three Israeli security men
arranged themselves in a loose triangle around the senior
man. Moshi withdrew a handkerchief from his suitcoat
pocket and nonchalantly dusted the crumbling step next to
Fairchild before sitting.

"Getting a little finicky aren't we?"

"More out of reverence to the historic setting, than out
of concern for my clothes," nodded the Israeli.

"I sense a history lesson coming."

"Ah no, Thomas," smiled the Mossad officer, "I chose the spot for security reasons—look at us, two foreigners, quite alone yet in the center of the civilized world circa one hundred B.C."

"I don't imagine it has anything to do with the fact that it's God-awful hot, the middle of August, and all sensible Italians are taking a nap."

"That too," nodded Moshi, a mischievous twinkle in his eye. "But just in case, I brought along my friends."

"I noticed," shrugged Fairchild exhaling on his cigarette. He glanced around at the three bodyguards. "You Katsas must be very important people Moshi, they protect you like gold."

"They insist, I think Tel Aviv wants us to feel special . . . but maybe they're just afraid we'll defect." The Israeli permitted himself a quiet chuckle. "So tell me, when did you start smoking again?"

"Recently," nodded the American, "your message sounded important."

"It is . . . did you know that when Sulla issued his proscriptions, he hung the heads of his victims right here on the Rostrum for everyone to see?"

Fairchild looked up at the decaying stone platform from which Roman orators would speak to the crowds.

"That shows a certain sense of style."

"Yes," laughed the Israeli, "I suppose it does . . . what do you think Sulla was really saying?"

Fairchild sucked on his cigarette. It was never the direct route with the Israeli. There was always a conundrum. "I don't know. I suppose he was sending a message to his enemies."

"Yes, I agree . . . and the message?"

The American exhaled a long stream of smoke. He field-stripped the cigarette, and rolled the filtered tip into a ball. "He was saying: 'don't fuck with me'."

Moshi laughed again.

"Yes, my interpretation exactly; which brings us to your problem . . ."

Fairchild rolled his wrist several times, motioning the Israeli to continue.

". . . if my sources are correct, you not only hired the American Jaycott to act as a Probe, you also hired the Greek to act as his Second."

Fairchild remained silent.

"I thought Theodori had retired," continued the Israeli undaunted.

"I wouldn't know," lied Fairchild.

"Of course you wouldn't," nodded Moshi amused, "but he was very good. We've used him several times ourselves . . . anyway," Moshi continued quickly, sensing Fairchild's growing impatience, "it seems that the Greek had a live-in girlfriend. Quite a beautiful woman I am told. When word went through the community that your two Contracts were involved in the Cairo incident, someone decided to make a statement."

"A warning, like Sulla?"

"Possibly, or maybe they had another purpose."

"Such as?"

"Well since there's no way to get to Jaycott, they went after his partner."

Fairchild feigned his most inquisitive expression. "And?"

"The woman was snatched two days ago."

The American signed deeply. "Any leads?"

"None yet, but it was a very smooth operation, very profession. A *Kidon* style team." The Israeli used the Hebrew term for bayonet, but it referred to a special type of combatants who performed executions and kidnappings.

"Is she alive?"

"Yes, but they eliminated Theodori's housekeeper and a carpenter in the process."

"Is she being dangled as bait?"

"It seems that way. My guess is that your two bloodhounds were having some success, and they decided to slow their progress."

"Where is she now?"

"Algiers."

Fairchild exhaled, his frustration evident—although in reality, this was the break they needed, and had—in fact—set in motion. "Algiers . . ."

"The Casbah to be exact." Moshi handed the American a sealed manila envelope. "They're *not* making it difficult Thomas; a little too obvious in their desire to bring your team out in the open."

"Zero hour must be close."

"My thoughts exactly."

Fairchild mused in silence for a moment. He looked over at the older Israeli. "How do you read this Moshi?"

The Mossad officer bit his lip before answering. "Moscow sponsored, I should think. It shows all the patterns; deliberate, heavy-handed, obvious disinformation . . . but there's a twist—something not quite right . . ."

The Israeli just shook his head, a genuine look of puzzlement crossed his face.

"I'd like to give it some thought."

Moshi stood, and motioned towards the Rostrum. "To Sulla." Cane in hand, he started back up the Via Sacra.

SAOUD ISSAN STOOD looking at the three Palestinians seated around the table in his hotel suite. Spread out in front of them, were the two blue nylon shoulder bags, the two oblong-shaped explosive charges, and the three leather pouches—each separately containing electric blasting caps, detonating cord, and the remote control firing devices.

As the control agent for the operation, Saoud's job was to prepare the four Palestinians that had left Algiers three weeks earlier for the actual mission. They were the "go" team, the mules, the agents that would assume the physical risk of transporting, placing, and initiating the explosive charges at the target site. Saoud on the other hand was the control agent, the cutout, who would pass the necessary equipment from the GRU illegals to the mules. He would give these men their final briefing and adjust for any unforeseen obstacles. Everything was proceeding on schedule except for one minor problem. Instead of four mules, there were now only three.

Saoud grimaced impatiently. Each of the Palestinians had departed Algiers within days of each other, using different routes, different identities, and different points of entry into the United States. The necessity of such a security measure also caused a lapse in contact; and now, as Issan passed important last minute information on to his team— only days before the strike—he was one man short. And to make matters worse, the status of that man—Abd-al Rahman—was unknown.

Saoud had no way of determining the fate of Rahman. For security reasons, he did not even know any of their false identities. He did recognize, however, that the absence of Abd-al Rahman from this meeting constituted a breach of security, and as such, the possibility existed that their mission was compromised. Nonetheless, Issan's instructions were quite specific: If the necessary explosives were obtained from the GRU illegals, then the mission would continue at *any* cost. And since Saoud himself would not even be in the country, much less on the target site, his personal risk was minimal. These young men were prepared to die for Allah.

"You will act alone, without assistance," nodded Issan to the man seated on the right. "Are you capable of completing your mission?"

"Aiwa," nodded the mule confidently.

"Are there any questions regarding the arming of the explosive charge?"

The young Palestinian, filled with the bravado and bluster of youth, answered in a cocky manner.

"No. It is like our training school. The assembly is simple, and I will personally place and activate the explosive precisely on schedule—using this . . ."

He touched the small remote control firing device on the table. Satisfied, Saoud turned towards the two Palestinians on the left and leaned over the table.

"Have you any questions?"

Both men shook their heads speaking in unison. "La."

He handed each of them a small colored map. "You must study your objectives, walk the grounds, know the target. Several days of reconnaissance are essential. You must use your time wisely between now and zero hour."

All three men nodded as Saoud absentmindedly stroked his gold necklace. He looked at his watch, a gold Rolex. "I show precisely four twenty-six in the afternoon. Today is August 20th."

Each of the mules adjusted their watches accordingly.

"There will be no further contact between any of us. Stay on schedule. Barak Allah fik."

Saoud bowed his head reverently with the last phrase.

"Allah Akbah," nodded the three Palestinians in unison.

The two mules on the left packed one explosive charge and their assorted equipment into a nylon shoulder bag and the leather pouches. The man on the right repeated the actions for the other explosive charge and his equipment. Issan went to the door of his hotel room, glanced quickly through the peep hole and then motioned to the first two men.

They stood and crossed the room. Saoud hugged each man, kissing them alternately in a platonic way on both cheeks. They nodded.

"Fi Aman illah."

"Ma'a as-salama."

Quickly they passed through the doorway into the corridor and were gone.

Issan looked back at the lone Palestinian. "We know not what has become of Abd-al Rahman. But from this point forward, Allah has chosen you to continue the Jihad as a team of one. Are you committed?"

"Aiwa, I shall not fail the Jihad. In-shall Ah." He touched his chest with an open hand.

Saoud grunted and summoned the mule forward. "Barak Allah fik." He hugged the Palestinian and then kissed him ritualistically on each cheek.

"Shukran, Saoud Issan. Fi Aman illah."

"Ma'a as-salama."

A last glance through the peephole to check the corridor and Saoud opened the door. Quickly, the young mule exited the hotel room.

THE ROOM WAS stuffy and hot, and the cracked stone walls smelled with the mustiness of age. One naked light bulb hung from the ceiling, illuminating what was otherwise a dark and sparsely furnished chamber.

Katerina drowsed between fits of sleep and moments of heightened sensation. There had been no contact since her

kidnappers had first dropped her—bound and blindfolded—
on what felt like a mattress; although her cursory movements
determined that it was on the floor rather than a bed frame.
She had recovered from the shock of that initial
confrontation, and with the disorientation that followed,
Katerina now tried to piece together the circumstances
surrounding her situation. Her throat was parched and her lips
dry, but she was hungry, and in a reflective moment Kat
reasoned there was value in this admission.

Katerina heard the sliding of a lock and the heavy oak
door swung inward. Several people seemed to enter the room,
and then a hand reached down and roughly tugged away the
blindfold. Standing over her, his expression blank, was a flat-
faced man in a business suit. Katerina looked up at the Soviet
Rezidentura. She found his choice of attire odd, considering
the heat, but found his European features more curious when
compared to the two Arabic looking men that stood behind
him.

The GRU officer studied Katerina contemplatively, as
if he was evaluating her, and the deference that the two Arabs
showed him made it clear that he was in charge.

"Neró," she said quietly in Greek, summoning all of
her courage.

He didn't respond; rather the flat-faced man cocked
his head slightly to one side and continued gazing, as if he
was studying a specimen in a laboratory. Without a word, the
Rezidentura reached forward and held the back of his fingers
against Katerina's cheek. Then he repeated the movement at
her forehead and the nape of her neck.

Turning slightly, the Soviet mumbled something undiscernible to the man over his right shoulder. There was a nod. The Rezidentura bent over and examined the rope that secured her ankles, assessing the pallor of Katerina's skin along the top of her naked foot. Gently, he squeezed at her large toe, watching to see the blood flow back into the toenail. Then he nudged her forward, and with the same calculating movements, checked the ropes that secured her wrists together behind her back, and checked Kat's fingernails for turgor. Finally, the Soviet stepped back from the mattress and continued gazing. Katerina met his eyes and repeated her request, "Neró."

The Rezidentura turned without responding and led the two young Arabs from the room. Several minutes passed and then an old *ma-ra* entered the chamber. She carried an assortment of towels, a pitcher of water, and a wash basin. The woman undraped Katerina's torn nightgown and began to give her a sponge bath—all the while careful not to disturb the ropes that secured Kat's wrists and ankles.

The water was a bit cool, but refreshing, and the old woman worked herself around Katerina's body with a practiced focus; neither gentle, nor rough, her movements were mechanical, and although the ma-ra wouldn't respond to Kat's questions, the physical contact added a sense of reassurance to an otherwise bleak situation.

After patting her dry, the old woman redressed Katerina in the torn nightgown and exited. Several minutes later she returned, carrying a fresh pitcher of water and a bowl of hot couscous; a cracked wheat and bean dish.

For the next twenty minutes, the ma-ra fed Katerina and nursed her through several full cups of water. Then finally, with one last check of the ropes, the old woman replaced the blindfold on Kat's eyes, and walked from the chamber.

TOM FAIRCHILD SAT patiently in the study of Rochelle Listach's upper M Street residence. His mind wandered. From the beginning, Tom knew that the unique risks posed by this assignment would require unique solutions. However, during the flight back from Italy, Fairchild tossed in a fitful sleep. He had reservations over the very turn of events that he had set in motion. Katerina Terass, an innocent, had been used as bait to flush out the perpetrators of a terrorist strike. They kidnapped her, and now were dangling Katerina themselves to flush out his team. One side hoped to identify a target site, the other side hoped to delay, or interrupt, the progress of identifying that target site.

Fairchild glanced at his wristwatch. He held few illusions about his profession. The charade that it was staffed by 'Men of Honor' never set with Tom, but the kidnapping of Katerina cut too close to the bone. It forced him to recall the murder of Ellie Jaycott two years earlier. A woman who knew little and cared less about her husband's assignment in Central America. Now Tom feared that Katerina could suffer the same fate.

The door opened, and Rochelle Listach entered the study. She paused for a moment, studying the weary Case Officer. "You look tired, Tom."

"I am." He stood, more out of courtesy to her gender and age than to her position as his supervisor. The CIA was still a very chauvinistic organization.

Listach took a seat opposite Fairchild and motioned for him to sit back down.

"It's a bit warm in here, I'm afraid the air conditioning has been on the blink. May I get you something cold to drink?"

"No thank you."

Fairchild acknowledged the humidity by loosening his tie and popping open the top button of his dress shirt. "Are we secure?"

"Very," nodded the old woman. She gazed serenely at her subordinate. Rochelle looked quite unaffected by the heat. "Have you been abroad?"

"Yes. I just flew in from Rome," answered Fairchild. "I met with Moshi."

She nodded. "And does the Mossad bring some news?"

The Case Officer paused before answering, taking a moment to study Listach's demeanor. "Katerina Terass has been snatched from Theodori's home on Corfu by—as yet— an unidentified team of specialists. She is purportedly alive and being held captive in the Old Quarter of Algiers."

Rochelle's face remained passive, but her eyes told the story. She was excited. Her sole demonstrative act was to clasp both hands together gently and nod. "It worked Thomas. They took the bait."

"Yes ma'm," agreed Fairchild.

"Have you had a chance to verify the information?"

"Not yet. I came straight here from the airport. But we have an address established by an Israeli *Marats* team."

"Oh . . . an *address* even . . . how interesting." Rochelle shook her head in admiration. "Moshi's assets in North Africa are quite impressive. How is he?"

"Good," nodded Fairchild, "but he never goes anywhere alone."

"Yarids," offered the Operations Officer in a knowing way. "Moshi's a very important Katsa. The security is standard."

"Can we trust him?"

Listach's face lightened in surprise as she removed her glasses. "Moshi?! Certainly not; but insofar as we are promoting an agenda that is beneficial to Israel, he will help us, and his information will be accurate."

She sat forward. "Tom, he has probably deduced that we set Theodori's woman up, and that we are using his 'black' agents to locate the perpetrators. We are using him. And he knows that we are using. And he knows, that we know, that he's aware of being used. But ultimately it all works towards the same goal. To identify T, H, O, T, M—the target."

Fairchild considered his thoughts before finally meeting the old woman's eyes. "And Katerina Terass, what of her?"

Rochelle Listach looked at Fairchild evenly. *"What* of her?"

"Do you think she'll survive?"

The Operations Officer shrugged indifferently. "In the big picture, does it really matter?"

The two CIA staffers looked at each other in silence. Despite the heat, Tom felt a noticeable chill in the room. Rochelle stood.

"I have some work to do. Keep me posted on new developments. Benjamin will show you out."

She turned, and with a youthful step, the old woman walked from the study.

XVIII

"SABAAH IL-KHAIR."

Jaycott stood in the doorway of the small tool and die shop at the east end of Habib Bourgihba Boulevard, and addressed the proprietor. The man looked up at the taller American, and assessed him silently for a moment. He noted Jay's Italian sportscoat, the dress slacks, and aviator sunglasses.

"Sabaah il-Khair," he mumbled politely.

"Tatakallum Inglizi?" asked Jay.

"Aiwa," nodded the merchant.

Jaycott removed his sunglasses and looked down at the merchant. The eye contact made the Tunisian shift uneasily under the gaze.

He was at it again; poking, prodding, stirring the pot. This was a calculated risk, but ever since the firefight in Cairo, Jay sensed that the terrorist net that planned the strike in the U.S. would be very impatient. They—as much as Jay and Theo—were playing against the clock. Thus, with little to lose, he took a deliberate and direct approach to reestablishing contact. He needed them to know that he had escaped, survived, and was determined to continue.

"I seek Rachid Ghannouchi," said Jay in a low voice. It is a matter of great importance."

The tool shop proprietor studied Jay's face. He couldn't help but notice the small white scar that ran along his cheek.

"I don't know Rachid Ghannouchi," answered the Tunisian warily.

"Yes you do," stated Jay calmly. There was something very serious in his voice.

The door to the tool and die shop opened again, and Theodori—as if on cue—strolled in. He fixed the proprietor with an even look and then walked down an aisle filled with shelves of supplies. The Tunisian looked from Jay, to Theo, then back to Jay.

Jaycott reached into his pocket and removed a large roll of Tunisian Dinars while the merchant considered the alternatives. The softening of the implied threat allowed the Tunisian to save face. The money made the request a business matter.

"Please," continued Jay politely, "a friend has sent me, and it is a matter of great importance."

The Tunisian relented. "Wait."

He turned and walked through a door at the rear of the shop.

Slowly, Jaycott turned from the counter and glanced unobtrusively over his shoulder. He caught Theo's eye, and saw the burly Greek move to another aisle stocked with screwdrivers, bolts, and metal braces.

Several minutes passed before the merchant returned. He handed Jay a folded piece of paper, making a point to leave his open hand on the countertop. Jaycott peeled off a couple of twenty Dinar notes. He stuffed them into the proprietor's palm and nodded, "Shukran."

It was the same story, different chapter. Fairchild's list of known cutouts, black marketeers, and minor players again proved accurate. If one spread enough glue, the purveyors of information would point them in the right direction. Hopefully, they could penetrate one of the nets that had knowledge of T, H, O, T, M.

Jaycott turned from the countertop and exited the shop.

"MRS. RONALD HOCH?"

The GRU officer looked at the two men in dark suits that stood at her front door. Her suburban home on a tree-lined street in Hackensack, New Jersey didn't often experience salesmen or solicitation. In the few seconds that it took the somber men to present identification, her mind raced through a series of memories, realities, and lost dreams. She squeezed her eyes shut.

"FBI, ma'm."

They both offered their badges. "May we come in?"

She nodded, fighting the urge to end it all and respond in Russian.

"Ronald . . ." she called out, ushering the two Federal Agents into her foyer. ". . . Ronald . . ."

"Yes, yes, I'm coming," answered the civil engineer from the kitchen. "Give me a . . ."

The explosives expert stopped short, surprised at the two men flanking his wife. One look at her face quickly confirmed his fear. Nonetheless, the professional in him played out the role.

"What is this?"

"FBI Mister Hoch," said the first man raising his identification to eye level. "Special Agent Lloyd. We were wondering if you and your wife would accompany us down to the Federal Building. We'd like to ask you some questions."

"Why, concerning what?!"

"We'd rather not talk here sir."

"But I have to go down to the hardware store. I have a business to run."

"Yes, we understand, but it's really very important," added the second Agent.

The GRU officer got indignant. "Are we under arrest?"

"No," shrugged the first Agent, "We would like you to come voluntarily, but if you prefer, we can arrest you."

"On what charge?"

"Conspiracy to commit murder."

"Murder?!" exclaimed the married couple in unison. Clearly they were very surprised. The wife gave her husband a puzzled frown.

"And interstate flight to avoid prosecution."

"What?! This is absurd," huffed the GRU officer.

"It must seem that way," acknowledged the first Agent, "that's why we'd like you to come voluntarily. I'm sure that we can clear this right up—after all, you weren't even *in* Miami when the assault took place."

"Miami?!"

Again, the married couple exchanged confused glances. It was enough to assure their cooperation. They were unaware of Saoud Issan's beating of the prostitute in a Miami hotel room, and although they had received one telephone call to confirm their meet, they never suspected Issan placed that call from the scene of a crime.

The civil engineer nodded to his wife and retrieved a set of keys from a side table. He motioned for the two Agents to lead the way. Special Agent Lloyd smiled and deferred the lead to Mrs. Hoch. They exited the home and waited as the civil engineer closed and locked his front door. Then as they walked towards the sidewalk a second sedan pulled up and two more men in dark suits jumped out. The first two Agents each tugged at the married couple's elbows, guiding them gently to separate automobiles. At first the action surprised the Hochs, but as the wife began to protest, the husband gave a quick, stern shake of his head. Quietly, they climbed into the rear seats of the two sedans and the automobiles drove away.

JAYCOTT ENTERED THE crowded Bistro off the Rue de la Re'volution, and scanned the unfamiliar faces. He was apprehensive. Two hours earlier, Jay had received a coded message requesting an emergency contact. The message instructed Jay to meet his Case Officer, Tom Fairchild, at this particular pub at precisely six p.m.—the height of the early evening party time.

Everywhere groups of Tunisians drank, argued, and ate; in essence they did everything but go home to their families. And it agitated Jay that Fairchild—an experienced staff officer—would violate operational security by having a face to face meet; much less in such a public place.

After a few seconds, Jay's eyes adjusted from the bright sun outside to the dark but noisy Bistro. He noticed Fairchild sitting in the corner under a haze of thick smoke. The Case Officer motioned with a nod of his head and Jay crossed the room to the rickety wooden table.

"Greetings," smiled Fairchild sucking on a filtered cigarette. "Would you like a drink?"

Tom raised a hand and jabbed two fingers in the air before Jaycott could answer.

Jay glanced around before sitting. "Hello Tom, when did you start smoking again?"

"What?" challenged Fairchild sarcastically. "You too? Everybody is a health critic." The words came out with just a touch too much bite. Jaycott paused as two tumbler glasses of scotch were set between them on the table. The waiter grunted and ambled off.

"And how long have you been drinking?" continued Jay undaunted.

"Not long enough," snapped the Case Officer. "Do you want to play doctor or get on with this?"

Jay removed his sunglasses and looked Fairchild hard in the eyes. His voice was very low, but serious.

"This must be pretty important."

"It is. But before we get started, let me ask: Where's your Greek friend?"

Something in Fairchild's demeanor made Jay cautious. Clearly, the Case Officer was under stress, the cigarettes and whiskey were longstanding crutches. But the way that Tom hesitated increased Jay's discomfort; that, and the fact that he was concerned with pinpointing Theodori.

"He's around Tom, why?"

Fairchild shrugged as Jay studied him closely. "This concerns him too."

Jay nodded. "You seem a little uncomfortable Tom, you doing something bad?"

"Bad?!" blurted Fairchild in surprise. "Such as?"

"Such as setting us up."

"What?!" Fairchild scowled, his shock genuine. He leaned forward. "You know Jay, you are one paranoid fuck . . . if I didn't know you better, I'd say that when Ellie went—you lost it."

Jay's eyes turned cold. Then he stood. "I'm out of here. This meet's over."

"Wait, wait . . ." blurted Fairchild.

"Fuck you Tom."

"Please . . ." The Case Officer motioned for Jay to sit back down. ". . . I'm sorry, really . . . I apologize. It was out of line." Fairchild's eyes implored Jaycott to stay. As a sign of good faith, he pushed his drink away and stubbed out his cigarette. "Please, sit . . ."

Jay took a wary look around the Bistro, then back at Fairchild. In one smooth motion he quickly but unobtrusively removed his pistol from the small of his back and held it under the table.

"Okay Tom, I'm sitting."

Fairchild swallowed and thought for a moment before continuing.

". . . This one's going to be tough . . ." He took a deep breath. ". . . two days ago, a snatch team went to Theodori's home on Corfu and kidnapped his woman."

Fairchild allowed Jay to digest the information. There was only the narrowing of his eyes into two small slits, and then they seemed to glaze over with a thin film.

"Is she alive?"

"Last we knew," nodded Fairchild, "although they killed the old woman and a carpenter from the village."

"Tell me about it."

The Case Officer shrugged. "Very professional . . . quick, smooth, thorough . . . they negated the alarm system, jammed the doors, triple tapped the house staff. In and out. No noise, no lights, minimal signs of struggle, vehicle in waiting. The bodies of the old woman and the carpenter were discovered the next morning by a local delivery boy who was dropping off some groceries. By then, Theodori's woman was probably already off the island on a boat halfway to Africa."

Jaycott remained silent, quietly piecing the facts together.

"Who?"

"We're not sure," admitted Fairchild, "but it would seem to be connected to our problem."

Jay squinted. "A pre-emptive strike?"

The Case Officer shrugged. "Maybe you were closer than we realized on penetrating the net."

"Or maybe we're close to zero hour, and they need to slow us down just a little bit longer."

"That too," mumbled Fairchild.

Jaycott leaned back for a moment and considered the information. After a few seconds, he leaned forward again. "You think that the snatch team is directly related to the net and they're baiting us."

"We don't know," answered Fairchild obliquely. "It makes as much sense as anything. But it could be a very subtle diversion."

"So why are you telling me Tom?"

Fairchild leaned forward, the alcohol and cigarette haze suddenly gone.

"Because of what happened to Ellie. I won't have Theodori's woman hanging over my head."

"It's a gamble either way. They're testing us."

"It's your call," answered the Case Officer putting both hands in the air, palms forward.

Jay sat motionless for a few seconds. "Do you have any leads on her location?"

"Yes," nodded Fairchild, "a precise fix."

Jaycott's eyes widened. Then they narrowed again. "This sucks."

"I agree. It smells to high heaven. They're feeding us."

"You've confirmed the fix?"

"Yes."

Jay nodded and backed away from the table. "I have to talk to Theo."

"I understand," nodded Fairchild. He slid a folded piece of paper across the table. Jay quickly palmed the note. "If you decide to go after the woman, be at this address in Bizerte by midnight. I'll take care of the logistics and set up assets 'in-country'."

"Where's 'in-country'?"

"Algiers."

Jaycott exhaled.

"It could have been worse," shrugged Fairchild.

"I suppose," conceded Jay, "at least we have *some* freedom of movement."

"Just remember Jay," added Fairchild, "if you decide to abort the Probe and go after Theodori's woman, none of the help came from me. Officially I know nothing. You broke contact without my knowledge or permission and went freelance. Agreed?"

"Agreed."

Jaycott gave Fairchild a final nod. Then he stood and quickly walked from the Bistro.

Three minutes later, from deep in the crowd, Fairchild noticed a man that looked like Theodori exit the noisy bar.

SAOUD CLIMBED THE crumbling, pocked-marked steps of the third floor apartment tucked deep in the Casbah. He was euphoric; riding a wave of energy that transcended any excitement he had ever known. They were there—barely days away—from a long awaited strike deep in the heartland of the great Satan, the United States.

Issan bounded the steps two at a time, hardly noticing the familiar whitewashed alabaster, the wall murals, the ornately painted wooden doors. On the flight back from Florida, Saoud's mind whirred continuously. He was awed by the magnitude of the upcoming event, the 'burn' that he would help etch in the pages of history. His time was *now*.

Issan paused at the top of the stairs and turned left. At the end of the hall, flanking a small wooden table, sat two young Arabs clutching AKM assault rifles. Saoud sneered and approached the Palestinians.

"Masar il-Khair," offered the nearest guard.

"Kaif halak, a-shlon-ak?"

"Bi kheyr, il-Hamdulilleh."

Saoud motioned for the guards to unlock the door that they sat protecting. The two young Arabs exchanged nervous glances.

"Open the door," commanded Issan in a testy voice. The Palestinians shifted uneasily in their seats. They didn't know precisely who Saoud was, or how he was connected to the various actions of the cell, but they did know that he held influence with the Soviet Rezidentura. This in itself made him a force to be recognized. In addition, his demeanor had grown increasingly caustic; the once cocky bluster that cloaked a pronounced insecurity, now proved dangerously overbearing. As zero hour approached, Saoud abused his position and its power.

"Open the door," repeated Issan venomously.

Just then, the old Ma-ra approached from the far end of the hallway.

"Qif, la, la," cautioned the woman, "it is *not* permitted. You must go—no men allowed."

She reached up to pull Issan's elbow, attempting to steer Saoud from the door when suddenly he whirled and lashed out with a backhand.

Do *not* touch me you old hag."

He turned his venomous snarl back to the closest of the two Palestinians. The man stood, a bit uneasily, and withdrew a set of keys. He hesitated, his eyes shifting furtively from Issan to the old Ma'ra.

"Open the door," whispered Saoud in a low growl, "or as Mohammed is my Prophet, I will cut off your hands."

Fumbling nervously, the young guard twisted a large skeleton key in the lock and turned the dead bolt. The huge oak door swung inward. Saoud entered the room and quickly slammed the door shut. His message was clear. *Do not disturb.*

From across the room, Issan surveyed Katerina. She lay, bound and blindfolded in her torn negligee atop the soiled mattress. Slowly, Saoud crossed the room, watching the rise and fall of her chest as she breathed uneasily. Katerina's head arched slightly, her ears perked to pick up sounds from the visitor. Issan paused at the foot of the threadbare mattress, hovering above Katerina, tugging at the single light bulb that dangled limply from the ceiling. He shifted the glare of the light and studied the prisoner; intrigued by Katerina's features, her smooth skin, her supple limbs. Issan recognized that despite the stuffy, claustrophobic, perspiring pit of a room, she was quite beautiful.

Saoud reached down and placed an open hand on the nape of Katerina's neck. She gasped involuntarily, surprised by the touch, unable to discern movements through the blindfold. Her fear excited Issan, and he allowed his hand to continue down to Katerina's breast. He groped her nipple through the thin, cotton negligee, and this caused Katerina to squirm uncomfortably.

Suddenly, the huge oak door swung inward and the Soviet Rezidentura stood in the center of the room.

"Issan, Aish fi?!" snapped the flat-faced man in Arabic. Saoud instantly recognized the voice. He turned towards the door.

"Ma a'arif," shrugged the Palestinian.

"Then come with me, Ta'al . . . we have much to discuss."

"Na'arn," nodded Saoud. He turned back towards Katerina, and with a deft hand he stroked her naked thigh where the negligee was torn and whispered, "I'll be back."

Then he straightened and followed the Rezidentura from the room.

XIX

24 August 1989
Moscow, USSR

COLONEL GENERAL ALEKSANDR Grigorevich Pavlov, First Deputy Chief of the GRU, leaned back in his chair and recradled the telephone. He thought in silence for a moment. Then he leaned forward and punched at the intercom on his desk.

"Yes Comrade General," came the male reply.

"Summon Guryenko at once."

"Da, Comrade General."

Pavlov resettled himself back in his chair and slowly began to strum his fingers on the desktop. It took four minutes for the head of the Illegals Training Centre to arrive.

"Comrade General," nodded the short, bespeckled Guryenko upon entering the corner office. He quickly noted the immaculate—as always—desktop of his superior.

"Vyacheslav Tikhonovich, thank you for coming," offered Pavlov graciously, as if Guryenko had a choice. "Please sit."

Pavlov stretched in his highbacked leather chair, assuming an overly casual demeanor. "I just got off the telephone with Comrade Gorbachev . . ."

"I thought he was on vacation?"

"He is," nodded Pavlov, a slight smile curving his upper lip, "but I had his private number in Sevastopol." Pavlov enjoyed flaunting a sense of self-importance to subordinates.

"The Crimea?"

"Da, Vyacheslov . . . as you know, the Politburo conservatives and neoStalinist Right has been particularly outspoken during his absence."

"Da," nodded Guryenko."

"Comrade Gorbachev was particularly stung by the sharp tongue of Nina Andreyeva in Leningrad, who, actually called him a 'bourgeois' . . ."

Guryenko tried to suppress a chuckle, knowing how the anti-Socialist label would rankle *any* Communist Party member, much less the Head of the Party.

". . . therefore," continued Pavlov, "before Ligachev, Chebrikov, and their supporters launch a coup, we must act."

"Zero hour is at hand," confirmed Guryenko. "Our Illegals are positioned, the Executive Agents have the explosives, and the strike is set for the American Labor Day weekend. It marks the official end to their summer, when the children return from holiday and prepare for school. We expect overflow crowds and maximum exposure."

"Harasho," nodded Pavlov satisfied. "You have prepared the channels of disinformation?"

"Da, Comrade General. The KGB will receive total responsibility for the attack. It will clearly swing the tide away from the hardliners. All known associates of the Ligachev-Chebrikov faction will avoid them like the plague."

Pavlov nodded again, confident that his subordinate had planned and would execute a successful operation.

"Comrade Gorbachev will be most pleased. And . . . you and I Vyacheslov Tikhonovich, have positioned ourselves perfectly during these perilous times. If it succeeds, then the hardliners will be decimated, Comrade Gorbachev will be eternally grateful, and *our* power assured. If it fails, our influence will continue unabated, and our hands scrupulously clean from any knowledge or involvement. We are Vyacheslov, straddling the fence with a safety net on either side."

"Da, Comrade General."

Pavlov leaned forward and picked up the telephone. It was an act of dismissal. "Spasseba Comrade, Dos veedanya."

Guryenko nodded politely, stood, and walked from the office.

THE SIX MEN sat huddled around the large kitchen table. As Jaycott spoke, the other five listened, each striving to absorb every bit of information he imparted. Occasionally, Jay would point to a photograph or the tattered blueprint that lay spread across the tabletop. After several minutes, Jaycott paused and looked up from his recital, taking a moment to survey his makeshift team.

In addition to himself and Theodori, sat four other men. Each was an unknown—and in Jay and Theo's mindset—untested commodity. But Fairchild swore they were seasoned professionals; and based on their overall intensity and demeanor, Jay surmised Fairchild told the truth—not that he and Theo had a good deal of choice in the matter.

These six men would surreptitiously enter the three story building in the middle of the Algerian Casbah in search of Katerina. None of the men—with the exception of Jay and Theo—had ever worked together. He didn't know their names or even their country of origin. Yet given the speed of unfolding events, it would have to do. They all seemed to absorb his briefing, and as is often the case, when unknown professionals are thrown together to work in a dangerous situation, they study each other quietly; watching for the little cues or habits that demonstrate experience—and hopefully reliability.

There was a pause in Jaycott's monologue, and the man designated number two excused himself to go to the toilet.

Fairchild had assembled the four men from a short list of North African Contract Agents. He and Jay agreed that only number designations would be used to differentiate between the Agents. There were three teams of two men each, with Jay and Theo the last two men in the assault file, designated numbers five and six respectively. The four Contracts and Jay would each carry a MP5SD, a nine millimeter submachine gun fitted with a special silencer.

Theodori, however, would carry a very noisy, very powerful Franchi SPAS12. The Franchi was a ferocious 12-gauge automatic shotgun, with a pistol grip and folding stock that collapsed to a length of 28 inches. It would be crossloaded with slug, '00 Buckshot, and Hatton rounds—the latter specially developed to blow hinges off locked or barricaded doors. Clearly, once Theo used the Franchi, the element of surprise would be lost.

Jaycott's plan of attack was simple: the first two teams of two men each would quickly leapfrog their way through the building, floor by floor, eliminating any and all occupants until they had located Katerina. Jay and Theo would follow in close support, lending backup and directing the search. Should a locked door or barrier present an obstacle, Jay would make an onsite tactical decision if Theo should cut loose with the Franchi. Much would depend upon their success up to that point, because once non-silenced weapons were used, the scenario changed dramatically.

In addition to the submachine gun and Theo's shotgun, each man would take along his personal choice of a sidearm and two stun grenades. 'Flash-Bangs' as they were commonly called, were special grenades designed for hostage rescue. Typically, they used a rubber or plastic body that contained a special explosive designed to produce an immense bang and blinding flash. The idea was to disorient and stun the terrorist in a room, while not harming the hostage.

Finally, each of them would wear a set of PVS-7 night vision goggles and an earphone-throat microphone headset. The passive illumination system allowed them to extract ambient light and virtually see in a darkened building, while the radio receiver-transmitter allowed them quiet, but continuous, communication. Jay and the team members could pass information and carryout instructions without losing their advantage of surprise.

The single biggest risks to the operation was the location of the apartment building, and the lack of a larger assault force. Situated in the heart of the Casbah, Katerina's 'prison' was surrounded by hundreds of sympathetic Islamic neighbors. Despite the assurance of Fairchild that he would seal-off the kill zone, Jay recognized that they'd be operating in hostile territory. The goal was to get in, get Katerina, and get out before someone sounded an alarm. The thought of having only six men to penetrate, search, and recover a hostage from a decrepit building, not knowing precisely the number of guards, their locations, the prisoner's location, or the internal precautions in place, disturbed Jay. It was an operation fraught with risks, yet one that he knew must be undertaken for Theo.

Jay looked over at his trusted friend. He had made a judgment call, and aborted their mission to penetrate the Tunisian Islamist cell to focus their time and energy on saving Theo's woman. In doing so, he realized he had probably foreclosed any opportunity to locate the Strike Target. He was sure that Fairchild's superiors at the CIA would now never allow him to read the After Action Report on Colón. Jay would never know who arranged the leak that got Ellie killed, or why such a cold-blooded decision was made. But in retrospect, it almost didn't matter. They had a chance—albeit a small one—to save Theo's woman from a similar fate. And as fond as Jay himself was of Katerina, he was truly happy that Theodori's life would now be complete—provided of course, they could locate and free her.

Theodori returned Jay's glance and nodded. There was an uncharacteristic bit of tension in the burly Greek's face. Unknown to the other four men, the rescue of Katerina was a personal matter. The others had been given a picture and a description of the hostage, but had no idea of her connection to Jaycott, and especially Theo.

A knock at the door broke Jay's reverie. He motioned and one of the men, number 'Four', stood and walked from the kitchen. He returned with Fairchild.

"Everything on schedule?", asked the Case Officer as he entered the room.

"Yes," nodded Jay. Then he stood as Fairchild motioned towards the hallway.

"What have you got for me?", asked Jaycott in a hushed voice.

"You're still a *Go*. It's been quiet. They rotated the guards an hour ago. The first floor dining area is noisy, probably a half dozen cell operatives chatting away. The second floor Radio Room has at least one man, and several of their senior officers are in the room across the hall—what we believe to be their Operations Center. One of the bedrooms on the third floor still looks like the most promising place to hold someone prisoner. Several guards are outside the door and at least one, if not two old women are up there all the time."

Fairchild handed Jay a packet of information. He leafed through several photographs until the Case Officer pointed specifically at one. It depicted a flat-faced man in an expensive business suit who looked to be of Eastern European heritage.

"We haven't seen him in several days, but the Marats team gave us an identity."

Jay looked skeptically at his Case Officer.

"It's okay," continued Fairchild, "Langley confirmed the I.D."

"Who is he?"

"The Soviet Rezidentura."

Jaycott caught his breath, a bit surprised by the revelation. "You think Moscow's mixed up in this?"

Fairchild shrugged. "We've had our suspicions . . . let's say for argument, that they're behind the strike."

Jay frowned. It was common knowledge that the Soviet Union loosely sponsored and generally supported the international web of terrorism; money, supplies, and training were always available to anyone that would destabilize a western nation. But to suggest that an official arm of Mother Russia would actively involve themselves in an operational strike against a sovereign country was a big leap.

"Okay," nodded Jay, "go on . . ."

"He's been seen entering and leaving the building on several occasions, as have several other known Palestinians tied to various Islamist splinter groups."

Fairchild allowed Jay to leaf through the packet of photographs before stopping him at a second picture. It was a black and white photo of Saoud Issan.

"This man is a confirmed Cell Commander for the Islamist Jihad. That is why it's so important to get into that second floor Operations Center."

Jay's eyes narrowed. "Tom, our mission is to save the woman."

"I know Jay, but it's Quid pro Quo. The Marats team gave us the location, they've been pulling on-site surveillance, and they'll seal off the kill zone. We told them we'd share the intel."

"If we get any."

"Jay . . ."

"Fuck the Israelis," snapped Jaycott in a harsh whisper. "Our mission is the woman, anything else is gravy. You got it?"

Fairchild relented. He quickly realized that this was emotional territory for Jay. Too many ghosts were surfacing. "Whatever you can do," mumbled the Case Officer obligingly. "The vehicle will be here at precisely twenty-two, thirty hours to pick up your men. At twenty-three, ten you will meet with a member of the Marats team at Checkpoint Charlie. He will feed you any last minute updates. You'll decide then if it's a 'go' or an 'abort'. Good Luck."

Jaycott nodded, pausing to take a long look at Fairchild before he ushered the CIA staffer from the safehouse. Back in the kitchen he addressed the other five men. "We're a 'Go'. Take ten minutes to do a final equipment check and hit the latrine. Then we'll rehearse our 'Actions at the Objective'."

Theodori took a long, hard, appraising look at Jay while sliding home the magazine to his Desert Eagle pistol. Their eyes met, and Jay gave his friend a confident wink.

LIEUTENANT COLONEL GENNADI Kozlov, Soviet Intelligence Officer of the GRU, also known as Ronald Hoch of Hackensack, New Jersey, sat and sighed. The jig was up. Clearly, despite their pretense at politeness and civility, the FBI did not accept his story.

He shifted in his seat, attempting to view the sidewalk from between the long floor length drapes of his living room. Somewhere out there, Gennadi knew with certainty, Counter Intelligence Agents of the United States Government were watching. The trashmen, utility workers, landscape service employees—everyone was suspect; and he feared that his wife would soon crack under the strain.

Gennadi replayed in his mind the interview. The FBI agents had been most cordial, all of them exuding a relaxed, polished demeanor—nothing the civil engineer was certain— like the KGB would have demonstrated had the situation been reversed. But after three years at the Illegals Training Centre (really more a remote Dacha on the outskirts of Moscow than a centralized training facility) followed by ten years of living and working in the United States, such deference to the rights of the individual was not unexpected. The U.S. law enforcement officials exuded a different approach to their citizens than most countries. Gennadi realized that the investigating officers had to be much sharper than their counterparts in Russia, for here, strongarm methods were unacceptable. In the USSR, the favored method of interrogation was physical; drugs, brutality, deprivation. In the United States, the method was mental; discussion, trickery, and boredom. He applauded their technique, but sensed that despite his performance, they didn't accept his answers.

Gennadi stretched, his vision following the mailman amble by under the weight of his heavy brown shoulder sack. The FBI, true to their word, never arrested him. But the dubious expression on their faces when they listened to his responses, said a great deal. The GRU officer found himself challenged by the whole interview process; a kind of cat and mouse game where the FBI relayed certain facts – or what they claimed were facts, of this Gennadi could not be certain—and he did his best to offer believable explanations to the various questions that followed. He backstopped his story of taking a short vacation with his wife by relating various innuendos. This was possible, because they made a point to actually *do* all of the activities they claimed to have done. The Illegals Centre had trained them well; and so, with the exception of one afternoon spent briefing Saoud Issan in their hotel room, the Hoch's from Hackensack, New Jersey, had actually enjoyed a vacation.

The GRU officer saw his neighbor, Mrs. Wentworth, pull her station wagon into the driveway across the street. The one sticking point, as he saw it, was a reasonable explanation as to why Saoud's telephone call to set up their meet, took

two minutes and six seconds. Gennadi claimed in was a
wrong number. One of the FBI men blandly acknowledged
that two minutes and six seconds seemed an extraordinary
length of time to advise someone that they had dialed an
incorrect telephone number. They presented him with a
computerized copy of the phone bill.

Gennadi's wife entered the living room. Her face was
taunt and her long, grey-streaked hair pulled back into a tight
bun. The stress in her features was obvious. She didn't speak,
but upon gaining eye contact, she scratched several words on
a notepad. *Ride? Talk?* The GRU officer nodded.

From the onset, the FBI agents had separated the
married couple, making a point to prevent any discussion
between them, much less further development of a cover
story. Gennadi knew his wife was well-trained, but no
amount of conditioning could offset the mental anguish of a
mother too far from home, too long separated from her sons.
The policy of the GRU to hold children of Illegals posted
abroad as polite hostages took its toll.

She had said little. Stuck to their well-rehearsed cover
story, told the FBI agents numerous boring details of her
vacation, and even acted mildly offended at the thought that
she and her husband would be involved in the attempted
murder of a prostitute in a Miami hotel room. She didn't
know a Raul Fazio, nor did she recall *any* telephone calls to
their hotel room in Daytona, much less a wrong number.

In summation, Gennadi's wife played her part well—
at least verbally. But her eyes told the story; and he feared
that these investigators read that defeat. For if the eyes were

the windows to the soul, then *her* eyes were a huge, transparent picture frame of glass.

The civil engineer stood, and silently followed his wife towards the kitchen. It had been two days since their interviews, and he suspected that during their time at the Federal Building, the FBI agents had planted listening devices. Gennadi knew that in the United States it took a court order to place a wiretap. However, he had to assume this had occurred, just as surely as he believed they were being watched. His problem was that he could not take the risk of contacting Moscow, nor could he afford not to. His mind raced. Gennadi *must* contact his Control Officer, Lieutenant General V. T. Guryenko, and advise him of developments. Unlike most Illegals who are controlled by one of the four geographic Directorate Heads, Gennadi and his wife reported to the Head of the Illegals Training Centre himself. This was an honor—or so they thought. And now it appeared that his entire Illegal Residency—to include the three agents he had recruited during their years in New Jersey—was at risk of compromise. Guryenko needed to know. The conundrum was intensified by the fact that Gennadi provided an Arabic cutout with two small, dangerously powerful, conventional explosives. For the GRU officers, the final destination of the bombs was unknown, and would only be recognized by Gennadi and his wife after the fact. But in the meantime, he needed to warn his Control Officer, that the FBI seemed to be sufficiently aware of the strike. He also needed to contain his wife. For if she unraveled now, their lives—and that of their children—would be horribly ruined.

~~~

"IT'S TIME."

There was a quiet pause as each of the five men glanced up at Jaycott, nodded, and stood. Their collective look of calm resolution suddenly changed. As if on cue, a subtle brew of energy began to surface, an intensity—still under control—that bubbled to the surface in the ensuing moment. For men of action, waiting was always the worst part. Now, finally, they were moving, and unimpeded lines of concentration could flow.

Jay's vision roamed the room, exchanging eye contact with each member of his team before finally settling on Theodori. For ten seconds the two friends passed a steady reassuring gaze. It had come down to this. Jaycott's wife Ellie was dead, and now Theo's woman, Katerina, was similarly threatened. They were alone, on the ropes, expendable; and the only solace either had, was the dependability of the other. In the brief span of the moment, Jay mused on the vagaries of male bonding. It developed in the strangest places and between the oddest men. Clearly, at face value Jaycott and Theo were the most unlikely pair; but when it came to work they meshed; a complimentary, glove to fist, unspoken trust that resulted from several forays to the edge.

Jay winked reassuringly as Theo crooked his head. Then the burly Greek yanked back on the upper receiver of his massive Desert Eagle pistol and cocked a round into the chamber. His face tightened as he slid the receiver back into battery with a thud. If danger was the ultimate aphrodisiac between opposite sexes, then it was also the ultimate bonding solution amongst the same sex. It defined friendships in ways that lesser experiences only hinted at.

Quietly, the team filed from the safehouse, down the back staircase, to a waiting truck parked at the rear of the building. Each of the men was dressed in black, carrying an assault weapon, a personal handgun, both stun and white phosphorus grenades, night vision goggles, and a combination earphone-throat transmitter radio headset.

As the last man climbed into the rear of the 1¼ ton Mercedes, the driver covered the back with a canvas tarpaulin. Then he jumped into the cab, shifted gears, and the truck slowly rumbled away.

It took twenty minutes of slow, winding turns to snake the Mercedes through the back alleys of the Casbah. It was half past eleven in the evening, and most civilized Algerians were asleep. The choice of the time was to permit the truck to move unobtrusively. Although Jay would have preferred waiting several hours more, this time of night found vehicular traffic sparse, but not nonexistent.

Finally, the Mercedes slowed, and a knock on the cabin wall by the driver signaled their arrival. Jay slipped over the tailgate in a smooth motion and drifted into the shadows.

"Shalom," mumbled an Israeli from the Marats team.

"And you," nodded Jay. "How does it look?"

"Two men out front, at least six inside, maybe more . . . one old woman, and a Cell Commander who just entered ten minutes ago: Saoud Issan—he's important."

Jay considered the information. "What posture are they in?"

"Relaxed. No visible signs of alert."

"You'll seal-off the kill zone?"

"Yes," assured the Israeli. "We have the entire block covered, to include your route of escape. There will be adequate time, but you must get to the Operations Center on the second floor. It is across the hall from the Communications Room."

"We'll do our best," mumbled Jay.

The Marats Agent gripped Jay's wrist. "Fairchild promised . . ."

"I *said* we'll do our best," snarled Jay in a quiet voice. He ripped his arm free. "You just do *your* job."

The Israeli relented. He didn't wish to alienate Jaycott at this point.

"Give us four minutes to get into position," added Jay.

The Israeli nodded. Jaycott turned and returned to the truck. He drew back the tarpaulin covering the rear of the Mercedes. "It's a go."

One by one the other five men slipped over the tailgate and assembled into a single file line. They moved to the edge of the alley, backs flat against the alabaster wall, and waited.

The lead man withdrew a rigid borescope from the cargo pocket at his thigh and worked it slowly around the corner of the wall before peering into an eye loop connected to a long stethoscope tube. A picture leaped into view, and he noted two sentries lazily smoking cigarettes in front of the three story target building. His right hand raised and two fingers jutted skyward. He spoke quietly into his throat transmitter.

"Two bogeys, AK-47's, twelve o'clock."

"Copy," acknowledged Jay into his mouthpiece. "All units?"

The second man in file raised his hand in acknowledgement, then in order the third, fourth, and Theo to Jay's rear tapped him on the shoulder. The point man replaced the borescope in his cargo pocket and gripped the silenced submachinegun in both hands. "Twenty seconds," said Jay.

They waited.

Jay calmly watched his wristwatch, allowing the illuminated sweep dial to tick off the remaining seconds.

"Go."

The point man moved out, turning the corner in an even, but fast-paced walk, immediately followed by the others. The six men automatically fanned out in a wedge, creating a diamond, each member of the team covering a firing sector, but also the flanks of the men to their left and right. It must have been an incredible sight to the two Arabs, who slouched nonchalantly in front of the building, smoking, and chatting aimlessly. Suddenly to their front appeared something unexplainable; six men, clad in black, looking every bit like aliens with night vision goggles protruding from their faces, carrying strange weapons with elongated barrels. The specter was enough to give pause to the two sentries as they wrestled with their AK-47's. This allowed the team to draw within twenty feet, and it proved disastrous.

The point man and number two simultaneously raised their submachineguns, and squeezed off several three round bursts apiece. The silenced MP5's spat subsonic bullets with deadly accuracy. The nine millimeter projectiles tore into the chest and abdomen of each sentry, knocking them backwards into the front wall of the building, before they crumbled into a heap on the ground.

In the center of the wedge, Jay spoke calmly into his mouthpiece. "One and two post at twelve o'clock, three and four sterilize the AO, six post at six."

In movement techniques, whether in an urban setting or out in the woods, small units worked off the clock method. Twelve o'clock was always the direction of travel, and security was always posted facing the other cardinal directions. Thus, the first two shooters in the wedge who had just eliminated the sentries continued moving towards the entrance to the building. The third and fourth men in the assault team fanned out to either side, each grabbed the torso of a dead Arab, and quickly dragged the limp bodies off into the shadows at the far side of the building. Theodori as the last man in the diamond, turned, and took a knee to cover the rear of the wedge. It took twenty seconds, time in which the point man again extracted his rigid borescope, and snaked it under the heavy door of the ground floor entrance. He signaled with a thumbs up, indicating that the hallway inside was clear. The second man gently tested the latch on the door and signaled that it was unlocked. Jay exhaled, relieved.

The initial reports passed on from the Marats team, to Fairchild, to Jay, stated that the ground floor entrance was never locked. The cell members seemed to come and go, at will, and evidently the building's location deep in the Casbah, when complimented by the sentries at the door, and the numerous visitors, lulled them into a false sense of confidence. Just as well. Jaycott had planned for the contingency of blowing the barrier, but of course that would immediately compromise their efforts. The deeper they penetrated into the building without telegraphing their presence, the better their chances of success.

When the third and fourth men returned to the wedge they assumed their positions on the flanks at nine and three o'clock respectively. Jay spoke again. "Let's go."

The second man lifted the latch and pushed the heavy oak door inward as the point man stepped deep into the foyer. Fortunately, the ambient light that spilled from the ground floor lounge made their night vision goggles quite useful, and the team heard several noisy, chattering inhabitants conversing down the hall. The smoke of stale, bitter tobacco wafted through the corridor.

Silently, the team paced off seven or eight steps before a stairwell opened to their right. All of the men had studied blueprints of the layout of the building. Jay knew that one of his first on-site decisions would be whether or not to eliminate any cell members lingering in the ground floor lounge, or whether to bypass the obstacle. Either way, there were risks, but thus far their presence had been undetected. He opted to bypass the lounge.

"One and two right flank, three post at nine, six secure the door."

Immediately, the first two men turned right and climbed several steps before stopping, occupying the stairwell by force, prepared to shoot anyone they confronted.

The third man peeled off and positioned himself in the center of the hallway, his silenced submachinegun aiming down the corridor towards the lounge. Theodori gently closed and latched the front door, before turning and catching up with the team at the stairwell entrance. He tapped Jay on the shoulder. With a nod, Jaycott spoke again. "Go." The first two men started up the stairs, quickly joined by the other four.

The team fanned out, scattered at various levels on the stairwell, their weapons covering each other in interlocking patterns. As they ascended, eyes straining through the blackened pitch of the building, the lack of useable ambient light degrading their goggles, Jay calculated his next move. He had already decided that since their primary goal was to find Katerina, and since she was most likely held captive on the third floor—if held in the building at all—he would, if possible, avoid any and all contact until she was rescued. The Operations Center, despite whatever treasures of information it may afford, could wait. This penetration was about friendship.

At the second floor landing, the point man paused behind the stairwell wall and snaked his borescope around the corner in either direction. He signaled all clear before speaking. "No activity. Two lights under closed doors, right corridor, left side."

Jay nodded.

"Bypass. One and two left flank, three post at three. Proceed to third floor. Acknowledge."

All of the men raised their hands to signal their understanding except for Theo who stood to the rear. He tapped Jay's shoulder. The point man pocketed his borescope and they started again.

The team climbed the seventeen steps to the third floor quickly, careful to watch their footing, and grateful that the old buildings of the Casbah used very little wood. Alabaster and concrete crumbled, but it seldom creaked. At each turn they were prepared to engage the enemy, but thus far, their luck and preparation had held out. Jay reasoned that if no one went searching for the sentries in the three minutes that they had been inside the building, his team just might locate and rescue Katerina before the shit hit the fan.

Two steps from the third floor landing, the point man again retrieved his borescope, snaked the optical device around the corner, and scanned the corridor in either direction. This time he lifted his right hand with two fingers pointing towards the ceiling. Peering into the eyeloop he watched as the sentries sitting outside the bedroom leaned forward. They seemed to be absorbed, eavesdropping on the room they guarded. The point man spoke quietly into his throat transmitter. "Two bogeys, sitting, left side, AK-47's, alert, light under door."

"Copy," said Jay, "acknowledge."

Each member of the team raised a hand toward the ceiling indicating that they had heard the lead man's information. Jay spoke again. "One, two, and three left flank, engage . . . four post at three. Six stay close."

The hands went up again. As soon as the point man replaced his borescope he gave Jay a thumbs up. "Go."

Quickly, the first three men mounted the last few steps and turned left into the darkened corridor. Immediately, they fanned out and raised their silenced MP5's. As the fourth man turned right and covered the rear, the sentries noticed the approach of the strange interlopers. Both men jumped to their feet, their eyes straining in the dimly lighted hallway. There was a muffled exclamation as the sentries grappled for their weapons. Too late. All three members of the assault team cut loose with their submachineguns, walking forward, holding their lanes, spitting rounds in three shot bursts. One of the Arabs, his torso riddled with bullets, fell back onto his chair and it tumbled over with a crash.

Jay and Theo were in tight proximity. Immediately, Jaycott rushed forward and tested the door. Locked. He knocked sharply and spoke in clipped, clear Arabic.

"Min faD-lak, sa-id nee."

There was a muffled plea from inside the room that sounded like a woman. Then a man's voice bellowed from behind the door.

"Im-shee!"

Theodori's ears perked as he grimaced standing next to Jay. His mouth contorted and he motioned with his shotgun. Jaycott shot one finger in the air, instructing the Greek to wait, aware that falling furniture in the old stone building was not nearly as noisy as the report of a Franchi twelve gauge. He tried one more time to coax the occupants of the bedroom to unlock the door from the inside.

"Min FaD-lak, sa-id-nee."

Just then, the old ma-ra exited a room at the far end of the corridor carrying a kerosene lamp. She took two steps before noticing the fourth man, clad in his alien-looking attire, posting security amid the shadows at the top of the stairs. Startled, the woman gasped and dropped the lantern. It crashed at her feet, and the kerosene and flames splashed the bottom of her ankle-length galabiyya. In seconds, the flammable cotton robe caught fire. The old ma-ra became a torch. She started to scream as number four squeezed the trigger on his submachinegun. The bullets stitched a vertical pattern up the woman's chest. Number four walked forward while speaking into his throat transmitter. "I've got a fire."

Jay looked to his right, his attention split between the locked door and the burning ma-ra. "Copy four, handle it. Three post his position."

The team shifted as the noise in the hallway alerted the occupants in the bedroom. Again they heard the muffled plea from inside. It was high-pitched, like a woman, and immediately the guttural voice of a man bellowed.

"Sib-nee fi Heh-lee. Im-shee!"

Jay made a decision, stepped back, and motioned to Theo. "Blast it."

The Greek raised his SPAS-12 shotgun and with a tight grip aimed and squeezed the trigger twice. The semi-automatic Franchi let two rounds fly, one a solid slug, the other double-O buckshot. The recoil was massive, but both the top and bottom door hinges disintegrated. Theo kicked the splintered oak barrier inward, and immediately fanned out in a low crouch inside the poorly lighted bedroom with Jay and the others. The four men automatically angled off the room into quadrants, the same way they had practiced at the safehouse. Each had an interlocking sector of fire to the man beside him. It was Jay, in a low crouch at the center right position, that held a target in his sights.

Saoud Issan stood naked, straddling a soiled mattress, a bulging erection protruding from his lower abdomen. In his right hand, the Palestinian held some type of needle, and his face was contorted in disbelief.

At Saoud's feet, laying bound and gagged spread-eagle atop the mattress was a woman. A torn night gown was hiked up about her hips, exposing naked legs. Despite her matted hair and blindfold, Jay realized the captive woman was Katerina. In the second that followed, Saoud and Jaycott locked eyes, and the Arab's lip curled in a defiant sneer. Jay squeezed the trigger on his MP5. Subsonic bullets from the submachinegun tore into Issan's ribcage, twisting his body in the air, and crumpling him in a heap at the foot of the mattress.

"We've got bogies," said number three over his headset. He was posted at the top of the staircase out in the corridor.

"Copy," answered Jay as Theo leaped forward towards the mattress. The burly Greek spoke to Katerina, reassuring her as he removed the blindfold and cut the ropes binding her wrists and ankles.

"Three and four post. We've secured the package. We're moving," continued Jay.

Katerina recognized Theo's voice, and in one quick motion, he flung her sideways over his brawny shoulder and stood. The four men charged from the room and regrouped in the hallway. They started down the stairs, moving fast, but never running, aware that the element of surprise was lost as several shouts emanated from below.

"One, two, and three take six and the package to the truck. Leave immediately. Four come with me, we're going to the second floor."

Theo looked sideways at Jay, his head shaking beneath the night vision goggles. Jay punched Theo on the arm. "Go."

For a brief moment, he saw Katerina look up, her head bobbing as they descended the stairs. She seemed to single him out amidst the noise and confusion. As if in the darkness and beneath his goggles and headset, she could discern it was Jay. He touched her arm, acknowledging her presence, and then peeled off with number four at the second floor landing.

A brief firefight erupted in the stairwell as cell members from the first floor lounge reacted. Jay turned down the corridor as the distinct chatter of AK-47's on full auto echoed from the walls. Then he heard the muffled bursts from two silenced MP5 submachineguns and the explosion of Theo's shotgun.

A man exited the radio room disoriented, obviously interrupted from his nap. Immediately, number four cut him down with a short burst of the MP5. As Jay passed the slumping body in route to the Operations Center, number four kicked the partially opened door of the radio room and began indiscriminately spraying the equipment with nine millimeter bullets. Then he tossed a white phosphorus grenade into the room and closed the door.

Across the hall, Jay fired two short salvos at the door knob of the Operations Center. Several return shots pierced the wooden door from the inside and number four spun to the wall clutching his shoulder. Jay reloaded a fresh magazine and splintered the door with a long stream of bullets. As the barrier creaked under the fuselage, he quickly kicked the door inward and tossed in a stun grenade. The 'flash-bang' erupted and Jaycott burst into the room immediately shooting the two occupants who squirmed, blinded and shell-shocked on the floor.

"You okay?" asked Jay through his mouthpiece. Number four motioned half heartedly and positioned himself just inside the door. Jay opened a canvas satchel draped over his shoulder and started stuffing it with the papers, documents and computer printouts that lay spread across the desk. There was no time to pick through the material. This was purely mass collection. Others would interpret the value.

Next Jaycott opened and emptied the drawers, grabbing any folders or files that looked important. Then he yanked a series of photographs off a peg board blotter mounted on the wall. Finally, he rummaged through the open floor safe, tossing bundles of foreign currency and gold coins aside, laying his hands quickly on documents, operational briefs, several passports, and a codebook. He didn't stop until his wide canvas satchel brimmed with material, threatening to split from the haul.

"I'll lead," he nodded to number four, and together they exited the room. "Willy Pete."

The wounded team member popped a white phosphorus grenade and tossed it back into the Operations Center. As the charge burst, the chemical fragments made contact with the air and began burning furiously. A thick cloud of toxic white smoke billowed and they ran down the hall.

Jay heard more shouting and explosions from outside. Then the distinct report of AK-47's on full automatic. They negotiated the stairs quickly, Jaycott aware that number four favored his shoulder, and was somewhat limited. Several Arab bodies lay scattered in various positions about the stairwell, and then Jay stepped over the torso of number two laying on his stomach, his side perforated by four gaping bullet holes. He reached down and quickly felt for a pulse on the man's neck. Nothing. They stepped over the body and continued through the carnage.

The building was on fire and the first floor looked worse than the stairwell. The neighborhood seemed to be awake outside, and Jay heard the occasional crack of a sniper rifle in the distance. They turned left and made for the front door which was half open and dangling disjointed on its hinges. Jay took a quick peek outside, noting the street and motioned to number four. They darted into the shadows hugging the side of the building.

More bodies lay scattered near the entrance to the alley. Throughout the ordeal, Jay's headset had been a crackling tempo of noise and confusion. Now suddenly, distinctively, he heard a voice inquire: "Number five, status?"

Before Jay could answer, the voice repeated the request: "Status, number five?"

"Ten seconds . . ." answered Jay.

They darted down the alley to the end of the wall and much to Jay's chagrin he saw the Mercedes truck parked and waiting. For some unexplainable reason, this picture filled him with dread. More bodies lay crumpled about the truck and Jay noted their driver on the ground outside the open cab door his face half shot away. Number three crouched beside the lowered tailgate, gesturing wildly with one hand.

Jaycott leaped into the rear of the truck, turning to cover as number four was boosted in beside him. The tailgate was raised with a clang and the canvas tarpaulin lowered. He heard numbers one and three climb into the cab, the gears shifted, and the 1¼ ton truck lurched forward.

Jay looked up to see Katerina, her face flushed and eyes aglow. She cradled Theodori's head in her lap. Jaycott ripped off his night vision goggles and headset, imploring with his eyes for an explanation. She shook her head, fighting hard to maintain composure, tears rolling down her cheeks.

Theo coughed and a mouthful of blood splattered Jay. Then his eyes seemed to focus as he saw his friend and the burly Greek smiled. "Ishmael . . . I wouldn't let them leave . . ."

"I said not to wait," mumbled Jay.

"I owed you . . . remember Tangiers?"

Theo wheezed as the fluid buildup in his lungs began to drown him. ". . . a Spartan never forgets."

The Greek's body shook in an uncontrollable spasm as he fought to maintain control. Kat stroked his face.

"My Katerina, a good woman . . ."

She looked down at Theo fondly. "Shhh . . . don't speak. Rest."

He waved her off with a smile.

". . . and Jaycott, my good friend . . ."

Theo gripped at Jay's forearm, demonstrating surprising strength.

". . . remember your promise Ishmael. I hold you to it."

Their eyes met and Jay nodded.

Suddenly a deep gurgling sound emanated from Theodori's throat and he lurched forward. Then his body went limp. Immediately, Jay checked Theo's carotid for a pulse. Nothing. For a moment, he sat in silence, numb, aware that Katerina watched him for a sign. Jay shook his head and leaned back. He heard a muffled cry and then Kat's soft lips trembled in realization. The floodgates opened, and they each descended into their own private hell.

XX

MIKHAIL GORBACHEV SAT calmly in a wooden chair, enjoying the warm sun and idle haze of a Black Sea August. He was nearing the end of a long holiday, one month into a five week summer vacation.

Nikolai Shishlin, one of Gorbachev's speech writers, approached his boss with a first draft of the important Central Committee plenum on nationalities issues, to be held in Moscow on September 19th and 20th. Shishlin kept his distance, politely waiting beyond voice range, watching as the seated Gorbachev spoke in hushed tones to a tall, familiar looking man. Shishlin tried to place the visitor—surely he had seen this man in Moscow.

The speech writer watched as the tall man walked away. There was an air of confidence in the walk; power; it was the walk of a man used to controlling.

"Nikolai", summoned Gorbachev jovially, motioning the speech writer closer. "How is our plenum speech?"

"It goes slowly, Comrade Chairman," nodded Shishlin honestly as he curiously watched the visitor step into a waiting limousine.

"Da, da," nodded Gorbachev, obviously warmed by whatever news the visitor had offered. "But we must turn our attention to another matter now . . . we are scheduled to return to Moscow on September 10th, yes?"

"Da, Comrade Chairman," nodded Shishlin.

"Nyet, we have just changed our plans. We will return on Friday, September 8th and you will prepare for me a very important speech that I will deliver to the nation on Saturday, September 9th. It will be an open request to the people for support during these perilous times."

"But Comrade Chairman . . ."

"Tsk, tsk," nodded Gorbachev clucking his teeth like a school teacher mildly admonishing a student, "I know your thoughts. I will meet privately with Chebrikov, Ligachev, and their rabble before the speech. I will quell their dissent. I now have the chance to dispel their power once and for all." Gorbachev took the typed pages from the speech writer and casually motioned him away. "Compliments of Dyadya Petya," he mumbled as a triumphant afterthought, unaware that Shishlin had heard him.

The speech writer walked back towards the Dacha. Nikolai Shishlin had been around Moscow politics long enough to know that 'Dyadya Petya' was the official pseudonym for Army General Petr Ivanovich Ivashutin, Deputy Chief of the General Staff of the Soviet Armed Forces. Head of the entire GRU.

JAY SAT ON the veranda, aimlessly looking out at the rolling green hills and olive groves that swept through the valley below. It was a beautiful view; serene; the late afternoon sun mischievously darting between tree branches as it fought to remain aloft, bouncing its last orange streamers toward the ocean in the final minutes before sunset.

Jaycott sipped at a glass of wine, the beverage provided by the house servant when asked for something cold to drink. He was foggy, but not so disoriented as to miss the serious demeanor of their staff—a gardener who didn't garden, a house servant who barely served. They carried weapons and they roamed the grounds, but scant attention was paid to functions other than the safety of Jay and Katerina.

It had been a jumbled itinerary that took them from Kat's rescue in the middle of the Casbah, to this European villa. Jay had drifted between fits of weariness, sleep, and glassy-eyed alertness. Ninety minutes of bouncing in the back of the Mercedes truck, alternately cradling a despondent Katerina and a dead Theodori, gave way to a two hour flight aboard a Porter. The high performance, single-engine, STOL aircraft crossed a wide expanse of the Mediterranean only to land before dawn on a remote airstrip cut along a mountain ridge. Dazed and listless, Jay and Katerina were piled into the back of a large Peugeot and driven to this secluded villa where they were bathed, fed, and secured in separate bedrooms. Each succumbed to hours of fitful sleep.

A set of French doors to Jay's rear opened, and Katerina stepped onto the veranda dressed in a simple, cotton negligee. Quietly, she slid into the iron chair beside Jay, and without asking, helped herself to his glass of wine. It was at once a familiar, if not intimate gesture. Then she kicked off her slippers, and curled both knees up under her chin, stretching the nightgown down to her ankles.

They sat in silence for several minutes, as Kat followed Jaycott's gaze out towards the scene below. So much had transpired in the past few hours, days, and weeks, that they both seemed to relish the solitude. The strange intimacy that first developed back on Corfu now resurfaced, and Jay knew that the shared tragedy of Theo's death would forever remain a special bond between them, regardless of whatever else might or might not transpire in their lives. Words somehow seemed inadequate, and they each dealt with the burly Greek's loss privately, yet together, comforted in the knowledge that although the emotions they felt towards Theodori were different, they were equally deep.

Finally, still gazing off at the sunset, Katerina sighed quietly and spoke. "Where are we?"

"I'm not sure," admitted Jay, "but I think Corsica."

"Corsica?"

He nodded absently. "I saw a road sign last night on the drive here." It said Calvi, eight kilometers. If I'm not mistaken, Calvi is on the island of Corsica."

Katerina folded her arms around her legs and propped her chin atop her knees. She seemed to shiver, which surprised Jay, because the early evening air was quite warm.

"That would be appropriate. Wasn't Theodori stationed on Corsica when he was with the Foreign Legion?"

Jay's eyebrows raised in surprise and he looked over at Katerina. The coincidence had never occurred to him.

"You know," nodded Jay slowly, "you're right. He would have been here when he was with the Second Rep."

Kat spoke in a resigned, unfazed manner. "Theo always said that life was a series of interconnecting circles. The patterns never change, just the size of the circle."

Jay mused silently, a bit intrigued by his old friend's philosophy. Katerina looked over at Jay, and for the first time, their eyes met. Her face was drawn and her complexion pale. The ordeal had clearly taken a toll, but despite Kat's fatigue, a radiance surfaced. More importantly, the thick wall of reserve crumbled, permitting a hidden vulnerability to creep forward. Katerina's features—for all their natural beauty— softened, and the affect was strangely overpowering. Her pain tugged at Jay's heart, and when compounded by his own feelings of loss, Jaycott found himself unable to hold her gaze. Jay looked away. "What will you do?"

"I will go back to Corfu and settle Theo's affairs." She paused, "And you? Will you continue this assignment with a new partner?"

Jay shook his head. "No, it's over. I'm done."

She frowned. "Well, I hope you found whatever it was you were looking for."

"I'm afraid I didn't," sighed Jay, "and unfortunately the price we paid was very high."

They lapsed into silence for a moment before Jay spoke again. "Will you bury him on Corfu?"

"No, Theo's wish was to be cremated. He wanted his ashes spread along the Ionian Sea."

"If you don't mind, I'd like to be there."

"Of course," nodded Katerina, "Theo would want that."

Jay paused again, wrestling with his thoughts. "If there's anything you need . . . I mean, I promised Theo that I would take care of you."

Katerina studied Jay for a few seconds. "You promised, or he made you promise?"

"Well . . . does it really matter," shrugged Jay.

She smiled self-consciously, mumbling to herself. "He knew; with people, Theo was always so wise."

Jay's eyes squinted. "Knew what?"

Kat just shook her head. "Thank you Jaycott, you are a true friend to Theodori; but I am quite capable. I release you from your obligation."

The look of dejection on Jay's face told the story. He paused, momentarily fixing her eyes. "Well what if I offered my help—not out of obligation to Theo, but out of personal desire. Would that make a difference?"

Kat's face seemed to brighten for a brief instance. Then she stood, slipping her feet back into the borrowed slippers, and walked behind Jay's chair.

As Jaycott turned to face Katerina, she bent over and hugged him from behind, wrapping her arms around his shoulders in a way that pinned him to the chair, and didn't allow Jay to face her and return the embrace. Kat nestled her face deep in the crook of his neck and kissed him lightly.

"Yes Jaycott, it would make a difference. But be patient with me, it will take some time . . ."

Jay started to speak, but Kat placed her fingers over Jay's lips. "Shhh . . . we all knew, all three of us, but none of us ever mentioned it. That is friendship Jaycott. That is loyalty."

Katerina straightened and with a light touch on the back of Jay's head, walked into her bedroom and closed the French doors.

ROCHELLE LISTACH CAREFULLY set down the Intelligence Brief on her coffee table and leaned back. She permitted herself a smile. At her fingertips was the initial analysis of the reams of raw information that Jaycott had stolen from the operations center in the Algerian old Quarter. That two minutes of madness in the middle of a rescue operation had produced a gold mine of data, and the good-old-boy Ivy Leaguers had Rochelle to thank. She made the tough calls that produced results; they and their countrymen owed her for the win. Listach's lips curled smugly.

Over the next several months, the desk jockeys from the Directorate of Intelligence would pour over the pile of information collected by Jaycott; but the key—once again confirmed to the elderly Operations Officer—was that hard assets on the ground, humans, were still the single best source of obtaining secrets. Her probe team, Jaycott and Theodori, controlled by a Case Officer outperformed all the satellites, fancy airplanes, and expensive eavesdropping equipment that the United States could foster.

Rochelle scribbled out in long hand a short message for Tom Fairchild. He would be elated that Jaycott's haul had helped to identify the Target. It would ease her Case Officer's conscience. She stood and moved towards the desk.

"Benjamin," said Rochelle in a deliberate tone into the intercom.

"Yes ma'm?"

"Please call Langley and have them dispatch a courier. I'll have an encrypted message to be transmitted to the Rome station immediately.

"Very good, ma'm."

Listach sat at her desk and pulled a "one time" Encryption Pad from her top drawer. Then, savoring the moment, she began to write.

JAYCOTT SAT IN the study, idly nursing a Scotch on the rocks, casually snapping playing cards from a deck and then flipping them face-up on a pile atop the desk. The door to the study slid open and Tom Fairchild entered the room. Without raising his head, Jay's eyes shifted. Then he flipped another card onto the pile.

"Where have you been?"

"Around," nodded the Case Officer. He reached over and sniffed at Jaycott's drink. "High test; that's unlike you."

"Things change . . ."

Fairchild sat and lighted a cigarette. "That they do Jay . . . I'm sorry about the Greek."

Jaycott looked at his Case Officer, then carefully set the playing cards down. "Theodori. His name was Theodori."

Fairchild hesitated, analyzing Jay's mood, then exhaled a long stream of smoke. "Yes, I'm sorry . . . Theodori . . ." he leaned forward, a sincere expression on his face and whispered, ". . . I *am* sorry."

Jay took a long pull on his Scotch. "Well, thank you for that . . ." He studied Fairchild in silence before continuing "where are we?"

"A safehouse, about six clicks outside of Calvi, the island of Corsica . . . how's the woman doing?"

Jay shifted his head from side to side as if to say 'so-so'.

"I know they were pretty hard on her," acknowledged Fairchild, "the Doc said she'll be okay—at least physically . . ." He grimaced as an afterthought.

"She's pretty tough," mumbled Jay, "it takes time . . . she'll be going back to Corfu to settle Theo's affairs . . . I'll be going with her."

"Oh?" Fairchild's eyebrows raised as he took another long drag on the cigarette.

Jaycott shrugged, refusing to offer further explanation.

"Are you sure you want to do that?" pressed Fairchild.

Jay fixed the Case Officer with a perturbed look. "Why would you care?"

"Because," smiled Fairchild smugly, "we owe you a look at an After Action Report."

"What?" Jay's face lighted in surprise. "What are you talking about?"

"Colón. The Intelligence Officer leaned forward and stubbed out his cigarette. "That *was* the deal wasn't it?"

Jaycott's eyes squinted as his face tightened. Fairchild lowered his voice into a conspiratorial whisper, quite enjoying the drama of the moment. "You asked where I was Jay . . . well after I dropped you off here, I immediately beat feet to the Rome station to process that satchel full of goodies you lifted from the Ops Center in Algiers."

"And?"

"And," smiled Fairchild, "it was an early Christmas."

Jay leaned back in his chair. "The target?"

"And more—incredible stuff! Langley's been pouring over the material like a dog in heat—of course, we'll have to share some of the product with Tel Aviv, and naturally the Brits will get a good chunk . . ."

"So where is it," asked Jay incredulously, a bit impatient at Fairchild's rambling.

"Where's what?"

"The *TARGET*," blurted Jay sitting forward again, "20-8-15-20-13 . . ."

"Oh," smirked the Case Officer standing, "they used a numeric-alphabetical sequence, but it was symbolic. A great choice actually, given their desire to strike at the very essence of America . . ."

"Tom . . ."

"T, H, O, T, M, " blurted Fairchild finally, as if it was the most obvious clue in the world, "is *The House of The Mouse*."

XXI

26 August 1989
Orlando, Florida

Disney World.

Viktor Papaha walked down Main Street, USA and laughed. Nothing in twenty-three years of military training had prepared the Colonel for the Magic Kingdom. He stopped every few feet and momentarily drank in the atmosphere of the colorful theme park. Papaha was amazed, dumbfounded, stupefied and delighted—all at the same time. But most of all he was awed. Viktor knew that if somehow he tried to describe this scene to the average Soviet citizen, they would scoff. Russians had no point of reference to such a place. Walt Disney World was unique; and to think that he, a hardened professional soldier who traveled the world and experienced much, would be captivated by this picture of America—it was unnerving.

In the four weeks since the Spetsnaz Officer had illegally crossed from Canada to the United States in Syracuse, Viktor had gradually immersed himself in the rhythm of America. At first, the transition was marked by a pronounced defensiveness. He continued to make excuses to himself as to why hotel rooms were abundant, gas was inexpensive, and the supermarket shelves burst with fresh meats, milk, and vegetables. Papaha had read much about life in the United States, but having never traveled to America, Viktor was totally unprepared for the truth. For several reasons, his route had been a long and winding journey from upstate New York to Florida—but no amount of Communist Party indoctrination could prepare the Spetsnaz Colonel for the obvious abundance of everyday amenities in America. The Capitalists *did* enjoy a better life, and to that end, it made Viktor question the deep ideological rift that separated the two Superpowers.

But Disney World iced his dismay. This was a special place; a place that every child should see, a place that every parent should feel. It was an illusion that transcended the physical barriers of age, language, and culture—but most of all it eclipsed ideology. Disney World was a beckoning mistress that pulled her guests through enchanting portals with the promise of happiness; wrapping their worries in a long shoulder length shawl of contentment, forcing them to abandon their cares at the door.

Papaha stopped outside the Penny Arcade and surveyed the crowd. This was peak season. Parents smiled, and children sparkled. Eyes were aglow at the moving kaleidoscope of costumed employees; balloons, ice cream, cotton candy; a strange life-sized duck with a long yellow bill and expressive eyes; a quartet of straw hat wearing men in bright bowties harmonizing a song; cameras everywhere.

Viktor sat at a park bench on the sidewalk. He unfolded the complimentary Magic Kingdom guide map and spread it on his lap. A mother pushing a baby stroller eased by, her child clutching at a strange stuffed animal that resembled a mouse. The scent of fresh flowers, shrubbery, and trees wafted through the air.

In seconds, the Colonel located the Hall of the Presidents. It was situated in the section of the theme park known as Liberty Square. Viktor calculated an azimuth up Main Street towards Cinderella's Castle, and then a left turn at about a 300 degree angle. A short walk, a pleasant walk. In typically methodical fashion, Papaha had started his target site reconnaissance several days earlier with a survey of the perimeter. Highways, parking lots, modes of transportation— all were compared to every known map of the Orlando area. Now, finally inside the theme park, Viktor knew that he would need several more days of walking, time to cover every piece of ground in the Magic Kingdom. Civilian targets made for an easy strike, but the professional in him would leave nothing to chance.

The Spetsnaz Officer refolded his guide map and repacked it in his nylon shoulder bag. The latter resembled the backpack that the 'mules' would use to transport the explosives. He stood and lighted a Marlboro cigarette. For a moment, Papaha turned melancholy. Viktor realized that when this assignment was complete, no one would ever experience the wonders of Disney World in quite the same way again.

~~~

A NERVOUS ENERGY crackled through the air. Room number forty in the old Executive Office Building hummed with a vibrant expectation. Tom Laughlin, the defacto Chairman of the Forty Committee had called a special session. Several weeks earlier, as the impending date with destiny drew near, the Committee had begun meeting every third day—until now. Suddenly and without notice, they had been assembled.

Tom paused, savoring the moment. He took an extra minute to glance around the large rectangular conference table, individually exchanging a glance with each member of the Committee. Tom had earned this brief respite, and in a world of secrets, the moments came seldom enough.

"Thank you all for coming on such short notice."

Then Tom looked straight across the long conference table to his fellow CIA employee, John Mullins. "John?"

The Deputy Director (Operations) inhaled on his cigarette, melodramatically stalling to increase the drama that Laughlin had begun. Several furtive glances shot back and forth between the two men seated at opposite ends of the table. "We have determined the target site," began the legendary spy master. He nodded evenly as several committee members sat forward in their seats. "And to use the vernacular code numbers of this case: 20-8-15-20-13 . . . also known as T, H, O, T, M, is a symbolic code to identify the target—which we correctly deduced as being in Florida . . ."

Mullins took another long drag on the cigarette and exhaled a thick stream of smoke. ". . . T, H, O, T, M stands for The House Of The Mouse."

Silence ensued, even puzzlement as five seconds elapsed, and then the first dawn of realizations crossed several faces. George of the Secret Service spoke first. "Oh my God . . ."

Paul of Customs, just shook his head, muttering despondently, but it was Russell of the FBI who blurted the one word aloud that had entered the collective thoughts of several committee members simultaneously. "Disney World."

The Rear Admiral from the Joint Chiefs slid his chair back from the conference table and abruptly stood. His face was a contorted web of frustration. "Cowards . . . the fucking cowards . . ."

The next thirty seconds produced a blur of activity as each man digested the significance of the target and all of its ramifications. Finally, Tom Laughlin raised a steady hand skyward and signaled. The commotion ceased.

"I think we will all agree," said the Deputy Director (Intelligence) "that their choice of a target is . . . well . . . perfect."

"Any possibility this could be a misdirection?", asked Rudy of the DIA.

"No," answered Laughlin, "my people analyzed all the raw data—and there's a bunch of it; codes, files, photographs, maps, computer printouts . . . we've broken a major operational cell of the Palestinian Islamic Jihad."

"How," interrupted Bob of the State Department, "did you physically lay your hands on that much Product?"

Laughlin looked at Mullins, and the eyes of the other committee members shifted again to the other end of the conference table.

"You don't want to know," said the DDO, "I'll take the responsibility." The allusion to the Congressional Oversight Committee caused several of the members to grumble. "Suffice to say, we used every means at our disposal—some practical, some expensive, and some even *un*orthodox."

Several faces lighted in acknowledgement.

"John," said Russell again, "does this success have anything to do with that *Probe* of yours?"

Mullins exchanged a long, pensive gaze with Tom Laughlin at the other end of the table before exhaling a long stream of smoke. Then he stubbed out his cigarette. The motion exhibited a distinct air of finality. Laughlin answered the question for Mullins.

"Gentlemen, we have a great deal to do, and precious little time. Can we move on?"

ANNA LYALIN STEPPED from the red double-decker bus at EPCOT Center and checked her watch. She jotted the time in a small notebook. Then she took a picture of the boat dock adjacent to the German Pavilion at the World Showcase Lagoon.

The former Olympic athlete had studied every aspect of the Walt Disney World theme park for the past ten days;

she knew the employee entrances, transportation route, support services, park attractions, and performance schedules.

Anna started walking at an unhurried pace towards the Italian Pavilion. Everything about this assignment confused her; there were cross currents of good and bad, hot and cold, black and white. From the beginning, Anna's unique position as a Spetsnaz trained GRU officer attached to the Soviet Swim & Dive Team gave her a unique perspective—she had travelled the world, and never had she been tasked to support a strike against a 'soft' target. Certainly nothing as nonthreatening as Disney World. Yet as an experienced Intelligence Officer, Anna knew that her involvement was but a very small portion of a very large picture. Thus, despite whatever philosophical misgivings Lyalin had, she knew that ultimately the professional in her would rule. Anna would do her job, reliable to the last.

She paced to the right and paused to snap a photograph of a gondola moored in the lagoon. The life size reproduction of the Venetian canal vessel rested across from the Italian Pavilion, a long anchor line tied to the brightly colored, red-striped barbershop pole jutting up from the water. Anna noticed several men admire her shapely figure, which even in her loosely fitted shorts and blouse, was difficult to hide. Lyalin knew that her greatest asset was also her greatest liability. Blonde, trim, and healthy good looks helped to seduce men, but it also drew unwanted attention. Especially now, when a proper reconnaissance demanded multiple visits to the target site. Anna knew all the tricks, and altered her appearance and clothing continuously, however, there was always the risk of being remembered, and the need to do her work alone increased the odds of exposure.

Lyalin turned to her left and started walking towards the *American Adventure*. Situated at the southernmost point of the man-made lagoon, the American Pavilion served as the host nation hub to the world showcase section of the EPCOT Theme Park.

The former bronze medalist stopped for a moment outside Liberty Inn, the large restaurant on the eastern side of the American Pavilion. She watched a small crowd of tourists walk through the triple glass colonial-style front doors of the main entrance to the rotunda; small children, mothers, grandparents. The next performance would start in four minutes, twenty seconds. Anna knew—she had sat through fourteen presentations of the show; each time changing her seat in the large auditorium, timing the different sequences, memorizing the movements of the staff. The folks at Disney were nothing if they weren't efficient and reliable.

Slowly, lazily, Lyalin waltzed past the main doors to the *American Adventure* and circled out towards the *Theatre by the Shore*, a covered amphitheatre directly in front of the Pavilion at the edge of the Showcase Lagoon. She pulled out her complimentary EPCOT Center Guidemap and as unobtrusively as possible studied the brochure for the fiftieth time.

CHIEF OF STAFF John Sununu opened one of the double wooden doors that led to the Oval Office and scanned the reception area. He recognized the distinguished looking Director of Central Intelligence sitting patiently next to a silent Secret Service Agent.

"Come in Judge," nodded Sununu, motioning towards William Webster. The Senior Intelligence Officer of the United States stood and followed the former University Professor into the inner sanctum of the White House. President George Bush finished signing some documents and looked up. "Bill . . ."

"Mister President," nodded Webster as Bush stood and circled the huge desk filled with pictures of his extended family. "Thank you for seeing me on such short notice."

"Of course."

They shook hands as the President guided Webster to the small sitting area to the right. Always a gracious man, George Bush settled his tall, lean frame into the closest wing chair and waited until Webster and Sununu settled themselves onto the couch and the other wing chair respectively.

"Some coffee Bill?"

"No sir, thank you . . . I know you wanted to be kept abreast of our progress on the Islamist strike."

"Yes."

"We'll we've identified the target."

Bush paused, momentarily looking across the coffee table at his Chief of Staff before focusing on William Webster. His wire rimmed eyeglasses reflected the light in an odd way, somehow increasing the intensity in his expression. The President nodded.

"It's Disney World, sir."

The obvious surprise in George Bush's face was matched only by the Chief of Staff's expression.

"Judge," asked Sununu, "are you quite sure?"

"Yes," nodded William Webster turning to face the Chief of Staff, "the information is well corroborated . . . we are quite sure."

With all the potential targets considered and analyzed by the experts, the thought of a terrorist attack against Disney World seemed incomprehensible. George Bush remained silent for a few seconds before speaking.

"Bill, are we doing everything possible to prevent this?"

"Yes sir, and I might add, the interagency cooperation has been excellent."

"How soon?" pressed Bush.

Webster shifted uncomfortably on the couch. "A matter of days, Mister President."

George Bush nodded and stood, extending his hand toward the Director of Central Intelligence, while addressing his Chief of Staff. "Anything he needs John . . . anything."

"Yes Mister President," acknowledged Sununu standing on cue as George Bush shook Webster's hand.

"I suppose," continued Bush rising to the full height of his six foot, two inch frame, "that from their perspective, it makes perfect sense."

"Yes Mister President," nodded Webster.

"We're counting on you Bill, this one could change us forever."

"Yes sir."

George Bush turned and walked back towards the huge refurbished Presidential desk, first introduced to the Oval Office by JFK. He looked out the large colonial window towards the Rose Garden, as the Chief of Staff escorted William Webster from the room. One of the two Secret Service Agents standing in the reception area, pulled the door closed behind the DCI.

"John," asked Bush when they were alone again, still looking out the window, "do you know how many grandchildren I have?"

The Chief of Staff paused in the middle of the room, considering the questions before answering. "Not precisely, Mister President."

Bush turned and sat back down at the desk, his poignant question hanging in the air. Then he picked up a document and mumbled two words—more to himself than to his Chief of Staff: "Disney World."

XXII

DEEP IN A remote corner of the U. S. military
reservation at Fort Bragg, is a large hidden compound known
as Range 19. Two fences, topped with barbed wire and
electronic sensors, surround the nearly six miles of restricted
grounds, adding security to the tall man-made grass berms,
pine trees, and thick red clay indigenous to the area. Since
1987, this facility has been the home of the 1st Special Forces
Operations Detachment—Delta (SFOD-D), more commonly
known as Delta Force.

The facility at Range 19 is quite self-sufficient and
very unique. It contains a cafeteria, an isolation center with
sleeping quarters, a sauna, an Olympic-sized pool, one
basketball and three racquetball courts, a gymnasium, a
nautilus weight room, and several lounges for socializing. But
the key to the $75 million construction cost of the facility, is
its use as the ultimate counter terrorism training complex.
When it comes to high tech combat, Range 19 has it all. The
specialized equipment includes a live fire "house of horrors"
with computerized targets and moving robots, three-

dimensional holograms of terrorists, voice activated posters, a forty-foot climbing wall, a ceiling suspended midsection of a hijacked jetliner, trick elevator shafts, and more video equipment than the boardroom of IBM.

In addition, a series of smaller, equally specialized sites are spread out about the Range 19 compound; Alpha for demolitions and explosives, Bravo for long distance sniper practice, Charlie for short range room clearing techniques, Delta for pistol, shotgun, and submachine gun training, and Echo for engaging moving vehicular targets. There are also jungle lanes for patrolling in thick foliage, and a 'skid pad' to practice evasive driving.

The fact that the Pentagon denies the existence of Delta Force is a bit of necessary subterfuge. Any acknowledgement would only spur more questions. Thus, the actual organization of Delta becomes even more oblique.

At the heart of the unit is the Operators or 'Shooters' as they are called. Each is a volunteer, career Army, and multitalented. Most are drawn from the elite Special Forces (Green Berets) Groups and Ranger Battalions. The selection and assessment process is both long and challenging—from a physical as well as mental capacity.

The Operators are placed into four or six man teams, which are then assigned with three or four other teams to a Troop. Three or four Troops make up a Squadron of about seventy-five Shooters. Three Squadrons are designated for Assault. The flexibility afforded this arrangement allows Delta to be focused according to the needs of each mission, and since the face of terrorism has many appearances, the unit can configure her Operators to best suit the situation.

The array of capabilities and specialized education the Operators demonstrate spans the full spectrum of modern warfare, from the esoteric to the practical; military free fall parachuting, assault and rescue training, advanced climbing techniques, body guard instruction, clandestine tradecraft, lock picking. They are by nature quiet, married men who socialize together, adopting the low profile persona that their relaxed grooming standards allow. But most of all the Operators of Delta are professionals, a clannish collection of free spirits bound by an unspoken bond of patriotism and performance. No man can fail to deliver at the point of action, no one can let down the team; and because of this, the men of Delta train—and they train, and train, and train . . .

"Hey Rosco . . ."

Sergeant First Class John Rosconovitch ignored the tall, broad shouldered man with long hair who stood six paces to the rear. The senior NCO continued to peer through the Leupold Ultra M3 ten-power sniper scope. Slowly, without breathing, he squeezed the trigger on the Remington bolt action rifle until the actual discharge of the weapon surprised him. His teammate, Paul O'Malley, also a SFC, lay next to Rosconovitch peering through a spotter scope. He called out the accuracy of the shot.

"High and right."

Both men, dressed in jeans and t-shirts, turned from their positions as Rosconovitch addressed the man to their rear.

"Yeah Boss?"

"Does your beeper work?"

Sheepishly, Rosconovitch stood brushing sand off his jeans and approached the tall man who stood sweat drenched in gym shorts and running shoes.

"Yeah Boss," he admitted, looking down at the alert beeper clipped to his belt, "but I couldn't let it break my concentration."

"Ten mikes is a lot of concentration," frowned the Troop Commander, consulting his wristwatch.

"High right," wisecracked O'Malley to Rosconovitch, needling his teammate over the less than perfect shot. "Must be the weapon, huh?"

"Eat shit," mumbled Rosconovitch to O'Malley handing him the rifle.

"Let's shake a leg," said the Major calmly, "we're *on . . .*"

Both NCO's eyes lighted as the Troop Commander turned, ". . . and find Jensen, he obviously doesn't answer his fucking beeper either."

"He's probably on Alpha Boss," offered O'Malley.

"Whatever, find him, Squad Room, five mikes."

O'Malley winked at Rosconovitch and they started to disassemble the M24 sniper system.

THE GLOW IN Jaycott's eyes expressed more than words ever would. Through all the years and despite all the training, Jay could only muster enough passive expression to cloak the rest of his face. But his eyes burned like two red embers plucked from a smoldering fire. He strode through the front door of the bustling M Street bar, his head shifting sideways to survey the crowd. There, positioned in a far corner, nursing a drink and smoking a cigarette, sat Tom Fairchild.

Jaycott turned and made a beeline for his Case Officer. Like the Red Sea and Moses, the cluster of social drinkers instinctively parted, swaying from the path of the very intense Contract Agent. At the table Jay leaned forward, prepared to sit just as Fairchild looked up and raised a tumbler glass to his lips. Suddenly Jay's right arm snapped from his hip, and in one quick, short, chop he punched Fairchild square in the mouth. The Case Officer tumbled backwards, his drink glass crashing to the table.

The sound of shattering glass and spewing ice cubes pierced the din of the crowd, and a sudden hush fell over the room. Fairchild sat stunned, a nervous twitch in his eyes as he tried to focus on Jaycott. He watched as the dangerous agent spun an empty chair around and sat inverted, calmly resting his elbows across the back of the chair.

"That's so you know I'm in no mood to play fuck around," started Jay quietly. There was an extra edge of intensity in his voice. "Who is R. Listach?"

Five seconds elapsed as Tom Fairchild slowly removed a handkerchief and dabbed at the trickle of blood that rolled down his chin. The calmness seemed to settle the other bar patrons, and within a moment they had turned their eyes away from the two men in the corner and re-engaged their interrupted conversations.

"An Operations Officer in PM Branch," acknowledged the Case Officer haltingly. He inspected his bloodied handkerchief.

"Where can I find him?" pressed Jay.

"Her."

"What?! What are you . . ."

"R stands for Rochelle. He is a She. Listach is a woman."

The revelation caught Jaycott by surprise. He leaned forward. "Your boss for the Colón Operation was a woman?"

"Is that so hard to accept?" blurted the Case Officer sarcastically. "After all, the Agency *is* an equal opportunity employer."

Jay sat in silence for a moment. He had come directly from the CIA's suburban headquarters in the Virginia countryside, having spent the last two hours studying the After Action Report from Central America that resulted in the sudden and unexplained compromise of a very deep cover Probe team. Jaycott and his associates had been tracing and identifying the different couriers in a Panamanian drug-money laundering network. He now understood that the leak which exposed the identities of his Probe team, and also culminated in the reprisal murder of his wife Ellie, had been intentional.

"Ok," nodded Jay, "so where do I find her?"

"Why?"

"Why do you *think*?!" snarled the Agent.

"Well," said Fairchild in a matter-of-fact tone. He leaned forward, "That makes sense, you might as well cap the bitch, she's only about seventy years old."

"What?!" Jay jerked instinctively, "You're kidding . . ."

"Afraid not . . ." shrugged the Case Officer. Tom grabbed at a paper napkin and jotted down an address. ". . . knock yourself out, I really don't give two fucks anymore."

Jaycott hunched forward again. "Tip her off Tom, and I'll be back for you."

Fairchild rolled his handkerchief in a ball and stuffed it in his pocket. "Of that I have no doubt . . . your problem Jay, is you never could figure out who your friends were."

"Theo was my friend," acknowledged Jay poignantly, "that much I know."

Jaycott stood and walked from the bar.

QUIETLY, THE THREE men entered the large, private hotel suite located at the northern edge of Interstate Route #4 in downtown Orlando. The hotel was specially selected for its close proximity to the airport, and also its discreet distance from the Walt Disney World complex. No one from their company knew they were here. The three had flown in commercially from the Burbank, California headquarters under complete anonymity.

The first man through the door was the Chairman and Chief Executive Officer. He was tall and confident, but the boyish grin that usually lighted his youthful face was absent, a somber tone in keeping with the gravity of the meeting. The CEO was the dreamer; the manchild; as comfortable in a pinstriped business suit as he was in a cast member costume. He, more than anyone else, typified the prodding, tweaking, excited wonder of Walt the founding visionary. His enchantment was infectious.

"Hello Mike," nodded Tom Laughlin, of the CIA, "thanks for coming." He steered the CEO into the hotel suite as they shook hands. Then he passed the CEO towards Russell Porter of the FBI.

The second man through the door was the President and Chief Operating Officer. He was ten years older than the CEO, but had the lean, athletic build of a runner. Pragmatic and well-educated, smart as a whip yet possessed of great humility, the President was the consummate team player who shared a unique interchangeable relationship with the CEO. Together, they were the duo appropriately credited with the impressive revival of one of the world's great consumer franchises. Arriving together in October 1984, the two had taken a moribund, stale company from the doldrums of despair to new heights of energy, enthusiasm, and financial success. In five short years they had tripled the revenues, quadrupled profits, and enriched their shareholders by increasing the market value of the stock tenfold.

"Hello Frank," offered Laughlin, continuing his greetings as he shuttled the executives into the hotel suite.

The third man was the Vice Chairman; quiet, mustached, unassuming. As the nephew and son of the two founding brothers, Walt and Roy, he was the direct link to the dream—and one of the driving forces in bringing the first two men together as CEO and President.

On seeing the Vice Chairman, Laughlin paused. The family resemblance was unmistakable. Tom patted the Vice Chairman on the back while shaking his hand and closed the hotel door.

Russell motioned to a side table of coffee, soft drinks, and fruit. "Please help yourselves." A minute later, the five men were seated comfortably around a coffee table.

"At the onset," started Laughlin, "let me thank you for meeting us on such short notice, and under such mysterious circumstances. In short order, you'll understand—and I hope—appreciate our sense of discretion on this."

The three executives quietly nodded.

"Was the use of Judge Rybech as a medium to pass the message appropriate?"

"Yes," nodded the President, adjusting his square-rimmed glasses, "he was an old Stanford Law School classmate. A trusted friend."

"Good," nodded Laughlin satisfied.

Then, both federal employees, as if on cue, pulled their identification from suitcoat pockets and lay them open on the coffee table.

"I'm Tom Laughlin, a Deputy Director for the Central Intelligence Agency in Washington, D.C.—a career Intelligence Officer."

"And I'm Russell Porter, a Deputy Director for the Federal Bureau of Investigation in Washington, D.C., a career Law Enforcement Officer."

They paused, allowing the three Disney executives to inspect the official identification. The company President, looked curiously from Laughlin to Porter, then back at the identification.

"Sort of an odd couple, aren't you?"

"That we are," nodded Laughlin. "It's rare that our jurisdictions overlap. I suppose it should suggest the severity of the situation."

Finally, the CEO sat forward. "Gentlemen, please cut to the chase."

Laughlin nodded, and spoke in a very clear, concise voice. "We have reason to believe that there will be a terrorist attack at one of your properties.

Dead silence.

Laughlin allowed a few seconds, permitting the impact of his statement to sink in. The only discernable movement was that the CEO blinked. The President removed his eyeglasses, and set them on the coffee table. The Vice Chairman seemed to stop breathing.

"How reliable is this information?" asked the CEO.

"Very," answered Russell. "We can't share sources and methods Mike, but we're convinced of the accuracy."

"You *must* address it," added Laughlin.

"Where?" asked the President.

"Here in Florida."

"When?"

"Our best estimates are less than two weeks."

Laughlin looked to his right to see the Vice Chairman stare quietly at the two federal employees. His complexion had blanched a ghostly white, as if someone had aimed a loaded weapon at his family. And in essence, someone had.

The CEO appeared calm, but one could see the sharp mind racing behind the passive eyes. He stood and removed his suitcoat, rolled up his sleeves, and poured himself a cup of coffee. With his back to the others, he spoke to the President.

"Frank, can you give them an idea of the complexity of our holdings."

The President cleared his throat and began reciting facts from memory. "We are finishing our 1989 fiscal year shortly, and we will break four and a half billion dollars in revenues. Our ROE, return on equity, is 25%—outstanding by any financial yardstick. We currently have five theme parks in operation, our flagship Disneyland in Anaheim, California, Tokyo Disneyland in Japan, and three theme parks right here at the Walt Disney World complex—the Magic Kingdom, Epcot Center, and the just opened Disney-MGM Studio. Add to that the hotels, restaurants, transportation systems . . ." the President paused to catch his breath, ". . . we own nearly 30,000 acres of land right here in Florida alone—that's larger than the entire burrough of Manhattan—and this is peak season, filled day and night with guests and employees . . ."

The Vice Chairman finally spoke, interrupting the President, the incredulity in his voice palpable. "I am having a very difficult time accepting that someone—anyone—would actually target us. Why?!"

"Politics," answered Laughlin.

"Politics!? We're *not* political. My God, Walt Disney is for families."

He nervously stroked his moustache, trying in a sane man's way to comprehend the irrational.

"Precisely," nodded Russell quietly. "Which is why it will accomplish their political agenda." The FBI man stood and poured himself a mineral water. "What you must understand about terrorists Roy, is that they often times attack 'soft' targets because of both the ease in the strike, and because it will stun the world with outrage. Everyone will be talking about the group that was responsible. It will give them what they desire most: visibility and credibility—ostensibly for their cause, whatever it is."

The Vice Chairman silently shook his head. He backed away from the table and walked to the window, deep in thought.

The President continued ". . . we have, in essence, our own government, chartered by the state of Florida. It's called the Reedy Creek Improvement District. It was cut out from portions of Orange and Osceola counties. We own and operate our own Power Company, Water Treatment Facility, Highway Contractors, Fire Department, Tree Farm, Food Service Division, Transportation Company, Laundromat, Security Service, Sewage Disposal Plant, and fifty-four miles of waterways and canals. Needless to say, when Walt and Roy Senior started buying up land here in central Florida twenty-five years ago, there wasn't much by way of infrastructure. We had to be self-sufficient—and we are."

"The obvious question," interjected the CEO carrying on the thought process, "considering our extensive exposure, where specifically will these terrorists attack?" He sat down again at the coffee table, cup and saucer in hand.

"We're not sure," answered Laughlin honestly, "but we suspect that they will target one of the theme parks for maximum propaganda value. We have specialists who will take a very hard look at all of your properties to best determine the most likely site."

The Company President fingered his eyeglasses and for the first time exhibited a tightening of his lean face. He exchanged a knowing glance with the CEO. The youthful looking Chairman scratched his chin before speaking. "At this time of year, we are talking a combined average daily attendance of over 120,000 guests between the three gates here at the complex. Add to that cast members, facility employees, auxiliary workers . . ."

"Who would do this?!" blurted the Vice Chairman still standing at the window.

"We think it's an Islamist Group," answered Porter quietly. "Middle East in origin, probably supported by a host nation."

"You see," added Laughlin, "Walt Disney is synonymous with all that is good, wholesome, and inspirational in America. From their perspective—which I agree is warped by our standards—Disney is the perfect 'soft' target."

"Sick," mumbled the Vice Chairman returning to the coffee table.

There was another lull in the conversation before the President spoke. "We will assist you in any way that we can. You're the experts . . . how long should we close the parks for?"

Laughlin and Porter both grimaced before the FBI man shook his head. "Quite the contrary Frank, you *can't* close the parks."

"What?!' chimed the three surprised executives in unison.

The CEO leaned forward. "Please explain."

"You can't close the theme parks," repeated Porter. "In fact, you can't change anything—at least not visibly. Our best chance of intercepting them and forestalling their success is to continue to operate under the status quo. We must *lull* them. To close the parks will tip our hand. It will warn them, and they will go underground—only to resurface at a later date when we are caught blind and unprepared. You *must* keep the parks open *and* operating as if everything is normal."

"But what about our guests, our employees?!" demanded the Company President.

"Everything stays the same," emphasized Laughlin, "you *must* trust us on this matter. We will have an entire task force down here, but you must do it our way."

"No," mumbled the CEO, "I can't take the risk . . ."

"The *children*," interjected the Vice Chairman, "My God man, think of what you're suggesting?!"

"I'm sorry," nodded Porter, "we insist." He thought for a moment, changing tactics. "When was the last time you closed the doors?"

"Of a theme park?" asked the President looking towards the Vice Chairman for confirmation. The younger Roy shook his head.

"Never," answered the CEO, "we've closed sections from time to time, certainly different attractions, but never a whole park. Occasionally a private group will have a special function for an evening or afternoon, but we've never closed an entire gate for any period of time to the public."

"That's precisely our point," whispered Laughlin as gently as he could." "You can't. If you succumb to the fear, then they win—and you will have allowed them to win on a mere threat. More importantly, they will only resurface and strike when we do not have our resources massed and in position. At that point you will most certainly have a catastrophe."

"We must prevent the occurrence *and* apprehend the guilty parties so as to send the message that they *cannot* succeed," added Porter. "They prey on weakness. We must prove larger than life, so as to dissuade all future occurrences."

"Remember," summarized Laughlin, "there has never been a successful, foreign inspired terrorist strike on U.S. soil. This is a first."

"I suppose we should feel lucky," snapped the Vice Chairman. He stroked his moustache in an agitated manner.

"In a perverse sort of way," acknowledged Laughlin. "When they chose 'Disney' they were making a statement. They are attacking a symbol that the world will recognize as quintessential American. It is a tribute to what your company stands for."

"It's a tribute from hell," mumbled the President, reaching forward to retrieve his eyeglasses.

"Gentlemen," said the CEO standing, "you will have our full cooperation. Tell us how to proceed."

"For now," answered Porter, "assemble the names of the handful of executives that absolutely *need* to know. Tell them nothing, but have them prepared to meet our advance team here in 24 hours. Also, we'll need to identify an off-site Command Center here in the Orlando area that can sustain a large group. Finally, tell *no one*—and I mean *no one*; not your wives, not your trusted secretaries, not your best friends. We have the advantage, let's not lose it."

The three executives nodded their agreement. The President and Vice Chairman also stood. Then the five men shook hands all around and started for the door.

Before leaving the hotel suite, the Vice Chairman paused and turned back towards Laughlin and Porter. He had a twinkle in his eye that was oddly reminiscent of his Uncle Walt. "You know, when I was growing up, and the success of 'Disney' as a company was evident, my uncle used to keep things in perspective by reminding everyone that it all began with a mouse. Let's not forget that 'Disney' is more than a name or a place. It represents a *special* kind of magic. Don't let these Islamists ruin the dream."

With a nod, he was gone.

JAYCOTT STOOD IN the shadows watching the old Georgian Revival. He knew from the beginning that if Rochelle Listach was a senior staffer for the Agency working the Paramilitary Branch, she would have protection. PM

Operations Officers were in a high risk category—and the
folks at Langley would protect those staffers if for no other
reason than to protect themselves. There was too much dirty
linen wrapped in the bed clothes of PM, and the potential
compromise of that information dictated the need for
precautions.

Jay shifted in the shrubbery as the innocuous blue
sedan pulled up to the side entrance of Rochelle's home.
Right on cue, two men in conservative suits stepped from the
car and paced to the door. Jaycott saw the upstairs curtains
part and a shadow peer from the window above. Then he
heard the wall mounted camera turn and the intercom buzz.
"Yes?"

It was the voice of Benjamin, Rochelle Listach's
manservant-bodyguard.

"John Duggan, Office of Security. We have an urgent
communiqué from Headquarters."

The explanation was accompanied by the two men
routinely holding official-looking identification up to the
camera. They did their best to look bored. Another buzz and
the French doors popped open. Quickly the first man stuck a
wooden wedge under the door and jammed the portal open.
The second man rushed past him into the foyer and shot the
dapper manservant with a dart gun. The powerful tranquilizer
struck Benjamin in the chest, and he fell backwards against a
small sidetable. Bursting from the shrubbery, Jaycott rushed
past the two impostors and leaped over Benjamin's prone
body.

He moved with a thoroughness, confident in his preparations and knowledge of the home. At the end of the hall, Jay burst through the library door and stopped short. Across the room on the divan behind the Queen Anne coffee table sat Rochelle Listach. From ten paces they stared at each other, and then very slowly Rochelle lowered her cup of tea.

The anger in Jaycott's eyes was unmistakable, and though he was surprised by the diminutive physique of the elderly lady, the cool, detached look in Rochelle's face confirmed his suspicions. She was an ice woman, a glacier.

"I've been expecting you," said Listach. She moved slowly, deliberately, making a point not to startle Jay into a defensive action. "Did you kill Benjamin?"

Her voice was steady, controlled; the question void of any sense of emotion.

"No," replied Jay, "moving slowly towards Listach, taking a wide arc around the outside of the library so as to observe everything in the room. He held a small automatic pistol at his side. "But I could have . . ."

"I know," Listach acknowledged the small Walther PPK resting calmly against Jaycott's thigh, "however, you are a professional, and Benjamin is not the focus of this exercise—I am."

Jaycott didn't respond, rather he circled to Listach's far side so that he observed her from every angle before settling over the old woman's right shoulder.

"I'm sorry about your friend, Theodori . . ."

Jay squinted hard at Listach. "He understood the risks."

The answer was Jay's way of dismissing the topic.

"Yes," continued Listach unperturbed, "and the woman, Katerina, how is she doing?"

Rochelle was deliberately letting Jaycott know the extent of her knowledge. She possessed first-hand information, which in a world of secrets and compartmentalization, could only mean that she was also involved in this most recent operation.

He paused for a moment, his mind racing, before changing the subject. "Tell me about Colón."

Listach had to swivel to her right in order to face Jaycott; for he had positioned himself to observe the entire room at a glance. The need to shift her torso towards Jaycott if she wished to confront him made the old woman squirm uncomfortably.

"You've read the After Action Report, what needs clarification?"

"The leak . . . why the intentional leak?" asked Jay.

It was a statement more than a question, and not one that encouraged denial. There was a long pause as the elderly Operations Officer considered all of the ramifications of her answer.

"There were bigger issues."

"Such as?"

"We are preparing an invasion of Panama," she said matter-of-factly. "The operation is codenamed: *Just Cause*, and it is—needless to say—highly classified. We expect to be in-country within six months. The focus of the invasion will be the Noriega government, and the entire infrastructure the drug cartels have provided . . ."

Listach studied Jaycott's face for a sign that the revelation surprised him. ". . . when we began the probe with your team in Central America, there were no plans for such an invasion. When the preliminary discussions for 'Just Cause' turned finite, we—I—made a decision. That decision was to offer the other side something plausible as a throw-off, to lull them, to encourage their friendship. We needed to win their trust."

"You sacrificed my team," clarified Jaycott.

"I made a tactical decision to protect the bigger operation."

"People died," responded Jaycott angrily.

"Yes," admitted Listach firmly, secure in her logic. " I made the hard decision to give up a few, to save the many."

"Good men . . ."

"And how many Soldiers, Sailors, and Marines will *live* when we enter Panama in a few months because Noriega's clan is sitting smugly in their piles of cocaine money thinking the CIA will protect them. 'Just Cause' will *be* the surprise invasion we need it to be, because they *trust* us."

She spoke the final phrase with a touch of assuredness.

"My *wife* is dead . . ." spat Jay finally broaching the subject.

"*Yes*," snarled Listach, exhibiting her first sign of emotion, "and that's *really* what this is all about, isn't it?"

Jaycott instinctively raised the pistol to hip level and aimed it at the old woman.

"She was an innocent," whispered Jay, "she *didn't* know the risks . . ."

Rochelle eyed the pistol objectively. "The Colombians are animals—obviously we didn't expect them to take things so far . . . your wife's death was . . . unfortunate."

"As will yours be," whispered Jaycott in a menacing tone. He closed the distance between them in one quick movement, and held the handgun next to Rochelle's forehead.

Listach remained absolutely still. She exhaled very slowly, her expression outwardly calm. "I have no doubt you could make this look like a suicide," she said quietly. "That would be convenient for the Agency. I'm sure many of the old boys would like to see me *permanently* retired."

"Maudlin doesn't suit you," suggested Jay, "you're much too cold-blooded."

His index finger tightened on the trigger.

"I prefer to think of myself as pragmatic," offered Listach, "which is why you have to kill me, or you'll never be out . . ."

"What?!"

The pistol now arched menacingly as Jay's wrist locked, and his elbow prepared for a recoil.

"You're too valuable Ishmael, if you don't kill me, I'll find a way to drag you back . . . this isn't about vengeance—this is about freedom—your freedom. l have too many resources, too many contacts, and the *will* to use them."

"I'm out!" grimaced Jaycott fervently. The muzzle of the pistol ground into the old woman's temple.

"No," whispered Rochelle in solemn disagreement, baiting Jay with a challenge. "I'm old, I've lived a life, it doesn't matter, pull the trigger . . ."

For ten seconds, Jaycott wrestled with the conflicting emotions of conscience, hate, love, anger, and desperation. For reasons in which he would never totally understand, Jay didn't squeeze the trigger the final ounce of pressure it would take to discharge the weapon and blow the diminutive woman's brains across her coffee table. At that time, in that room, in the heat of that moment, with all the disjointed passions of a lifetime, Jay didn't kill Rochelle Listach. He blinked, and the reaction was as if the elderly lady had called his bluff—and won.

Jaycott lowered the Walther PPK, and without saying a word, walked from the library.

XXIII

THE GRU REZIDENTURA sat in his office at the Soviet Embassy in Algiers. He encrypted the final paragraph of his long After Action Report and sealed it in a large manila envelope along with a dozen black and white photographs. Then the Rezidentura placed the envelope into a special canvas carrying bag. This would then be placed in the Diplomatic Pouch for overnight delivery to Moscow.

The incident at the Islamist Safehouse in the middle of the Casbah had been quite successful—beyond the Rezidentura's wildest hopes. The snatch team that recovered Theodori's woman, ransacked the Operations Center, and killed eleven terrorist cell members, had been brutally efficient. Now, days before the strike at T, H, O, T, M, the prospects for complete success were in motion.

The plan, contrived by Colonel General Aleksandr Grigorevich Pavlov, First Deputy Chief of the GRU, was brilliant, and it demonstrated an uncanny grasp of the subtleties in planning a complex covert operation. The Islamists would never understand that they were pawns in a much bigger game. They were expendable, and their Koran-thumping, epitaph-spitting, religious fanaticism made them the perfect dupes for such an operation.

The Rezidentura lighted an imported French cigarette and leaned back in his chair. His job was done, and his superiors at the Khodinka Field Headquarters of the GRU would be quite pleased.

JAYCOTT LEANED BACK in his airline seat and closed his eyes. The Boeing 747 cruised effortlessly at 36,000 feet and seemed to suspend time. He had come full circle.

The period since Ellie's murder had produced a flood of emotions, passions, and feelings; and through it all, Jay knew that to close the door, to resolve the unyielding frustration of his wife's cruel and senseless death, he would have to somehow identify both the rationale as well as the responsible parties to her brutal slaying. Now, as he reflected on both the perpetrator, as well as the impetus for Ellie's murder, he understood.

Accept was another matter.

Jay had been in the game a long time, and he understood how pragmatic, hard-ball decisions were made. He had no doubt that at some point in the near future, the United States would successfully invade the Republic of Panama, depose the Noriega Regime, arrest the drug lords—and in so doing, somehow justify the convoluted rationale that led to "blowing" his Probe Team, that in a retaliatory sense, led to Ellie's death. But he didn't accept that it had to happen; that an innocent had to be involved, had to be murdered. Which brought him back to Rochelle Listach; an elderly, diminutive, ladylike—but ultimately—ice-veined Operations Officer. She made the call. She accepted the ramifications—yet *he* suffered the consequences. Ellie was *his* wife, and when confronted by the hard facts, and in a position to exact retribution, when Jaycott stood at 'checkpoint Charlie', the symbolic point of no return, holding a loaded pistol to Rochelle Listach's head, prepared to resolve Ellie's senseless murder—he passed. Jay didn't pull the trigger. Why?

He did not know. For some reason, despite numerous past experiences down that path, Jaycott 'passed'. Why? He didn't hate Listach, however, he certainly didn't like—or trust—her. Maybe it was the futility of the act that prevented its occurrence. What would it accomplish? Ellie was dead, his mission was over, the target was identified, and Jay was *out*. Somewhere deep in the recesses of Jaycott's mind the opportunity for a new life glimmered. Maybe it was the possibility of a contented life with Katerina that beckoned. Somehow, someway, Jay believed that happiness was again possible. He could live, and laugh, and love again; and the strangely amoral world of covert operations could become a distant memory. It was his opportunity to pursue. He would leave it all behind once and forever. Jaycott would bury the body of his good friend Theodori, bury the memory of his loving wife Ellie, and bury the drama of his now, past profession. Time to begin anew. He would carve a sense of normality out of an otherwise abnormal existence, and savor whatever intimacies life with Katerina would offer. To do any less, would indicate that the confrontation with Madame Listach was a defeat. By walking away under his own power, on his own terms, with her life hanging on the mere twitch of his index finger, Jay had won—and in so doing, Listach's physical life was spared, and Jaycott's emotional balance was preserved.

MICHAEL EISNER, THE youthful CEO of the Walt Disney Company, sat across from his trusted friend and co-worker, and signed. "You know Frank, I get it . . . but then I really don't. I think what haunts me about the whole thing, is the absurdity of it all. I see Roy sitting in the back of the limo, repeating the question, 'but what about the children?' And the more I think about it Frank, that really *is* the issue, isn't it?"

Attorney Frank Wells, President of the Walt Disney Company, removed his glasses and nodded. He was senior in age to Eisner, yet second-in-command; but the two men shared a unique professional bond that transcended protocol, and now tasked them with their greatest challenge to date— they confronted a crisis borne on distinctly unfamiliar territory. The first ever terrorist strike sponsored by foreign nationals was targeted at them. It *was* absurd. Wells rubbed tired eyes. Who would think that with all the potential military, industrial, and governmental targets available to a group of terrorists, why would anyone ever even *consider* attacking Disney World? But then Wells' logical mind saw the true genius in the selection—precisely because it was absurd.

"The perception *is* the reality Mike. Not in a factual sense, but in a *defacto* sense. We *are* the perfect target. It will put their cause on the map—whatever that cause is."

Eisner adjusted one of the baseball caps he was fond of wearing, and shuffled over to a large map of the Walt Disney World complex that he had spread across the coffee table. "You know, with three of my own, that could just as easily be one of my kids sitting in the wrong place when the bombs go off."

"I know," nodded Wells in agreement.

"My youngest is ten," continued Eisner, almost to himself, "I feel like there's something else we should be doing . . ."

"No," said the President, "there isn't. Let the professionals do their job Mike. We'll continue to support them every way that we can. They're obviously on top of this—don't forget, they came to us."

Eisner nodded absentmindedly, his eyes furtively searching the large map for something they hadn't considered. Finally he looked up. "Did you talk to Roy?"

Wells shook his head. "Not since this afternoon. He's not doing well . . ."

Eisner frowned. "Such a gentle soul. It's almost like a personal attack on his family."

"It is Mike. In a strange sort of way, this is very much a personal attack—on our way of life, our values, our sense of morality . . . it's a very deliberate strike at our happiness, our resolve to laugh and play and feel secure again. I can now understand—as much as I deplore the concept—why Tom Laughlin says we *are* the perfect choice: Disney World, the quintessential *American* dream."

Eisner stood again and stretched. His restlessness was quite apparent. "I think I'll call home." He sighed "You know Frank, last March, I turned 47. Every year I keep promising Jane that we'll spend more time smelling the roses . . . and then you and I start hatching our plans, Roy has the creative side clicking, we get caught up in the dreams for Euro Disney, and suddenly I look up and ask where did the time go?"

"There's a lesson in all that Mike," acknowledged Wells, "and if we somehow get through this, promise me you'll remember that."

Eisner nodded at his friend and reached for the telephone.

THE TALL MAN dressed in a casual nylon warm-up suit approached the podium and paused. He scanned the rows of serious faces in the auditorium before beginning. "I'm Special Agent John Crawford of the Federal Bureau of Investigation. For the sake of brevity, let me acknowledge who is collectively represented in this room. We have members of the FBI Hostage Response Team, Agents of the Treasury Department's Secret Service, Customs, and ATF. The Army's EOD and Delta Force, the Navy's Seal Team Six, the State Department's Office to Combat Terrorism, the CIA's

Counter Terrorist Center, the National Security Agency, and select members of the Florida State Police, and both the Orange and Osceola Counties Sheriff Departments. In all, there are over four hundred specialists in this auditorium to augment the three hundred twenty-one non-armed Disney World security staff. 'Posse Comitatus' is in effect for *all* unlicensed, non-law enforcement personnel. Rules of engagement are strict. This is a federal operation, and the FBI is the senior service."

John Crawford looked to his left and nodded. A lean, square-jawed man in tan khaki pants and running shoes approached the podium. He shifted the microphone and consulted a notebook.

"I'm Colonel Franklin. I am the S-3 for SFOD-Delta out of Fort Bragg. Please hold all questions to the end of the five paragraph operations order, as we have several annexes that may promote clarity and save time. Situation, enemy forces . . ."

XXIV

30 August 1989
Corfu, Greece

THE SERVICE HAD been simple, quiet, and very private. Jaycott and Katerina stepped onto the dockside patio behind the Dorian Gray Restaurant and sat at a corner table. Katerina solemnly placed the urn with Theodori's ashes to the side and ordered two Ouzos from the bartender.

"Tomorrow, I will charter a boat and we will go to Glyfada. It was one of Theodori's favorite places to swim. We will scatter his ashes there."

Jay nodded. Taking charge of Theo's affairs gave Katerina a sense of control. It was her way of dealing with the loss. The drinks arrived, and Jay sipped slowly at the white, licorice tasting liquor.

"I never did hear how you met?"

The question surprised Katerina. It seemed to dislodge her from the mental checklist of Theo's funeral. She paused before answering.

"It was a long time ago," reminisced Katerina. She rolled the Ouzo-soaked ice cubes in a gentle semi-circle. "I was young, and head strong, and caught between some very unsavory characters . . ."

Jay shifted his sunglasses and looked hard at Katerina. "What were you doing?"

"Working," admitted Katerina.

There was another pause as Jay's chagrin surfaced. "For who?"

"Governments."

The hard eyes squinted beneath the sunglasses. "You're in the Community?"

"Yes . . ." nodded Katerina, a bit uneasily.

"Doing what?" pressed Jaycott.

"I was a courier for several western alliance countries . . . usually the Mossad, sometimes MI-6 . . ."

The revelation seemed to hang in the air between them.

". . . occasionally they used my ability with languages to set up a False Flag." Katerina shrugged, "Theo and I worked together once or twice on small operations. He was very good to me, very protective . . . our relationship evolved over time."

Jay digested the information. In retrospect, Katerina's admission made perfect sense. Kat was much too self-sufficient to be a 'kept' woman. She stayed with Theodori out of choice, not need.

"Well, at least now with Theodori's money, you don't have to work. You can walk away."

Kat looked quietly at Jay and set her drink down. For a moment, Katerina bit her lip, not quite wanting to disagree, but not accepting his statement. "We can *never* really get out Jaycott—you know that."

"I did," said Jay with finality. He thought back to his confrontation with Rochelle Listach. "If they lose their leverage, they lose their control. They have nothing I want— or *need* anymore."

Katerina reached forward and took both of Jay's hands in her own. She squeezed. "Do you think so Jaycott? Will they leave us alone?"

He nodded, returning her intense gaze. "It's over Kat. We paid our dues—we're out."

SERGEANT FIRST CLASS Paul O'Malley of the Special Forces Operational Detachment—Delta sat outside the Liberty Tree Tavern at the Magic Kingdom, and sipped at a soft drink. His hand absentmindedly reached up towards his ear microphone as he surveyed the tourists strolling through the Square.

O'Malley's partner, John Rosconovitch, made eye contact from across the Square. Rosco shrugged, watching as a mother and two small boys entered the Hall of Presidents minutes before the next show. On average, twice each hour, hundreds of tourists—many of them children—would crowd into the small auditorium to watch the life-size robots known as audio animatronics. Although the thinktank terrorism specialists had identified several probable targets within the Walt Disney complex, in truth, there was no way to predict precisely where—or how—the Islamists would strike.

Rosconovitch looked off to his left and made eye contact with a Disney World Security Officer dressed as an ice cream vendor. The portable refreshment stand was occasionally moved during the day, permitting the unarmed Disney employee to refocus on different angles in Liberty Square. The combination of static and mobile surveillance disguises available to the counter terrorist forces made for an easier setup. In such a crowded, vibrant amusement park, there were a multitude of potential throwoffs available. The difficulty, was in a sustained vigilance. Focus, became the key.

Rosco studied a swarthy looking man and woman strolling hand-in-hand towards the huge replica of the Liberty Bell. They paused, took several photographs, and then started off again out of the Square towards Frontier Land.

"PAUL?" THE SURPRISE in Anna Lyalin's voice was genuine. She stood flat-footed, folded clothes in one hand, the bureau drawer opened.

The CPA looked first at the open suitcase on the bed half-filled with clothes, then at his beautiful blond lover.

"What are you doing here?", she blurted. The mental checklist in the Spetsnaz Officer's head did not provide for this contingency. Paul Hersch never came home from work at mid-morning. Now she was faced with the prospect of a long drawn out argument that Anna neither wanted, nor had time for.

"Britt, what are *you* doing?" demanded Hersch. "Are you leaving?"

"An urgent business trip," offered Anna without hesitation. She turned and stuffed her clothes into the open suitcase.

"Where?!" "When?!", pressed Hersch aggressively. The pain in his voice palpable. "Were you going to tell me?"

"Of course," answered Anna in a distracted fashion. Her mind quickly calculated the options. She had little time and less inclination to provide the long reassuring explanations that Paul Hersch's fragile ego required. "I was going to leave you a note with my address and phone number at the hotel where I'll be staying. This all happened so quickly."

His expression fixed on the former Olympic swimmer. He walked up and grabbed Anna's shoulders from behind. She bristled, then snapped the suitcase shut as her eyes furtively scanned the bedroom.

"What, what is it?", implored the CPA. Anna Lyalin turned.

"Please Paul. This is a business emergency. I must not miss my plane to Dallas."

"Dallas?!"

She turned now, regretting her coolness towards him the last few days; but Anna had long since grown bored making love and feigning attraction to Paul Hersch. Although he was the perfect 'mark', he was also everything she found unappealing in a man—insecure, possessive, doting. She kissed him warmly, her fingers groping expertly for Paul's zipper, reaching in to free his arousal, starting to kneel down when Hersch grabbed at her elbows.

"No, not now . . . we need to talk."

"Paul, there's no time, please . . ."

He tried to guide her to sit down at the bed. Anna realized that there would be no expediting the process. This was a battle against Hersch's insecurities; an emotional minefield fraught with tension, reassurance, and endless discussion. Most importantly, it would eat up valuable time on Anna's operational clock—time which she did not have.

"Ok, ok," she relented. "You wait here and I'll be right back."

Anna picked up the suitcase from the bed. "Just let me pack this in the trunk."

Hersch grabbed for the suitcase. "Here, let me carry that for you."

"No," snarled Anna more intensely than she wanted. "Please Paul, just stay, I'll be right back." Her voice softened. "Please . . ."

The CPA relented. He cognitively realized that he was smothering his beautiful Swede, but emotionally Paul was unable to relax. He sat on the bed, a jumble of nerves, watching as Anna Lyalin carried her suitcase out to the car in the driveway.

Ninety seconds elapsed, and it seemed like an eternity. Finally, Paul heard the kitchen door open and reclose, and the soft patter of Anna's footsteps return. He started to relax. Paul would have a chance to hold his beautiful Britt and tell her again how much he needed her; loved her.

A smile crossed Paul Hersch's face as the familiar blonde hair swung back from her shoulders. Yet as Anna took a step into the bedroom and raised her head, the CPA confronted features that scared him. Anna's jaw was set in a rigid pose and her deep green eyes seemed to blanch white.

Paul Hersch sat stunned on the edge of the bed as his lover effortlessly settled into a practiced stance, feet spread at shoulder width, knees slightly bent, both arms extended outward aiming a large handgun.

The automatic pistol coughed and Paul Hersch felt a burning sensation as the noise suppressed bullet tore into his sternum. The weapon coughed again, followed by another burn in his chest, and he felt a spot of blood leap into his throat. The third bullet penetrated Paul's forehead, and his final thought in this world was that Britt was angry with him.

LIEUTENANT COLONEL OLGA Kozlov, Intelligence Officer for the GRU, opened the door to her suburban home in Hackensack, New Jersey and her heart sank.

"Mrs. Ronald Hoch?", asked a man dressed in a business suit. His voice was polite, but sure. It was more of a statement than a question.

"Yes," nodded the wife, running her hands through the tight bun of grey streaked hair.

"FBI ma'm," said Special Agent Lloyd. He offered his identification in a confident, practiced way.

"We have a Federal Warrant to search the premises." He handed Olga an official looking document. "Of course, you are free to call an attorney, but I'm sure you'll find everything is in order."

The FBI man stepped past the Soviet Illegal and motioned towards the retinue of agents that lined up behind him at her front door.

The engineer's wife sighed and followed them into her living room, just as Gennadi walked from the kitchen.

"What is this?!", blurted the explosives expert, his eyes quickly focusing on the agents as they started popping open suitcases.

"FBI, Mister Hoch," repeated Special Agent Lloyd, again offering his identification.

Gennadi watched as several forensic experts assembled audio probes, complete with earphones and electronic power sources. Another agent, trained in architecture and civil engineering, unfolded a large blueprint of the house and started tapping randomly at several walls.

"You?! This is an outrage!", bellowed the GRU Officer at Agent Lloyd. "How dare you!"

"Please Mister Hoch," shrugged Lloyd, "it's a little late in the game for that. You can save us all a lot of trouble if you or your wife could just point us in the right direction."

"Get out!"

Three Special Agents moved past Kozlov and started methodically and systematically touching, opening, perusing, and discarding every book in the floor to ceiling bookcase.

"We are not going anywhere until every brick in this house is separated. You cannot leave. There are twenty New

Jersey State Troopers sealing off the street and surrounding the house."

"You will pay," growled the engineer, snatching the search warrant from his wife's hand. "My lawyers will sue the Justice Department for millions—and *you*," he pointed defiantly at Agent Lloyd, "*you* will be chasing Eskimos in Alaska!"

The Agent shrugged, popping a piece of gum into his mouth. "I heard Anchorage was good duty." He loosened his tie.

Two more agents moved past the couple. Each carried a small metallic box. They started towards the stairs that led to the basement.

Gennadi and his wife exchanged a long gaze. Then they sat on the couch and prepared for the inevitable.

XXV

31 August 1989
Moscow, USSR

V YACHESLOV G URYENKO, HEAD of the GRU Illegals
Training Centre, entered the spacious office of his boss,
Colonel General Pavlov, First Deputy Chief of the GRU.

"Comrade Tikhonovich," nodded Pavlov using
Guryenko's middle name. His desk, as always, was
immaculate. He waved the shorter Guryenko to a seat. "It
sounded urgent . . ."

"Most urgent, Comrade General," admitted Guryenko.
He removed his glasses and nervously started cleaning them
with a handkerchief. "Two of our deep cover assets in
America have been arrested by the FBI."

"Your Illegals?"

"Da."

"Who?"

"Comrade Kozlov and his wife."

Guryenko handed Pavlov two thick files, the entire
dossiers on the New Jersey engineer and his spouse. "Both
are Lieutenant Colonels in my department. For ten years they
have been controlled directly from here. Most recently, I used

them to provide logistical training and support to the Islamist Executive Agents who would initiate the strike in the United States."

Pavlov grew pensive for a few minutes, quietly perusing the thick personnel files of the two arrested GRU officers. He turned in his seat, leaning forward at the desk and read. It seemed like a very long time before the First Deputy Chief looked up.

"They have two sons."

"Da," nodded Guryenko.

"Both are students, one is at the University," continued Pavlov flipping a page, "pick them up."

"I have already issued orders," offered Guryenko, knowing immediately that their ultimate control was in leveraging an Illegal's family.

Pavlov studied the dossiers a bit longer. "Are they reliable?"

"Their work has been solid, consistent, and accurate—but not spectacular. I believe they will hold up."

Pavlov leaned back in his leather chair and folded his hands, extending and touching both index fingers together. A minute lapsed before he spoke again. "We have assets at the target site?"

"Da," nodded Guryenko.

"Good ones?"

"Da," said the Head of the Illegals Training Centre, replacing his eyeglasses, "Spetsnaz."

Alekansandr Pavlov grunted, his mind set on the course of action. "Roll it up Vyacheslov, eliminate the Islamists, abort the strike.

Guryenko sat stunned.

"Abort?"

"Da, immediately, and bring me the entire operational file. I must contact Comrade General Ivashutin. He may wish to apprise Gorbachev."

Guryenko's features turned glum. All his work, his planning, his efforts; it was all being abandoned at the last moment. A touch of fear swept Guryenko. "Comrade General, the time . . ."

"Use the emergency cutout Vyacheslov. We must abort . . .*time* is critical."

Pavlov's eyes turned cold, looking back at the two thick dossiers that lay spread across his desk. He spoke quietly, almost to himself. "Ultimately, if we handle the channels of disinformation correctly, aborting the operation will achieve the same ends."

A wave of his hand and Guryenko was dismissed.

UNKNOWN TO MOST visitors at Walt Disney's Magic Kingdom, the true genius is behind the scenes. Walt created the sprawling amusement park with an incredible eye for detail. Everything that a guest to the park saw, heard, smelled, tasted, and felt supported the illusion. Thus, a visitor should never notice an employee dressed in Frontierland attire wander through Tomorrowland at the end of their workshift; garbage should never pile on the sidewalk; cast member meals should be taken beyond public view; fresh costumes needed to be accessible for a quick change; food and drink required resupply. At no time could any of the normal, necessary logistical functions of the sprawling, continuously-open enterprise risk a sensory interruption. Continuity was the key.

Walt Disney solved this dilemma by digging a massive tunnel complex under the Magic Kingdom, complete with trap doors, hidden entrances, and special access routes to all parts of the park. He called it the Utilidor. All employees to the Magic Kingdom leave their cars in staff facilities far from the tourist entrances. They arrive in civilian clothes and board special buses which bring them to the main Utilidor tunnel entrance located beneath the 'Fantasy Faire' attraction at the far end of the park. Inside, one notices a buzzing web of color-coded, concrete tunnels spraying in various directions. Massive power, plumbing, climate control, and sewage pipes hug the ceiling as golf carts race by carrying maintenance workers and supplies. The tunnels provide cafeterias, cleaning services, tailors, locker rooms, make-up artists, wardrobes, equipment rooms, and power generators. It also houses a computer center located directly below the theatre which faces Cinderella's Golden Carousel. From this computer center, every single attraction from a note of music, to a flashing light, to a movement of one of the numerous robots known as Audio Animatronics is controlled. Everything. The entire amusement park is synchronized to the split second.

For obvious reasons, access to this sensitive area is highly restricted, and numerous closed circuit televisions and special cameras keep the staff appraised of the status of each attraction. It was here in the computer room, deep in the

Magic Kingdom tunnel complex, that Special Agent John Crawford of the FBI's Hostage Response Team placed his Crisis Center. A second TOC (Tactical Operations Center) was prepared in the regular Magic Kingdom Security Office located above the Penny Arcade on Main Street, USA. Three other control points were located in the Carousel of Progress, the Pirates of the Caribbean, and the Haunted Mansion. In all, four hundred thirty seven, three-man teams—both mobile and stationary—roamed the three amusement parks in various guises of cast members, tourists, food vendors, and entertainers. If Disney World was impossible to secure, at least it was reasonably simple to patrol; because the very same factors that made it difficult to monitor crowds, made it equally easy to penetrate them.

"Agent Crawford?"

"Yes," nodded the FBI Supervisor, turning from a closed circuit monitor.

The Disney Security Officers motioned towards the alert telephone that connected the Crisis Center with Bureau Headquarters in Washington, D.C. Agent Crawford, dressed casually in slacks and a polo shirt, snatched at the telephone.

"Command Post, Operation Intruder, this line is secure, Special Agent Crawford."

"Crawford," came the terse reply over the telephone, "this is Deputy Director Porter. Listen closely . . ."

There was a pause on the line to ensure that Crawford's attention was focused.

". . . we arrested two Soviet Illegals—a husband and wife team—up in New Jersey, after serving them with a search warrant. They had been under surveillance for a week. The lab boys took the home apart. In the basement, behind a false wall, was a communications room. They also turned up bits of wiring, reworked circuit boards, and residue from chemical composition-four . . ."

"Plastique?" interrupted Crawford, mildly surprised.

". . . yes," confirmed Porter, "C-4. Obviously the two Illegals are not talking, but this changes the complexion of the operation. The forensic guys think you should be very sensitive to remote control-detonated shaped charges. They feel there's ample evidence of customized bomb construction."

Crawford nodded, more to himself, than the non-visible Deputy Director. "Thank you Sir, I'll pass it along." He hung up the telephone and turned to the Walt Disney World Security Officer. "Alert the Watch Commanders on the FM. Advise them to call in on a land line immediately. We'll conference call on my phone."

The Disney Security Officer nodded. The last few days had proven the most stressful and yet exciting moments of his nine years at the Magic Kingdom. His life moved in a blur, and he could barely contain his enthusiasm in watching the very serious, very calm Federal and Military personnel who operated around him. With a sense of dramatic urgency, the Disney employee—there because he knew the layout of the amusement park better than anyone—rushed towards the Motorola wireless radio transmission console.

COLONEL VIKTOR PAPAHA slowly backed away from
the telephone and turned towards the Tomorrowland Terrace.
To his right was Cinderella's Castle and to his left the Grand
Prix Raceway. He had intentionally avoided the area
immediately surrounding Liberty Square as zero hour
approached. Now, barely fifty-one minutes before the strike,
he made his final contact to the telephone message retrieval
system that served as the emergency cutout. He had called
this number every twelve hours since arriving in Orlando;
always from a different pay telephone, and always received
the same taped message which was a recitation of the time,
the weather, and the wind speed. His pre-operational briefing
specified the need to make a final contact within sixty
minutes of zero hour, however, after twenty-seven separate
telephone calls to the cutout, the routineness of the message
lulled Papaha, and he felt quite unprepared for the coded, last
minute change. Viktor lighted a cigarette and sat at an empty
park bench. He needed to think.

It was standard GRU operating procedure to place an
independent asset on the ground when using Executive
Agents. From the beginning, Viktor knew what the
Palestinian mules looked like, how they would hit the target,
and when and where they would strike. Usually, the GRU
asset was used to observe and report on the completeness of
the operation—a first person BDA (Bomb Damage
Assessment). The three word voicemail message startled the
Spetsnaz Colonel while radically altering his assignment:

"*Uskoreniye, fizicheskoye ustraneniye.*"

Papaha's new mission was to eliminate the Executive Agents, the mules, *before* they initiated the strike on the target. It was a clear abort. Something had gone wrong, something had changed, and the Spetsnaz Colonel needed to quickly locate, intercept, and eliminate the two Palestinians who were currently somewhere in the amusement park before they exploded a very lethal charge in the Hall of the Presidents.

Viktor pensively inhaled on his Marlboro cigarette, blowing a long stream of smoke skyward. Since he didn't know their exact route of approach, he would have to intercept the mules at Liberty Square outside the auditorium—preferably before they entered the Hall. Papaha stood, field stripped the cigarette, rolled the yellow filter into a ball, and dropped the butt into the trash receptacle. Time was short.

DEEP IN THE bowels of the Disney World Utilidor resides the main telephone switch room or PBX (Private Branch Exchange) for the Magic Kingdom. This telephone computer switch system receives all of the internal phone lines, corporate phone lines, and public pay telephone lines in the amusement park. It is a BellSouth system which then reroutes calls both local and long distance to their proper destination.

Crowded in the small room were seven FBI technicians sitting around three very powerful laptop computers connected by hardware coaxial cables. The first laptop retrieved all calls directed into the PBX, providing a data stream that was intentionally programmed to disregard all internal and corporate telephone calls. Only the public pay telephone calls were processed.

The second laptop used a computer program written with a special table that provided locator numbers for all AT&T street files; in other words, a telephone directory. This was then downloaded onto a third laptop computer with an address for the destination call that was matched against the FBI's main database known as FOIMS (Field Office Information Management System). The addresses were cross-referenced against all known Islamist Terrorist or Soviet Intelligence safehouses, control points, and operational facilities throughout the continental United States. Thus, literally, within seconds, the Southern Bell PBX identified the terminal or pay phone within the Magic Kingdom where a telephone call originated, and the AT&T street file provided the destination address of the receiving telephone. A blinking light signaled a match to a suspicious address. In addition, regardless of suspicion, every conversation was routinely taped and stored, and the FBI techs took turns randomly replaying every conversation placed from a pay telephone in the park.

The Bureau's use of state of the art technology was the easy part; the most difficult aspect of the operation was convincing a federal judge to issue a warrant of sufficient breadth permitting the FBI to wiretap such a broad-based, all-encompassing system. Typically, wiretaps—as invasions of privacy—are narrowly designated and very specific as to time, purpose, persons involved, and exact location. It took considerable arm twisting, and ultimately a personal request by the Attorney General of the United States to the federal magistrate in Orlando, to expedite the issuance of the warrant.

Ultimately, the whole process was a long shot; but given the circumstances, every conceivable method of data collection made sense.

"Flag," said Keith Dyson sipping on a soft drink. He sat forward in his chair, suddenly alert, and adjusted his earphones. Several technicians looked towards Dyson. He replayed the digitally recorded telephone call and made a notation in the yellow legal pad on his makeshift desk.

"*Uskoreniye, fizicheskoye ustraneniye*," said a voice in a clear, non-accented cadence, immediately followed by a dial tone.

Dyson stopped the tape and rewound. "Frank?" He beckoned towards a linguist across the small room. The man approached Dyson and took the headset from Keith. He adjusted the earphones and nodded. The short message was replayed again.

"Acceleration . . . physical removal . . ." translated the linguist, ". . . classic Russian."

The FBI men exchanged a look. Quickly Dyson wrote down the words, and pointed at his computer screen as he consulted his wristwatch.

"Origination point; Magic Kingdom, terminal I.D. B-forty-one, a pay telephone station outside the Enchanted Grove, across from the Tomorrowland Terrace . . . Destination point; Orlando, terminal I.D. D-eight-seven-six, a private telephone station at an apartment complex located at fifteen-sixty Edgewater Drive near Interstate Four . . . Time of call thirteen zero-nine hours or one-oh-nine p.m. Eastern Standard Time—six minutes ago."

ANDREW PRATT, SPECIAL Agent for the Bureau of Alcohol, Tobacco, and Firearms, stood beside the tall Movieland Memorabilia Monument just inside the turnstiles of the main entrance to the Disney-MGM Studios. Dressed in a sportscoat and tie, Pratt politely nodded at each adult entering Disney's newest theme park, and handed them a complimentary ticket entitling them to a 20% discount to any purchase made at the Keystone Clothiers. The offer was real, but the hidden intent was to give the Treasury Agent an excuse to approach and assess every individual entering the Disney-MGM Studios.

To Pratt's left and right, stood the other two members of his team—an unarmed Disney Security Officer and a fellow ATF agent. Each wandered unobtrusively inside the broad receptionway, blending into the crowd as they intently studied guests entering the park.

In the distance, at the far end of Hollywood Boulevard, perched in the tower of the Great Movie Ride, sat two more ATF agents, alternately peering through high-powered telescopic sights mounted on tripods. Everyone was in contact via Motorola FM radios.

There were one hundred sixteen, three-men teams covering the Disney-MGM Studios, and the task facing them, similar to their counterparts at the other two theme parks at the Orlando complex, was in identifying suspects and eradicating suspicions without alarming the thousands of legitimate guests—or alerting the real terrorists. Unlike airports or other high-profile security areas, the use of metal detectors, X-ray machines, and other magnetometer-type instruments as guests entered the theme park would only telegraph an advance warning to the perpetrators. It was contrary to the entire Disney persona, and such behavior would be instantly noted. For the very same reasons, spotter-sniffer dogs were not used. This of course, made their task that much more difficult.

Pratt's earphone, disguised to look like a walkman radio set, crackled as the static observers in the Tower of the Great Movie Ride directed a mobile team to check out an adult couple lingering outside the Brown Derby Restaurant to his rear.

Each of the theme parks of the Disney World complex had been separated into grids. The grids were then cordoned off into zones of responsibility accented by colored corridors, which were then overlaid with clean map acetate that delineated specific static and mobile patrol routes. At any given time, Supervisory Special Agent John Crawford of the FBI could pinpoint any attraction in any of the three theme parks and descend with an armada of personnel. The entire coordination of the massed forces was run through his Crisis Center in the bowels of the Magic Kingdom's Utilidor; however, due to the disjointed nature of the three 'stand alone' gates at Disney World, each of the theme parks maintained a separate Command and Control structure on sight. This greatly expedited speed, response time, and decision making—all crucial elements if a terrorist strike was to be thwarted.

Agent Pratt marveled at the crowds as they swarmed through the turnstiles. The Labor Day guests seemed oblivious to the Central Florida heat, as parents and children alike enjoyed the final vestiges of summer. The ATF agent smiled, nodded, and offered his souvenir store discount tickets, sizing up each adult for an instant. Early afternoon, and the Treasury man was already hot, tired, and mentally weary—all products of suspecting everyone. It was the thousand meter stare scenario that he remembered from his four years in the Marine Corp.; when mental tiredness replaced physical tiredness and in many ways took a heavier toll. Pratt was thankful that the Disney-MGM Studios would close at nine p.m. that evening, allowing guests to board a bus for a fireworks display at EPCOT Center, or a parade at the Magic Kingdom. Let his co-workers at the other theme parks manage the people flow. Pratt and his team needed a break.

ANNA LYALIN TAILED her mark in front of the French Pavillion at EPCOT Center, and felt that something was drastically wrong. Her pre-operational briefing had specified *two* Executive Agents, not *one*. The discrepancy bothered her. Unfortunately, each time she stopped to use a public telephone to check the message retrieval system, the mule started moving again.

The Spetsnaz officer slid the sunglasses back up the bridge of her nose and paused as the Palestinian stopped to examine souvenirs in the window at *Plume et Palette*. It was Paul Hersch's fault. Ever since Anna's sudden elimination of the CPA, her schedule condensed. She took unplanned time to sterilize his home, hide his body in a utility closet, and set the central air conditioning to an extremely cool level. The colder the home, the slower the decomposition of his body—and hence, the longer before any telltale stench to the outside. Although Anna was well-trained and quite efficient, the delay was unplanned, and thus threw off her rhythm. She had telephoned the emergency cutout every twelve hours since arriving in Orlando; however now, with forty-three minutes remaining before zero hour, Lyalin had yet to make her final telephone call—and something was wrong.

The former Olympic swimmer drifted off to the side, keeping the mule and his blue nylon shoulder bag in view. The Palestinian turned and started walking again.

"PENCILS?"

"Yes," smiled Viktor Papaha," the kind with the Disney characters on them." He pointed to a shelf behind the cash register filled with Theme Park memorabilia.

The young clerk smiled in return and reached for a package of long, yellow, #2 lead pencils embossed with the characters of Mickey and Minney Mouse, Goofy, Donald Duck, Cinderella, and Snow White. She gave them to the Spetsnaz officer. "That will be a dollar ninety-nine plus tax."

As Viktor handed her a five dollar bill he motioned to the package." Would it be possible to get them sharpened?"

"Sure," nodded the girl as she rang the purchase. She handed Papaha his change and receipt, tore open the cellophane, and moved to the countertop where she quickly ran each pencil through an electric pencil sharpener for a few seconds. Then she handed the box with six sharpened pencil tips back to Viktor.

For a moment the Spetsnaz office checked each sharpened pencil, reviewing her work before smiling again. "Thank you." he winked. "Word puzzles for the kids, this should keep them busy tonight."

"Have a nice day," smiled the young clerk, waving as Viktor exited the Emporium Store on Main Street, USA.

THE THREE CAR convoy made record time from the offsite TOC (Tactical Operations Center) up Interstate Route #4 to the apartment complex at fifteen-sixty Edgewater Drive; two FBI Agents, two Osceola County Sheriffs' Deputies, and a Florida State trooper.

The apartment manager was just finishing lunch when the cadre yanked him from his kitchen and half-prodded, half-pulled him to the small one bedroom on the second floor in the South Wing. He never did see the "warrant" that they mentioned and his nervousness was only heightened by their serious demeanor, such that he nearly dropped the massive master-key chain to the property.

Within a minute, three of the five law enforcement officers burst through the door, weapons drawn.

Empty. The apartment was vacant. Sterile. Uninhabited. Unused. The only sign of life was a large answering machine sitting squarely on the countertop next to the wall mounted telephone, and a series of connecting wires to a ring-activated tape recorder.

Special Agent Dan Johnston looked towards the Apartment Complex manager with a perturbed expressions. "Tell me about the tenants."

The nervous complex manager shrugged. "I only met the man once . . . he paid for three months rent in advance, plus first month, last month, and a damage deposit . . . said he traveled a lot . . . well dressed I guess . . . quiet . . ."

"What does he look like?"

"I don't remember," protested the manager defensively. "I have two hundred units . . . my job is to keep the property rented . . ."

Johnston's hand shot skyward, cutting off the explanation. He turned to the second FBI Agent, "You stay with one of the Deputies, I will get back to the TOC and get a forensic team down here."

"Think anyone will come back?"

"No," conceded Johnson. "This is a pure cutout . . . six months rent in advance . . .," he grimaced, ". . . but we will want to analyze the tapes."

Johnston nodded to the State Trooper and the second Sheriff's Deputy Trooper and motioned towards the door as he led the apartment manager by the elbow. "We will need to see the rental file on your quiet tenant.

~~~

ANNA LYALIN HUNG up the telephone and let out a
deep sigh. She had just completed her final call to the
message retrieval system, and instead of hearing a taped
monotone message that recited the time, the weather, and the
wind speed, she heard instead three clear Russian words:
"Uskoreniye, fizicheskoye, ustraneniye"

Anna paused for a moment, deep in thought, her mind
a brief collection of muddled concerns. With thirty-one
minutes remaining before zero hour, she had been given a
coded advisory to abort the mission. In addition, she had to
eliminate the mules, the Palestinian Executive Agents, who
transported the explosives and would detonate the bomb.
Precious little time, mused the Olympic swimmer.
Instinctively she fingered the large Beretta automatic pistol
and the silencer that lay in her wide canvas purse. Upon
eliminating Paul Hersch, and securing his apartment, Anna
had wrestled with the risk of entering the Epcot Center theme
park with the handgun. But her pre-mission reconnaissance
had served Anna well, as the routine of multiple entrances
and exits from the park in previous visits, had demonstrated
no visible signs of searches or metal detectors. This was a
family place, and evidently such an intrusion was deemed
inappropriate.

Anna started for the American Adventure at the far
end of the World Showcase side of the Epcot Center. She
knew the target, she knew the mule, and she knew the
timeline. Anna also knew that the explosive was an arm-on-
site remote–controlled device. She would intercept the

Palestinian either in route or at the Pavilion. Lyalin looked sideways at the Executive Agent as he paused to look at the boat dock in front of the Moroccan Pavilion. Her one nagging concern was why there was only one mule. Of course, Anna could not know that Abd-al Rahman, the second mule, traveling under a false identity, had managed to kill himself in a traffic accident on Interstate Route #10 east of Mobile, Alabama nearly three weeks earlier.

THE TELEPHONE RANG in the vacant apartment at Edgewater Drive. The startled FBI Agent and Sheriff's Deputy stood, moving quickly towards the tape recorder. The Agent held up a hand and both men stopped and listened as the answering machine clicked on:

"Uskoreniye, fizicheskoye Ustraneniye" repeated the monotone message. Just as quickly the line clicked dead.

"Call it in," instructed the Agent to the uniformed Sherriff.

The Deputy raised his FM two-way radio and spoke: "Just received a call, destination point . . . request immediate trace on origination point.

PAPAHA COULD NOT believe his good fortune. He noticed the two mules just off the center island that led to Cinderella's Castle, slightly past the Main Street, USA Bookstore. Their distinctive attire and back pack assisted the process, but still, the Park was crowded.

Viktor fell into step behind the Executive Agents. He had come prepared. Long ago the Spetsnaz officer learned that the best disguise was to hide in plain sight. Thus he dressed like a tourist; khaki pants, running shoes, a white short sleeve open collar shirt worn untucked over a black t-shirt, and sunglasses. He draped a camera over his neck-although today he had not taken any pictures. Papaha fingered the bright red bandanna stuffed in his front pocket, and the opened case of sharpened pencils-erasers up in his rear pocket.

The Palestinians would not know Papaha, and in fact, it was doubtful they would be aware of a GRU presence. But instead of turning left and taking the access bridge at the ten o'clock position to Liberty Square, the mules continued straight, angling towards Cinderella's Castle. The Spetsnaz Colonel frowned and glanced at his wristwatch. He picked up the pace. Twenty-two minutes.

"FLAG," JUMPED KEITH DYSON, holding his earphones in the basement PBX of the Utilidor, "origination point; Epcot center, terminal I.D. C-thirty-seven, a pay telephone station outside the French Pavilion, in the World Showcase . . . destination point the apartment at fifteen-sixty Edgewater Drive."

"Just received a call from the TOC," confirmed FBI Supervisory Special Agent Crawford, "same locations, same message . . . it's Russian, we have men on site and a forensic team in route . . . scramble the team at Epcot Center."

ANNA LYALIN KNEW that the lone mule would have to find a secure location to connect the electric circuit board to the detonating device. It was not the type of thing one did in public. She walked in front of the Palestinian now, past the Japanese Pavilion, sure in her knowledge of his final destination. Lyalin approached the American Pavilion. The attraction was in the center of the World Showcase, a proud, public display of American ingenuity and industry. It featured a large theatre style auditorium where two lifelike audio animatronic robots of Mark Twain and Ben Franklin discoursed widely on the virtues and challenges of the young nation.

Anna entered the pre-show reception lobby of the Pavilon. If the mule did not lose his nerve and kept to the plan, then he would detonate the explosive while positioned in the middle of the crowded theatre. This would produce maximum death, destruction, and fear-all preconditions for a successful terrorist strike.

"ROSCOE, WE HAVE a shake," mouthed SFC O'Malley of Special Forces Operational Detachment Delta into the microphone in his sleeve.

Across Liberty Square, John Rosconovitch his military partner, touched his ear piece and nodded, "What's up?"

"They are scrambling outside the Enchanted Grove near Tomorrowland . . . also, outside the French Pavilion at Epcot . . . stay alert."

"Roger that," nodded Rosconovitch.

~~~

PAPAHA'S DILIGENCE DURING his days of reconnoitering the Theme Park paid off. The two Palestinians had reappeared on the far side of Cinderella's Castle in the middle of Fantasy Land. They turned left, angling between the Magic Journey's Motion Picture and the Golden Carousel Ride. Viktor checked his watch. If they were to stay on schedule, the Executive Agents would either turn back now and approach Liberty Square from beside the Sleeply Hollow Sandwich shop, or continue through Fantasy Land to enter the Square under the archway next to Peter Pan's Flight. Papaha closed the distance, prepared to reverse direction when the two mules turned left at the Mad Hatter clothing store.

Viktor nodded to himself. It would be from the North. He tugged the red bandanna from his pocket and rolled it into a sweat band, then wrapped it around his forehand and tied the kerchief into a knot.

ANDREW PRATT OF ATF listened intently. Then he stepped to his right and loosened his tie. "All units," began Pratt calmly, "be advised we have a scramble at the other two Gates . . ."

He tried to smile at the guests streaming past him
down Hollywood Boulevard but it was difficult to
concentrate. ". . . something is live, and we could be next,"
he continued over his mouthpiece.

Pratt stepped back from the Movieland Memorabilia
Monument and took a long appraising look at the throngs of
children, baby strollers, and parents that flooded the wide
avenue. He shook his head, tired and frustrated, but mostly
angry.

THE LONE PALESTINIAN crossed in front of the
American Pavilion and walked towards the lavatory that
adjoined the restaurant. Anna followed. The mule would
arm the explosive by connecting the detonator to the circuit
board in the privacy of a toilet stall. Quickly she veered into
the companion ladies room and entered a toilet stall herself.

In seconds Lyalin had pulled the Beretta pistol from
her bag, screwed the noise suppressor on the barrel, and
tucked the weapon into her waistband. Next she dumped the
contents of her handbag into the toilet-cosmetics, perfume,
eyeliner, mascara, lipstick-and covered the pile with tissues.
Finally Anna gripped the pistol and chambered a round by
snapping back and releasing the upper receiver. She placed
the silenced automatic, by itself, into her canvas bag,
straightened her hair, and exited the ladies room.

THEIR TARGET WAS the Hall of the Presidents in Liberty Square, a popular theatre-style attraction, where full-size Audio Animatronic robots of the Presidents of the United States came to life. The Spetsnaz officer knew the Park layout cold, and he watched as the two mules entered the men's lavatory next to Peter Pan's Flight. This would be his chance. Papaha paused for a moment, looked around in all directions, and then followed them into the toilets.

A father and son exited as Viktor turned the corner. One of the Palestinian's leaned over a sink, methodically washing his hands over and over. The man eyed Papaha suspiciously, and then looked away as Viktor ignored him. His trained eye noted the middle toilet stall with its three quarter door closed, and a man's legs exposed beneath. He would be arming the explosive, the second Palestinian.

The Spetsnaz officer approached the row of sinks and made a point to leave a space between himself and the Executive Agent. He turned on the water.

It happened so quickly that the Palestinian never reacted. Before getting his hands wet, Papaha reached back and pulled a long lead pencil from the cardboard case in his back pocket and in a blur, thrust the pencil into the mule's right eye. The man screamed but before he could move, Viktor jammed a second sharpened pencil into the soft pallet beneath the man's chin. Blood spurted sideways. Then Papaha grabbed a fist full of the Palestinian's hair and slammed his head—face first—into the hard porcelain sink. The guardian went down.

In seconds, Viktor crossed the lavatory and kicked open the door to the toilet stall. The second mule sat frozen on the commode, the circuit board spread on his lap, wires and the electronic detonator in opposite hands. The Executive Agent tried to stand, but Papaha pushed him back while stabbing a pencil into the man's neck just above his carotid artery. A second pencil found its mark, and bright arterial blood spurted like a water fountain. A third entered the man's throat, and Viktor heard the Palestinian gurgle as he tore at the circuit board. Wires, electronic receptors, copper connections—all pulled apart to insure the explosive remained inert. Then Papaha stuffed the device into the mules backpack and bounded from the Men's Room.

At the door, two men nearly collided with Viktor. Aghast at his disheveled blood spattered white shirt and face. "Get help," he bellowed, "please, a man is bleeding . . . get a doctor, quick . . ." He pushed them from the entrance to the Men's Room. They turned right and Papaha moved left. As he ducked under the Archway that separated Fantasy Land from Liberty Square, he ripped off his blood streaked white shirt, camera, and red bandanna, rolled them into a ball, wiped his face and arms, and stuffed the pile into the backpack on top of the explosive. This he dropped into a trash receptacle before slowing to a walk. Without looking back, Viktor donned his sunglasses and melted into the crowd.

Anna Lyalin stood quietly in the reception center of the American Experience Pavilion, and examined the historic displays. The lone Palestinian fidgeted nervously to her left. He kept on tugging at the backpack. A few minutes passed, and then the inner doors to the theatre opened electronically, and the crowd started to file into the huge auditorium.

Anna positioned herself behind the mule, careful to pace so that she could close quickly. Lyalin managed to file into the row directly behind the mule, in the middle of the large theater. The crowd had spread out, spacing itself comfortably, allowing several seats between guests.

The Palestinian lay the backpack across his lap as the lights dimmed, and a musical overture started from the stereo speaker system. During her reconnaissance, Anna had clocked the show multiple times. She had to act quickly. As the room turned black, Lyalin positioned her canvas bag against the back of the Palestinian's chair, reached through the zipper, gripped her Beretta, and squeezed the trigger. The supersonic round cracked inside the bag, louder than she feared, and felt the mule tense upright as the metal jacketed nine millimeter bullet tore into his spine. A flourish of music and Anna squeezed the trigger two more times, coughing bits of canvas into the air, riveting the back of the theatre seat. Immediately, Anna reached over his shoulder as the Palestinian slumped, grabbed the remote control detonator from one hand, and the backpack from his lap.

"Excuse me," apologized Anna moving down the row bumping guests, stepping on toes as she ambled from the middle of the auditorium to the aisle. The intrusion went unnoticed; the other guests were enthralled in the "Imagineering" on the stage.

Lyalin turned left, pacing upward, scaling the gentle slope of the aisle back towards where they had first entered. She gripped the backpack and her canvas bag against her stomach. At the top an usher stopped Anna and pointed towards the exit signs at the front of the theatre.

"Sick . . . sick, please . . ." pleaded Anna clutching her midsection. ". . . throw up, please . . ."

The usher stepped away, quickly opening the rear door for Anna, and she pushed into the reception area, bounding through the new crowd waiting for the next show, and out the front doors.

Past the fountain, through the gardens, and towards the Lagoon, Lyalin paused to throw the canvas bag with the pistol into a trash bin on the way to the water. Twenty steps later she wound-up and threw the backpack as far as she could, into the Lagoon, aiming for a striped barber pole that moored a gondola beside the Italian Pavilion.

Finally Anna turned right, pulled her long blond hair into a bun, donned her sunglasses, tied a green kerchief around her neck as she walked, and rolled up her pants above her knees. Then she joined the crowd that assembled near the boat dock at the German Pavilion.

XXVI

JUDGE WILLIAM WEBSTER, Director of the CIA, removed his glasses and set them on the coffee table. He looked first at Chief of Staff John Sununu, and then leaned back in his chair.

"Incredible effort Judge," said the President. "You and your team are to be commended."

"Thank you Mister President," nodded Webster looking at George Bush, "in fairness, we had a lot of help . . . the interagency cooperation was excellent."

"Yes," nodded the President thoughtfully, "and yet I can't help but think just how close we came . . . will there be problems with the media?"

"We don't think so Mister President," interjected Sununu, "the first responders were quick and thorough, and clearly the folks at Disney have a big stake in this situation . . . they have a franchise to protect."

"In essence Mister President," added the CIA Director," there are pockets of people who know that something happened, but no one is in a position to put the whole picture together."

George Bush stood, stretching to the full height of his 74 inch frame and paced quietly in thought. "So it was Islamists . . . we are sure of this?"

"The dead Executive Agents on the scene were certainly illegals of Middle Eastern ethnicity . . . forensics has confirmed this," nodded Webster. He watched the President move quietly around the Oval Office. "But undoubtedly they had sponsors with means, motive, and infrastructure."

"And you think it could be the Soviets?"

"The trendline and peripheral data does indicate Moscow, but I'm not sure we will ever find the smoking gun."

George Bush paused and looked pensively at the CIA Director. "Thank you Judge, I will want daily updates as you develop more information."

"Of course Mister President," He stood, knowing the request was an act of dismissal. Webster reached forward and gathered his briefing file before turning.

"And Judge, please convey to everyone our deep appreciation for their efforts . . . our country is in their debt."

They shook hands.

"I will Mister President," nodded Webster respectfully. "Thank you."

The CIA Director paced to the door accompanied by the Chief of Staff and exited the Oval Office.

George Bush sat back down in the Edwardian chair, removed his eyeglasses and rubbed his tired eyes.

"Can I get you anything Mister President?" asked Sununu.

"No," mumbled Bush pensively, his thoughts miles away. Thirty seconds of silence ensued and then the President repositioned his glasses and sighed. "John, I have this incredible knot in my stomach . . . we will never be the same."

"Yes Mister President," agreed the former Academic, "the simple truth is, we got lucky."

". . . AND IN SUMMATION," concluded Tom Laughlin," the spin doctors are at work, and there is a 'Spike' on all media inquiries. The Fifth Estate is frustrated but silent. We had scrub teams sealing off the kill zones and sterilizing the locations throughout the night . . . witnesses were identified and isolated . . . stories varied, recollections distorted, memories confused . . . sometimes accidents happen and people get sick—even at Disney World . . . people know that something happened, but no one can really conceive of the intended atrocity . . . thus families, with some prodding, move on to continue their holiday . . . our good fortune is that the Mules were eliminated by professionals in manners not wholly visible or expected . . . no one can get a clear picture . . . collection has produced remote control detonated explosive material and bloody clothing . . . we are discreetly searching every crevice, corner, and pile of garbage . . . dredging of the Lagoons continues nightly . . ."

Laughlin sat back and closed the file ". . . gentlemen, we dodged the proverbial bullet."

There was a quiet, reflective moment shared by all the members of the Forty Committee as they considered the incidents at the Walt Disney World Theme Parks.

"And the next time Tom," asked Paul from Customs, "What about the next time?"

Before Laughlin could answer, John Mullins his fellow CIA employee interrupted while exhaling a long stream of cigarette smoke. "In so far as this Committee only convenes in times of a serious national emergency, I for one, hope that I don't see you guys for a very long time."

Mullins snubbed out his cigarette with a distinct air of finality. Then he made a fist, before extending his thumb and index finger barely an inch apart, as if to say: 'we came this close.'

XXVII

9 September 1989
Moscow, USSR

MIKHAIL GORBACHEV CLIMBED from the rear seat of his chauffeur-driven Volga limousine. It was a balmy Saturday in Cathedral Square, and the last vestige of summer fought to retain the little warmth that remained. Soon, the oppressive cold of a bitter Russian winter would surface. Time to rest, although this morning the General Secretary of the Communist Party of the Soviet Union had serious matters occupying his attention.

He entered the huge, ornate portal of the Great Kremlin Palace and turned right, pacing down a long high-ceilinged hallway towards the Romanov Room tucked in the far corner of the building. With a flourish, Mikhail flung open the door and strode to a chair placed at the head of a long, rectangular mahogany-stained table. Gorbachev paused, allowing his eyes to search out the face of each man seated around the room, and then very slowly, with a studied motion, Mikhail set a leather brief case on the brightly polished conference table.

Gorbachev had planned to return from his five week Crimea vacation on Sunday, however, allies in Moscow convinced the Soviet leader to return two days early—trouble was afoot. Thus, Mikhail raced back on Friday afternoon, and met that evening with Army General Petr Ivashutin, Deputy Chief of the General Staff of the Soviet Armed Forces. Ivashutin presented the Party Secretary with the highly sensitive, vastly incriminating documents contained in the leather brief case. Petr went by the pseudonym *Dyadya Petya*. He was chief of Soviet Military Intelligence, the GRU.

The tension in the room grew. Seven pair of eyes studied Gorbachev's every move; there was Viktor Chebrikov, former head of the KGB and a Politburo hardliner; Yegor Ligachev, leader of the Central Committee; Vladimir Shcherbitsky, the ironfisted boss of the Ukraine; Viktor Nikonov, an economic right winger; current KGB Chief Vladimir Kryuchkov; Prime Minister Nikolai Ryzhkov, and defense Minister Dmitri Yazov.

Gorbachev sat, calm and oddly confident for this impromptu plenum meeting of the Politburo.

"How was the Crimea, Mikhail Sergeyevich," inquired Yazov conversationally.

Gorbachev's penetrating gaze sliced through the Defense Minister. As is often the case in these situations, personal chemistry counted; and Mikhail was the establishment leader. "You didn't *request* this meeting Dmitri, to inquire of my vacation."

"Nyet," agreed Viktor Chebrikov brusquely, "we did not. We *requested* this meeting Comrade Gorbachev, to advise you it's time for a change."

Mikhail's face tightened. He surveyed the room, filled with right wing neoStalinists, and listened as Chebrikov launched a bold, verbal attack against his policies of *perestroika* and *glasnost*. The virulent former head of the KGB ranted for a full three minutes, calling into question every reform that Mikhail Gorbachev's four years in power had produced.

The other Politburo members studied the General Secretary, watching closely for signs of weakness. There was none. Quite the contrary, the embattled Party Leader absentmindedly scratched the large purple birthmark on the right side of his forehead—all the more prominent due to his receding hairline—and smiled. It was the toothy smile of a predator, and Mikhail paused to look around the conference table as Chebrikov bellowed. Finally, he raised a hand, beckoning the *apparatchik* to silence. There was such poise in the movement, that the former KGB Chief abruptly ceased talking.

"I've heard enough Viktor Mikhailovich" said Gorbachev. He reached forward and opened the leather briefcase. Then he withdrew a large handful of classified documents; photographs, diplomatic cables, transcripts of telephone conversations, sworn statements, and intelligence reports. He threw them across the table at Chebrikov and simultaneously addressed the group in a clear, concise voice. "*This* is irrefutable proof, that splinter elements of the Committee for State Security, sponsored a terrorist strike against the United States."

The seven men in the room sat stunned. The shock of Gorbachev's revelation coupled with the apparent preponderance of proof that lay scattered before them, had quickly and decisively altered their agenda. They were rendered—quite literally—speechless.

"They launched an unprecedented, irresponsible operation, targeting innocent women and children at an amusement park . . ." Mikhail paused, sighing for effect, ". . . to say that World condemnation for this atrocity would be insurmountable, should it have succeeded, is an understatement."

Mikhail slowly scanned the room to see what expressions confronted him. Their surprise was evident.

"Just this morning," he continued, admonishing them in a clear tone, "I spoke with George Bush regarding the situation. He was quite . . ." Gorbachev paused again, searching for the proper word ". . . *disturbed* by the entire development. I assured the American President that it was *not* the Committee for State Security itself who was to blame, but rather various rogue elements of the Politburo formerly associated or aligned with the KGB. Am I wrong?"

The Party Secretary waived an arm over the conference table, referring to the piles of evidence that lay before them. Thirty seconds passed. In a challenging tone, Mikhail posed a question: "Who else among you agrees with Viktor Mikhailovich's assessment of my tenure?"

The question, with all of its implications hung in the air, floating above the stacks of incriminating paperwork scattered on the conference table. Gorbachev fixed his most penetrating glare at Chebrikov. The former chairman of the

KGB shifted uneasily. He had taken the lead, but suddenly the Politburo hardliner found himself alone on a limb; his support had vanished.

In minutes, the agenda of this special session of the Politburo—a planned and bloodless *perevorot*, or coup— never materialized. Chebrikov knew, that despite the shock of being implicated in a terrorist strike of which he knew absolutely nothing, the reams of information before him would suggest otherwise. He had been ambushed, and his career—for all intents and purposes—was over.

Quickly the other Politburo hardliners seated around the conference table assessed their personal positions. No one had the courage to sift through the stacks of documents and evidence that lay before them. Mikhail Gorbachev's confidence set the tone. They waited for the General Secretary to play his hand.

"You Vladimir Aleksandrovich," said Gorbachev addressing Kryuchkov, the current KGB Chief, "will abolish the Fifth Directorate, and create a new Directorate at the KGB for the Defense of the Soviet Constitutional System. Its purpose will be to coordinate the struggle *against* terrorism. You will also contact William Webster, your counterpart at the CIA in Washington; he is expecting you to dispatch several senior officers to meet with his counter terrorist experts at a private conference in California next month. We *will* collaborate with the United States on this issue of terrorism, to demonstrate our resolve. Have you any questions?"

Kryuchkov sighed and shook his head. His career—at least for the moment—seemed spared. Mikhail looked around the conference table. "Over the next week, I will be meeting with each of you individually, to discuss how I think you can best serve the Rodina."

He looked at Chebrikov. "Except you, Viktor Mikhailovich; I will meet with you *now*."

The Party Secretary waived his hand in the air. "This plenum session of the Politburo is adjourned."

EPILOGUE

20 November 1989
Corfu, Greece

THREE MONTHS; TIME to rest, time to heal, time to develop an intimacy that would last a lifetime. For the first time in a very long time, Jaycott was happy. The irrepressible void that engulfed him following Ellie's death, was now replaced with hope; a renewed sense of optimism that love and contentment were again possible. Katerina filled Jay with a special warmth that made each day worth living.

They strolled down Polichroni Konstanta towards the small cottage they had rented. The murder of Lenoris at the time of Kat's kidnapping, coupled with the flood of memories from years of living with Theodori, made his home on Mitropolitou Athanasiou quite uninhabitable. Katerina gripped Jay's free arm between both hands, leaning her head on his shoulder as they walked. They whispered quietly, sharing a private moment, having long since ignored pretenses of their budding passion. But the locals didn't mind, and in a sense, the islanders facilitated Jay and Kat's romance by permitting them the courtesy to be themselves.

As they turned the corner near Margariti, Jay noticed two police cars parked on the street in front of their cottage. Instinctively, he stiffened. The change in demeanor caused Katerina to look away from Jay and focus on the distinctly decaled police cars.

"Katerina, Katerina," nodded the crisply uniformed Commissiar of Police. He stepped forward and clicked his heels respectively at the island's newest millionaire. "Kalimerá," answered Kat warily.

The Commissiar tugged at Katerina's elbow attempting to steer her away from both Jay and two very serious looking men in suits who stood outside the cottage.

"No," protested Kat calmly, "he is with me." She referred to Jaycott. "What you have to say, is said here."

The Commissiar shrugged. The appropriate courtesy had been extended—and rejected.

"Very well Katerina," he jerked his head towards the two men in suits. "They are from Athens. Both are inspectors with the Special Branch of the Guard de Nationale. You must accompany us down to Police Headquarters on Ioannou Romanou."

"Why," asked Kat in irritation, "what is the problem?"

The Commissiar lowered his voice, again demonstrating a respectful deference to Katerina. "They claim there are charges of smuggling."

"What?!" blurted Jay as surprised as Kat was quiet.

A look of initial confusion swept over her beautiful face, and then Jay saw a look of resignation in Kat's eyes.

"That's absurd," he snapped at the Commissiar.

"Ne," nodded the Police official, "please Katerina, if you could come with us down to headquarters, I'm sure we can clear up the misunderstanding."

She looked at Jay with a pained expression.

"Do we have a choice?" asked Jaycott for both of them.

The Commissiar frowned, searching for the diplomatic solution to preserve a local's reputation. "I would like to send the inspectors back to Athens . . . alone."

Jay took Katerina's hand and looked deeply into her eyes. He searched for an explanation, needing Kat to reassure him; knowing full well that years in intelligence work—especially as a Courier—could easily have pushed Katerina across the line to which she was now being charged.

The Commissiar touched both their elbows and politely separated Jay's grip. "Please, just Katerina . . ."

She reached up and touched Jaycott's cheek with an open hand. There was defeat in Kat's eyes, and that disturbed Jay more than any charges. They separated, and as the Commissiar led Katerina to the rear seat of the second police car, Jay ran towards Theodori's Jaguar parked on the side of the rented cottage. He followed them to headquarters.

An hour passed, and during that time, Jaycott sat waiting with several other locals in the lobby of the Kerkyra Police municipal building. The inactivity and lack of information on Kat's status frustrated Jay. He started to pace. Several times the Commissiar circled between the reception area, his private office, and a rear interrogation room where Katerina was being questioned by the Federal Inspectors.

Whenever he passed by Jay, he shrugged somewhat helplessly, thus offering little by way of encouragement.

Another twenty minutes passed before the Commissiar led Katerina and the two Federal Inspectors from the rear interrogation room.

"I'm sorry," he offered deferentially, approaching Jay before the others. "Katerina has been placed under arrest. She is to be transported to the mainland this afternoon."

"This is a setup," protested Jay grimly as Kat shuffled by. She tried to stop, but the two inspectors prompted Katerina forward, the handcuffs and leg irons slowing her progress.

Kat turned, her eyes fixing on Jay, she spoke over her shoulder. "I told you," there was quiet resignation in her voice, "we are *never* out . . ."

The Inspectors prodded Katerina towards a rear door.

Jaycott stood in the middle of the lobby, numb, his newfound life suddenly and inexplicably crumbling down around him.

"Mister Jaycott?"

Jay turned and noticed a short, mustached man in his early sixties, leaning on a polished cane.

"Mister Jaycott," continued the man quietly, "perhaps I can be of some assistance?"

Jay's mind churned, his attention drawn to the final steps of Katerina as the rear door closed behind her. He tried to focus on the shorter man. "What?!"

"Assistance," repeated the man. "Perhaps I can offer help."

Jay was vaguely aware of two younger men hovering protectively in the background, but his mind was so emotionally muddled over the turn of events in the last hour, that he couldn't consciously connect the dots. He looked at the man squarely for the first time. "Listen, there will be plenty of time for lawyers, but right now . . ."

The short man chuckled, stroking his moustache, his laugh interrupting Jay. "I assure you Mister Jaycott, I am *not* a lawyer."

"Whatever," mumbled Jay dismissing the man, "another time. Right now, I have to catch a plane to Athens."

Jaycott turned, his eyes searching for a public phone, his attention still drawn to Katerina's plight.

"My name is *Moshi*," interjected the short man, as Jay started moving away. "I am *not* Greek." He said the final words in a barely audible voice, confident that no one else in the lobby heard him.

The distinctly Jewish name hung in the air. Jay paused and turned back to look at the diminutive man resting on his polished cane. There was an easy confidence here. Moshi dressed unobtrusively like a retiree; slacks, walking shoes, a dress shirt buttoned to the collar with no tie, and a cotton jacket.

"Perhaps I can help," repeated the Katsa a third time, pausing for emphasis, "Oh, and . . . Rochelle Listache sends her regards."

POST EPILOGUE

December 1989

In a surprise military operation codenamed *Just Cause*, the United States armed forces invaded the Republic of Panama, deposed the corrupt drug cartels of the ruling Junta, and arrested General Manuel Noriega, military Dictator of the Central American country. Noriega is currently serving a 40 year sentence at the Miami Metropolitan Correctional Center.

September 1990

Michael Eisner, Chief Executive Officer of the Walt Disney Company, announced a sixth year of record revenues, profits, and return on shareholder equity.

August 1991

Vladimir Kryuchkov, Chairman of the KGB, masterminded a right wing coup attempt that failed. The ill-fated takeover led to the downfall of Mikhail Gorbachev's historic reign, and the dissolution of the Soviet Union.

June 1992

Two imprisoned Intelligence Officers, Gennadi and Olga Kozlov, were quietly exchanged in a repatriation agreement for a detained CIA Officer and a Canadian Diplomat outside the U.S. Consulate in Budapest Hungry.

February 1993

A group of Islamic terrorists detonated a massive car bomb in the garage of the World Trade Center in New York, killing five.

September 2001

A group of Islamic terrorists hijacked four commercial jetliners and intentionally crashed them into the twin towers of the World Trade Center, the Pentagon, and a field in Pennsylvania, killing 2,793.

In the years that followed, there has never been a news article, media bite, incident report, or Government acknowledgement of the events that occurred at the Walt Disney World Theme Parks over the Labor Day weekend of 1989.

ABOUT THE AUTHOR

Steve Dimodica spent nearly 20 years on Active and Active Reserve status in the US Army Special Forces and Military Intelligence.

Following three mission deployments to North Africa where he served as a Weapons Leader and Medical Specialist on a Special Forces A Team, Steve then received a Direct Commission as a Military Intelligence Officer.

For the next fourteen years, Steve had numerous mission deployments to Europe and Central America, serving first as a Counter Intelligence Officer, and then as both an Executive Officer and Detachment Commander on Special Forces A Teams.

Steve lives in the Philadelphia suburbs with his wife Marianne and his dog Gregor. This is his first novel.

Printed in the United States
145139LV00005B/6/P

9 781933 598369